SLIGHTLY SHADY

Amanda Quick

BANTAM BOOKS
New York   Toronto   London   Sydney   Auckland

SLIGHTLY SHADY

A Bantam Book/April 2001
All rights reserved.
Copyright © 2001 by Jayne A. Krentz

Book design by Lynn Newmark

Library of Congress Cataloging-in-Publication Data
Quick, Amanda.
Slightly shady / Amanda Quick.
p. cm.
ISBN 0-553-80188-0 (HC)
1. Italy—Fiction. 2. Romantic suspense fiction. I. Title.

PS3561.R44 S55 2001
813'.54—dc21
00-058528

Published simultaneously in the United States and Canada

PRINTED IN THE UNITED STATES OF AMERICA

RRH   10   9   8   7   6   5   4   3   2   1

For Frank, with all my love

prologue

The intruder's eyes blazed with a cold fire. He raised a powerful hand and swept another row of vases off the shelf. The fragile objects crashed to the floor and shattered into a hundred shards. He moved on to a display of small statues.

"I advise you to make haste with your packing, Mrs. Lake," he said as he turned his violent attention to a host of fragile clay Pans, Aphrodites, and satyrs. "The carriage will leave in fifteen minutes, and I promise you that you and your niece will be aboard, with or without your luggage."

Lavinia watched him from the foot of the stairs, helpless to stop the destruction of her wares. "You have no right to do this. You are ruining me."

"On the contrary, madam. I am saving your neck." He used a booted foot to topple a large urn decorated in the Etruscan manner. "Not that I expect any thanks, mind you."

Lavinia winced as the urn exploded on impact with the floor. She knew now that it was pointless to berate the lunatic. He was intent on destroying the shop and she lacked the means to stop him. She had been taught early in life to recognize the signs that indicated it was time to stage a tactical retreat. But she had never learned to tolerate such annoying reversals of fortune with equanimity.

"If we were in England, I would have you arrested, Mr. March."

"Ah, but we are not in England, are we, Mrs. Lake?" Tobias March seized a life-size stone centurion by the shield and shoved it forward. The Roman fell on his sword. "We are in Italy and you have no choice but to do as I command."

It was useless to stand her ground. Every moment spent down here attempting to reason with Tobias March was time lost that should be spent packing. But the unfortunate tendency toward stubbornness that was so much a part of her nature could not abide the notion of surrendering the field of battle without a struggle.

"Bastard," she said through her teeth.

"Not in the legal sense." He slammed another row of red clay vases to the floor. "But I believe I comprehend what you wish to imply."

"It is obvious that you are no gentleman, Tobias March."

"I will not quarrel with you on that point." He kicked over a waist-high statue of a naked Venus. "But then, you are no lady, are you?"

She cringed when the statue crumbled. The naked Venuses had proved quite popular with her clientele.

"How dare you? Just because my niece and I got stranded here in Rome and were obliged to go into trade for a few months in order to support ourselves is no reason to insult us."

"Enough." He whirled around to face her. In the lantern light,

his forbidding face was colder than the features of any stone statue. "Be grateful that I have concluded that you were merely an unwitting dupe of the criminal I am pursuing and not a member of his gang of thieves and murderers."

"I have only your word that the villains were using my shop as a place to exchange their messages. Frankly, Mr. March, given your rude behavior, I am not inclined to believe a single thing you say."

He pulled a folded sheet of paper from his pocket. "Do you deny that this note was hidden in one of your vases?"

She glanced at the damning note. Only moments ago she had watched in stunned amazement while he shattered a lovely Greek vase. A message that looked remarkably like a villain's report to his criminal employer had been tucked inside. Something about a bargain with pirates having been successfully struck.

Lavinia raised her chin. "It is certainly not my fault that one of my patrons dropped a personal note into that vase."

"Not just one patron, Mrs. Lake. The villains have been using your shop for some weeks now."

"And just how would you know that, sir?"

"I have watched these premises and your personal movements for nearly a month."

She widened her eyes, genuinely shocked by the infuriatingly casual admission.

"You have spent the past month *spying* on me?"

"At the start of my observations, I assumed that you were an active participant in Carlisle's ring here in Rome. It was only after much study that I have concluded you probably did not know what some of your so-called customers were about."

"That is outrageous."

He gave her a look of mocking inquiry. "Are you saying you *did*

know what they were up to when they came and went in such a regular fashion?"

"I am saying no such thing." She could hear her voice climbing but there was little she could do about it. She had never been so angry or so frightened in her life. "I believed them to be honest patrons of antiquities."

"Did you indeed?" Tobias glanced at a collection of cloudy green glass jars that stood in a neat row on a high shelf. His smile was devoid of all warmth. "And how honest are you, Mrs. Lake?"

She stiffened. "What are you implying, sir?"

"I'm not implying anything. I am merely noting that most of the items in this shop are cheap replicas of ancient artifacts. There is very little here that is truly antique."

"How do you know?" she shot back. "Never say you are an expert in antiquities, sir. I will not be taken in by such an outlandish claim. You cannot pass yourself off as a scholarly researcher, not after what you have done to my establishment."

"You are correct, Mrs. Lake. I am not an expert in Greek and Roman antiquities. I am a simple man of business."

"Rubbish. Why would a simple man of business come all the way to Rome in pursuit of a villain named Carlisle?"

"I am here on behalf of one of my clients who employed me to make inquiries into the fate of a man named Bennett Ruckland."

"What was the fate of this Mr. Ruckland?"

Tobias looked at her. "He was murdered here in Rome. My client believes it was because he learned too much concerning the secret organization that Carlisle controls."

"A likely story."

"Nevertheless, it is my story and mine is the only tale that matters tonight." He hurled another pot to the floor. "You have only ten minutes left, Mrs. Lake."

It was hopeless. Lavinia took two fistfuls of her skirts and started up the stairs. But she paused midway as a thought struck her.

"This business of making inquiries into murders on behalf of your clients—it seems a rather odd sort of profession," she said.

He smashed a small Roman oil lamp. "No more odd than selling false antiquities."

Lavinia was incensed. "I told you, they are not false, sir. They are reproductions designed to be purchased as souvenirs."

"Call them what you wish. They look remarkably like fraudulent imitations to me."

She smiled thinly. "But as you just said, sir, you are no expert in rare artifacts, are you? You are merely a simple man of business."

"You have approximately eight minutes left, Mrs. Lake."

She touched the silver pendant she wore at her throat the way she often did when her nerves were under a great strain. "I cannot decide if you are a monstrous villain or merely deranged," she whispered.

He looked briefly, chillingly, amused. "Does it make any great difference?"

"No."

The situation was impossible. She had no choice but to concede the victory to him.

With a soft exclamation of frustration and anger, she whirled and rushed on up the stairs. When she reached the small, lantern-lit room, she saw that, unlike herself, Emeline had made good use of the time allotted to them. Two medium-size and one very large trunk stood open. The smaller trunks were already crammed to overflowing.

"Thank goodness you are here." Emeline's words were muffled,

as her head was inside the wardrobe. "Whatever took you so long?"

"I was attempting to convince Mr. March that he had no right to toss us out into the street in the middle of the night."

"He is not tossing us into the street." Emeline straightened away from the wardrobe, a small antique vase cradled in her arms. "He has provided a carriage and two armed men to see us safely out of Rome and all the way home to England. It is really very generous of him."

"Rubbish. There is nothing at all generous about his actions. He is playing some deep game, I tell you, and he wants us out of his way."

Emeline busied herself rolling the vase into a bombazine gown. "He believes we are in grave danger from that villain Carlisle, who used our shop as a place to send and receive messages from his men."

"Bah. We have only Mr. March's word that there is any such villain operating here in Rome." Lavinia opened a cupboard. A very handsome, extremely well endowed Apollo gazed out at her. "I, for one, am not inclined to put much faith in anything that man tells us. For all we know, he wants the use of these rooms for his own dark purposes."

"I am convinced he has told us the truth." Emeline stuffed the cushioned vase into the third trunk. "And if that is the case, he is right. We are indeed in danger."

"If there is some villainous gang involved in this affair, I would not be surprised to discover that Tobias March is their leader. He claims to be a simple man of business, but it is obvious to me that there is something distinctly diabolical about him."

"You are allowing your ill temper to influence your imagination,

Lavinia. You know you are never at your most clearheaded when you allow your imagination to run wild."

The sound of shattering pottery echoed up the staircase.

"Damn the man," Lavinia muttered.

Emeline paused in her packing and tilted her head slightly, listening. "He certainly is intent on making it appear that we were the victims of vandals and thieves, is he not?"

"He said something about destroying the shop so this villain Carlisle would not suspect he had been discovered." Lavinia wrestled with the Apollo, struggling to get it free of the cupboard. "But I believe it is just another one of his lies. The man is enjoying himself down there, if you ask me. He is quite mad."

"I hardly think that is the case." Emeline went back to the wardrobe for another vase. "But I will admit it is a good thing we stored the genuine antiquities up here so we could keep them safe from street thieves."

"The only bit of luck in this entire affair." Lavinia wrapped her arms around Apollo's chest and hauled him out of the cupboard. "I shudder to think what might have happened if we had put them on display alongside the copies downstairs. March would no doubt have destroyed them too."

"If you ask me, the most fortunate aspect of this thing is that Mr. March concluded we were not members of Carlisle's ring of cutthroats." Emeline shrouded a small vase in a towel and stored it in the trunk. "I tremble to think what he might have done to us had he believed us to be consorting with the real villains and not just innocent dupes."

"He could hardly have done worse than to ruin our only source of income and throw us out of our home."

Emeline glanced at the old stone walls that surrounded them

and gave a delicate sniff. "You can hardly call this unpleasant little room a home. I shall not miss it for a moment."

"You will most certainly miss it when we find ourselves penniless in London and forced to make our living on the streets."

"It will not come to that." Emeline patted the towel-wrapped vase she held. "We will be able to sell these antiquities when we return to England. Collecting old vases and statues is all the rage, you know. With the money we receive for these items we shall be able to rent a house."

"Not for long. We will be fortunate to make enough from the sale of these objects to support ourselves for six months. When the last of them is gone, we will be in desperate straits."

"You will think of something, Lavinia. You always do. Just look at how well we managed when we found ourselves stranded here in Rome after our employer ran off with that handsome count. Your notion of going into the antiquities business was nothing short of brilliant."

Lavinia managed, by dint of sheer willpower, not to scream in frustration. Emeline's boundless faith in her ability to recover from every disaster was quite maddening.

"Give me a hand with this Apollo, please," she said.

Emeline glanced doubtfully at the large nude statue Lavinia was attempting to haul across the room. "It will take up most of the space in the last trunk. Perhaps we ought to leave it behind and pack some of the vases instead."

"This Apollo is worth several dozen vases." Lavinia stopped halfway across the room, breathing hard from the exertion, and changed her grip on the figure. "He's the most valuable antiquity we've got. We must take him with us."

"If we put him in the trunk, we won't have room for your books," Emeline said gently.

A sick sensation twisted Lavinia's insides. She stopped abruptly and looked at the shelf filled with the books of poetry she had brought with her from England. The thought of leaving them behind was almost too much to bear.

"I can replace them." She took a tighter hold on the statue. "Eventually."

Emeline hesitated, searching Lavinia's face. "Are you certain? I know how much they mean to you."

"Apollo is more important."

"Very well." Emeline stooped to grasp Apollo's lower limbs.

Booted footsteps rang on the staircase. Tobias March appeared in the doorway. He glanced at the trunks and then he looked at Lavinia and Emeline.

"You must leave now," he said. "I cannot risk allowing you to remain here even another ten minutes."

Lavinia longed to hurl one of the vases at his head. "I am not leaving Apollo behind. He may be all that stands between us and life in a brothel when we return to London."

Emeline made a face. "Really, Lavinia, you mustn't exaggerate so."

"It's nothing short of the truth," Lavinia snapped.

"Give me the bloody statue." Tobias came toward them. He hoisted the sculpture in his arms. "I'll put it into the trunk for you."

Emeline smiled warmly. "Thank you. It is rather heavy."

Lavinia gave a snort of disgust. "Don't thank him, Emeline. He is the cause of all our troubles tonight."

"Always delighted to be of service," Tobias said. He wedged the statue into the trunk. "Anything else?"

"Yes," Lavinia said instantly. "That urn near the door. It is an exceptionally good piece."

"It will not fit into the trunk." Tobias gripped the lid and looked at her. "You must choose between the Apollo and the urn. You cannot take both with you."

She narrowed her eyes, suddenly suspicious. "You intend to take it for yourself, do you not? You plan to steal my urn."

"I assure you, Mrs. Lake, I have no interest in that damn urn. Do you want it or the Apollo? Choose. Now."

"The Apollo," she muttered.

Emeline hurried forward to stuff a nightgown and some shoes in around the Apollo. "I believe we're ready, Mr. March."

"Yes, indeed." Lavinia gave him a steely smile. "Quite ready. I can only hope that one of these days I shall have an opportunity to repay you for this night's work, Mr. March."

He slammed the lid of the trunk. "Is that a threat, Mrs. Lake?"

"Take it as you will, sir." She seized her reticule in one hand and her traveling cloak in the other. "Come, Emeline, let us be off before Mr. March decides to burn the place down around our ears."

"There is no call to be so disagreeable." Emeline picked up her own cloak and a bonnet. "Under the circumstances, I think Mr. March is behaving with admirable restraint."

Tobias inclined his head. "I appreciate your support, Miss Emeline."

"You must not mind Lavinia's remarks, sir," Emeline said. "Her nature is such that when she is feeling hard-pressed she is inclined to become somewhat short of temper."

Tobias settled his cold-eyed gaze on Lavinia again. "I noticed."

"I pray you will make allowances," Emeline continued. "In addition to all of the other difficulties tonight, we are obliged to leave her books of poetry behind. That was a very difficult decision for her. She is very fond of poetry, you see."

"Oh, for pity's sake." Lavinia swung her cloak around her shoulders and strode briskly toward the door. "I refuse to listen to any more of this ridiculous conversation. One thing is certain, I am suddenly quite eager to be free of your unpleasant company, Mr. March."

"You wound me, Mrs. Lake."

"Not nearly so deeply as I could wish."

She paused on the staircase and looked back at him. He did not look wounded. Indeed, he looked magnificently fit. The ease with which he hoisted one of the trunks testified to his excellent physical condition.

"Personally, I'm looking forward to going home." Emeline hastened toward the stairs. "Italy is all very well for a visit, but I have missed London."

"So have I." Lavinia jerked her gaze away from Tobias March's broad shoulders and stomped down the stairs. "This entire venture has been an unmitigated disaster. Whose idea was it to travel to Rome as companions to that dreadful Mrs. Underwood in the first place?"

Emeline cleared her throat. "Yours, I believe."

"The next time I suggest anything so bizarre, I pray you will be so kind as to wave a vinaigrette under my nose until I come to my senses."

"It no doubt seemed quite a brilliant notion at the time," Tobias March said behind her.

"It did indeed," Emeline murmured in very neutral tones. " 'Just think how delightful it will be to spend a season in Rome,' Lavinia said. 'Surrounded by all those wonderfully inspiring antiquities,' she said. 'All at Mrs. Underwood's expense,' she said. 'We shall be entertained in grand style by people of quality and taste,' she said."

"That is quite enough, Emeline," Lavinia snapped. "You know very well it has been a very educational experience."

"In more ways than one, I should imagine," Tobias said rather too easily, "judging by some of the gossip I have heard concerning Mrs. Underwood's parties. Is it true they tended to evolve into orgies?"

Lavinia gritted her teeth. "Granted there were one or two minor incidents of an unfortunate nature."

"The orgies were somewhat awkward," Emeline allowed. "Lavinia and I were obliged to lock ourselves in our bedchambers until they ended. But in my opinion, matters did not become truly dire until we woke up one morning to discover that Mrs. Underwood had run off with her count. That course of action left us stranded and penniless in a foreign clime."

"Nevertheless," Lavinia continued forcefully, "we managed to come right again and we were doing quite nicely until you, Mr. March, chose to interfere in our personal affairs."

"Believe me, Mrs. Lake, no one regrets the necessity more than I," Tobias said.

She paused at the foot of the stairs to take in the sight of the shop full of shattered pottery and statuary. He had destroyed everything, she thought. Not a single vase had been left unbroken. In less than an hour, he had ruined the business it had taken nearly four months to establish.

"It is inconceivable that your regret equals my own, Mr. March." She tightened her grasp on her reticule and walked through the rubble toward the door. "Indeed, sir, as far as I am concerned, this disaster is entirely your fault."

———

It was not yet dawn when Tobias heard the shop's rear door open at last. He waited on the unlit stairs, pistol in his hand.

A man carrying a lantern turned down low emerged from the back room. He came to a halt when he saw the wreckage.

"Bloody hell."

He set the lantern down on the counter and crossed the room swiftly to examine the shattered remains of a large vase.

"Bloody hell," he muttered again. He swung around, studying the ruined objects. "Bloody damn hell!"

Tobias went down one step. "Looking for something, Carlisle?"

Carlisle went very still. In the weak, flaring light of the lantern, his face was a mask of chilling evil. "Who are you?"

"You don't know me. A friend of Bennett Ruckland sent me to find you."

"Ruckland. Yes, of course. I should have anticipated this."

Carlisle moved with blinding speed. He raised his hand, revealing the pistol he held, and prepared to fire without a second's hesitation.

Tobias was ready. He pulled the trigger of his own gun.

The explosion was all wrong. He knew at once the pistol had misfired. He reached into a pocket, grabbed his second gun, but it was too late.

Carlisle fired.

Tobias felt his left leg go out from under him. The impact threw him back and to the side. He dropped his unfired pistol in favor of grabbing the banister. Somehow he managed to keep himself from falling headfirst down the stairs.

Carlisle was already preparing to fire his second pistol.

Tobias tried to scramble back up the staircase. Something was very wrong with his left leg. He could not get it to move properly.

23

He turned onto his stomach and hauled himself up the steps using his hands and right leg in a crablike movement. His foot slipped in something wet. He knew it was the blood seeping from his thigh.

Down below, Carlisle moved cautiously toward the foot of the stairs. Tobias knew the only reason the other man hadn't fired the second gun was because Carlisle could not see him clearly in the shadows.

The darkness was his only hope.

He made it to the landing and more or less fell through the doorway into the unlit room. His hand struck the heavy urn Lavinia had left behind.

"Nothing so annoying as a misfire, is there?" Carlisle asked pleasantly. "And then to drop your second gun. Clumsy. Very clumsy."

He was coming up the stairs now, quickly, more confidently.

Tobias gripped the urn, pulled it onto its rounded side, and tried to breathe very shallowly. The pain had started to burn in his left leg.

"Did the man who sent you after me bother to tell you that you probably would not return to England alive?" Carlisle inquired from halfway up the stairs. "Did he tell you that I am a former member of the Blue Chamber? Do you know what that means, my friend?"

He would have only one chance, Tobias told himself. He had to wait until the right instant.

"I do not know how much you were paid to hunt me down, but whatever it was, it was not enough. You were a fool to agree to the bargain." Carlisle had almost reached the landing. There was hungry excitement in his voice. "It will cost you your life."

Tobias shoved the large urn, using most of what little strength he had left. The plump vessel rumbled toward the staircase.

"What's that?" Carlisle froze on the top step. "What's that noise?"

The urn crashed into his legs. Carlisle yelled. Tobias heard him clawing at the wall in an attempt to regain his balance but to no avail.

There was a series of dull, jolting thuds as Carlisle tumbled down. His scream stopped with awful suddenness near the bottom.

Tobias yanked the sheet from the bed, ripped a long strip from it, and bound up his left leg. His head swam when he hauled himself to his feet.

He swayed and almost fainted halfway down the staircase, but he managed to stay upright. Carlisle lay sprawled at the foot of the steps, his neck twisted at an unnatural angle. The shards of the urn were scattered around him.

"She chose the Apollo, you see," Tobias whispered to the dead man. "In hindsight, it was clearly the right decision. The lady has excellent intuition."

one

*T*he nervous little man who had sold him the journal had warned him that blackmail was a dangerous business. Some of the information in the valet's diary could get a man killed. But it could also make him rich, Holton Felix thought.

He had made his living in the gaming hells for years. He was well acquainted with risk and he had long ago learned that there was no reward for those who lacked the resolve and the sheer bloody nerve required to roll the dice.

He was no fool, he told himself as he dipped his quill in the ink and prepared to finish the note. He did not intend to pursue a career in blackmail for long. He would abandon it just as soon as he collected enough money to pay off his most pressing debts.

He would keep the diary though, he thought. The secrets it contained would be useful in the future should he ever find himself in dun territory again.

The knock on the door startled him. He stared at the last line of the threat he had just penned. A blob of ink marred the word *unfortunate*. The sight of the ruined sentence irritated him. He took pride in the wit and cleverness of his notes. He had worked hard to tailor each message to the appropriate recipient. He could have been a famous writer, another Byron perhaps, had circumstances not obliged him to support himself in the hells.

Old rage shot through him. Everything would have been so much easier if life had not been so damnably unfair. If his father had not got himself killed in a duel over a disputed hand of cards; if his desperate and despairing mother had not died of the fever when he was but sixteen; who knew what he might have achieved? Who knew how high he could have risen had he been given even some of the advantages other men possessed?

Instead, he was reduced to blackmail and extortion. But someday he would finally reach the position that should have been his, he vowed. Someday . . .

The knock sounded again. One of his creditors, no doubt. He had left his vouchers in every hell in town.

He crumpled the letter in his fist and stood abruptly. Crossing the room to the window, he eased aside the curtain and peered out. There was no one. Whoever had knocked a moment ago had abandoned the attempt to make him respond. But there appeared to be a parcel on the step.

He opened the door and stooped to pick up the package. He caught only a glimpse of the hem of a heavy greatcoat when the figure moved out of the shadows.

The poker struck the back of his head with killing force. For Holton Felix, the world ended in an instant, canceling all of his outstanding debts.

two

The stench of death was unmistakable. Lavinia caught her breath on the threshold of the firelit room and hastily fumbled in her reticule for a hankie. This was the one possibility for which she had made no allowance in her plans tonight. She placed the embroidered square of linen over her nose and fought the urge to turn and flee.

Holton Felix's body lay sprawled on the floor in front of the hearth. At first she could see no sign of injury. She wondered if his heart had failed him. Then she realized there was something dreadfully wrong with the shape of his skull.

Evidently one of Felix's other blackmail victims had arrived before her. Felix had not been a particularly clever scoundrel, she reminded herself. After all, she had managed to determine his identity shortly after receiving the first extortion note from him,

and she was quite new and inexperienced at this business of making private inquiries.

Once she had learned his address, she had talked to some of the maids and cooks who worked in the neighborhood. Satisfied that Felix had a nightly habit of taking himself off to the gaming hells, she had come here tonight intending to search his lodgings. She had hoped to find the diary he claimed to be quoting in his notes.

She surveyed the small room, uncertainty twisting her stomach. The fire still burned cheerily on the hearth, but she could feel icy perspiration trickling down her spine. Now what was she to do? Had the killer been satisfied with Felix's death, or had he taken the time to go through the villain's possessions to discover the diary?

There was only one way to learn the answers to those questions, she thought. She must carry on with her original scheme to search Felix's rooms.

She forced herself to move. It took an effort of will to push through the invisible wall of dread that curtained the hellish scene. The flickering light of the dying flames cast ghastly shadows on the walls. She tried not to look at the body.

Breathing as shallowly as possible, she considered where to start her search. Felix had furnished his lodgings in a simple manner. Given his fondness for the hells, that came as no great surprise. He had no doubt been obliged to sell the occasional candlestick or table to cover his debts. The servants she had questioned had assured her that Felix was rumored to be forever short of the ready. One or two had implied he was an unscrupulous opportunist who would stoop to any means to secure money.

Blackmail had very likely been only one of a number of

unpleasant financial schemes Felix had concocted in his career as a gamester. But evidently it had been a losing stratagem.

She looked at the desk near the window and decided to start there, although she suspected the killer had already gone through the drawers. It was certainly what she would have done in his place.

She circled Felix's body cautiously, keeping as far away from it as possible, and hurried toward her goal. The surface of the desk was littered with the usual paraphernalia, including a penknife and an inkstand. There was also sand for blotting and a small metal dish for melting sealing wax.

She bent down to open the first of the three drawers on the right side of the desk. And froze when a shiver of premonition stirred the fine hairs on the nape of her neck.

The soft but unmistakable scrape of a boot sounded on the wooden floor behind her. Fear crashed through her, stealing her breath. Her heart raced so swiftly she wondered if she was about to faint for the first time in her life.

The killer was still here in these rooms.

One thing was certain. She could not afford the luxury of a swoon.

She stared at the items on the desk for a horrified instant, searching for a weapon with which to defend herself. She put out a hand. Her fingers tightened convulsively around the handle of the small penknife. It looked so tiny and fragile. But it was all that was available.

Clutching the tiny blade, she whirled around to face the murderer. She saw him at once, looming in the darkened doorway that opened onto the bedchamber. She could see the outline of his greatcoat, but his face was concealed by the shadows.

He made no move to close the short distance between them, however. Instead he lounged there, one shoulder propped negligently against the frame of the door, arms folded across his chest.

"Do you know, Mrs. Lake," Tobias March said, "I had a feeling that you and I would meet up again one day. But who could have guessed that it would be under such interesting circumstances?"

She had to swallow twice before she could speak. When she did eventually manage to utter a few coherent words, her voice sounded thin and it easily cracked.

"Did you murder that man?"

Tobias glanced at the body. "No. I got here after the killer, just as you did. From what I can determine, Felix was killed on his front step. The murderer must have dragged him back into this room."

The news did little to reassure her. "What are you doing here?"

"I was about to ask you the same question." He contemplated her with a considering air. "But I have a hunch I already know the answer. You are obviously one of Felix's blackmail victims, are you not?"

Outrage temporarily overcame fear. "The horrid creature sent me two notes this week. The first arrived on Monday. It was delivered to the kitchen door. I could not believe my eyes when I read his ridiculous demands. He wanted a hundred pounds. Can you imagine? One hundred pounds to ensure his silence. Of all the unmitigated gall."

"On what point did he promise to maintain silence?" Tobias watched her intently. "Have you been into more mischief since we last met?"

"How dare you, sir? This is entirely your fault and yours alone."

"My fault?"

"Yes, Mr. March. I blame the entire affair on you." She gestured

toward the body with the tip of the penknife. "That wretched man attempted to blackmail me over that business in Rome. He threatened to reveal everything."

"Did he indeed?" Tobias straightened with an oddly stiff movement. "Now, that is most interesting. What, precisely, did he know?"

"I just told you, he knew it all. He threatened to make it known that I had operated a shop in Rome frequented by a band of villains. He implied that I was an accomplice to their schemes and had allowed the cutthroats to use my establishment as a communications post. He even went so far as to infer that I had very likely been the mistress of the gang's leader."

"Was that all he said in his note?"

"All? Isn't that enough? Mr. March, in spite of your best efforts, my niece and I managed to survive your assault on our business in Rome. Barely."

He inclined his head. "I rather thought you might come about again. Yours is a spirit that does not sink easily."

She ignored that. "Indeed, things are going rather well at the moment. I have every hope of giving Emeline a taste of a real Season. With luck, she may even meet an eligible gentleman who can support her in the manner to which I wish to see her accustomed. This is a rather delicate time, if you see what I mean. I cannot allow her name to be tainted by the least hint of gossip."

"I see."

"If Felix had bruited it about that she had at one time been involved in a shop that catered to villains in Rome, the damage would be incalculable."

"I suppose gossip to the effect that she was the niece of the mistress of a notorious criminal lord would complicate your scheme to launch Miss Emeline into the social whirl."

"*Complicate* it? It would ruin everything. This is all so very

unfair. Emeline and I had nothing to do with those villains and the man you called Carlisle. I don't see how any person possessed of even a small measure of refined sensibilities could leap to the conclusion that my niece and I consorted with thieves and murderers."

"I leaped to that conclusion for a short time at the start of the affair, if you will recall."

"I do not find that particularly surprising," she said grimly. "I was referring to persons possessed of refined sensibilities. That group would hardly include you, sir."

"Or Holton Felix, apparently." Tobias looked at the body. "But I think it would be best to save this discussion of my lack of exquisite sensibilities for another occasion when we will have the leisure to examine my flaws in detail. At the moment, we have other problems. I assume we are both here for the same purpose."

"I don't know why you are here, Mr. March, but I came to search for a certain diary that apparently once belonged to the valet of Mr. Carlisle. The man you claimed was the leader of the criminal gang in Rome." She paused, frowning. "What do you know of this affair?"

"You know the old saying 'No man is a hero to his valet.' It seems that Carlisle's faithful servant kept a private record of his employer's most damning secrets. After Carlisle's death—"

"Carlisle is dead?"

"Quite. As I was saying, the valet sold the diary to purchase passage back to England. He was killed, apparently by a footpad, before he got out of Rome. From what I was able to determine, the diary was sold twice after that. In both instances, the temporary possessors have suffered fatal accidents." He angled his head toward Felix's body. "And now there is a third death associated with the damn thing."

Lavinia swallowed. "Good heavens."

"Indeed." Tobias left the doorway to walk toward the desk.

Lavinia watched him uneasily. There was something odd about the way he moved, she thought; a slight but detectable catch in his gait. A limp, actually. She could have sworn there had been no such hesitation in his stride the last time she saw him.

"How do you come to know so much about this diary?" she asked.

"I have been on the trail of the damned thing for the past few weeks. Followed it across the Continent. I arrived in England a few days ago."

"Why have you chased after it?"

Tobias jerked open a desk drawer. "Among other interesting bits of gossip, I believe it to contain information that may answer some questions for my client."

"What sort of questions?"

He glanced at her over his shoulder. "Questions of treason and murder."

"*Treason?*"

"During the war." He opened another drawer and rifled through some papers. "We really do not have time to go into the details of the matter. I shall explain later."

"Never say you failed in your endeavors in Rome, Mr. March. Surely, after all you put us through that dreadful night, you did not fumble the prize? What, precisely, happened to that man Carlisle? You claimed he would show up in our shop to collect the message from his minion."

"Carlisle arrived after you left."

"Well?"

"He tripped and fell on the stairs."

Her eyes widened in disbelief. "He tripped and fell?"

"Accidents do happen, Mrs. Lake. A staircase can be treacherous."

"Bah. I knew it. You mishandled matters after Emeline and I left that night, did you not?"

"There were complications."

"Obviously." For some reason, in spite of the horrific situation, she was able to take a perverse satisfaction in laying the blame at his feet. "I should have guessed the truth immediately after I received Holton Felix's first extortion note. After all, things had been going along quite smoothly until that moment. I should have known that when problems arose, you would be at the root."

"Damnation, Mrs. Lake, this is not the time to take me to task. You know nothing of the intricacies of this affair."

"Admit it, sir. This problem with the valet's diary is entirely your fault. If you had dealt properly with the situation in Rome, we would not be here tonight."

He went very still. In the hellish light cast by the fire, his eyes were very dangerous. "I assure you, the serpent who controlled that band of vipers in Italy is dead. Unfortunately, that was not the end of the matter. My client wishes to see the entire affair resolved. He has engaged me to do so, and that is precisely what I intend to do."

She went cold. "I see."

"Carlisle was at one time a member of a criminal organization known as the Blue Chamber. The gang had tentacles throughout England and Europe. For many years the organization was controlled by a leader who styled himself Azure."

Her mouth went dry. For some inexplicable reason she sensed he was telling her the truth. "How very theatrical."

"Azure was the undisputed head of the organization. But from what we can discern, he died about a year ago. The Blue Chamber

26

has been in chaos since his death. Azure had two powerful lieutenants, Carlisle and another man whose identity remains a mystery."

"Azure and Carlisle are both gone, so I assume your client wants you to discover the identity of the third man?"

"Yes. The diary may contain that information. With luck, it will also tell us who Azure was and clear up a few other questions as well. Now do you see why it is so dangerous?"

"Indeed."

Tobias picked up a sheaf of papers. "Rather than just standing there, why don't you make yourself useful?"

"Useful?"

"I did not have an opportunity to search the bedchamber before you arrived. Take a candle and see what you can discover in the room. I will finish in here."

Her first impulse was to tell him to consign himself to Hades. But belatedly it occurred to her that he had a point. They were both after the same thing, it seemed. The advantages of dividing up the task of searching Felix's rooms were self-evident. In addition, there was another extremely compelling reason for following his instructions. If she took the bedchamber, she would not have to work in sight of the bloody body.

She picked up a candle. "You do realize that there is a very good chance that whoever murdered Mr. Felix found the diary and took it away?"

"If that is the case, our problems are considerably compounded." He cast her a cold-eyed look. "One step at a time, Mrs. Lake. Let us first see if we can discover that damned diary. It would certainly simplify matters."

He was right, she thought. March was irritating, provoking, and extremely annoying, but he was correct. One disaster at a

time. That was the only way to get through this affair. It was, in point of fact, the way she got through life.

She hurried into the small room adjoining the parlor. There was a book on the table beside the bed. A tingle of excitement sparked within her. Perhaps luck was with her, after all.

She crossed the room to examine the title in the glow of the flame. *The Education of a Lady.* On the off chance that the leather binding might conceal a handwritten diary, she opened the cover and thumbed through a few pages. Disappointment drowned her small burst of hope. The volume was a recently published novel, not a personal journal.

She replaced the book on the table and went to the washstand. It took only moments to search the small drawers. They contained the things she would have expected to discover in such a location: a comb and brush, shaving items, and a toothbrush.

She tried the wardrobe next. There were a number of expensive-looking linen shirts and three stylish coats inside. Evidently on the occasions when he had done well at the tables, Felix had spent his winnings on fashionable clothing. Perhaps he saw the costly apparel as a business investment.

"Have you found anything?" Tobias called softly from the other room.

"No," she said. "You?"

"Nothing."

She heard him shift a large item of furniture in the outer room. The desk, perhaps. He was certainly being thorough in his search.

She opened the drawers inside the wardrobe and discovered only a selection of gentlemen's smallclothes and cravats. She slammed the doors and turned around to study the sparsely furnished chamber.

Desperation grew until she could hardly breathe. What on earth would she do next if they did not find the evidence that had led Felix to attempt to blackmail her?

Her gaze fell again on the leather-bound volume on the night-stand. There were no other books in evidence here in Felix's lodgings. If it were not for *The Education of a Lady,* she would have said he had not been given to amusing himself with literature. Yet he had kept the one novel beside his bed.

She went slowly across the room to take another look at the book. Why would a gamester take an interest in a novel that had no doubt been written for young ladies?

She picked up the book again and flipped through a few more pages, this time pausing to read a sentence here and there. It did not take long to see that the story had most definitely not been written for the edification of young ladies.

. . . her elegantly sculpted buttocks
quivered in anticipation of my velvet whip . . .

"Good grief." Hastily she slammed the book closed. A small slip of paper fluttered to the floor.

"Did you find something of interest?" Tobias inquired from the other room.

"I most certainly did not."

She glanced down at the small sheet of paper that had landed on the toe of her half boot. There was handwriting on it. She grimaced. Perhaps Felix had enjoyed the novel to such an extent, he had resorted to making notes on the text.

She bent down to retrieve the paper, glancing at the words scrawled on it as she did so. Not notes on *The Education of a Lady,* but an address. Number Fourteen, Hazelton Square.

Why would Felix keep an address tucked in this particular novel?

She caught the faint but telltale slide of Tobias's boot on the floor of the parlor. On impulse she tucked the note into her reticule and turned toward the door.

He appeared in the opening, silhouetted against the dying firelight. "Well?"

"I found nothing that even remotely resembles a diary," she said firmly and, she reflected, quite honestly.

"Neither did I." He swept the bedchamber with a grim expression. "We are too late. It appears that whoever murdered Felix had the presence of mind to take the diary."

"Hardly a surprising turn of events. It's certainly what I would have done under the circumstances."

"Hmm."

She scowled. "What is it?"

He looked at her. "It seems we must now bide our time until the new blackmailer makes his move."

"The *new* blackmailer?" Shock held her motionless for a few seconds. She had to work to get her jaw closed. "Dear heaven, whatever are you saying, sir? Do you suppose that Felix's killer intends to set up shop as an extortionist?"

"If there is a promise of money in the enterprise, and I'm certain there is, then we must assume the answer to that question is yes."

"Bloody hell."

"My sentiments exactly, but we must look on the positive side, Mrs. Lake."

"I fail to see one."

He gave her a humorless smile. "Come now, the two of us managed to track down Felix independently, did we not?"

"Felix was an incompetent fool who left all sorts of clues. I had no problem bribing the urchin he used to deliver his blackmail notes. The lad gave me the direction in exchange for a few coins and a hot meat pie."

"Very clever of you." Tobias looked back into the other room, where the dead man lay on the carpet in front of the fire. "I do not believe that whoever succeeded in murdering Felix will be quite so inept. Therefore, we had best combine forces, madam."

A fresh wave of alarm shot through her. "Whatever are you talking about?"

"I'm sure you comprehend my meaning." He switched his gaze back to her. One brow rose. "Whatever else you are, you are not slow-witted."

So much for hoping he would want them to go their separate ways after this meeting.

"Now see here," she said crisply. "I have no intention whatsoever of forming any sort of partnership with you, Mr. March. Every time you appear, you cause me no end of trouble."

"There have been only two occasions when we have been obliged to spend time in each other's company."

"Both have been disastrous, thanks to you."

"That is your opinion." He took an uneven stride toward her and grasped her arm firmly in his large gloved hand. "From my perspective, it is you who possess a most remarkable talent for complicating a situation beyond belief."

"Really, sir, this is too much. Kindly take your hands off me."

"I fear I cannot do that, Mrs. Lake." He guided her out of the room and down the back hall. "Given that we are both enmeshed in this web, I must insist we work together to untangle it."

three

I can't believe you encountered Mr. March again. And under such odd circumstances." Emeline put down her coffee cup and regarded Lavinia across the breakfast table. "What an astounding coincidence."

"Rubbish. It is no such thing, if his tale is to be believed." Lavinia tapped her spoon against the side of her plate. "According to him, this affair of blackmail is connected to that business in Rome."

"Does he think that Holton Felix was a member of this criminal gang called the Blue Chamber?"

"No. Apparently Felix came into possession of the diary more or less by chance."

"And now someone else has it." Emeline looked thoughtful. "Presumably whoever murdered Felix. And Mr. March is still on the trail. He is really quite tenacious, is he not?"

"Bah. He is doing this for the money. So long as someone is willing to pay him to make inquiries, it is in his own best financial interests to be tenacious." She made a face. "Although why his client continues to purchase his services after his shockingly incompetent performance in Rome defeats me."

"You know very well we must be grateful for the way he carried out his inquiries in Italy. Another man in his position might well have concluded that we were, indeed, members of that gang of cutthroats and acted accordingly."

"Anyone engaged in such inquiries would have had to be a fool to imagine we were involved in criminal activities."

"Yes, of course," Emeline said soothingly, "but one can certainly see how another, less intelligent, less observant gentleman than Mr. March might have concluded that we were members of the gang."

"Do not be so quick to credit Tobias March with any positive qualities, Emeline. I, for one, do not trust him."

"Yes, I can see that. Why ever not?"

Lavinia spread her hands. "For heaven's sake, I found him at the scene of a murder last night."

"He found you at the same scene," Emeline pointed out.

"Yes, but he had got there before me. Felix was already dead when I arrived. For all I know, March was the one who killed him."

"Oh, I doubt that very much."

Lavinia stared at her. "How can you say that? March was quite free with the information that Mr. Carlisle did not survive the encounter in Rome."

"I thought you said something about an unfortunate accident on the stairs."

"That was March's version of events. It wouldn't surprise me in the least to discover that Carlisle's death was not an accident."

"Well, that is neither here nor there now, is it? The important thing is that the villain is dead."

Lavinia hesitated. "March wants me to help him find the diary. He wants us to combine our efforts."

"That makes perfect sense, does it not? You are both determined to find it, so why not form a partnership?"

"March has a client who is paying him a fee for his efforts. I do not."

Emeline studied her over the rim of her coffee cup. "Perhaps you can negotiate with Mr. March to give you a portion of the money his client pays him. You developed a distinct talent for bargaining while we were in Italy."

"I have given the matter some consideration," Lavinia admitted slowly. "But the notion of a partnership with March makes me extremely uneasy."

"It does not appear that you have much choice. It would be a trifle inconvenient for us if the gossip about our business in Rome began to circulate here in London."

"You have a gift for understatement, Emeline. It would be more than inconvenient. It would utterly destroy my new career, to say nothing of your chance to enjoy a Season."

"Speaking of your career, did you happen to mention the nature of your new profession to Mr. March last night?"

"Of course not. Why would I do that?"

"I merely wondered if, in the intimacy of the setting in which you and Mr. March found yourselves, you perhaps felt called upon to confide in him."

"There was nothing *intimate* about the setting. For heaven's sake, Emeline, there was a dead man in the same room with us."

"Yes, of course."

"One does not become *intimate* under such circumstances."

"I understand."

"In any event, the last thing I would want to do is become intimate in any way with Tobias March."

"Your voice is rising, Aunt Lavinia. You know what that means."

Lavinia slammed her cup down onto the saucer with a great deal of force. "It means that my nerves have been sorely tried."

"Indeed. But it is clear to me that you have no choice but to do as Mr. March suggests and join together to search for the diary."

"Nothing can convince me that forming a partnership with that man would be wise."

"Calm yourself," Emeline said gently. "You are allowing your personal feelings about Mr. March to interfere with sound judgment."

"Mark my words, Tobias March is once again playing his own deep game, just as he was the last time we had the misfortune to encounter him."

"What game would that be?" Emeline asked, showing the first hint of exasperation.

Lavinia contemplated the question for a moment. "It is entirely possible that he is seeking the diary for the same reasons that Holton Felix wanted it. For purposes of extortion and blackmail."

Emeline's spoon clattered loudly on the saucer. "Never say you actually think that Mr. March intends to set himself up as an extortionist. I refuse to believe he has anything in common with a creature like Holton Felix."

"We know nothing about Tobias March." Lavinia flattened her palms on the table and shoved herself to her feet. "Who can guess what he would do if he managed to gain possession of the diary?"

Emeline said nothing.

Lavinia clasped her hands behind her back and began to pace around the table.

Emeline sighed. "Very well, I cannot give you any reason to trust Mr. March, beyond the fact that he did see to it that we got safely back to England after the disaster in Rome. It must have cost him a small fortune."

"He wanted us out of the way. In any event, I very much doubt March paid the expenses of that journey. I'm sure he sent the bill to his client."

"Perhaps, but my point is that you have no choice in this affair. Surely it is better to work with him than to ignore him. At least that way you will be in a position to learn whatever he discovers."

"And vice versa."

Emeline's expression tightened. An uncharacteristic anxiety flickered in her gaze. "Have you got a more cunning plan?"

"I don't know yet." Lavinia came to a halt and reached into the pocket of her gown. She removed the piece of paper that had fallen out of *The Education of a Lady*. She examined the address written on it. "But I intend to find out."

"What have you got?"

"One small clue, which may well lead nowhere." She put the address back into her pocket. "But if that proves to be the case, I can always consider the merits of a partnership with Tobias March."

"She found something important in that bedchamber." Tobias shoved himself up out of the chair and walked around to the front of the wide desk. He leaned back, bracing his hands on either side. "I know she did. I sensed it at the time. Something in the extremely innocent look in her eyes, I believe. Quite an unnatural expression for the woman."

His brother-in-law, Anthony Sinclair, looked up from the depths of a large tome dealing with the subject of Egyptian antiquities.

He lounged in his chair with the negligent ease that only a healthy young man of twenty-one can achieve.

Anthony had moved into his own lodgings last year. For a time, Tobias had wondered if the house would seem lonely. After all, Anthony had come to live with him while still a child when his sister, Ann, had married Tobias. After Ann died, Tobias had done his best to finish raising the boy. He had gotten accustomed to having him underfoot, he thought. The house would seem odd without him.

But within a fortnight of setting up in his own lodgings a few blocks away, it had become clear that Anthony still considered this house an extension of his own rooms. He certainly seemed to be around a lot at mealtime.

"Unnatural?" Anthony repeated neutrally.

"Lavinia Lake is anything but innocent."

"Well, you did say that she was a widow."

"One can only wonder about the fate of her husband," Tobias said with some feeling. "I wouldn't be surprised to learn he spent his last days chained to a cot in a private asylum."

"You have mentioned your suspicions about Mrs. Lake at least a hundred times this morning," Anthony said mildly. "If you are so certain she found a clue last night, why did you not confront her?"

"Because she would have denied it, of course. The lady has no intention of cooperating with me in this matter. Short of up-ending her and giving her a shake or two to empty out her pockets and reticule, there was no way to prove she had discovered some clue."

Anthony said nothing. He just sat there gazing at Tobias with an expression of grave inquiry.

Tobias tightened his jaw. "Don't say it."

"I fear I cannot help myself. Why did you not upend the lady and shake out whatever it was you thought she had found?"

"Bloody hell, you make it sound as if turning respectable females upside down is in keeping with my normal mode of behavior toward the opposite sex."

Anthony raised his brows. "I have pointed out on more than one occasion that your manners where women are concerned could do with some refinement. Nevertheless, they generally fall within the boundaries expected of a gentleman. With the exception of Mrs. Lake. Whenever her name is mentioned, it never fails but that you sink into a fit of extreme rudeness."

"Mrs. Lake is a most exceptional creature," Tobias said. "Exceptionally strong-minded, exceptionally stubborn, and exceptionally difficult. She would give any sane man fits."

Anthony nodded with an air of sympathetic understanding. "It is always so damnably irritating to see one's most pronounced traits mirrored so clearly in another, is it not? Especially when that other person is a member of the fair sex."

"I warn you, I am in no mood to serve as a source of amusement for you this morning, Anthony."

Anthony closed the large book he had been reading with a soft snap. "You have been obsessed by the lady since the incidents in Rome three months ago."

" 'Obsessed' is a gross overstatement of the situation and well you know it."

"I don't think so. Whitby gave me a full account of your ramblings and ravings during that period when he tended to the fever caused by your wound. He said you conducted several lengthy, one-sided, mostly incoherent conversations with Mrs. Lake. Since your return to England, you have found a reason to mention her name at least once a day. I would say that borders on obsessed."

"I was obliged to spend nearly a month trailing around behind the wretched woman in Rome, watching her every move." Tobias gripped the carved edge of his desk. "You try following a female around for such an extended period, keeping track of every person she greets on the street, every shopping expedition. And all the while wondering if she consorts with cutthroats or if she herself is in danger of having her throat slit. I assure you, that sort of thing takes its toll on a man."

"As I said, you developed an obsession."

" 'Obsession' is far too strong a term." Tobias absently rubbed his left thigh. "She leaves an indelible impression, however, I'll grant you that much."

"Evidently." Anthony propped his right ankle on his left knee and carefully adjusted the pleats of his stylish trousers. "Is your leg aching badly today?"

"It's raining outside, in case you haven't noticed. It is always more uncomfortable when the weather turns damp."

"There is no need to snap at me, Tobias." Anthony grinned. "Save your temper for the lady who inspires it. If the two of you do form a partnership to find the diary, I expect you will have ample occasion to vent your ill humors on her."

"The very thought of a partnership with Mrs. Lake is enough to send chills down a man's spine." He paused at the sound of a brisk knock on the door of the study. "Yes, Whitby, what is it?"

The door opened to reveal the short, dapper figure of the man who served as his faithful butler, cook, housekeeper, and, when necessary, doctor. In spite of the occasionally precarious state of the household's income, Whitby always managed to appear elegant. Between Whitby and Anthony, Tobias usually felt at a grave disadvantage when it came to matters of masculine fashion and style.

"Lord Neville is here to see you, sir," Whitby said in the ominously weighted tones he employed whenever called upon to announce persons of high rank.

Tobias knew that Whitby did not actually consider such beings to be superior by virtue of their social status; rather, he reveled in the opportunity to indulge his personal flair for melodrama. Whitby had missed his calling when he had failed to become an actor.

"Send him in, Whitby."

Whitby vanished from the doorway.

Anthony uncoiled slowly from his chair and got to his feet.

"Bloody hell," Tobias said very softly. "I dislike having to deliver bad news to clients. It never fails to annoy them. One never knows when they will decide to stop paying one's fee."

"It is not as though Neville has a great deal of choice," Anthony said just as quietly. "There is no one else to whom he can turn."

A tall, heavily built man in his late forties strode into the room, not bothering to conceal his impatience. Neville's wealth and aristocratic lineage were evident in everything about him, from his hawklike features and the way he carried himself to his expensively cut coat and gleaming boots.

"Good day to you, sir. I did not expect you so early." Tobias straightened and waved a hand in the general direction of a chair. "Please, sit down."

Neville did not respond to the formalities. He searched Tobias's face, his eyes narrowed and intent. "Well, March? I got your message. What the devil happened last night? Any trace of the diary?"

"Unfortunately, it was gone by the time I arrived," Tobias said.

The tight twist of Neville's lips made his disgruntled reaction to the news blazingly clear.

"Damnation." He stripped off a glove. The black stone in the

heavy gold ring on his right hand glittered when he shoved his fingers through his hair. "I had hoped to have this matter resolved quickly."

"I did turn up some useful clues," Tobias continued, striving to project an image of professional expertise and confidence. "I expect to locate it in the near future."

"You must find it as soon as possible. So much hangs upon this matter."

"I am aware of that."

"Yes, of course you are." Neville went to the brandy table and seized the decanter. "Forgive me. I am well aware that we have a mutual interest in finding the bloody diary." He paused with the bottle in midair and glanced at Tobias. "D'you mind?"

"Of course not. Be my guest." Tobias tried not to wince at the sight of the large quantity of brandy that Neville poured into a glass. The stuff was expensive. But it generally paid to be gracious to the client.

Neville took two quick swallows and put down the glass. He studied Tobias with a grim expression. "You must find it, March. If it falls into the wrong hands, we may never know who Azure really was. Worse yet, we will not learn the name of the single surviving member of the Blue Chamber."

"Another fortnight at most and you will have the diary, sir," Tobias said.

"Another fortnight?" Neville stared at him with an appalled expression. "Impossible. That is too long to wait."

"I will do my best to uncover it as soon as possible. That is all I can promise."

"Damnation. Every day that passes is another day in which the diary may be lost or destroyed."

Anthony stirred and politely cleared his throat. "I would remind

you, sir, that it is only because of Tobias's efforts that you are even aware the diary exists in the first place and is somewhere here in London. That is a good deal more information than you had last month at this time."

"Yes, yes, of course." Neville prowled the room with long, restless strides and massaged his temples. "You must forgive me. I have not slept well since learning of the diary's existence. When I think of those who died during the war because of the actions of those criminals, I can scarcely control my rage."

"No one wants to find the damned thing more than I do," Tobias said.

"But what if whoever has it destroys it before we can get hold of it? Those two names will be lost to us."

"I doubt very much that whoever has possession of the diary will consign it to the fire," Tobias said.

Neville stopped rubbing his temples and frowned. "What makes you so certain it will not be destroyed?"

"The only person who might conceivably want it destroyed is the one surviving member of the Blue Chamber, and it is highly unlikely that he has got hold of it. To anyone else, it is worth a great deal of money as a source of blackmail. Why burn potential profits?"

Neville thought about that. "Your logic seems solid," he finally admitted, somewhat grudgingly.

"Give me a little more time," Tobias said. "I will find that diary for you. Perhaps then we shall both sleep better at night."

four

The artist always worked near the hearth. The warmth of the flames together with a pan of hot water and the natural heat of the human hand softened the wax so it could be sculpted and shaped.

Most of the initial modeling was done with thumb and forefinger. It required a strong, sure hand to mold the thick, pliant wax. In the initial stages of creation, the artist often worked with eyes closed, relying on a keen sense of touch to form the image. Later a small, sharp, heated tool would be used to add the all-important fine details that breathed vigor and energy and truth into the waxwork.

In the artist's opinion, the ultimate effect of the finished piece always hinged on the smallest details: the curve of the jaw, the details of the gown, the expression of the features.

Although the viewer's eye rarely focused on such tiny elements, those bits and pieces of reality were the very factors responsible for

eliciting the thrilling shock of comprehension that was the mark of all great art.

Under the artist's hands, the warm wax seemed to pulse as though blood ran beneath the smooth surface. There was no material so perfect for capturing an imitation of life. None so ideal for preserving the instant of death.

five

*L*avinia paused beneath the leafy branches of a tree to check the address on the small slip of paper. Number Fourteen, Hazelton Square, was in the middle of a row of very fine town houses that fronted one side of the lush green park. Elegant colonnades and new gas streetlamps marked the entrance of each residence.

A sense of unease trickled through her as she took in the sight of the two gleaming carriages waiting in the street. They were horsed with glossy, well-matched teams. The grooms who held the reins were attired in expensive livery. As she watched, a lady emerged from Number Sixteen and came down the steps. Her pale pink walking dress with its matching pelisse had obviously come from a modiste who catered to a wealthy, stylish clientele.

This was not quite the sort of neighborhood she had expected to find herself in when she had set out this morning, Lavinia reflected. It was difficult to believe that Holton Felix had been acquainted with, let alone had actually tried to blackmail, a person who lived at such a fashionable address.

She studied the colonnaded residences warily. It would not be easy to talk her way into the front hall of one of these houses. Nevertheless, she could not see any other choice but to make the attempt. The address she held in her hand was the only clue she possessed at the moment. She had to start somewhere.

Steeling herself for the task, she crossed the street and went up the white marble steps of Number Fourteen. She raised the heavy brass knocker and rapped it with what she hoped was an authoritative strike.

Muffled footsteps sounded from the hall. A moment later the door opened. An imperious-looking butler built along the lines of a large bull gazed down at her. She could see by the expression in his eyes that he was already planning to close the door in her face. Hastily she extended one of the crisp, new cards she had ordered from a printer last month.

"Kindly present this to your employer," she said briskly. "It is most urgent. My name is Lavinia Lake."

The butler glanced disdainfully at the note. He clearly harbored grave doubts about the wisdom of accepting it.

"I believe you will find that I am expected," Lavinia said in her iciest tones. It was a bald-faced lie, but it was all she could think of at the moment.

"Very well, madam." He stood back to allow her into the hall. "You may wait here."

She drew a deep breath and stepped hastily over the threshold. She had jumped the first hurdle, she thought. She was inside.

The butler disappeared down a shadowy hall. Lavinia took the opportunity to assess her surroundings. The black and white tiles

beneath her feet, together with the elaborately framed and gilded mirrors on the walls, spoke of fashionable taste and a great deal of money.

She heard the footsteps of the returning butler and held her breath. When he appeared, she knew immediately that her card had worked.

"Mrs. Dove will see you. This way, if you please, madam."

She started to breathe again. So much for the easy part. Now she faced the infinitely more delicate task of persuading a stranger to talk to her about blackmail and murder.

She was shown into a large drawing room done in shades of yellow, green, and gilt. The furnishings were covered in striped silks. Heavy green velvet drapes tied back with yellow cords framed the view of the park. Her footsteps were hushed by a thick carpet woven in the same hues.

A strikingly elegant woman occupied one of the gilded sofas. She was dressed in an exquisitely stylish gown cut from the palest of silver-gray silk trimmed with black. Her hair was caught up at the back of her head in a graceful style that subtly emphasized the graceful length of her neck. From a distance she could have been easily mistaken for a woman in her early thirties. But as Lavinia drew closer she noticed the fine lines at the corners of the intelligent eyes and an unmistakable softness around a throat and jaw that had once no doubt been quite firm. There was a fair amount of silver in the honey-colored hair. The lady was closer to forty-five than thirty-five.

"Mrs. Lake, madam." The butler bowed curtly.

"Do come in, Mrs. Lake. Pray be seated."

The words were spoken in a cool, refined voice, but Lavinia could hear the tension in them. This woman had been living under a great deal of strain.

Lavinia sat down in one of the striped gilded armchairs and tried to look as if she were accustomed to holding conversations in the midst of such fine furnishings. She was very much afraid that her plain muslin gown, once a vivid, reddish brown but now closer to the shade of weak tea, betrayed her. The recent attempt to dye the fabric back to its original hue had not been entirely successful.

"Thank you for seeing me, Mrs. Dove," Lavinia said.

"How could I refuse after you presented such an intriguing card?" Joan Dove raised her elegantly arched brows. "May I ask how it is that you are acquainted with my name when I am well aware we have never met?"

"There is no great secret to that. I simply asked one of the nannies in the park. I was informed that you are a widow who lives here with your daughter."

"Yes, of course," Joan murmured. "People will talk."

"In the course of my new career, I frequently rely on that particular tendency."

Joan tapped the little card absently against the arm of the sofa. "What, precisely, is the nature of your career, Mrs. Lake?"

"I shall explain later, if you are still interested. First, allow me to tell you the reason for my visit here today. I believe we have, or rather I should say, had, a mutual acquaintance, Mrs. Dove."

"Who would that be?"

"His name was Holton Felix."

Joan's brows drew together in a frown of polite bewilderment. She shook her head. "I am not acquainted with anyone by that name."

"Really? I found your address in a book that he kept next to his bed."

She saw that she had Joan's full and unwavering attention. She

was not certain that was a good thing. But she was committed now, Lavinia told herself. There was no turning back. A woman in her profession had to be prepared to take the bold course.

"In a book next to his bed, you say?" Joan sat very still on the sofa, her gaze unwavering. "How very odd."

"Actually, that is not nearly so odd as his profession. He was a blackmailer."

There was a beat of silence.

"Was?" Mrs. Dove repeated with subtle emphasis.

"When I made the acquaintance of Mr. Felix last night, he was dead. Murdered, to be precise."

At that, Joan stiffened ever so slightly. The reaction amounted to no more than a small, involuntary intake of breath and a faint narrowing of the eyes, but Lavinia knew the other woman had received a shock.

Joan recovered quickly, so quickly, in fact, that Lavinia wondered if she had misjudged her reaction to the news of Felix's death.

"Murdered, you say," Joan said as though Lavinia had made a passing remark on the weather.

"Yes."

"You're quite certain?"

"Absolutely certain. It is not the sort of thing that is easily mistaken for other conditions." Lavinia folded her gloved hands together. "Mrs. Dove, I will be frank. I know very little about Holton Felix, but what I do know does his memory no credit. He attempted to blackmail me. I came here today to ask if you were also among his victims."

"What a perfectly outrageous question," Joan said swiftly. "As if I would pay blackmail."

Lavinia inclined her head slightly in polite agreement. "I was equally repelled by the attempt at extortion. In fact, it was because

I was so incensed that I took the trouble to discover Mr. Felix's address. It is why I went to his lodgings last night. I was careful to choose a time in the evening when I had every expectation that he would not be at home."

Joan looked unwillingly fascinated. "Why on earth did you do such a thing?"

Lavinia gave a small shrug. "I went there with the intention of retrieving a certain diary Mr. Felix claimed to possess. It transpired that he was at home for the evening, after all. But by the time I arrived, someone else had already paid him a visit."

"The murderer?"

"Yes."

There was another short, tense silence while Joan appeared to contemplate the news.

"How very adventurous of you, Mrs. Lake."

"I felt I had little choice but to take some action."

"Well," Joan said eventually, "it would seem your problem has resolved itself. Your blackmailer is dead."

"On the contrary, Mrs. Dove." Lavinia smiled coolly. "The matter has grown more complicated. You see, the diary I had hoped to retrieve was not in Mr. Felix's rooms. I was left to conclude that the killer now has it in his or"—Lavinia paused delicately—"her possession, as the case may be."

Joan was not in the least slow-witted, Lavinia noted. She caught the implications immediately. They seemed to amuse her.

"Surely you do not believe I am the person who killed Mr. Felix and took the diary," Joan said.

"I was rather hoping you were the one. It would make things ever so much more simple and straightforward, you see."

An odd expression lit Joan's eyes. "You are a most extraordinary woman, Mrs. Lake. This career you mentioned a moment ago.

Does it by any chance involve treading the boards in Drury Lane or Covent Garden?"

"No, Mrs. Dove, it does not, although I find myself called upon to do a bit of acting now and again."

"I see. Well, this has all been quite entertaining, but I assure you I know nothing of murder and blackmail." Joan made a show of looking at the clock. "Dear me, it is rather late, is it not? I fear I must ask you to leave. I have an appointment with my modiste this afternoon."

This was not going well. Lavinia leaned forward slightly.

"Mrs. Dove, if you were being blackmailed by Holton Felix and if you are not the person who killed him, you are now in a somewhat precarious position. I may be able to assist you."

Joan gave her a look of polite bemusement. "Whatever do you mean?"

"We must consider the possibility that the person who murdered Holton Felix and stole the diary may attempt to set himself up in the extortion business."

"You expect new threats?"

"Even if there are no new blackmail notes, the fact remains that someone out there has the bloody diary. I find that a very disturbing notion, don't you?"

Joan blinked once, but she gave no other sign that the picture Lavinia painted alarmed her. "I mean no offense, Mrs. Lake, but you are starting to sound like a candidate for Bedlam."

Lavinia gripped her hands together very tightly. "Holton Felix must have known something about you, madam. There is no other reason why he would have had your address stuck inside a perfectly dreadful novel devoted to the subject of the debauching of an innocent young woman."

Rage flashed in Joan's expression. "How dare you imply that I

would be acquainted with such an individual. Please remove yourself at once, Mrs. Lake, or I shall ask one of the footmen to perform the task."

"Mrs. Dove, please listen to me. If you were one of Holton Felix's blackmail victims, then you may well possess information that, combined with what I already know of the matter, will enable me to determine the identity of whoever now possesses the diary. Surely you are as interested as I am in recovering it, madam."

"You have wasted enough of my time."

"For a small fee, just enough to compensate me for my time and expenses, you understand, I will be happy to make inquiries into the matter."

"Enough. You are clearly a madwoman." Joan's eyes were as hard as gemstones. "I must insist that you take your leave or I will have you thrown out into the street."

So much for the direct approach, Lavinia thought. It was not always easy finding clients in her new profession.

With a small sigh of frustration, she got to her feet. "I shall see myself out, Mrs. Dove. But you have my card. If you should change your mind, please feel free to call upon me. I suggest you do not delay too long, however. Time is of the essence."

She walked quickly to the door and let herself out of the drawing room. In the front hall the butler gave her a chilling look and opened the front door.

Lavinia tied her bonnet strings and went down the steps. Overhead the sky was leaden. With her luck this afternoon, the rain would no doubt start again before she got home.

She crossed the street and hurried past the park. She hated to admit it, but Emeline had been right. Her niece had warned her that whoever lived at the residence in Hazelton Square was highly

unlikely to admit to being a victim of blackmail and even less eager to employ a stranger to make discreet inquiries into the matter.

She would have to come up with another scheme, Lavinia thought. She turned a corner and went along a narrow walk between two rows of town houses. There had to be a way of convincing Joan Dove to confide in her. She was certain the woman knew a great deal more than she had let on during the short interview.

The shadows in the small passageway darkened abruptly. A chill that had nothing to do with the impending rain shot down Lavinia's spine. She sensed the presence behind her.

Perhaps it had been a mistake to take this shortcut. But she had used it on the way to Hazelton Square and there had been nothing the least bit ominous about the small walk. She stopped and turned quickly.

The large, looming figure of a man garbed in a heavy greatcoat blocked a good deal of what little light entered the tiny passage.

"Imagine finding you here, Mrs. Lake." Tobias March came toward her. "I have been looking everywhere for you."

She was still fuming a short time later when she swept into the small hall of the little house in Claremont Lane. Tobias March was right behind her.

Mrs. Chilton appeared, drying her big, competent hands on the hem of her apron.

"There ye are, ma'am. I was afraid ye wouldn't get home ahead of the rain." She eyed Tobias with unconcealed curiosity.

"Luckily, I made it without getting soaked to the skin." Lavinia stripped off her bonnet and gloves. "That is, however, the only piece of good fortune I have had today. As you can see, we have an

53

uninvited guest, Mrs. Chilton. I suppose you had best prepare a tray and bring it into the study."

"Aye, ma'am." With a last, searching glance at Tobias, Mrs. Chilton turned to go down the hall to the stairs that descended into the kitchen.

"Do not waste the fresh oolong I purchased last week," Lavinia called after her. "I'm sure we still have some of the old, less expensive tea left in the chest."

"Your gracious hospitality is overwhelming," Tobias murmured.

"My gracious hospitality is reserved for those who are invited into my home." She slung the bonnet onto a hook and turned away to stalk down the hall. "Not those who invite themselves."

"Mr. March." Emeline leaned partway over the upstairs railing. "How lovely to see you again, sir."

Tobias looked up and smiled for the first time. "I assure you, the pleasure is mine, Miss Emeline."

Emeline came lightly down the stairs. "Did you go to the address in Hazelton Square too? Is that where you met up with Lavinia?"

"In a manner of speaking," Tobias said.

"He *followed* me to Hazelton Square." Lavinia went through the doorway of the small study. "He was spying on me again, just as he did in Rome. It is really a most irritating habit."

Tobias moved into the cozy room. "It would be an entirely unnecessary habit if you would simply keep me informed of your intentions."

"Why on earth should I do any such thing?"

He shrugged. "Because if you do not, I shall continue to follow you about London."

"This is too much. Absolutely insupportable." She went quickly

toward her desk and sat down behind it. "You have no right to intrude into my personal affairs, sir."

"Nevertheless, that is precisely what I intend to do." Tobias settled himself into the largest chair in the room without waiting to be asked. "At least until this affair of the diary is finished. I strongly suggest that you cooperate with me, Mrs. Lake. The sooner we combine forces, the sooner the matter will be brought to a satisfactory conclusion."

"Mr. March has a point, Lavinia." Emeline walked into the study and took the one remaining chair. "It makes great sense for you two to work together to resolve this business. I told you that this morning before you left the house to find the address in Hazelton Square."

Lavinia glared at both of them. She was trapped and she knew it. Combining forces was only logical. Had she not made precisely the same argument to Joan Dove a short time earlier?

She narrowed her eyes at Tobias. "How do we know that we can trust you, Mr. March?"

"You don't." Unlike the smile he had bestowed on Emeline, the one he gave her held no warmth, only cool amusement. "Just as I have no way of knowing whether or not I can trust you. But I see no sensible alternative for either of us."

Emeline waited expectantly.

Lavinia hesitated, hoping for inspiration. None struck. "Bloody hell." She drummed her fingers on the desk. *"Bloody hell."*

"I know precisely how you feel," Tobias said neutrally. " 'Frustration' is the word that comes to mind, is it not?"

"Indeed, the word 'frustration' does not begin to convey the full depth of my feelings at the moment." She leaned back and gripped the arms of the chair very tightly. "Very well, sir, as

everyone seems to agree that it is the *sensible, logical* thing to do, I am prepared to explore the possibilities of a partnership."

"Excellent." Tobias's eyes gleamed with a triumph he made no attempt to conceal. "It will make matters much simpler and more efficient."

"I sincerely doubt that." She sat forward abruptly. "Nevertheless, I shall attempt the experiment. You may go first."

"First?"

"To show your good faith, of course." She gave him the sweetest smile she could manage under the circumstances. "Tell me what you know of Joan Dove."

"Who is Joan Dove?"

"Bah. I knew it." Lavinia turned to Emeline. "You see? This is pointless. Mr. March possesses even less information than we do. I fail to comprehend how a partnership with him will benefit me."

"Come now, Lavinia. You must give Mr. March a chance."

"I just did. He is quite useless."

Tobias looked at her with an expression of grave humility. "I like to think I have something to offer to you, Mrs. Lake."

She did not trouble to hide her suspicion. "Such as?"

"I presume Joan Dove is the identity of the person who lives in Hazelton Square."

"A brilliant deduction, sir."

Emeline winced at the sarcasm but Tobias appeared undaunted.

"I admit I know nothing about her," he said, "but it should not prove too difficult to uncover a fair amount of information in a relatively short time."

"How do you intend to do that?" Lavinia asked, unwillingly curious. She still had a lot to learn about this new profession, she reminded herself.

"I have a network of informants here in London," Tobias said.

"Spies, do you mean?"

"No, merely a group of reliable business associates who are willing to sell information when it comes their way."

"Sounds like a gang of spies to me."

He let that go. "I can make inquiries, but I'm sure you would agree that it would be a waste of time to duplicate your efforts. If you will tell me what you learned today, matters will progress far more quickly."

"Our conversation was somewhat limited in nature."

Emeline gave a start of surprise. "Lavinia, never say you actually spoke with this Joan Dove?"

Lavinia waved a hand in a casual manner. "Well, yes, as it happens, the opportunity presented itself and I took advantage of it."

"You assured me that you were only going to locate the residence and watch it for a time to see if you could discover anything useful." Emeline frowned with concern. "You said nothing about introducing yourself to anyone in the house."

For the first time, Tobias looked more than irritated. He looked a bit dangerous. "No, Mrs. Lake, until now you did not mention that you actually spoke with Joan Dove."

"It was clear to me that she was very likely another one of Holton Felix's blackmail victims." Lavinia could feel Tobias's cold disapproval. She did her best to ignore it. "I decided to strike while the iron was hot, as it were."

"But, Aunt Lavinia—"

"What the devil did you say to her?" Tobias interrupted much too quietly.

"It is obvious," Emeline said somewhat testily, "that my aunt saw an opportunity not only to gain some information about the mystery but also to acquire a client."

"*Client?*" Tobias looked stunned.

"That is quite enough, Emeline," Lavinia said firmly. "There is absolutely no need to tell Mr. March everything about my personal affairs. I'm certain they are of no concern to him."

"On the contrary," Tobias said, "I assure you that at the moment I have the utmost interest in everything about you, Mrs. Lake. Even the smallest detail is of acute concern to me."

Emeline frowned at Lavinia. "Under the circumstances, I fail to see how you can keep Mr. March in the dark on this matter. He is bound to discover the truth sooner or later."

"Rest assured," Tobias said, "it will be sooner. What the devil is going on here, madam?"

"I am merely struggling to secure a livelihood for myself and my niece that does not involve selling myself on the street," she said.

"And just how are you going about securing this livelihood?"

"The fact that I was obliged to enter a new profession is entirely your fault, Mr. March. It was because of you, sir, that I was forced to embark upon a new business venture, one which has yet to produce a reliable income, I might add."

He was on his feet now. "Damnation, what is this new career of yours?"

Emeline gave him a gentle look of reproof. "There is no need to be alarmed, sir. I'll admit that Lavinia's new profession is a trifle unusual; nevertheless there is nothing actually illicit about it. Indeed, you were her inspiration."

"Bloody hell." Tobias took two strides toward the desk and flattened his palms on the surface. "Tell me what is going on here."

He spoke in a tone of voice that struck Lavinia as all the more unnerving for its extreme softness.

She hesitated, then shrugged and opened the small central drawer of her desk. She removed one of her new cards. Without a

word, she placed it on the polished mahogany surface in front of him where he could see it clearly.

Tobias glanced down. She followed his gaze, reading silently along with him.

PRIVATE INQUIRIES CONDUCTED
DISCRETION ASSURED

She braced herself.

"Of all the bloody nerve." Tobias snatched the card off the desk. "You've gone into my line. What the devil made you think you were qualified?"

"As far as I was able to determine, there are no particular qualifications required in this career," Lavinia said. "Merely a willingness to ask a great many questions."

Tobias narrowed his eyes. "You tried to induce Joan Dove to employ you to find the diary, didn't you?"

"I suggested that she might want to consider giving me a commission to make inquiries into the matter, yes."

"You're quite mad, aren't you?"

"How odd that you should question my sanity, Mr. March. Three months ago in Rome, I had serious doubts about yours."

He sent the small card sailing back across the desk with a flick of his hand. It fluttered in the air and landed directly in front of her.

"If you are not mad," he said without inflection, "you must be a featherbrained idiot. You have no notion of the damage you may have done, do you? You have no concept of the danger involved in this affair."

"Of course I know there is some danger involved. I saw Mr. Felix's skull last night."

He circled the edge of the desk with surprising speed, given his limp. He reached down, grasped her arms, and hauled her out of the chair. He lifted her right off her feet.

Emeline leaped out of her own chair. "Mr. March, what are you doing to my aunt? Please put her down."

He ignored her. His entire attention was focused on Lavinia. "You are a meddling little fool, Mrs. Lake. Do you even begin to comprehend what you have put in jeopardy? I have spent weeks crafting my plans and now you come along and throw everything into a muddle in a single afternoon."

The undisguised fury in his eyes made Lavinia's mouth go dry. The knowledge that he had the power to unnerve her so ignited her temper.

"Unhand me, sir."

"Not until you agree to a partnership."

"Why would you want to work with me when you have such a low opinion of me?"

"We are going to work together, Mrs. Lake, because today's events prove that I cannot take the risk of allowing you to continue on your own. You require close supervision."

She did not like the sound of that. "Really, Mr. March, you cannot hold me here in midair indefinitely."

"Do not depend upon that, madam."

"You are no gentleman, sir."

"You have already mentioned that fact on a prior occasion. Do we have an agreement to work together on this affair of the diary?"

"I have very little interest in forming any connection whatsoever with you. Nevertheless, as I cannot seem to turn around without tripping over you, I am willing to pool our resources and exchange information."

"A wise decision, Mrs. Lake."

"However, I must insist that you refrain from this sort of rude behavior." He was not hurting her, but she was intensely aware of the strength in his hands. "Now set me down, sir."

Without a word, Tobias lowered her until her feet touched the floor, then released her.

She shook out her skirts and put a hand to her hair. She felt flustered and angry and oddly breathless. "This is an outrage. I expect an apology, Mr. March."

"I beg your pardon, madam. There appears to be something about you that brings out the worst in me."

"Oh dear," Emeline murmured. "This partnership is not starting off well, is it?"

Lavinia and Tobias both turned to look at her. Before anyone could speak, the door opened. Mrs. Chilton barged into the study with the tea tray.

"I'll pour," Emeline said quickly. She rushed forward to seize the tray.

By the time three cups had been filled, Lavinia had her temper back under control. Tobias stood at the window, hands clasped behind his back, and looked out into the tiny garden. The remnants of his rather dangerous and unpredictable mood were still evident in the set of his shoulders. She told herself that the fact that he had made no more remarks about featherbrained idiots was a good sign.

When the door closed behind Mrs. Chilton, Lavinia took a fortifying sip of tea and set down her cup with great precision.

The tall clock ticked heavily in the thick silence.

"Let us start again at the beginning," Tobias said flatly. "What, exactly, did you say to Mrs. Dove?"

"I was very forthright with her."

"Bloody hell."

Lavinia cleared her throat. "I merely said I had been a victim of blackmail and had tracked the extortionist to his lair, only to discover that someone else had got there first. I explained that the diary Holton Felix had mentioned in his blackmail notes was gone and that I had found her address tucked into a disgusting novel in the bedchamber."

Tobias turned swiftly to face her. "So that was what you discovered in that room. I knew you had found something. Damnation, why did you not tell me?"

"Mr. March, if you are going to berate me at every step of the way, we shall not make much progress."

His jaw tightened, but he did not argue. "Continue."

"Unfortunately, that's about all there is to tell. She admitted no knowledge of the blackmail affair, but I'm convinced she was one of Felix's victims. I offered to take her on as a client. She refused." Lavinia spread her hands. "I left the house."

There was no need to mention that she had been ordered to leave under threat of being physically tossed out the front door, she thought.

"Did you tell her that I was with you last night?" Tobias asked.

"No. I told her nothing about your involvement in the business."

Tobias contemplated the information in silence for a moment. Then he went to the small table near the big chair and picked up his cup and saucer. "She is a widow, you say?"

"Yes. One of the nannies in the park told me that her husband died nearly a year ago, shortly after the daughter's engagement was announced at a grand ball."

Tobias paused, the cup halfway back to the saucer. Acute interest gleamed in his eyes. "Did the nanny say how he died?"

"Some sort of sudden illness while he was visiting one of his estates, I believe. I did not inquire into the details."

"I see." Tobias set the cup very carefully into the saucer. "You say she did not admit to being blackmailed?"

"No." Lavinia hesitated. "She did not actually say she had received extortion threats. But her manner convinced me that she knew very well what I was talking about. I believe she is quite desperate and I would not be surprised to hear from her soon."

Six

*I*t was still early when Tobias walked into the club later that day. The hushed atmosphere was disturbed only by the faint rustle of newspaper pages being turned, cups clattering in saucers, and the occasional clink of a bottle of port against a glass. Most of the heads visible above the backs of the large, cushioned reading chairs were fringed with gray.

At this hour most of those present tended to be of an age when a man took more interest in whist and the funds than in mistresses and fashion. The younger club members were either shooting pistols at the targets set up at Manton's or paying calls on their tailors.

Their wives and mistresses were no doubt occupied with shopping, Tobias reflected. The two categories of females frequently patronized the same modistes and milliners. It was not unheard of for a gentleman's lady to come face-to-face with his ladybird over

a bolt of fabric. In such cases the wife, of course, was expected to ignore the demirep.

But if the wife in question happened to be of Lavinia's reckless, fiery temperament, he thought, the bit-o'-muslin would likely be well and truly shredded before the end of the encounter. For some reason the image amused him in spite of his dark mood. Then it occurred to him that when she had finished with the mistress, Lavinia would no doubt corner her husband, who would likely get the worst of it. He stopped smiling.

"Ah, there you are, March." Lord Crackenburne lowered his newspaper and peered at Tobias over the rims of his spectacles. "Thought I'd see you here today."

"Good day to you, sir." Tobias took the chair on the other side of the hearth. Absently he started to rub his right leg. "You are very wise to have taken up residence here by the fire. This is no afternoon to be running all over town. The rain has turned the streets to mud."

"I have not engaged in anything so strenuous as running all over town for over thirty years." Crackenburne's gray brows rose and fell above his spectacles. "I prefer to let the world come to me."

"Yes, I know."

Crackenburne had more or less lived here at his club since the death of his beloved wife a decade earlier. Tobias made it a point to visit with him often.

Their friendship went back nearly twenty years, to the day when Tobias, fresh from Oxford and quite penniless, had applied to become Crackenburne's man of business. To this day he did not know why the earl, a man of impeccable lineage, extensive resources, and personal connections to some of the highest-ranking members of Society, had agreed to employ an inexperienced young

man with no references and no family. But Tobias knew he would be eternally grateful for Crackenburne's trust.

He had ceased to handle Crackenburne's financial and business affairs five years ago when he had gone into the private inquiry line, but he continued to value the older man's advice and wisdom. In addition, Crackenburne's penchant for spending most of his time here in his club made him a useful source of rumors and gossip. He always seemed to know the latest *on dit*.

Crackenburne rattled his paper and turned a page. "Now then, what is this I hear about the murder of a certain gambler last night?"

"I'm impressed." Tobias smiled wryly. "How did you come to learn that piece of news? Is it in the papers?"

"No. I eavesdropped on a conversation that was conducted over a game of cards this morning. I recognized Holton Felix's name, naturally, since you had asked me about the man just two days ago. He's dead, then?"

"Most assuredly. Someone crushed his skull with a very heavy object."

"Humph." Crackenburne went back to his paper. "What of the diary Neville employed you to find?"

Tobias stretched out his legs toward the fire. "Gone by the time I arrived on the scene."

"I see. Unfortunate. Don't suppose Neville was pleased to hear that."

"No."

"Any notion of where to start looking for it next?"

"Not yet, but I have let my informants know I am still in the market for any and all information that might lead me to the damned thing." Tobias hesitated. "There has been a new development."

"What is that?"

"I have been obliged to form a partnership for the duration of this venture. My new associate has already come across a clue that may prove useful."

Crackenburne looked up swiftly, faded eyes glinting with astonishment. "A partner? Do you mean Anthony?"

"No. Anthony is my occasional assistant and I intend that he remain in that role. I've explained that I do not want him to become too involved in my business."

Crackenburne was dryly amused. "Even though he enjoys the work?"

"That is beside the point." Tobias steepled his fingers and studied the fire. "This is no field for a gentleman. It is only one step up from being a spy, and the income is, to say the least, unpredictable. I promised Ann that I would see to it that her brother pursued a respectable, stable career. Her greatest fear was that he would end up in the hells, as their father did."

"Has young Anthony demonstrated any interest in a respectable, stable career?" Crackenburne asked dryly.

"Not yet," Tobias admitted. "But he is only one-and-twenty. At the moment his attentions swing wildly among a number of subjects, including science, antiquities, art, and Byron's poetry."

"If all else fails, you can always suggest he try his hand at fortune hunting."

"I fear that Anthony's chances of meeting, let alone marrying, a wealthy wife are extremely small," Tobias said. "Even if he were to stumble across one by accident, his low opinion of young ladies whose conversation centers on gowns and gossip would no doubt sink the endeavor before it set sail."

"Ah well, I would not worry about his future too much, if I were you," Crackenburne said. "It has been my experience that young men tend to make their own decisions. In the end, there is

very little one can do but wish them well. Now, tell me about this new business associate you mentioned."

"Her name is Mrs. Lake. You may recall my mentioning her name to you."

Crackenburne's mouth opened and closed and then opened again. "Good God, man. Never say it is the same Mrs. Lake you encountered in Italy?"

"One and the same. It seems that she was on Felix's list of blackmail victims." Tobias regarded the fire over his steepled fingers. "Blames me for it."

"You don't say." Crackenburne adjusted his spectacles and blinked a number of times. "Well, well, well. What an interesting turn of events."

"It's a damnable complication, so far as I'm concerned. She has set herself up in the business of accepting commissions for private inquiries." Tobias tapped the tips of his fingers together. "I believe I was her inspiration."

"Astonishing. Absolutely astonishing." Crackenburne shook his head. He appeared torn between amusement and amazement. "A lady pursuing a career in the same odd profession you have created for yourself. I vow, it leaves a man quite stunned."

"I assure you that being left stunned is only one of a number of unpleasant effects the news had on me. However, since she intends to pursue the diary on her own, I have little choice but to engage myself as her partner."

"Yes, of course." Crackenburne nodded wisely. "It is the only way to keep an eye on her and control her actions."

"I'm not at all certain that anyone can control Mrs. Lake." Tobias paused. "But as it happens, I did not come here to talk about my problems with my new partner. I sought you out today to ask you a question."

"What would that be?"

"You have connections in Society and you keep track of rumors. What can you tell me about a woman named Joan Dove who lives in Hazelton Square?"

Crackenburne considered the question for a moment. Then he folded his newspaper and set it aside.

"Not a great deal, as it happens. Mr. and Mrs. Dove did not go about much in Society. There is very little gossip to relate. Nearly a year ago, I believe, the daughter got engaged to Colchester's heir. Fielding Dove died shortly afterward."

"Is that all you know of the woman?"

Crackenburne studied the leaping flames. "She was married to Dove for some twenty years. There was a considerable difference in age. He must have been at least twenty-five years older than she, perhaps thirty. I don't know where she came from, nor do I know anything about her family. But I can tell you one thing with great certainty."

Tobias cocked a brow in silent inquiry.

"When Fielding Dove died," Crackenburne said very deliberately, "Joan Dove inherited his extensive business interests. She is now an exceedingly wealthy woman."

"With wealth comes power."

"Yes," Crackenburne said. "And the more wealthy and powerful one is, the more one is tempted to do whatever it takes to keep one's secrets buried."

It was still raining heavily when the elegant carriage came to a halt in front of Number Seven, Claremont Lane. Lavinia peeked through the curtains and saw a muscular footman in handsome green livery spring down to open the door and raise an umbrella.

A heavy veil concealed the features of the woman who was handed down from the vehicle, but Lavinia knew there was only one lady of her acquaintance who could afford such an expensive equipage and who would have reason to come out in such dreadful weather.

Joan Dove carried a package wrapped in cloth. She went quickly up the steps.

In spite of the attentive footman and his umbrella, Joan's kid half boots and the skirts of her elegant dark gray cloak were damp by the time she was shown into the cozy parlor a few minutes later.

Lavinia hastily gave her a chair near the hearth and took the one across from her guest.

"Tea, if you please, Mrs. Chilton." She gave the order briskly, trying to sound as though receiving such a distinguished visitor was an everyday occurrence here in Claremont Lane. "The new, fresh oolong."

"Yes, ma'am, right away, ma'am." Mrs. Chilton, clearly awed, nearly fell over her own feet when she tried to curtsy her way out of the room.

Lavinia turned back to Joan and sought an appropriate comment. "The rain appears to be here to stay for a while." She blushed instantly at the inanity. Not precisely the way to impress a potential client, she thought.

"Indeed." Joan reached up with one black-gloved hand and raised her veil.

Any remaining remarks concerning the nasty weather died in Lavinia's throat when she saw Joan's pale face and stark eyes. Alarm swept through her. She rose quickly and seized the small bell on the mantel.

"Are you all right, madam? Shall I send for a vinaigrette?"

"A vinaigrette will not help me." Joan's voice was amazingly even, given the dread in her eyes. "I am hoping you can, Mrs. Lake."

"What is it?" Lavinia sank slowly back into her chair. "What has happened since we last spoke?"

"This arrived on my doorstep an hour ago." Very deliberately, Joan unwrapped the square package she had brought with her.

The cloth fell away to reveal a small waxwork scene framed in a wooden box that was approximately a foot square. Without a word, Lavinia stood again and took the picture from Joan's hands.

She carried the little waxwork to the window, where the light was better, and studied the artfully wrought, finely detailed scene.

The focal point of the picture was a small but precisely executed wax sculpture of a woman in a finely detailed green gown. She lay crumpled on the floor of a room, her face turned away from the viewer. The high-waisted bodice of the dress was cut very deeply in the back. The hem was trimmed with three rows of small flounces accented with small roses.

But it was the color of the strands of the real hair used on the head of the tiny sculpture that riveted Lavinia's attention. They were blond, streaked with silver. Just like Joan's, she thought.

She looked up from the picture. "This is a most unusual and excellently made waxwork, but I don't understand why you have brought it to me."

"Look closely at the image of the woman." Joan clasped her hands together very tightly in her lap. "Do you see the red on the floor beneath her?"

Lavinia examined the scene. "She appears to be lying on a crimson scarf or perhaps a scrap of red silk." She trailed off as the reality of what she was seeing finally sank in. "Dear heaven."

"Yes," Joan said. "It is a dab of red paint beneath the figure. It

is obviously meant to represent blood. The woman is clearly dead. It is a scene of murder."

Lavinia slowly lowered the horrid little picture and met Joan's eyes. "The lady in this waxwork is intended to be you," she said. "It is a death threat."

"I believe so." Joan looked at the picture in Lavinia's hands. "That green gown is the one I wore on the night of my daughter's engagement ball."

Lavinia thought about that for a few seconds. "Have you worn it on any other occasion?" she asked.

"No. It was made especially for the affair. I have had no other occasion to wear it."

"Whoever created this image must have seen the gown." Lavinia studied the figure. "How many people attended your daughter's engagement ball?"

Joan's mouth curved humorlessly. "Unfortunately, the guest list had well over three hundred names on it."

"Oh dear. That does give us a long list of suspects, does it not?"

"Yes. Thank heavens my daughter is out of town for the month. This would upset her greatly. She is still not entirely recovered from the shock of her father's death."

"Where is she?"

"Maryanne is visiting some of her fiancé's relatives at their estates in Yorkshire. I want this matter resolved before she returns to London. I trust you will begin your inquiries immediately."

One had to be very careful when dealing with persons of quality, Lavinia reminded herself. They could afford one's fees but they were also adept at not paying their bills.

"You wish to give me a commission to discover the identity of the person who sent you this picture?" she asked carefully.

"Why else would I have come here today?"

"Yes, of course." Persons of quality could also be extremely brusque and quite demanding, she reflected.

"Mrs. Lake, you indicated that you were already in the process of conducting inquiries into this affair. Your conversation and your card gave me to understand that you would be willing to accept a commission from me. Is the offer still open?"

"Yes," Lavinia said hastily. "Indeed it is. I will be pleased to accept your commission, Mrs. Dove. Perhaps we should discuss my fees."

"There is no need to go into the details. I do not care what you charge for your services so long as I receive satisfaction. When you have concluded the affair, send the bill, whatever it is, to me. Rest assured, you will be paid." Joan smiled coldly. "Just ask any of the people who do business with me or who supply my household. They will tell you that they always receive their payments in a timely manner."

It would be simple enough to discover the truth of that statement, Lavinia thought. In the meantime, the last thing she wished to do was jeopardize the commission by irritating the client with a discussion of fees.

She cleared her throat. "Well, then, let us begin. I must ask you several questions. I hope you will not feel that I am intruding unnecessarily into your private life."

She broke off at the sound of the front door being opened in the hall.

Joan tensed and glanced toward the closed parlor door. "It appears you have another visitor. I must insist that you do not tell anyone about my reasons for calling on you today."

"Do not distress yourself, Mrs. Dove. That will likely be my niece returning from a call on her new acquaintance, Priscilla

Wortham. Lady Wortham invited her to tea this afternoon. She was so kind as to send her own carriage for Emeline."

Lavinia hoped she did not sound as if she was boasting. She knew very well that an invitation from Lady Wortham would mean little to a person who moved in Joan Dove's wealthy circles. But the invitation to tea had been a social coup for Emeline as far as she was concerned.

"I see." Joan did not take her eyes off the door.

An all-too-familiar masculine voice rumbled in the hall. "Never mind, I'll see myself in, Mrs. Chilton."

"Bloody hell," Lavinia muttered. "His timing is, as always, extremely annoying."

Joan glanced quickly at her. "Who is this?"

The parlor door opened. Tobias walked into the room. He came to a halt at the sight of Joan Dove and made her a surprisingly graceful bow.

"Ladies." He straightened and raised one dark brow in Lavinia's direction. "I see you have made some progress in my absence, Mrs. Lake. Excellent."

"Who is this gentleman?" Joan asked again, very sharply this time.

Lavinia gave Tobias her most repressive glare. "Allow me to introduce my *associate*, Mrs. Dove."

"You made no mention of an associate."

"I was just getting around to it," Lavinia said soothingly. "This is Mr. Tobias March. He is assisting me in my inquiries."

"In point of fact," Tobias said with a meaningful look at Lavinia, "Mrs. Lake is assisting me."

Joan searched his face and switched her gaze to Lavinia. "I do not understand."

"It is really very simple." Lavinia deliberately turned her back

on Tobias. "Mr. March and I are partners in this endeavor. It is actually something of a bargain for you. As my client, you will enjoy the services of both of us for no additional cost."

"Two for the price of one," Tobias said helpfully.

Lavinia managed what she hoped was a reassuring smile. "Mr. March has had some experience with this sort of thing. I assure you he is extremely discreet."

"I see." Joan hesitated. She did not look entirely satisfied, but she was clearly a woman who lacked choices. "Very well."

Lavinia turned back to Tobias and thrust the waxwork into his hand. "Mrs. Dove came here today because a short while ago she received this. She believes it to be a threat on her life, and I agree. The gown the figure is wearing is one of Mrs. Dove's and, as you can see, the hair is the same color as her own."

Tobias examined the picture for a long while. "Odd. One would expect a blackmailer to threaten to expose an old secret, not to send a death threat. Hardly logical to murder the source of one's income."

There was a short, charged silence. Lavinia traded glances with Joan.

"Mr. March has a point," Lavinia muttered ungraciously.

"Yes, he does," Joan said with a thoughtful expression.

Lavinia noticed that her new client was studying Tobias with considerably more interest than she had exhibited a moment ago.

Tobias lowered the picture. "On the other hand, we must bear in mind that we are dealing with a new villain now, one who has already committed murder. This cutthroat may feel that a threat of death is a more effective method of inducing his victims to pay."

Joan nodded in agreement.

It was time to regain control of this affair, Lavinia thought. Tobias was showing every sign of assuming command.

She looked at Joan. "I must ask you a very personal question, Mrs. Dove."

"You wish to know what Holton Felix found in the diary that made him think I would pay him for his silence."

"It would be helpful to know the specifics of his threat, yes."

Joan cast another assessing glance at Tobias. Then she contemplated Lavinia for a moment.

"I shall be as brief as possible," she said finally. "I found myself alone in the world at the age of eighteen and was obliged to pursue a career as a governess. When I was nineteen, I made the mistake of giving my heart to a man, a frequent visitor in the household where I was employed. I believed myself to be in love and assumed my sentiments were returned in full. I fear I was so foolish as to allow him to seduce me."

"I see," Lavinia said quietly.

"He brought me to London and set me up in a small house. All went well for a few months. In my naïveté, I assumed that we would be married." Joan's mouth twisted wryly. "I discovered my mistake when I learned he was already contracted to wed a wealthy heiress. He had never had any intention of marrying me."

Lavinia tightened one hand into a fist. "Dreadful man."

"Yes," Joan said. "Quite. But a rather common story. In the end, of course, he cast me aside. I was desperate and without funds. He stopped paying my rent. I knew I would be forced to move out of my home at the end of the month. My lover had given me nothing in the course of our affair that I could pawn or sell, and I had not thought to extract anything except promises from him. I could not obtain another position as a governess because I had no references."

"What did you do?" Lavinia asked softly.

Joan looked past her toward the window, as if there were something in the steady rain that fascinated her.

"It is difficult to think about it now," she continued quietly, "but at the time my spirits were very depressed. Every night for a week, I walked to the river and considered ending the nightmare. But every night, I walked home before dawn. I suppose one could say I lacked the courage."

"On the contrary," Lavinia said firmly, "you displayed remarkable strength of will in resisting the river. When one's spirits are extremely low, one sometimes cannot imagine getting through another day, let alone a lifetime."

She felt Tobias's gaze slide to her, but she did not look at him.

Joan flashed her a quick, unreadable look and then once more fixed her gaze on the rain. "One night on the way back from the river, I found Fielding Dove waiting for me in the doorway of my house. I had met him a few times in the course of my connection with my lover, but I did not know him well. He made it plain he was interested in forming a liaison. He said he had paid my rent for me and I was not to worry about it." Joan smiled wryly. "I understood he meant to become my new protector."

"What did you do?" Lavinia asked.

"I can hardly credit it now, but from out of nowhere, I recovered my pride. I told him I was not in the market for a lover but I would very much appreciate a loan. I promised to repay him as soon as possible. To my amazement, he merely nodded and asked me how I planned to invest the funds."

Tobias lowered himself somewhat stiffly into a chair. "Dove gave you the money?"

"Yes." Joan smiled wistfully. "And some investment advice. I put the money into a building venture he recommended. We met and talked many times while the houses and shops were being built. I came to think of Fielding as a friend. When the properties were sold a few months later, I received what seemed like a fortune at the time. I immediately sent a note to Fielding telling him I was in a position to repay him."

"How did he respond?" Lavinia asked.

"He called upon me and asked me to marry him." Joan's eyes were shadowed with memories. "By then, of course, I was deeply in love. I accepted his offer."

Lavinia felt the moisture gathering in her eyes. She sniffed twice in a vain attempt to keep the tears from streaming down her cheeks. Tobias and Joan looked at her.

"Forgive me, Mrs. Dove, but yours is a very affecting tale," Lavinia said.

She yanked a hankie out of her pocket and hastily blotted up the tears. When she was finished, she blew her nose as discreetly as possible.

She lowered the little square of embroidered linen and saw that Tobias was watching her with a derisive gleam in his eyes. She gave him a disgusted look. Obviously the man possessed no refined sensibilities. But then, she was already well aware of that fact, she reminded herself.

She wadded up the hankie and stuffed it back into her pocket. "Forgive me, Mrs. Dove, but may I conclude that Holton Felix threatened to expose the liaison in which you engaged prior to your marriage?"

Joan glanced down at her hands and then nodded. "Yes."

"What a horrid little man he was," Lavinia said.

"Huh," Tobias said.

Lavinia gave him another repressive look. He paid no attention.

"No offense, madam, but I fail to see how that particular threat

would have created much of a scandal," he said. "After all, the affair ended over twenty years ago."

Joan stiffened. "My daughter is engaged to Colchester's heir, Mr. March. If you know anything at all about the family, you will be aware that his grandmother Lady Colchester controls much of the family fortune. She is extremely high in the instep. The least hint of scandal would be more than enough to convince her to force her grandson to call off the marriage."

Tobias shrugged. "I would not have thought that such old scandal broth would have caused much of an uproar."

Joan sat motionless. "I will be the judge of what is at risk here. My husband was delighted with the Colchester alliance. I will never forget the happiness in his eyes when he danced with Maryanne at her engagement ball. And as for my daughter, she is deeply in love. I will not let anything get in the way of this marriage, Mr. March. Do you comprehend me?"

Lavinia rounded on Tobias before he could respond. "It is all very well for you to entertain doubts, sir, but I will thank you to keep them to yourself. What do you know of marital alliances formed in such elevated circles? A young woman's future is at stake. Her mother has every right to take precautions."

"Yes, of course." Tobias's eyes glinted with ironic amusement. "Forgive me, Mrs. Dove. Mrs. Lake is quite correct. I have not had a lot of experience with marital alliances formed in, uh, elevated circles."

To Lavinia's surprise, Joan actually smiled.

"I understand," Joan murmured.

"I assure you, the fact that Mr. March does not move in exclusive circles will not prevent him from being able to conduct his inquiries," Lavinia said hastily. She gave Tobias a speaking look. "Will it, sir?"

"I generally manage to find out what I need to know," Tobias said.

Lavinia turned back to Joan. "Rest assured we shall begin our inquiries immediately."

"Where do you propose to start?" Joan asked, genuine curiosity in her eyes.

Lavinia stood and walked to the table where Tobias had placed the waxwork death threat. She examined it closely again, noting the fine details.

"This is clearly not the work of an amateur," she said slowly. "I believe we should begin by seeking advice from some workers in wax. Artists often have distinctive styles and methods. With luck we may find someone who can tell us something about the unique elements of this particular sculpture."

Tobias regarded her with poorly veiled surprise. "That is not a bad notion."

She clamped her teeth together.

"How will you discover the names of these expert modelers in wax?" Joan asked, clearly oblivious to the byplay.

Lavinia drew a finger slowly along the frame of the picture. "I shall ask my niece for some advice in the matter. Emeline has been going about to a great many museums and galleries of all sorts since we returned to London. She will likely know the ones that exhibit waxwork sculptures."

"Excellent." Joan rose gracefully and adjusted her gloves. "I shall leave you to it." She paused. "Unless you have some more questions for me?"

"Only one." Lavinia hesitated, gathering her nerve. "I fear you will find it presumptuous."

Joan appeared dryly amused. "Really, Mrs. Lake. I cannot imag-

ine a more presumptuous question than the one concerning why I am being blackmailed."

"The thing is, my niece has received a small number of invitations, thanks to Lady Wortham. But Emeline requires some new gowns if she is to go about with Priscilla. I am wondering if you would be so kind as to supply me with the name of your modiste."

She could almost feel Tobias raising his eyes to the ceiling, but he had the good sense not to speak.

Joan contemplated Lavinia with a thoughtful expression. "Madame Francesca is very expensive."

"Yes, well, as to that, I have a plan to finance at least one or two nice gowns."

"I am sorry to tell you that she takes new clients only on recommendation."

Lavinia's spirits plummeted. "I see."

Joan walked toward the door. "I shall be happy to supply you with one."

They showed the malignant little waxwork to Emeline a short time later.

"If I were you, I would start with Mrs. Vaughn in Half Crescent Lane." Emeline studied the picture with a troubled expression. "She is by far the most proficient worker in wax in London."

"I have never heard of her," Lavinia said.

"Probably because she does not receive many commissions."

"Why not?" Tobias asked.

Emeline looked up from the waxwork. "You will understand when you see her creations."

Seven

I congratulate you on securing a client to pay your expenses in this affair." Tobias lounged in the hackney seat. "It is always pleasant to know that when one is finished one can send a bill to someone."

"I very nearly lost her, thanks to you, sir." Lavinia pulled her serviceable woolen cloak more snugly around herself, warding off the damp chill. "I do not believe you could have been any more rude if you had tried."

He smiled slightly. "At least I did not presume to inquire the name of her modiste."

Lavinia ignored him. Very pointedly she looked out the carriage window.

London was a study rendered in a thousand shades of gray today. Paving stones gleamed damply beneath a lowering sky. The rain had driven most people indoors. Those who braved the weather took

refuge in carriages or dashed from doorway to doorway. The coach-men huddled on their boxes, swathed in their many-caped great-coats, hats pulled down over their ears.

"Would you like a word of advice?" Tobias asked mildly.

"From you? Not particularly."

"Nevertheless, I am going to give you some words of wisdom, which you will do well to heed if you elect to continue in your new career."

Unwillingly she dragged her attention away from the gloomy street. He was an expert, she reminded herself.

"What advice do you have for me, sir?"

"It is never a good idea to cry when clients tell you their tales of woe. It gives them the impression that you will believe what-ever they say. In my experience, clients tend to lie quite regularly. There is no reason to encourage them with tears."

She stared. "Are you saying you think Mrs. Dove lied to us?"

He shrugged. "Clients always lie. If you continue in this profession for long, you will soon learn that simple fact of business."

She gripped the edges of her cloak very tightly. "I do not be-lieve for one moment that Mrs. Dove invented her story."

"How would you know?"

She raised her chin. "I have a keen sense of intuition."

"I shall take your word for it."

He never failed to annoy her, she thought.

"Allow me to tell you, sir, that my parents were both skilled practitioners of mesmerism. I became their assistant at a very early age. After their deaths I continued to make my living for some time giving therapeutic treatments. Intuition is a requirement for success in that field. Indeed, my father told me on a number of occasions that I had a talent for the business."

"Bloody hell. I have a practitioner of animal magnetism as a partner. What did I do to deserve this?"

She gave him a thin smile. "I am glad that you are amused, sir, but it does not change the fact that I believe Mrs. Dove's story." She paused. "Most of it in any event."

He shrugged. "I will allow that she probably did not invent *all* of it. I suspect she is smart enough to know that interweaving fact with fiction makes for a more genuine-sounding tale."

"You are very cynical, Mr. March."

"It is an asset in this business."

She narrowed her eyes. "I will tell you one thing for certain. She was not lying about her love for her late husband."

"If you remain in this career for long, you will eventually learn that all clients lie when it comes to the subject of love."

The hackney rattled to a halt before she could pursue the matter. Tobias opened the door and made to alight. He did not drop lightly to the street, she noticed. Rather, he eased himself out of the vehicle with the air of a man who was in some pain. But when he turned to assist her, his face was impassive.

A small shock of awareness went through her when she felt the strength in his hand. She allowed him to bundle her into the shelter of a doorway and tried to cover her unsettling reaction by pretending a deep interest in their surroundings.

Half Crescent Lane was a cramped, curved passage. It twisted through a narrow, densely shadowed valley formed by looming stone walls. It was probably never a sunny place, but on a day such as this it was drenched in stygian gloom.

Tobias rapped sharply on the door. Footsteps sounded from within. A moment later an aged housekeeper appeared. She squinted at Tobias.

"What is it ye want?" she inquired in the very loud tones used by those who were hard of hearing.

Tobias winced and took a step back. "We're here to see Mrs. Vaughn."

The housekeeper cupped her ear with one hand. "What's that?"

"We're here to see the modeler in wax," Lavinia said, enunciating her words very carefully.

"Ye'll 'ave to purchase a ticket," the housekeeper announced in ringing accents. "Mrs. Vaughn doesn't let anyone into her gallery without a ticket anymore. Too many folks takin' advantage, y'know. Claim they want to give her a commission but once they're inside they just have themselves a good look at the sculptures and then they leave."

"We're not here to view her waxworks," Lavinia said loudly. "We wish to speak with her on another matter."

"I've 'eard all the excuses. None of 'em will work with me and that's a fact. No one gets in without a ticket."

"Very well." Tobias dropped a few coins into the woman's hand. "Is that enough to get us two tickets?"

The housekeeper examined the coins. "That'll do, sir, that'll do."

She stepped back. Lavinia walked into the small, poorly lit hall. Tobias followed her. When the door closed behind him, the shadows intensified.

The housekeeper moved off down a darkened corridor. "This way, if ye please."

Lavinia glanced at Tobias. He made a slight movement with his hand, motioning her to precede him down the hall.

Without a word, they followed the housekeeper to the end of the passageway. She opened a heavy door with a theatrical flourish.

"Go right in," she shouted. "Mrs. Vaughn will be with you in a moment or two."

"Thank you." Lavinia stepped into the dimly lit chamber and came to an abrupt halt when she saw that a number of people were gathered there. "I didn't realize Mrs. Vaughn already had guests."

The housekeeper cackled and shut the door, leaving Tobias and Lavinia inside the crowded room.

Heavy drapes were drawn across the two narrow windows, shutting out what little light might have managed to seep into the chamber from without. The only illumination came from the two tapers in the large, ornately worked candelabra that sat atop the piano. There was a decided chill in the atmosphere. It seemed to emanate from the dense shadows around the visitors. Lavinia saw that there was no fire on the hearth.

The other guests stood and sat in a variety of poses. A man with an elegantly tied cravat read quietly in a wing-back chair, although he did not have a candle beside him to throw light on the page. His legs were casually crossed at the ankle. A comfortably rounded woman dressed in a long-sleeved gown trimmed with a crisp white ruff occupied the piano bench. She wore a large white apron. Her thick gray hair was pinned in a heavy knot beneath a lace cap. Her fingers hovered in the air just above the keys as though she had just finished one piece and was about to begin another.

Near the unlit hearth sat a man with a half-finished glass of brandy in his hand. Next to him two other gentlemen were engaged in a game of chess.

An eerie stillness cloaked the long, narrow chamber. No heads turned to look at the new arrivals. No one moved. No one spoke.

The piano remained silent. It was as if everyone in the chamber had been frozen forever in a moment of civilized pursuit.

"Good heavens," Lavinia breathed.

Tobias moved past her and crossed to where the chess players sat at a game that would never be finished.

"Astonishing," he said. "I have seen other examples of wax-works but none so close to life as these."

Lavinia walked slowly toward the figure reading the small volume. The waxwork head was tilted at a realistic angle. The glass eyes appeared to be absorbed with the print on the page. There was a small frown between the brows, and tiny hairs rose from the back of the veined hands.

"One almost expects them to speak or move," she whispered. "I vow, there is even a slight bluish tint to the veins, and just look at the pale cast of that woman's cheek. It is unnerving, is it not?"

"Your niece told us that most workers in wax use clothing and jewelry and other items to achieve the effect of a living image." Tobias moved to a woman dressed in a fashionable gown. The fingers of the figure's hand toyed negligently with a fan. She seemed to smile coyly. "But Mrs. Vaughn is a master in her profession, an artist who need not rely on tricks. These statues are brilliantly modeled."

The figure in the apron and cap seated at the piano bowed from the waist.

"Thank you, sir," she said with a merry chuckle.

Lavinia swallowed a small shriek and took a hasty step back. She came up against a dandy who frowned at her through a quizzing glass. She jerked herself aside as if the figure had reached out to touch her. In the process she nearly dropped the package she had brought with her.

She caught her balance, feeling foolish, then shook out the folds of her cloak and summoned a determinedly polite smile.

"Mrs. Vaughn, I presume?" she said briskly.

"Yes, indeed."

"I am Mrs. Lake and this is Mr. March."

Mrs. Vaughn rose from the piano bench. Her smile dimpled her cheeks. "Welcome to my exhibition chamber. I invite you to examine my figures for as long as you please."

Tobias inclined his head. "My congratulations, madam. This is an amazing collection."

"Your admiration is extremely gratifying, sir." Mrs. Vaughn looked at Lavinia, amusement sparkling in her bright eyes. "But something tells me that Mrs. Lake is more reserved in her opinion."

"Not at all," Lavinia said quickly. "It is just that the impact of your art is . . . unexpected. Striking, I should say. I mean, it is as if this room is filled with people who are . . . well . . . uh—"

"People who are not quite alive and yet not quite dead, is that what you mean?"

Lavinia smiled weakly. "Your skill is extremely impressive."

"Thank you, Mrs. Lake. But I can see you are one of those who are not entirely comfortable with my art."

"Oh, no, really, it is just that these figures are so very life-like." *Corpselike* would have been a more accurate description, she thought. But she did not want to appear critical. After all, the woman was an artist. Everyone knew they were eccentric and inclined to be temperamental.

Mrs. Vaughn's dimples appeared again. She waved a hand in a reassuring gesture. "You need not worry about offending me, Mrs. Lake. I am well aware that my work is not to everyone's taste."

"They are certainly interesting," Tobias said.

"Nevertheless, I gain the impression you are not proposing to give me a commission for a family portrait, either."

"You are a very astute woman, Mrs. Vaughn." Tobias studied the elegantly modeled throat of the woman with the fan. "Perhaps that is why your figures achieve such a semblance of life."

Mrs. Vaughn gave another bubbling chuckle. "I do pride myself on an ability to read the truth that lies just beneath the surface. You are quite right—that skill is key to achieving an accurate portrayal. But it requires more than insight to bring a figure to life. It takes a great amount of detail work. The little lines at the corner of the eye. The accurate placement of the veins so they appear to throb with blood. That sort of thing."

Tobias nodded. "I see."

Lavinia thought about the extraordinary degree of detail in the waxwork picture she clutched and went very still. What if fate had led them directly to the killer? Across the room, she caught Tobias's eye. He shook his head slightly.

She took a deep breath to compose herself. He was right, of course. It was simply too much of a coincidence to believe they had come straight to the killer seeking answers about a death threat she had sent. Then again, how many expert workers in wax were there in London? The number could not be large. Emeline had put Mrs. Vaughn at the top of the list of the most skilled without any hesitation.

As if she had read Lavinia's mind, Mrs. Vaughn glanced at her with a knowing expression and smiled broadly.

Lavinia shook off the cobwebs of unease that had settled over her senses. What on earth was the matter with her? She was allowing her thoughts to become disordered. It was impossible to envision this small, cheerful woman in the role of murderess.

"We came here today to consult with you about that very sub-ject, Mrs. Vaughn," she said.

"Artistic details?" Mrs. Vaughn beamed. "How intriguing. There is nothing I love to discuss more than my art."

Lavinia put the package on the nearest table. "If you would be so kind as to examine this waxwork and tell us what you can about the artist who created it, we would be extremely grateful."

"The work is unsigned?" Mrs. Vaughn moved closer to the ta-ble. "How unusual."

"I think you will comprehend why the artist did not inscribe his signature when you see the picture," Tobias said dryly.

Lavinia untied the string that bound the cloth. The material fell aside to reveal the unpleasant scene.

"Oh my." Mrs. Vaughn removed a pair of silver spectacles from the pocket of her apron and pushed them onto the bridge of her nose. She did not take her gaze off the picture. "Oh my."

Troubled lines appeared between her brows. She picked up the picture and carried it across the room to put it down on top of the piano. Lavinia followed. She stood behind Mrs. Vaughn and watched as the tapers in the candelabra cast a flaring light across the miniature ballroom and the dead woman in the green gown.

"Can I assume that this is not intended to illustrate a scene from a play or novel?" Mrs. Vaughn asked without looking away from the waxwork.

"You assume correctly." Tobias came to stand next to Lavinia. "We believe it was meant as a threat. We wish to find the artist who made it."

"Indeed," Mrs. Vaughn whispered. "Indeed. I can certainly understand your desire to do that. There is great malevolence in this little piece. Great anger. Great hatred. Was it sent to you, Mrs. Lake? No, that cannot be. The hair is blond caught in the process

of turning slowly silver. You are a younger woman and your hair is quite red, is it not?"

Tobias gave Lavinia's hair an enigmatic glance. "It is very red."

She scowled at him. "There is no need for personal remarks, sir."

"Merely an observation."

It was more than an observation, Lavinia thought. She wondered if Tobias was one of those men who disliked red-haired women. Perhaps he actually believed all that nonsense about fiery tempers and difficult dispositions.

Mrs. Vaughn looked up. "How did this little picture come into your hands?"

"It was left on the doorstep of an acquaintance," Tobias said.

"How odd." Mrs. Vaughn hesitated. "I must say, the piece is very elegantly modeled, for all its unpleasantness."

"Have you ever seen workmanship of this quality?" Lavinia asked.

"Other than my own, do you mean? No." Mrs. Vaughn slowly removed her spectacles. "I cannot say I have. I make it a point to tour the galleries and exhibitions of my competitors. I would have remembered such skill."

"Do you think we can assume, then, that the artist is not exhibiting to the public?" Tobias asked.

Mrs. Vaughn frowned. "I would not assume any such thing, sir. An artist possessed of this degree of talent would find it extremely difficult not to exhibit his creations. There is a need to have one's work seen and appreciated."

"One can hardly make a living otherwise," Lavinia said.

Mrs. Vaughn shook her head decisively. "It is not simply the money, Mrs. Lake. Indeed, if the artist is wealthy, the money is the least of it."

Lavinia glanced at the nearest of the fascinating waxworks. "I understand."

"There really are not that many expert modelers in wax, you know," Mrs. Vaughn continued. "I fear waxwork is rapidly declining from the level of true art to a type of entertainment meant to appeal primarily to bloodthirsty schoolboys and apprentice lads. I blame the late, unpleasant business in France. All those death masks Madame Tussaud was obliged to make after the guillotine had done its work. It gave the public a taste for art that produces horrid thrills in the viewer."

As if her own work did not create a few cold chills, Lavinia thought. "Thank you very much for giving us your opinion on this waxwork." She picked up the picture and began to rewrap it. "I had hoped you would be able to give us some clues. But it appears we shall have to pursue another avenue of inquiry."

Mrs. Vaughn's round face lost much of its bright-eyed good cheer. "You will be cautious, I trust."

Cold interest sparked in Tobias's expression. "What do you wish to imply, madam?"

Mrs. Vaughn watched Lavinia tie a knot in the string. "Whoever modeled that picture was clearly intent on inducing terror in the heart of the person who received it."

Lavinia thought about the stark dread she had seen in Mrs. Dove's eyes. "If that was, indeed, the artist's goal, I assure you he or she was successful."

Mrs. Vaughn pursed her lips. "I regret I cannot tell you the name of the artist who created this picture. But I can tell you that you are looking for someone who is consumed with a desire to inflict revenge or, perhaps, punishment. In my experience, there is only one thing that can turn so completely to hate."

Lavinia stilled. "What is that, Mrs. Vaughn?"

"Love." Mrs. Vaughn smiled again. The sparkling cheerfulness returned to her eyes. "It really is quite the most dangerous of all the emotions, you know."

Almost everyone had a strong opinion on love today, Lavinia reflected.

eight

"I don't know about you, Mr. March," Lavinia declared as she swept through the door of her study a short time later, "but I vow I am sorely in need of something of a medicinal nature to settle my nerves. Mrs. Vaughn and her collection of waxworks left me with a most unpleasant sensation."

Tobias closed the door very deliberately and looked at her. "For once, Mrs. Lake, we are in complete agreement."

"I do not believe that a pot of hot tea will be effective in this instance. A stronger tonic is required."

She crossed the room and opened an oak chest to reveal the cut-glass decanter inside. It was nearly full.

"We are in luck." She seized the decanter. "I believe I have found a remedy for what ails us. If you will see to the fire, sir, I shall pour us both a glass."

"Thank you." Tobias walked to the hearth and went stiffly down on one knee. His expression tightened.

Lavinia frowned, the sherry decanter tilted over a glass. "Did you injure your leg, sir?"

"A small misstep." He concentrated on setting the kindling ablaze. "The leg healed nicely, but on days such as this I am occasionally aware of my mistake."

"Mistake?"

"Pray do not concern yourself, Mrs. Lake." He finished his task, gripped the edge of the mantel, and pulled himself to his feet. When he turned toward her, his expression was politely unreadable. "It is nothing, I assure you."

It was clear to her that he did not want to make further explanations, and the condition of his leg was certainly none of her business. Furthermore, she had no cause to feel the least bit of sympathy for Tobias March. Nevertheless, she could not repress the twinge of concern.

He must have seen something in her eyes because his own hardened in annoyance. "The sherry will suffice to take care of the problem."

"There is no need to snarl at me, sir." She splashed the liquor into the second glass. "I was merely being polite."

"Between us, madam, there is no need for such niceties. We are partners, remember?"

She handed him one of the glasses. "Is there a rule in the private inquiry profession stating that partners do not have to be civil with each other?"

"Yes." He downed a large quantity of the contents in a single swallow. "I just invented it."

"I see."

She took a healthy sip from her own glass. The warmth of the sherry had a reviving effect on both her spirits and her temper. If the man did not want polite concern, she would certainly not go out of her way to smother him with the stuff.

She stalked to one of the chairs in front of the fire and dropped into it with a small sigh of relief. The heat of the flames drove out the damp chill that had clung to her after leaving Mrs. Vaughn's establishment.

Tobias took the large chair across from her without waiting for an invitation. They sat together in silence for several minutes, sipping from their glasses without comment. Tobias began to rub his left leg.

After a while, Lavinia got restless.

"If your leg pains you greatly, sir, I might be able to relieve some of the discomfort with a mesmeric treatment."

"Don't contemplate such a notion for even a moment," he said. "Do not take offense, Mrs. Lake, but I have absolutely no intention of allowing you to put me into a trance."

She stiffened. "As you wish, sir. There is no need to be rude."

His mouth twisted. "Forgive me, madam, but I do not believe in the so-called powers of mesmerism. My parents were students of science. They agreed with the results of the public inquiry conducted by Dr. Franklin and Lavoisier. The whole business of inducing therapeutic trances with the power of the gaze or with magnets is utter nonsense. Demonstrations of that sort are best suited to entertaining the gullible."

"Bah. That inquiry was conducted over thirty years ago, and bear in mind that it was held in Paris. I would not put too much stock in it if I were you. You will notice that it did nothing to lessen the public's interest in animal magnetism."

"I have noticed that fact," Tobias said. "It says little for the intelligence of the general public."

If she had any sense, she would let the conversation end there, she thought. But she could not resist probing deeper. "Your parents were students of science?"

"My father conducted researches in electricity, among other things. My mother was very taken with the study of chemistry."

"How very interesting. Do they continue to perform experiments?"

"They were both killed in an explosion in their laboratory."

She caught her breath. "How dreadful."

"From what I was able to make out from their last letter to me, I believe they had hit upon the idea of combining their two fields of research. They decided to conduct a series of experiments involving certain volatile chemicals and an electrical apparatus. It proved disastrous."

She shuddered. "Thank heaven you were not injured in the explosion."

"I was away at Oxford at the time. I came home to bury them."

"Did you return to Oxford after their deaths?"

"That was not possible." Tobias cupped the glass in his hands. "The explosion destroyed the house and there was no money. My parents had used all of their financial resources to fund their last great experiment."

"I see." Lavinia rested her head against the back of her chair. "Yours is a very tragic story, sir."

"It all happened a long time ago." He took another mouthful of sherry and lowered the glass. "What of your parents?"

"They were invited to America to give a series of demonstrations of mesmerism. They accepted. Their ship went down. All aboard were lost."

His jaw tightened. "I'm sorry for your loss." He glanced at her.

"You said you assisted them in their demonstrations. How did it happen that you were not with them?"

"I had recently married. The gentleman who had invited my parents to America was unwilling to pay for the cost of two additional passages. John was not keen on the notion, in any event. He was a poet, you see. He felt that America was not conducive to the practice of serious metaphysical contemplation."

Tobias nodded. "He was no doubt correct in that assumption. When did your husband die?"

"Eighteen months after we were wed. A fever took him."

"My sympathies."

"Thank you."

In the nearly ten years since his death, the sweet, gentle memories she had of John had taken on the wispy quality of an old dream, she reflected.

"Forgive me for asking," Tobias said, "but did your husband ever publish any of his poetry?"

She sighed. "No. His work was quite brilliant, of course."

"Of course."

"But as is so often the case with true poetic genius, it went unappreciated."

"I've heard that is a common occurrence." He paused. "May I ask how you survived financially? Did your husband have another source of income?"

"During the course of our marriage, I supported us by giving mesmeric treatments. After John's death, I continued in the profession for a few years."

"Why did you stop?"

Lavinia took a sip of sherry and lowered the glass. "There was an unfortunate incident in a small village in the north."

"What sort of incident?"

"I do not care to discuss it. Suffice it to say that I thought it best to pursue another career."

"I see. And when did Emeline come to live with you?"

"Six years ago, after her parents were killed in a carriage accident." It was time to change the subject, Lavinia thought. "Emeline said that after we viewed Mrs. Vaughn's waxworks, we would understand why she does not receive many commissions for her sculptures. I think I know now what she meant."

"Indeed."

"There may be such a thing as art that is too true to life. I found her statues . . ." She hesitated, searching for the right word. "Disquieting."

"Perhaps it is the very nature of wax." Tobias studied the remaining sherry in his glass with a thoughtful expression. "The material is not innately cold like stone or clay. Nor does it allow for a two-dimensional image as is the case with a painting. Nothing looks more like human flesh when it is well modeled and properly painted."

"Did you notice that Mrs. Vaughn went so far as to use real hairs on the hands and eyebrows and eyelashes?"

"Yes."

"Her work is extraordinary, but I would not want any of her figures sitting here." Lavinia shuddered. "It is one thing to have a painted portrait of one's grandfather hanging over the fireplace. Quite another to have a life-size, three-dimensional image of him occupying a chair in one's study."

"Indeed." Tobias gazed meditatively into the fire.

The flames leaped into the next pool of silence.

After a while, Lavinia got to her feet to fetch the sherry

decanter from its cupboard. She refilled the two glasses and then sat down again. This time she left the decanter on the table next to her chair.

She thought about what it was like to have Tobias here in her study. They had nothing in common, she told herself. Unless one counted a murdered blackmailer, a missing diary, and a business arrangement that would eventually end.

It was difficult *not* to count those things, she discovered.

After a while, Tobias stretched out his left leg in what appeared to be an attempt to make himself more comfortable.

"I suggest we return to the problem at hand," he said. "I have been thinking of how we should proceed in this matter. It strikes me that Mrs. Vaughn was not terribly helpful today. All that blather about love turning to hate was useless."

"That remains to be seen."

"It certainly did not give us any clues. I'm not at all sure this business of interviewing the proprietors of waxwork museums will lead us in the right direction."

"Have you got a better notion?" she asked bluntly.

He hesitated. "I have put the word out to my informants that I will pay well for any information on the diary. But, at this moment, I must admit I have heard nothing from that quarter."

"In other words, you do not have a better notion of how to proceed."

He tapped his fingers on the arm of the chair. Abruptly he pushed himself to his feet. "No," he said. "I do not have a better notion."

She watched him warily. "Then we may as well talk to the other museum proprietors."

"I suppose so." He gripped the edge of the mantel and looked

at her with an enigmatic expression. "But it might be best if I handle the remainder of the interviews alone."

"*What?*" She slammed the sherry glass down on the table and leaped to her feet. "Do not even *think* about proceeding on your own without me, sir. I will not hear of it."

"Lavinia, this situation grows more complicated and dangerous by the hour. It is clear to me now that it will not be easily resolved. I do not like the idea of your getting more deeply involved."

"I am already involved, sir. Lest you forget, in addition to having a client who has given me a commission to conduct inquiries into this matter, I was one of Holton Felix's blackmail victims."

"I would, of course, continue to consult with you and keep you advised."

"Rubbish. I know what this is about." She fitted her hands to her hips. "You're trying to steal my client, are you not?"

"Bloody hell, Lavinia, I don't give a damn about your client. I'm trying to ensure the safety of your person."

"I am quite capable of looking out for myself, Mr. March. Indeed, I have been doing so very successfully for a number of years. This is a ploy to get your hands on my client, and I will not allow it."

He took his hand off the mantel and caught her gently by the chin. "You really are the most stubborn, most difficult woman I have ever met."

"Coming from you, sir, I must take that as a compliment."

The warmth of his fingers held her as motionless as any mesmeric trance. An awareness that was almost painful in its intensity fluttered through her. She suddenly felt light-headed.

He was too close, she thought. She really ought to step back and put some distance between them. But oddly enough, she could not seem to summon the willpower to do so.

"There is something I have been meaning to ask you," he said very softly.

"If you think to talk me out of my client, think again."

"My question has nothing to do with Joan Dove." He did not take his fingers away from her chin. "I want to know if you truly despise me for what happened in Italy."

Her jaw would have dropped, she thought, but for the fact that he held it fast in his hand. "I beg your pardon, sir?"

"You heard me."

"I do not comprehend what you are about," she muttered.

"That makes two of us." He raised his other hand and cradled her face between his palms. "Do you despise me for the events in Rome?"

"You certainly could have handled matters in a less outrageous fashion."

"There was no time. I explained that I had very little warning that Carlisle intended to make his move the same night."

"Excuses, sir. Nothing but excuses."

"Do you *despise* me for them?"

She threw up her hands. "No. I do not despise you. Mind you, I believe matters could have been handled in a more civil fashion, but I can see that good manners are not your strong point."

He brushed his thumb across her lower lip. "Tell me again that you do not despise me."

"Oh, very well. I do not despise you, sir. I am aware you were overwrought that night in Rome."

"Overwrought?"

She felt a little dizzy. Too much sherry on an empty stomach, no doubt. She moistened her lips.

"I realize that, in your own demented fashion, you had

concluded Emeline and I were at some risk. I have made some allowance for your state of mind at the time," she said.

"What about my state of mind right now?"

"I beg your pardon?"

"I must be just as crazed this afternoon as I was that night in Italy." He leaned closer. "But for entirely different reasons."

His mouth closed over hers.

She really ought to have taken that step back, she thought. But it was too late to do so now.

His powerful hands tightened on her face. The kiss seemed to explode through her senses. He deepened the embrace. Intense sensations swept through her. She could hardly stand. It was as if she were a wax sculpture that had been placed too close to the fire. Something inside her threatened to melt. To steady herself, she was obliged to curl her fingers around his shoulders.

When he felt her clutching him, he groaned and folded her into his arms, tightening his hold until her breasts were crushed against his chest.

"God help me, I don't know why, but I have been wanting to do this since Italy," he muttered against her mouth.

The words were hardly poetic, she thought. But for some reason she found them almost unbearably thrilling. She was stunned by the violent strength of the emotions flooding through her.

"This is madness." She would have fallen had she not clung to him. "Absolute madness."

"Yes." He wound his fingers in her hair and tilted her head back so he could nibble on her ear. "But we both agreed that I may be demented."

She gasped when she felt him kiss her throat. "No, no, I think it's the sherry."

"It's not the sherry." He slid a knee between her thighs.

"It must be the sherry." She shivered beneath the wave of ravenous hunger she sensed burning in him. "We shall no doubt both regret this when we have recovered from the effects of the wine."

"It's not the sherry," he said again.

"Yes, of course it is. What else—ouch." She flinched as his teeth closed ever so carefully but very deliberately around her earlobe. "Good heavens, sir. What do you think you're doing?"

"It's not the bloody sherry."

She was quite breathless now. "I cannot think of any other reason for us to be behaving in such an odd fashion. It is not as if we were actually fond of each other."

He lifted his head abruptly. In his eyes, irritation warred with another, more heated emotion.

"Must you argue every damn point, Lavinia?"

She finally took the step back that she ought to have taken a few minutes ago. She struggled to catch her breath. She could feel tendrils of hair straggling down the nape of her neck. Her fichu was askew.

"It would seem, sir, that you and I cannot even do this sort of thing in a polite and civilized manner," she muttered.

"This sort of thing? Is that what you call what just happened between us?"

"Well?" She stabbed a pin back into her hair. "What would you call it?"

"In some quarters it is known as passion."

Passion. The word stole her breath again.

And then reality crashed through her.

"Passion?" She glowered furiously. *"Passion?* Did you think to *seduce* me into letting you have my client? Is that what this is all about?"

A terrible stillness gripped the study.

For a moment she thought he did not intend to respond. He contemplated her with unreadable eyes for what seemed an eternity.

He moved at last. He walked to the door of the study and opened it. He paused for a moment on the threshold.

"Believe me, Lavinia," he said, "it never once occurred to me that I could employ passion and seduction to influence you in any way. You are clearly a woman who puts matters of business ahead of all else."

He went out into the hall and closed the door much too softly.

She listened to his booted footsteps ringing on the wooden floor. She could not move until she heard him leave the house. When the front door closed behind him, she felt as if she had been released from a mesmeric trance.

She went to the window and stood looking out into the rain-soaked garden for a long time.

Tobias had been right about one thing, she thought after a while. It had not been the sherry.

The kiss had been a mistake, he thought as he went up the steps of his club. What the devil had he been thinking?

He winced. The problem was that he had not been thinking clearly at all. He had allowed the seething brew of anger, frustration, and desire to get the better of his common sense.

He tossed his hat and gloves toward the porter and made his way into the main room.

Neville was slumped heavily in a chair near the window. He had a glass of claret in one hand. The bottle stood nearby. At the sight of him, Tobias paused, wondering if it was too late to escape back into the street. Neville was the last man he wanted to deal

with today. There was no good news to give him, and Neville did not like bad news.

As if on cue, Neville raised his head at that moment to take another swallow from his glass. He caught sight of Tobias. His dark brows bunched together in a scowl.

"There you are, March. Wondered when you'd show up. I want to have a word with you."

Reluctantly, Tobias changed course and crossed the room to take the chair opposite the one in which Neville reclined.

"Bit early to see you here, sir," he said. "Come in to get out of the rain?"

Neville's mouth twisted. "Came in to fortify myself." He flicked a meaningful glance at the glass he held. "I've got an unpleasant task ahead of me this evening."

"What would that be?"

"Decided to end the affair with Sally." Neville gulped claret. "She's become too demanding. They all do sooner or later, don't they?"

Tobias had to think for a moment before the name rang a bell. Then he recalled Neville's occasional references to his current mistress.

"Ah, yes, Sally." He watched the rain come down in the street outside the window. "From what you have told me about her, I would think a couple of nice trinkets should smooth any ruffled feathers."

Neville snorted in disgust. "It will take some very nice, very expensive trinkets to convince her to end the matter without a nasty scene. She's a greedy little thing."

Curiosity made Tobias glance away from the rain to study Neville's expression. "Why end the connection? I thought you enjoyed Sally's company."

"Oh, she's a charming enough creature." Neville winked broadly. "Energetic and extremely creative, if you know what I mean."

"I believe you've mentioned those qualities on occasion."

"Unfortunately all that energy and creativity take a toll on a man." Neville sighed heavily. "Hate to admit it, but I'm not as young as I once was. In addition, her demands for jewelry lately have become excessive. Gave her some earrings last month and she had the gall to inform me the stones in them were too small."

Sally was a professional, Tobias thought. She had no doubt guessed that Neville was getting restless. Aware the affair was nearing its conclusion, she was working quickly to wring whatever she could out of her admirer before he cast her aside.

Tobias smiled humorlessly. "A woman in Sally's line of work must plan ahead for retirement. There are no pensions available to the ladies of the demimonde."

"She can go back to the brothel where I found her." Neville hesitated and then his gaze narrowed. "Perhaps you would care to take my place? Sally will be in the market for a new benefactor after tonight, and I can personally testify to her skills in the bedchamber."

He had no interest in inheriting another man's mistress, even if she was energetic and creative, Tobias thought. In any event, he doubted that Sally would be alone for long. Judging from the remarks Neville had made about her in the course of the past few weeks, she was a clever girl.

"From the sound of it, I cannot afford her," Tobias said dryly.

"She's a prime article, but not as expensive as the high-flyers." Neville gulped his claret and put down the glass. "Forgive me, March. Didn't mean to bore you. I am far more interested to discover what progress you've made. Any news of that damned diary?"

Tobias chose his words carefully. In his experience, clients often responded well to hunting and fishing metaphors.

"I can tell you this much," he said. "I have picked up the trail and the scent grows stronger."

A feverish excitement lit Neville's eyes. "What do you mean? What have you learned?"

"I would prefer not to be too specific at this juncture. But I can say that I have several lures in the water and there have been some nibbles. Give me another few days and I should be able to reel in our catch."

"Hell's teeth, man, what is taking so long? We must find that damned diary and we must do so soon."

Time to take a calculated risk, Tobias thought.

"If you are not satisfied with my efforts, sir, you are free to employ someone else to make inquiries for you."

Neville's mouth thinned in frustration. "There is no one else I can trust to handle this thing with absolute discretion. You know that as well as I do."

Tobias released the breath he had not realized he had been holding. "Calm yourself, sir. I will have news for you soon."

"I trust that will be the case." Neville set aside his empty glass and levered himself up out of the chair. "Regretfully, I must be off. Got to pay a visit to a jeweler this afternoon."

"Sally's farewell gift?"

"Indeed. A pretty necklace, if I do say so myself. Cost me a pretty penny, but I suppose one must pay for one's pleasures, eh? Told the jeweler I'd be around to pick it up and pay for it today. Don't want to take the risk of being late."

"Where's the risk in that?"

Neville snorted again. "Barton told me he ordered a sapphire brooch from the same shop for his ladybird last month. He

neglected to pay for it in a timely manner. The jeweler arranged to have the piece sent around to his town house, where it was delivered to Lady Barton instead of the sweet cyprian."

Tobias nearly smiled. "Quite by accident, I'm sure."

"So the jeweler claimed." Neville shuddered. "Nevertheless, I am not about to take any chances. Good day to you, March. Send word immediately when you have information concerning the diary. I do not care what time of day or night I hear from you."

"I understand."

Neville nodded once and walked off toward the front door of the club.

Tobias sat for a while, watching the carriages in the wet street. The gloom outside seemed to pass through the panes of the window, enveloping him in a gray mist.

It would be pleasant to think a mistress was the solution to this gnawing restlessness that gripped him whenever he contemplated the subject of Lavinia Lake. But he knew the truth. The kiss this afternoon had confirmed his deepest fear. A convenient bed and a willing female whose passion had been purchased would not suffice to ease the pangs of this deep hunger.

After a while he rose and went into the coffee room. En route, he picked up a copy of a newspaper that had been left atop a side table.

Crackenburne was in his customary position near the hearth. He did not look up from his copy of *The Times*. "Saw Neville lying in wait in the other room. Did he manage to corner you?"

"Yes." Tobias lowered himself into a chair. "If you would be so kind, I would appreciate it if you would refrain from employing the language of the hunt. It reminds me of the conversation I just had with Neville."

"Well? What news did you give him?"

"Let's just say I implied that things are going well."

"Are they?"

"No. But I saw no reason to inform him of that."

"Humph." The newspaper rustled in Crackenburne's hands. "Neville was satisfied with your implied progress?"

"I don't think so. But fortunately for me, he had other things on his mind. Tonight he plans to inform his current mistress that he is no longer in the market for her services. He's on his way to pick up an item from a jeweler that he hopes will ease the anguish of parting."

"Indeed." Crackenburne slowly lowered the newspaper. There was a speculative expression in his eyes. "Let us hope that his latest light-o'-love does not meet the same fate as the last one."

Tobias paused, the newspaper partially open. "What do you mean by that?"

"Several months ago Neville turned off another little demirep. I believe he kept her in a house on Curzon Street for nearly a year before he grew tired of her favors."

"What of it? It is hardly uncommon for a man of Neville's position and social status to maintain a mistress. It would be more unusual if he did not do so."

"True, but it is a bit odd when one of them throws herself into the river a few days after she has been cast aside."

"Suicide?"

"So they say. Evidently the woman's heart was broken."

Tobias slowly refolded the unread paper and set it on the arm of the chair. "That is a bit difficult to credit. Neville has told me on several occasions that he selects his mistresses from among the denizens of the brothels. Professionals, as it were."

"Indeed."

"Such women are not generally given to sentimentality. I doubt

they would make the mistake of falling hopelessly in love with the men who pay their bills."

"I'm inclined to agree." Crackenburne went back to his paper. "Nevertheless, the *on dit* several months ago was that his last mistress took her own life."

nine

The following afternoon Tobias arrived in Claremont Lane shortly before two o'clock. He made to alight the moment the hackney rattled to a stop. His fingers tightened briefly around the edge of the door when pain jolted sharply through his left thigh. He drew a deep breath and the ache eased.

He steadied himself and finished his descent to the pavement.

"We're in luck." Anthony vaulted gracefully down from the cab behind Tobias. "It has stopped raining."

Tobias eyed the leaden sky. "Not for long."

"Have I ever mentioned that one of the traits I most admire in you is your optimistic nature? I vow, you possess the sort of temperament that brings sunshine wherever you go."

Tobias did not dignify that with a response. The truth was, he was in a foul mood and he knew it. The cause was not the

dull ache in his leg. It was the sense of anticipation that hummed through him.

He had awakened to the odd sensation this morning, and he found it deeply disquieting. A man of his years and experience ought to have more control over his feelings, he told himself. His eagerness to see Lavinia again was more suited to a young blood of Anthony's age who was about to pay a call upon his sweetheart.

His unease turned to surprise and then flashed into outright irritation when he noticed the other hired carriage standing in the street outside the little house.

He came to a halt. "What the devil is she about now?"

Anthony grinned. "It would appear that your new business associate has plans of her own for the day."

"Devil take it, I sent word round to her this morning advising her that I would be here at two."

"Perhaps Mrs. Lake does not care to be commanded to wait upon your whims," Anthony offered a little too helpfully.

"It was her notion to visit some more waxwork museums." Tobias started toward the steps. "If she thinks I will allow her to set out on her own to interview the proprietors, she can bloody damn well think again."

The door of Number Seven opened wide just as Tobias and Anthony reached the bottom step.

Lavinia, garbed in a familiar brown woolen cloak and half boots, appeared in the opening. She had her back to the street as she spoke to someone inside.

"Have a care, Emeline. This is the best one of the lot."

Without turning her head, Lavinia backed cautiously out of the doorway. Tobias saw that she cradled one end of a bulky package swathed in cloth.

A few seconds later Emeline emerged from the hall. Her lustrous dark hair was partially covered by a pale blue bonnet framing her pretty face. She struggled with the other end of the long, shrouded object.

"It is very heavy," she said, peering down to watch her footing. "Perhaps we should sell one of the others instead."

Anthony sucked in his breath. Tobias felt him go very still.

Oblivious to the two men at the foot of the steps, Lavinia continued to maneuver the package backward.

"None of the others will fetch as much as this one," she said. "Tredlow hinted that he knew a collector who would pay a nice sum for an Apollo in excellent condition."

"I still say we should not sell this statue just to purchase some gowns."

"You must think of the new clothes as an investment, Emeline. I have explained that to you several times today. No suitable young man will take notice of you if you attend the theater in an old, unfashionable gown."

"I have told you that any man who cannot see the person beneath the clothing is not a man I would care to have notice me."

"Rubbish. You know very well that you will be ruined if you allow any man to view the person beneath your clothing before you are properly wed."

Emeline laughed.

"She is a sparkling brook dancing beneath a sunlit sky," Anthony whispered.

Tobias groaned. He was fairly certain that Anthony was not referring to Lavinia.

He watched the two women make their way down the steps. The physical contrast between the aunt and the niece could not have been more pronounced. Emeline was tall, graceful, and

elegantly formed. Lavinia was considerably shorter and smaller in all dimensions. It had, he reflected, been remarkably easy to hold her suspended off the floor.

"Where are you going?" Tobias said.

Lavinia gave a tiny, startled shriek and whipped about to face him. The mummylike package in her arms tilted precariously. Anthony made a heroic dash forward and caught her end of the statue before it crashed to the steps.

Lavinia glared at Tobias. "Just see what you nearly made me do! If I had dropped this statue, it would have been entirely your fault."

"It usually is," he said politely.

"Mr. March." Emeline gave him a warm smile. "How nice to see you today."

"A pleasure, Miss Emeline. Allow me to introduce my brother-in-law, Anthony Sinclair. Anthony, this is Miss Emeline and her aunt, Mrs. Lake. I believe I may have mentioned them to you."

"Delighted." Anthony managed a small bow without losing his grip on the statue. "Allow me, Miss Emeline." He took the full weight of the burden, freeing it from her grasp.

"You are very quick on your feet, sir." Emeline glowed at him. "I vow, there would be a dreadful crack in Apollo by now if you had not moved to rescue him."

"Always happy to be of assistance to a lady," Anthony assured her.

He regarded Emeline as if she were propped atop a pedestal and adorned with wings.

Lavinia rounded on Tobias. "You came very close to causing a disaster here, sir," she declared. "How dare you sneak up on a person in such a manner?"

"I was not sneaking. I am here at precisely the time I mentioned in my note this morning. You did receive it, I presume?"

"Yes, yes, I got your royal command, Mr. March. But as you did not trouble to inquire about whether the time of your visit was convenient to me, I did not bother to send word back that it was not at all convenient."

He deliberately loomed over her. "As I recall, madam, you were the one who insisted that we interview more wax museum proprietors together."

"Yes, well, as it happens, something more important has come up."

He leaned closer. "What is more important than getting on with this inquiry?"

She did not retreat. "Nothing less than my niece's entire future is at stake, Mr. March."

Emeline made a face. "That is something of an overstatement, in my opinion."

Anthony gave her a look of deep concern. "What has happened, Miss Emeline? Is there anything I can do to help?"

"I doubt it, Mr. Sinclair." She wrinkled her nose at him. Her eyes gleamed with wry amusement. "Apollo is to be sacrificed."

"Why?"

"For the money, of course." She chuckled. "The difficulty is that I have been invited to attend the theater tomorrow night in the company of Lady Wortham and her daughter. Aunt Lavinia sees this as an opportunity to parade me in front of some eligible gentlemen who, poor fools, have no clue that she has set her sights on them."

"I see." Anthony's expression darkened.

"Lavinia is convinced that an expensive, fashionable gown is necessary to display my wares to the best advantage. She has concluded that Apollo must be sacrificed to obtain the necessary funds."

"Forgive me, Miss Emeline," Anthony said with grave gallantry, "but any man who could not perceive that your unique charms are best displayed without a gown would have to be a benighted idiot."

There was a short pause. Everyone looked at Anthony. He turned a violent shade of red.

"I meant that your charms would be, uh, *charming* regardless of whether or not you were dressed," he stammered.

No one said a word.

Anthony looked truly stricken now. "That is to say, you would be spectacular in only an apron, Miss Emeline."

"Thank you," she murmured. Her eyes danced.

Anthony looked as if he would very much like to sink into the pavement.

Tobias took pity on him. "Well, then, if we have quite finished with the topic of Miss Emeline's charms, I suggest that we return to the matter of how we are to accomplish a variety of tasks this afternoon. I propose that Miss Emeline and Lavinia carry on with their plans to sacrifice Apollo. Anthony, you and I shall deal with the proprietors of the waxwork museums."

"Certainly," Anthony said.

"Hold on a moment." Lavinia stationed herself in Tobias's path. Deep suspicion glittered in her gaze. "I never said I did not wish to participate in the interviews."

Tobias smiled. "Forgive me, Mrs. Lake, but I was under the impression you had more important things to do today."

"There is no reason we cannot deal with both the statue and the interviews," she said smoothly. "Emeline plans to attend a lecture on Egyptian antiquities together with her friend Priscilla Wortham this afternoon. I intend to set her down at the Institute and then continue on to Mr. Tredlow's shop to deal with the Apollo. When that is done, you and I can proceed with the interviews.

When we are finished, we shall go back to the Institute to fetch Emeline."

Enthusiasm kindled in Anthony's eyes. "It would be my great pleasure to escort you and your friend to the lecture, Miss Emeline. I have a great interest in Egyptian antiquities."

"Do you indeed, sir?" Emeline floated down the steps and moved toward the hackney. "Have you read Mr. Mayhew's most recent article by any chance?"

"Yes, of course." Anthony fell into step beside her. "In my opinion, Mayhew made several excellent points, but I do not believe he is correct about the meaning of the scenes inscribed on the walls of the temples he examined."

"I agree with you." Emeline stood aside to allow him to stow Apollo in the carriage. "It is also clear to me that the hieroglyphs are the key. Until someone can properly translate them, we shall never grasp the significance of the pictures."

Anthony leaned into the vehicle to adjust the statue on the floor. "A proper understanding of the Rosetta stone is our only hope." His voice was slightly muffled by the interior of the cab. "I hear Mr. Young is making some progress in that regard."

Lavinia studied the pair for a moment as they continued to exchange views on Egyptian antiquities. Her brows formed a thoughtful line above her fine nose.

"Hmm," she said.

"I can vouch for Anthony's character," Tobias said in a low voice. "I assure you, your niece is safe in his company."

She cleared her throat. "I don't suppose there is any chance of an inheritance in that direction? The odd estate tucked away in Yorkshire, perhaps?"

"Not so much as a small cottage in Dorset," Tobias said, grimly cheerful. "Anthony's finances are in a similar state to my own."

"And that state would be?" she asked with great delicacy.

"Precarious. Like you, madam, I must depend upon attracting clients for my services in order to secure my living. Anthony assists me on occasion."

"I see."

"Now then," Tobias said, "shall we proceed with the business at hand, or do you intend to stand here in the middle of the street quizzing me on my finances for the remainder of the afternoon?"

She did not take her eyes off Emeline, who was still carrying on a lively discussion with Anthony. For a few seconds he thought she had not heard the question. Then she seemed to shake off whatever thoughts had distracted her. When she turned back to him, the familiar light of steely determination blazed anew in her eyes.

"I do not wish to waste another moment on your finances, sir. They are none of my concern. I have my own to worry about."

"A very nice Apollo, Mrs. Lake." Edmund Tredlow patted a bulging stone muscle in a well-sculpted thigh. "Very nice indeed. I should be able to get you as much as I managed to obtain for the Venus you brought in last month."

"This Apollo is worth considerably more than the Venus, Mr. Tredlow." Lavinia circled the nude statue and came to a halt on the opposite side. "We are both aware of that fact. It is quite genuine and in excellent condition."

Tredlow bobbed his head several times. Behind the lenses of his spectacles, a crafty gleam burned brightly in his eyes. Lavinia knew that he was enjoying himself immensely. She could not say the same for herself. Too much depended on this bargain.

Tredlow was a hunched, perennially rumpled little man of

indeterminate years who favored old-fashioned breeches and un-starched neckcloths. He looked as old and dusty as the statuary in his shop. Gray hair sprouted wildly from his balding pate. His whiskers bristled like untrimmed hedges.

"Please do not mistake me, my dear." Tredlow stroked Apollo's buttocks. "The condition of the statue is, indeed, very fine. It is just that there is very little call for Apollos these days. It won't be easy to interest a collector. I may be stuck with the thing for some months before I can sell it."

Lavinia gritted her teeth behind a cool smile. It was all very well for Tredlow to savor the bargaining process. For him it was a game as well as a matter of business. For her, on the other hand, the tense dance in which they engaged every time she came to his shop was always underlined with a desperation she knew she had to conceal at all costs.

Tobias watched the negotiations from the far side of the dusty shop. He stood leaning negligently against a marble pedestal, to all intents and purposes quite bored. But she knew he was listening to every word of the exchange with acute interest. It was infuriating. After all, it was largely his fault that she was obliged to come here and bargain like a fishwife with Tredlow.

"I certainly would not want to take advantage of your kindness and generosity," Lavinia said smoothly. "If you really feel you will not be able to lure a buyer who can appreciate the excellence of this statue, I suppose I shall have to take it elsewhere."

"I never said I could not sell it, my dear, only that it might take a considerable length of time." Tredlow paused a beat. "Of course, if you wish to leave it with me on consignment . . ."

"No, my intention is to sell it today." She made a show of adjusting her gloves, as if preparing to leave. "I really cannot

afford to waste any more time here. I shall be off to Prendergast's establishment. Perhaps he caters to a more discerning clientele."

Tredlow flapped a hand. "No need to do that, my dear. As I said, the market is not good for Apollos just now, but for the sake of our long-standing acquaintance, I shall attempt to find a collector who will accept this one."

"Really, sir, I would not want to put you to any trouble."

"No trouble at all." He gave her his gnomelike smile. "You and I have done a good deal of business together during the past three months. I am prepared to take a smaller profit than usual on your Apollo as a favor to you, my dear."

"I wouldn't dream of asking you to reduce your profit." She made to retie her bonnet strings. "Indeed, I would never forgive myself if I thought for one moment that I had used our long and mutually agreeable association to take advantage of your kind nature, Mr. Tredlow."

Tredlow eyed the well-endowed Apollo with a thoughtful expression. "Now that I think upon it, I believe I know a gentleman who will pay a goodly sum for this statue. He is not inclined to fret overmuch about price."

She concealed her sigh of relief and gave him a brilliant smile. "I was sure you would know just the right collector, sir. You are nothing if not expert in this field."

"I have had some experience," Tredlow said modestly. "Now, then, as to price, my dear."

It did not take long to arrive at a suitable figure.

Tobias took Lavinia's arm as they left the shop a short time later. "Nicely done," he said.

"The amount Tredlow gave me for the Apollo should cover the cost of the new gowns I ordered from Madame Francesca."

"You bargained well."

"I learned a few things about the fine art of negotiating during the time I spent in Italy." She did not trouble to conceal her satisfaction.

"They do say that travel is broadening."

She smiled coolly. "Fortunately, Emeline and I were able to salvage some of our best items the night you ransacked our shop and threw us out into the street. But I still regret having to leave behind that lovely urn."

"Personally, I thought you made a very wise decision when you decided to take the Apollo instead."

The resurrectionists toiled over the open grave at midnight. A dimly glowing lantern lit the macabre scene, revealing the shovels and ropes that had been employed to haul the new coffin out of the ground. A cart waited in the shadows.

"Another stolen body on its way to a medical school in Scotland," Tobias said cheerfully. "How reassuring it is to know that the march of modern science cannot be thwarted."

Lavinia shuddered and took a closer look at the figures arranged in the tableau. In terms of quality, the waxwork statues here in Huggett's Museum were typical of those she and Tobias had viewed in the two other establishments they had visited this afternoon. The artists had relied on scarves, hats, and flowing cloaks to conceal the poor modeling of the features. The horrid effect had been achieved largely through the aid of a realistic-looking coffin and eerie lighting.

"I must say, the exhibits here are a good deal more melodramatic than the others," Lavinia said.

She realized she had spoken in a whisper, but she was not sure why. She and Tobias were the only people in the museum. But something about the thick gloom and the grisly tableaux disturbed her in a way that the exhibits in the previous establishments had not.

"Huggett is obviously possessed of a flair for the theatrical," Tobias said. He walked down the shadowy aisle and came to a halt in front of the next illuminated tableau. It depicted a dueling scene. "And he appears to have a taste for blood."

"Speaking of Mr. Huggett, he is certainly taking his time, is he not? The ticket seller went to fetch him from his office several minutes ago."

"We will give him a few more minutes." Tobias walked off into another row of waxwork exhibits.

Finding herself alone, Lavinia hurried after him. She spared only a brief glance for the scene of a condemned murderer on the gallows before she rounded the corner and nearly collided with Tobias's solid frame.

She stared at the death scene that had caught his attention. It featured a man collapsed in a chair next to a card table. The figure's head had fallen forward in a manner that not only conveyed a disturbingly accurate imitation of death but also conveniently disguised the lack of artistry in the features. One of the statue's arms was flung out to the side. The figure of the killer stood at the edge of the scene, pistol gripped in a wax hand. Several playing cards were scattered across the carpet.

She glanced at the neatly lettered sign. *A Night in a Gambling Hell.*

"Something tells me we aren't going to learn any more here than we did at the first two museums," she said.

"You may be right." Tobias looked closely at the face of the killer and shook his head slightly. "Mrs. Vaughn was obviously correct when she said that the majority of waxwork museums cater to the public's desire for horrid thrills rather than a demand for fine art."

Lavinia looked around at the ranks of bloodcurdling scenes that loomed in the shadows. Grave robbers, murderers, dying prostitutes, and violent criminals filled the vast chamber. The quality of the art might not be high, she thought, but the proprietor had certainly been successful in creating an atmosphere of dread. She was not about to admit it to Tobias, but the place was affecting her nerves.

"I fear we are wasting our time," she said.

"No doubt." Tobias moved on to the scene of a man strangling a woman with a scarf. "Nevertheless, as we are here and it is the last museum on our list, we may as well interview Huggett before we go."

"Why bother?" Lavinia trailed after him. She grimaced at the tableau and glanced at the title, *The Inheritance*. "Tobias, I really think we should leave. Now."

He gave her an odd look. It occurred to her that she had just addressed him by his given name for the first time. She felt herself grow unaccountably warm and was very grateful for low light.

It was not as if they had not shared some degree of intimacy, she thought. They were business associates, after all. And there was that kiss in her study yesterday, although she had tried very hard not to reflect upon the passionate interlude.

"What the devil is wrong with you?" Amusement dawned in Tobias's eyes. "Never say that these exhibits are affecting your

nerves. I would not have thought you the sort to succumb to dark imaginings in a waxwork museum, of all places."

Outrage fortified her spirits as nothing else could have done. "My nerves are in excellent condition, thank you. I am certainly not the sort to be influenced by exhibits such as these."

"No, of course you aren't."

"It's just that I see no reason to stand about waiting for a rude proprietor who cannot make time to speak with two people who have paid good money to purchase tickets to his dreadful attraction."

She came to the end of an aisle and saw a narrow spiral staircase leading up to another floor. "I wonder what Mr. Huggett keeps up there."

A slithering sound in the darkness behind her froze her in her tracks. A low, sibilant voice spoke.

"The upstairs gallery is for gentlemen only."

Lavinia whirled around, peering into the gloom.

In the weak, flaring light that illuminated a nearby murder scene, she made out a tall, skeletally thin man. The skin of his face was tightly stretched across the bones. His eyes were caverns. Any spark of warmth that might once have blazed there had long ago been extinguished.

"I am Huggett. I was told you wished to speak with me."

"Mr. Huggett," Tobias said. "I am March and this is Mrs. Lake. We appreciate your taking the time to speak to us."

"What do you want from me?" Huggett rasped.

"We wish to ask your opinion of a certain waxwork," Tobias said.

"We are trying to find the artist who produced this." Lavinia held out the small scene of death and pulled aside the cloth. "We hoped you might recognize the style or some other aspect of

the workmanship that might help us learn the name of the modeler."

Huggett glanced at the picture. Lavinia watched his skull-like face carefully. She was almost certain that she saw a faint flicker of recognition, but it was gone in an instant. When Huggett looked up again, his face was devoid of expression.

"Excellent workmanship," he rattled. "But I do not believe I recognize the artist."

"The subject matter would seem to suit your museum," Tobias said.

Huggett gestured with bony fingers. "As you can see, I display life-size statues, not small pictures."

"If a name should occur to you after we leave today, please send word to me at this address." Tobias handed Huggett a card. "I can assure you that it would be worth your while."

Huggett hesitated and then accepted the card. "Who would be willing to pay for such information?"

"Someone who very much desires to make the acquaintance of the artist," Tobias said.

"I see." Huggett coiled in on himself, retreating into the darkness. "I shall give the matter some thought."

Lavinia stepped forward. "Mr. Huggett, one more thing, if you don't mind. You did not finish your explanation about your upstairs gallery. What sort of exhibits do you keep up there?"

"I told you, only gentlemen allowed upstairs," Huggett whispered. "The exhibits up there are not suitable for ladies."

He disappeared back into the shadows before she could ask any more questions.

Lavinia glanced at the spiral staircase. "What do you think he keeps up there?"

"I have a feeling that if you were to ascend those stairs," Tobias

said, taking her arm, "you would find an exhibit of naked wax-works engaged in erotic acts."

She blinked. "Oh." She glanced back at the spiral staircase one last time and then allowed Tobias to guide her toward the door.

"He knows something about our little waxwork," she said softly. "I sensed some recognition in the way he responded to it."

"You may be right." Tobias escorted her through the door. "There was something odd about his reaction."

She smiled with relief when they stepped out into the driz-zle. The hackney in which they had arrived stood in the street.

"Thank goodness the coachman waited for us," she said briskly. "I would not care to walk all the way home in the rain."

"Nor would I."

"This has been a very productive afternoon, has it not? I be-lieve I told you that interviewing people familiar with the styles of various modelers in wax would be useful. Thanks to my ap-proach, we have picked up the scent at last. It is time to sound the horns."

"If you don't mind, I would rather avoid the unnecessary use of the vocabulary of the hunting field." Tobias opened the hackney door. "I find it tiresome."

"Rubbish." Lavinia gave him her hand and bounced exuber-antly into the cab. "You're in a foul mood because it was my bril-liant notion that got us to this point in our inquiries. Admit it, sir. You are annoyed because none of your lures has drawn a nibble."

"I do not care for fishing cant either." He gripped the edge of the door and hauled himself into the vehicle. "If I am in an un-pleasant temper today, it is because I do not like the fact that there are so many unanswered questions."

"Cheer up, sir. Judging from the glint in Huggett's eyes, I sus-pect we will have news soon."

Tobias contemplated the wooden sign above the door to Huggett's Museum as the hackney pulled away. "That gleam you saw in his eyes might not have been an indication of his interest in our money."

"What else could it have been?"

"Fear."

ten

*T*he leather binding was cracked and charred from the flames. Most of the pages were burned to a crisp. But there were enough bits and pieces left in the ashes to enable Tobias to determine beyond a shadow of a doubt that he was looking at the remains of the valet's diary.

"Bloody hell."

He stirred the ashes with a poker. They were cold. Whoever had burned the thing had allowed plenty of time for the embers to die before he had sent the message.

He glanced around the small chamber. It was obvious no one lived here on a permanent basis, but there was enough clutter about to indicate that the room was frequented by those who made their living on the streets. He wondered if the book had been burned elsewhere and then brought here to be dumped on the hearth.

He did not know who had sent the summons to him. He doubted it was one of his usual informants, because no one had come forward to claim the money he had offered for information.

Someone, however, had very much wanted him to discover the diary here tonight.

Luckily he had been at his club when the note had arrived a short while ago. He had set out immediately, devoutly grateful that the bad weather and the lateness of the hour had given him the excuses he needed not to send word to Lavinia. She would no doubt be annoyed when he woke her up to tell her what he had found, but she would have to accept that time had been of the essence.

He looked around for something he could use to collect the burned diary and saw an old empty sack stuffed into the corner.

It did not take long to scrape up the remains of the valet's dangerous little journal.

When he was ready, he put out the smoky tallow candle he had found in the room. He picked up the sack and went to the window. There was no reason to expect any trouble. After all, someone had gone to a good deal of effort to ensure that he found the diary tonight. But others were searching for the journal. It was only prudent to take some precautions.

The rain that had been falling all evening had transformed the narrow lane into a shallow stream. The weak glow of a lantern emanated from a window across the narrow lane. The light did little to relieve the dense darkness.

He observed the shadows down in the lane, waiting to see if any of them shifted or moved. After a while he concluded that if anyone was watching the entrance he had used earlier, that person was not in his line of sight now.

He removed his greatcoat. After knotting the sack's ties, he

slung it on one shoulder. Satisfied the burden would stay dry, he pulled on the coat again and left the small chamber. There was no one about on the stairs. He descended to the cramped hall and let himself out onto the stone step.

He waited a moment longer in the minimal shelter of the doorway. None of the shadows across the way moved.

Setting his teeth, he waded into the shallow, filthy stream that was the lane. The paving stones proved surprisingly slippery. His left leg could not be trusted in such circumstances. He flattened a gloved hand against the wet stone wall to his left to steady himself.

Oily water splashed across the toes of the boots Whitby had labored so valiantly to bring to a high gloss. It would not be the first time he had been obliged to rescue badly treated footwear, Tobias thought.

He worked his way cautiously toward the end of the lane. He hoped the hackney that had brought him here still waited in the next street. There was little hope of finding another on a night like this.

Halfway to his goal, he sensed the other presence in the lane. He took another step, sought purchase with his left hand, and swung about very suddenly.

The outline of a man in a heavy greatcoat and hat was silhouetted against the weak lantern light that illuminated the window. The sight was vaguely familiar. Tobias was almost certain he had seen this particular greatcoat and hat earlier in the evening outside his club.

The man in the heavy coat froze when he saw that Tobias had halted. The figure whirled and fled in the opposite direction. Water splashed at his heels. The sound echoed down the lane.

"Bloody hell."

Tobias shoved away from the wall, throwing himself into pursuit. Pain shot through his leg. He gritted his teeth and tried to ignore it.

He was wasting his time, he thought as he struggled to maintain his balance. With his treacherous leg, he did not stand a ghost of a chance of catching the fleeing man. He would be lucky not to fall facedown into the murky stream.

His boots slipped and slid on the wet stones, but somehow he managed to stay on his feet. Twice he put out a hand in time to save himself.

But the running man was having troubles of his own. He lurched abruptly and flailed his arms. His greatcoat flapped as he tried to regain his footing. An object he had been carrying clanged when it struck the pavement. Glass shattered. An unlit lantern, Tobias thought.

The fleeing figure went down hard. Tobias was nearly upon him now. He threw himself forward and managed to grab one of the man's legs. He used the grip to raise himself and slam a fist into solid flesh. It had no immediate effect. The man struggled furiously.

"Be still or I'll use my knife," Tobias said roughly. He had no blade on him, but the man had no way of knowing that.

There was a groan and then the man slumped into the cold rainwater. "I was only doin' what I was told, sir. I swear it on my mother's honor. I was only following orders."

"Whose orders?"

"My employer's."

"Who is your employer?"

"Mrs. Dove."

"I received a message." Joan Dove picked up the delicate porcelain teapot. "I sent Herbert to see what it was about. Obviously he arrived shortly after you did, Mr. March, and saw you leave the building. In the shadows, he could not make out your identity. He tried to follow you. You spotted him and brought him down."

Lavinia was so angry she could barely speak. She watched Joan pour the tea into china cups. The act had all the practiced grace one expected from a wealthy, polished lady serving afternoon guests. But it was not three o'clock in the afternoon. It was three in the morning. She and Tobias had not come here tonight to exchange gossip about the latest scandals of the ton. They had come to confront Mrs. Dove.

Thus far she had done all the talking. Tobias lounged in a chair, a stony expression on his face, and said little. Lavinia was worried about him. He had taken time to stop by his house to change into dry clothing before he had arrived on her doorstep with the remains of the diary. She was certain his outer air of calm was deceptive. He had been through a great deal tonight. She could tell that his leg was causing him some discomfort.

"What did the message say?" Tobias asked, making one of his rare contributions to the conversation.

Joan displayed only the slightest hesitation as she set down the pot. "It was not a written note. A young street urchin appeared at my door and said that what I wanted could be obtained at Number Eighteen, Tartle Lane. I dispatched Herbert."

"Enough, Mrs. Dove." Lavinia's fury boiled over. "If you cannot bring yourself to tell us the truth, be good enough to say so."

Joan's mouth tightened. "Why do you doubt me, Mrs. Lake?"

"You received no message. You sent Herbert to follow Mr. March, did you not?"

Joan's eyes were cold. "Why would I do that?"

"Because you hoped Mr. March would recover the diary, and when he did, you intended for Herbert to steal it from him. Is that not the truth?"

"Really, Mrs. Lake. I am not accustomed to having my word doubted."

"Indeed?" Lavinia smiled coldly. "How very odd. Mr. March believes you have lied to us from the start. But I was prepared to credit your tale, or at least most of it. However, it would appear you have attempted to use us for your own ends, and that is intolerable."

"I do not comprehend why you are so angry." Joan's words were edged with reproof. "There was no harm done to Mr. March tonight."

"We are not pawns for you to move about on the board, Mrs. Dove. We are professionals."

"Yes, of course."

"Mr. March risked his neck to go down that lane and into that building. He was working on your behalf. But I am convinced your man, Herbert, would have tried to take the diary by force if he believed Mr. March had discovered it."

"I assure you, I had no desire for Mr. March or anyone else to be hurt." Joan's voice held a distinct edge now. "I instructed Herbert to keep watch on him. That is all."

"I knew it. You *did* assign him to spy on Mr. March."

Joan hesitated. "It seemed a prudent move."

"Bah." Lavinia squared her shoulders. "Mr. March is correct. You have lied to us from the start, and I, for one, have lost all patience. We have fulfilled our commission, madam. The diary has been recovered. It is quite unreadable, as you can see, but at least it can cause no further harm."

Joan frowned at the charred remains of the valet's diary. They filled a large silver platter.

"But you cannot halt your inquiries now," she said. "Whoever burned that diary no doubt read it first."

"Perhaps," Lavinia said, "but it is clear to Mr. March and to me that destroying the diary was someone's way of telling us the affair is ended. We suspect that the culprit was another one of Holton Felix's victims, very likely the person who murdered him."

Tobias glanced at the platter. "I believe the message was intended to convey more than mere reassurance that there will be no more blackmail threats."

"What do you mean?" Joan asked swiftly.

Tobias did not take his thoughtful gaze off the charred book. "I have a hunch we are being told in no uncertain terms to cease our inquiries into this affair."

"But what of the death threat I received?" Joan demanded.

"That is your problem now," Lavinia said. "Perhaps you will be able to find someone else to look into the matter for you."

"Uh, Lavinia," Tobias murmured.

She ignored him. "Under the circumstances, I cannot allow Mr. March to continue to take risks on your behalf, Mrs. Dove. I'm sure you understand."

Joan stiffened. "All you cared about was the diary, because it contained your secrets too. Now that it has been found, you are content to take my money and quit the affair."

Lavinia leaped to her feet, incensed. "*You may keep your bloody money!*"

Out of the corner of her eye, she saw Tobias wince. She went behind the sofa and gripped the elegantly curved wooden frame with both hands.

"Mr. March took great chances on your behalf tonight," she said.

"For all he knew, he was walking into a trap. The killer could have been waiting for him in that chamber where he found the book. I will not allow him to continue such dangerous work for a client who lies to us."

"How dare you? I have not lied to you."

"Well, you certainly have not told us the whole truth, have you?"

Anger flashed across Joan's face. It was under control in an instant. "I have told you everything I thought you needed to know."

"And then you employed a man to spy on us. You used Mr. March. I will not tolerate that." She whirled and pinned Tobias with a glance. "It is time to leave, sir."

Tobias obligingly pushed himself up out of the chair. "It is getting late, is it not?" he said mildly.

"Yes, it is."

Lavinia swept out of the drawing room and led the way down the hall to the front door. The bull-size butler ushered them out into the wet night.

She stopped short when she saw that the hackney that had brought them to the mansion was gone. In its place was a gleaming maroon carriage.

"Madam gave instructions earlier when you arrived that the hackney was to be dismissed, as she wished you to be conveyed home in her coach," the butler said without inflection.

Lavinia thought of the unpleasant conversation that had just taken place in the drawing room. She doubted that Joan Dove was still feeling quite so generous.

"Oh, we couldn't possibly accept such a—"

"Indeed we can." Tobias's fingers closed firmly on her arm. "I think you've said quite enough tonight, Mrs. Lake. You might

wish to stand out in the rain and attempt to summon a hackney, but I trust you will humor me. I would much prefer to travel in Mrs. Dove's very comfortable carriage, if you don't mind. It has been a long evening."

She thought of what he had been through and was immediately stricken with remorse.

"Yes, of course." She went smartly down the steps. If they hurried, she thought, they would get to the vehicle before Joan thought to rescind her offer.

A burly footman handed Lavinia up into the plush cab. The interior lights revealed soft, maroon velvet cushions and cozy blankets to keep out the chill. She reached for one of the latter as soon as she took her seat, and discovered that it had been heated with a warming pan.

Tobias sat down next to her. There was a stiffness about his movements that concerned her. She paused in the act of arranging the blanket around her knees and draped it over Tobias's legs instead.

"Thank you." There was rough gratitude in the words.

She frowned. "Have you noticed that Mrs. Dove has a number of very large men on her staff?"

"I've noticed," Tobias said. "Something of a small army."

"Yes. I wonder why she feels it necessary—" She broke off when she saw his hand slip under the blanket and begin to rub his leg. "You were not injured when you subdued Herbert, were you?"

"Do not concern yourself, Mrs. Lake."

"You cannot blame me for being concerned, under the circumstances."

"You have your own concerns, madam." He paused meaningfully. "Under the circumstances."

She huddled beneath the warm blanket and settled into the depths of the velvet cushions. The full implications of what had just happened struck her quite forcibly.

"I take your point," she said morosely.

Tobias did not respond.

"I do believe I just dismissed the most important client I have had to date."

"I believe so, yes. Not only that, but you also turned down her offer to pay you for the services rendered thus far."

"There is something to be said for the sort of client who can afford to send us home in nice, comfortable equipages."

"Indeed." Tobias rubbed his leg.

The silence hung heavily inside the cab.

"Well," Lavinia said eventually, "it is not as if there was any other course of action open to us. We certainly cannot continue to make inquiries on behalf of a client who withholds vital information and sets spies to follow us about."

"I fail to see why not," Tobias said.

"What?" She straightened in the seat. "Are you mad? You could have been hurt or badly injured tonight. I am convinced Herbert intended to take that diary from you by force."

"I have no doubt but that she instructed Herbert to take the diary from me if I managed to recover it. After all, her primary objective is to conceal her secrets."

She pondered that. "There is obviously something in the diary she does not want anyone to know, including us. Something potentially more damaging than the details of an affair that is more than twenty years old."

"I warned you, all clients lie."

She snuggled back under the blanket and thought about matters for a while.

"It occurs to me that Mrs. Dove is not the only one who failed to be completely forthcoming this evening," she muttered finally.

"I beg your pardon?"

She glowered. "Why didn't you send word to me the instant you received that message at your club? I should have accompanied you to find that diary tonight. You had no business going alone."

"There was very little time. You must not feel slighted, Lavinia. I was in such a hurry that I did not even attempt to get word to Anthony."

"Anthony?"

"In general, he is the one who assists me in such matters. But he was at the theater tonight, and I knew it would be extremely difficult to get a message to him in time."

"So you went alone."

"In my professional opinion, the situation required immediate action."

"Rubbish."

"I had a hunch you would hold that view," Tobias said.

"You went alone because you are not in the habit of working with a partner."

"Damnation, Lavinia, I went alone because there was no time to waste. I did what I thought best and that is the end of the matter."

She did not dignify that with a response.

Silence settled heavily on the cab once more.

After a while she realized he was still massaging his thigh.

"I expect you strained your leg when you ran after Mrs. Dove's footman."

"I expect so."

"Is there anything I can do?"

"I most certainly do not intend to allow you to put me into a mesmeric trance, if that is what you mean."

"Very well, sir, if you insist upon being churlish about the matter."

"I do. I am very skilled when it comes to behaving churlishly."

She gave up and lapsed back into silence. It was going to be a long drive home, she thought. The carriage was making slow progress, not only because the rain had become heavier but also because the streets were crowded at this hour. The glittering balls and sparkling soirees of the ton were ending. People were returning to their town houses and mansions. Drunken young rakes were drifting out of the hells and brothels and clubs and climbing into whatever vehicles they could find to convey them back to their lodgings.

A number of gentlemen were no doubt demanding to be driven to Covent Garden. There they would find prostitutes who, for a few coins, would get into their carriages to provide a few minutes of desultory pleasure. The hired coaches that accepted their custom would smell sour in the morning.

Lavinia wrinkled her nose at the thought. There was, indeed, a great deal to be said for a client who could afford to send one home in a fine carriage.

Beside her, Tobias shifted slightly in the seat, settling more deeply into the cushions. His uninjured leg pressed briefly against her thigh. She had no doubt but that the slight contact had been entirely accidental, but it set afire her already agitated nerves. Memories of the heated embrace in her study shivered through her senses.

This was madness.

She wondered if Tobias was in the habit of stopping off in Covent Garden late at night on his way home. Somehow she doubted it. He would be more selective, she decided. More particular.

That consideration led to another, even more disturbing question. What sort of female *did* Tobias prefer?

In spite of the kiss in the study, she was quite certain that she was not the type he generally found attractive. They had been thrown together by circumstances. It was not as if he had been attracted by her ravishing looks or entranced by her clever conversation. He had not glimpsed her across a crowded ballroom and been overwhelmed by her stunning beauty.

In point of fact, given her rather short stature, it was unlikely he would even be able to see her across a crowded room.

"You let your client go because of me, didn't you?" Tobias asked.

The remark, falling as it did into the deep pool of silence, startled her out of her reverie. It took her a moment to collect herself.

"It was the principle of the thing," she muttered.

"I don't think so. You let your client go because of me."

"I do wish you would stop repeating yourself, sir. It is a most annoying habit."

"I'm sure I have any number of habits you find annoying. That is not the point."

"What is the point?"

He slid one hand behind her neck and put his lips very close to hers. "I cannot help wondering how you will feel in the morning when you realize that because of me, you refused the handsome fee that Mrs. Dove would have paid you."

It was not her lost fee that she would be contemplating in the morning, Lavinia thought. It was the end of her uneasy partnership with Tobias that would weigh heavily on her mind. The diary had brought them together and now the diary was no more.

The full impact of this night's events finally struck her. A ghastly sensation of doom descended.

She might never see Tobias again after tonight.

The sense of impending loss that swirled through her was intense. What was the matter with her? She ought to be grateful to know that he would soon be out of her life. He had cost her the fee for this night's work.

But for some reason, all she could feel was regret.

With a soft cry, she released the blanket and threw her arms around his neck.

"*Tobias.*"

His mouth closed urgently over hers.

His last kiss had left smoldering embers. At the touch of his mouth now, the flames leaped into a searing, dazzling blaze. No man's embrace had ever had such an effect on her. What she had known with John all those years ago had been a sweet sonnet of delicate, insubstantial feelings too ethereal for this world. What she experienced in Tobias's arms, however, filled her with indescribably thrilling sensations.

Tobias tore his mouth from hers and trailed kisses down her throat. She fell back onto the velvet squabs. Her cloak spread out beneath her. She felt his hand on her leg and wondered how he had got it beneath the cloak and the skirts of her gown without her being aware of his action.

"We hardly know each other," she whispered.

"On the contrary." He slid warm fingers up the inside of her thigh. "I'll wager I discovered more about you during the time in Rome than a great many husbands know about their wives."

"I find that extremely difficult to believe."

"I shall prove it to you."

She kissed him hungrily. "How can you do that?"

"Let me see, where shall I begin?" He reached behind her and loosened the tapes of her bodice. "I know that you are very fond of long walks. I must have followed you for miles in Rome."

"Healthful. Long walks are excellent for the health, sir."

He lowered the bodice of her gown. "I know that you enjoy reading poetry."

"You saw the books on my shelf in Rome that night."

He touched the silver pendant she wore at her throat and then he kissed one stiff nipple. "I know that you would not allow Pomfrey to make you his mistress."

That piece of information was like cold rain dashed in her face. She went still, her hands on his shoulders, and stared up at him.

"You know about Pomfrey?"

"Everyone in Rome knew about Pomfrey. He seduced nearly every widow in town and a fair number of wives." Tobias kissed the valley between her breasts. "But you turned down his offer out of hand."

"Lord Pomfrey is a married man." Good grief, she sounded quite prim, even to her own ears.

Tobias raised his head. His eyes gleamed in the dim glow of the lamps. "He is also very rich and said to be exceedingly generous with his mistresses. He could have made your life a good deal more pleasant."

She shuddered. "I cannot think of anything more unpleasant than being Pomfrey's mistress. The man drinks heavily and when he is in his cups he has no control over his temper. I once saw him strike a blow at another man who had only teased him for being inebriated."

"I was there the day he saw you in the market. I heard him try to persuade you to let him set you up in a small apartment."

She was mortified. "You overheard that embarrassing conversation?"

"It wasn't particularly difficult to overhear your response to his offer." Tobias's teeth flashed briefly. "Your voice was somewhat elevated, as I recall."

"I was furious." She paused. "Where were you?"

"In the doorway of a small shop." He slid his hand higher along the inside of her leg. "I was eating an orange."

"You remember such a small detail?"

"I remember everything about that moment. After Pomfrey took himself off in high dudgeon, I decided that the orange I was eating was far and away the finest orange I had ever eaten in my entire life. Nothing else had ever tasted so sweet."

He closed his palm over the hot, damp place between her legs.

Heat swirled through her lower body, leaving her tingling and trembling in a storm of sensation. She could tell from the wicked satisfaction in Tobias's eyes that he knew full well what he was doing to her. It was time to turn the tables.

"Well, at least now I know something about you, sir." She clutched his shoulders very tightly. "You are fond of oranges."

"I like them well enough. But in Italy they say there is no fruit that can compare with a ripe fig." He stroked her deliberately. "I'm inclined to agree."

She nearly choked on a gasp that was a mix of outrage and laughter. She had lived long enough in Mrs. Underwood's household to learn that in Italy ripe figs were considered an earthy symbol of a woman's sex.

He covered her mouth once more with his own, silencing her. He used his hand to bring her to the brink of a sensation she had never known before. When she shivered and moaned in his arms, seeking something more, he unfastened the opening of his trousers.

And then he was between her legs, sliding slowly, relentlessly into her body, filling her completely. Without warning, the great tension within her suddenly exploded in glittering fragments of intense feeling that no poet could have even begun to describe.

"Tobias?" She clawed her hands down his back. "Bloody hell, Tobias. *Tobias.*"

A soft, husky laugh, more of a groan really, purred through him.

She wrapped her arms around him, repeating his name over and over again. He used his weight to sink himself deeper into her body.

Beneath her hands the muscles of his back went taut and rigid. She knew he was on the edge of his own release. Impulsively she tried to pull him closer.

"No," he muttered.

To her astonishment he wrenched his mouth from hers and jerked himself roughly, unceremoniously out of her body. He gave a muffled exclamation and convulsed violently.

She held him while he spent himself into the folds of her cloak.

eleven

$\mathcal{T}$obias came slowly back to his senses. The carriage was still in motion, he realized. He did not have to move just yet. He could indulge himself in her softness for a little while longer.

"Tobias?"

"Mmm?"

She shifted a little beneath him. "I think we are about to arrive at my house."

"I thought you might say that." He closed his hand over one breast. It was resilient and so beautifully shaped. A perfect apple.

It would probably be a good idea not to return to the subject of fresh fruit tonight. Lavinia was right, they must be very close to her little house in Claremont Lane.

"Hurry, Tobias." She wriggled agitatedly beneath him. "We must put ourselves to rights. Just think of how embarrassing it would

be to have one of Mrs. Dove's footmen discover us in this condition."

The alarm in her tone amused him.

"Calm yourself, Lavinia." He sat up slowly, reluctantly, pausing just long enough to drop a kiss on the inside of her bare thigh.

"*Tobias.*"

"I hear you, Mrs. Lake. So will the coachman and the footman up on the box if you do not lower your voice."

"Quickly." She sat up, fumbling with her bodice. "We shall be stopping at any moment. Oh dear, I do hope we have not damaged Mrs. Dove's cushions. What will she think?"

"I do not particularly care what Mrs. Dove thinks." He inhaled the tang their recent passion had left in the close confines of the carriage. "She is no longer your client, remember?"

"For heaven's sake, sir, she is an elegant lady." Lavinia adjusted the silver pendant with a small, anxious motion. "I'm quite certain she is not accustomed to having her lovely carriage treated like a cheap hackney."

He looked at her, unable to resist a rush of deep satisfaction. The yellow light of the lamp danced on her tousled hair, igniting red and gold sparks. Her cheeks were flushed. There was a warm glow about her that was unmistakable.

Then he noticed the panic in her eyes.

"You're embarrassed, aren't you?" he asked. "You're afraid Mrs. Dove will believe you to be something other than a lady, if she learns what happened here."

Lavinia was engaged in a full-scale struggle with her bodice. "She will likely conclude that I am no better than one of those women who hang about in Covent Garden at odd hours of the night."

He shrugged, still too satiated to work up any strong feelings on the matter. "Why do you care what she thinks of you now?"

"Having her believe me to be a light-skirt is not the sort of impression one wishes to leave with a client."

"Former client."

Her jaw tightened grimly. "Yes, well, word of mouth is important in this profession. One can hardly advertise in the papers, after all. One must rely on recommendations from satisfied clients."

"Personally, I am perfectly satisfied at the moment. Does that count?"

"Certainly not. You are a business associate, not a client. Do not tease me, Tobias. You know perfectly well I cannot have Mrs. Dove telling her fine friends that I am nothing but a . . . a—"

"You're not," he said flatly. "And we both know it. So why harp on the subject?"

She blinked, as if slightly dazed by the simple question. "It's the principle of the thing."

He nodded. "You mentioned principles earlier. I gather they are important to you. But this is something other than a matter of principle. It is a matter of common sense. I would not want you to get into the habit of throwing your clients' money back in their faces. If Mrs. Dove should decide to send you your fee in spite of what you said to her tonight, I strongly suggest you accept it."

She stopped fighting with the bodice and gave him a ferocious look. "How dare you find this the least bit amusing, sir."

"Forgive me, Lavinia." He reached behind her shoulders and adjusted the gown. "But you appear to be falling into a fit of hysteria."

"How can you accuse me of hysteria? I am concerned for my reputation. A perfectly reasonable concern, if you ask me. I do not wish to be forced to change careers again. It is a great bother."

He smiled. "Mrs. Lake, I assure you, if anyone dares to impugn your honor, I will defend it all the way to the dueling field."

"You are determined to make a joke of this, are you not?"

"Your cloak may be somewhat the worse for wear, but I think you will find that the cushions are in excellent condition. Even if they are not, I'm sure that the coachman will see to it that they are spotless in the morning. It is his job to keep the vehicle in excellent condition."

"My cloak." Fresh alarm stole the warmth from her face. She went decidedly pale. She scrambled awkwardly off the seat and plucked the cloak off the cushions. "Oh dear."

"Lavinia—"

She sat down on the opposite seat and shook out the folds of the cloak. Holding the garment out in front of her, she stared, aghast, at the lining.

"Oh no. This is dreadful. Absolutely dreadful."

"Lavinia, has the loss of your client affected your nerves?"

She ignored that. Whipping the cloak around, she displayed a dark, damp stain. "Look what you did to it, Tobias. You ruined it. I cannot possibly explain such a mark. I can only hope I will be able to remove it before anyone in the household notices."

Her overwrought concern about the cushions and her cloak was destroying his mood, he thought. The lovemaking had been the most exhilarating experience he had had in a very long time. He would have wagered a considerable amount that she had been amply satisfied also. In fact, the surprise that had laced her voice when her climax had stormed through her had convinced him that until tonight she was unfamiliar with the sensation of a sexual release.

But instead of reveling in the aftermath of mutually shared pleasure, she was carrying on about a damned stain.

"Congratulations, Lavinia. You do a very affecting Lady Macbeth. But I'm certain that when you consider the matter more closely, you'll agree it is far better to have the evidence of our recent exercise show up on your cloak than elsewhere."

She looked uneasily at the velvet cushions next to him. "Yes, of course. It would have been terrible if the stain had appeared on the seat. But it does appear to be unspotted, as you said."

The carriage was slowing. He pulled aside the curtain and saw that they had arrived in Claremont Lane. "I was not referring to the cushions."

"Really, sir, where else would a stain such as that matter as much as it would on Mrs. Dove's cushions?"

He met her eyes and said nothing.

She frowned. Confusion crossed her face a second before comprehension lit her eyes.

"Yes, of course," she said without inflection. Her gaze slipped away from his. She concentrated on bundling up the cloak.

"There is no need for embarrassment between us, Lavinia. We have both had some experience in the marital bed. Neither of us is newly emerged from the schoolroom."

She stared fixedly out the window. "Yes, of course."

"While we're on the subject, let us speak plainly. As you can tell from that damned spot on your cloak, I took what small precautions were available under the circumstances." He softened his voice. "But we both know there is no guarantee that there will not be unintended consequences."

Her hands tightened on the wadded-up cloak. "Yes, of course."

"If they occur, you will feel free to discuss them with me, will you not?"

"Yes, of course." This time she uttered the litany in a tone that was two octaves above her normal speaking voice.

"I admit I was caught up in the passions of the moment. Next time, however, I shall be better prepared. I will endeavor to procure some devices before we indulge ourselves in this sort of thing again."

"Oh, look, sir, we have arrived," she said much too brightly. "Home at last."

The sturdy footman opened the carriage door and let down the step for Lavinia. She moved toward the opening as though it were an escape route from a burning building.

"Good night, Tobias."

He reached out and caught her hand. "Lavinia, are you certain you are all right? You do not seem quite yourself."

"Indeed?"

The smile she gave him over her shoulder gleamed like polished steel. Very much a Lavinia sort of smile, he concluded. He did not know if that was a good sign.

"It has been a trying evening," he ventured cautiously. "Your nerves are obviously quite unsettled."

"I cannot imagine why my nerves should be the least unsettled. After all, I have merely lost my sole client and had a perfectly good cloak ruined. In addition, I shall be obliged to worry about some extremely *personal* matters for the next few days."

He met her eyes. "You can blame me for all of those concerns."

"Oh, I do." She gave her hand to the big footman. "Clearly my difficulties can be traced directly to your doorstep, sir. Once again, my problems are all your fault."

Why was it that everything involving Lavinia was always so damnably complicated? Tobias stalked into his study a short while later, poured himself a healthy measure of brandy, and dropped

into his favorite chair. He gazed morosely into the banked fire. Visions of a stained cloak danced in front of his eyes.

The door opened behind him.

"You're home at last." Anthony, cravat loosened and shirt open, sauntered into the room. "I stopped off an hour ago on my way back to my lodgings to see if you had any news. Helped myself to some of Whitby's leftover salmon pie. I must say, I miss his cooking."

"How could you possibly miss it? You seem to be around for every meal and a good many late-night snacks."

"Wouldn't want you to get lonely." Anthony chuckled. "Not like you to be out so late. An interesting evening, I presume?"

"Found the diary."

Anthony whistled softly. "Congratulations. I assume you tore out the pages that were of particular importance to you and Mrs. Lake and your client?"

"There was no need to remove them. Someone had thrown the damn thing into a fire before I found it. There was enough left to identify it but not enough to matter to anyone."

"I see." Anthony shoved a hand through his hair while he pondered that. "Whoever killed Felix and took the diary wanted to make it clear to you that your inquiries can be halted now, is that it?"

"I think so. Yes."

"You said at the beginning of this affair that a number of people were mentioned in the diary. Any one of them might have killed Holton Felix and then destroyed the journal."

"Yes."

"How did Neville take the news?"

"I haven't informed him of the latest developments," Tobias said.

Anthony looked curious. "What happens next?"

"Next? I'm going to bed. That's what happens next."

"I was about to walk back to my lodgings when I heard that very fine carriage arrive at our door." Anthony grinned. "Thought at first someone had mistaken the address. Then I saw you get out."

"The carriage belongs to Lavinia's client." Tobias swallowed some brandy. "Former client, as of tonight."

"Because the diary has been found?"

"No. Because Lavinia dismissed her. Told Mrs. Dove that she would not accept the fee they had agreed upon."

"I don't understand." Anthony went to stand in front of the slumbering fire. "Why the devil would Mrs. Lake reject her fee?"

Tobias downed more brandy and lowered the glass to the arm of the chair.

"She did it because of me," he said.

"You?"

"Matter of principle, you see."

Anthony gave him a puzzled look. "No, I don't see. No offense, Tobias, but you're not making a great deal of sense. How much have you had to drink tonight?"

"Not enough." Tobias tapped one finger against the side of the glass. "Lavinia dismissed her client because she blamed Mrs. Dove for putting me in jeopardy this evening."

"Explain, please."

Tobias explained. When he had finished, Anthony studied him for a long moment.

"Well, well, well," Anthony said at last.

Tobias could not think of an intelligent riposte, so he let it go.

"Well, well, well," Anthony said again.

"Lavinia has a temper. Mrs. Dove managed to set it alight tonight."

"Evidently."

Tobias swirled the remaining brandy in his glass. "I believe my partner is already regretting her action."

Anthony quirked a brow. "Why do you say that?"

"Her last words to me as she got out of the carriage were to the effect that I was once again to blame for all of her problems."

Anthony nodded wisely. "Sounds a sensible conclusion on her part."

"I thought you mentioned that you were on your way home."

"You are in one of your foul moods, are you not?"

Tobias thought about it. "I believe I am."

Anthony surveyed him from head to foot with an interested expression. "You said you changed your clothes after the scuffle in the lane?"

"Yes."

"Then can I assume that the reason you appear so disheveled is due to another, more recent tussle?"

Tobias narrowed his eyes. "If you think I am not in good temper now, pray continue with your quizzing. You will soon discover just how unpleasant my mood can become."

"Ah, so now we arrive at the heart of the matter. You kissed Mrs. Lake and she slapped your face for your trouble."

"Mrs. Lake," Tobias said very deliberately, "did not slap my face."

Anthony stared at him, eyes widening.

"Hell's teeth," he whispered. "Never say that you . . . that you actually . . . With *Mrs. Lake*? In a *carriage*? But she's a *lady*. How could you?"

Tobias looked at him.

Whatever Anthony saw in his face was sufficient to make him swallow and hurriedly turn his attention back to the embers on the hearth.

The tall clock ticked relentlessly toward dawn.

Tobias sunk deeper into his chair. It was annoying to be lectured by a younger man who had never been seriously involved with a woman in his life.

After a while, Anthony cleared his throat. "You know that she plans to attend the theater tomorrow evening." He glanced at the clock. "Actually, that would be tonight, would it not? In any event, you could arrange to be there too. She and Emeline will be in the company of Lady Wortham and her daughter. It would be quite appropriate for you to pay a call on them in their box."

Tobias put his fingertips together. "Indeed."

"Never fear," Anthony said very smoothly, "I wouldn't dream of sending you off on your own into such uncharted waters. You obviously need a guide. I shall be happy to accompany you to the theater."

"Ah, so that is what this is all about."

Anthony gave him a look of innocent inquiry. "I beg your pardon?"

"You wish to attend the theater tomorrow night because you know Miss Emeline will be there. You want a convenient excuse to pay a visit to the Wortham box."

Anthony's expression tightened. "Emeline is to be put on display in the marriage mart tomorrow night. Lavinia is hoping to attract an eligible suitor for her, remember?"

"The sacrificed Apollo. I remember."

"Precisely. Emeline is so charming and so clever, I fear that Lavinia's scheme will bear fruit."

Tobias winced.

Anthony paused in obvious concern. "Does your leg ache badly tonight?"

"It is not my leg that pains me. It is the reference to fruit."

His leg was actually feeling remarkably comfortable at the moment, Tobias thought. The brandy, no doubt. But now that he considered the matter, he realized he had stopped noticing the familiar discomfort earlier tonight. At about the time he had begun to make love to Lavinia. Nothing like a bit of distraction to take a man's mind off his aches and pains, he thought glumly.

Anthony looked blank. "I don't understand. What's this about fruit?"

"Never mind. I wouldn't worry about Lavinia's schemes if I were you. Emeline is an interesting young lady and she may attract some attention. But once word gets around that she is not an heiress, the shrewd mamas of the ton will make certain their sons do not look too long in that direction."

"That may well be true, but what about all the rakehells and professional seducers? You know as well as I do that no young lady is safe from that sort. They make sport of seducing the innocent."

"Lavinia can protect Emeline." Tobias thought about Emeline's coolheadedness in Rome. "Actually, I have a hunch that Miss Emeline can take care of herself."

"Nevertheless, I would prefer not to take any chances." Anthony gripped the mantel determinedly. "And as my goals appear to align with yours, we may as well work together on this project."

Tobias exhaled deeply. "We are a pair of fools."

"Speak for yourself." Anthony headed happily toward the door. "I will secure the theater tickets first thing tomorrow."

"Anthony?"

"Yes?"

"Did I tell you that Lavinia and her parents were practitioners of mesmerism?"

"No, but Miss Emeline mentioned it, I believe. What of it?"

"You took a brief interest in the subject some time back. Do you think it's possible for a skilled practitioner of the art to put a man into a trance without him being aware of the process?"

Anthony smiled slowly. "It's entirely possible that a weak-minded man might be vulnerable to the skills of a very proficient practitioner. But I cannot imagine for one moment that a man endowed with a strong, resolute will and keen powers of observation could ever be put into a trance."

"You're certain?"

"Not unless he wished to be entranced, that is."

Anthony went very quickly out the door and closed it behind himself.

Tobias heard him laughing all the way down the hall and out the front door.

twelve

"What on earth is wrong with you this morning?" Emeline reached for the coffeepot. "I vow, you are in a very strange mood."

"I have a right to be in a strange mood." Lavinia ladled eggs onto her plate. She was also unusually hungry, she realized. She had awakened with an extremely healthy appetite. All that exercise in Mrs. Dove's carriage, no doubt. "I told you, we are presently without a client."

"You were quite correct to terminate your association with Mrs. Dove." Emeline poured coffee into her cup. "She had no business instructing her man to spy upon Mr. March. Who knows what she intended?"

"I'm almost certain she ordered the footman to try to get to the diary first or take it from Mr. March by force. She wanted the book very, very badly. She did not want Tobias or me to read the passages that contained her secrets."

"Even though she had already told you about them?"

Lavinia raised her brows. "I am forced to agree with Mr. March. I think we can assume that whatever Mrs. Dove's secrets are, they amount to something more than the details of an indiscretion conducted in the distant past."

"Well, that is neither here nor there now, is it? The diary has been destroyed."

"I may have been a bit hasty in throwing her money back in her face," Lavinia said slowly.

Emeline's eyes sparkled. "It was the principle of the thing," she said.

"Yes, it was. Mr. March was an extremely difficult partner, but he was my associate in the affair. I could hardly allow a client to believe she could treat him like a pawn and perhaps take advantage of him. One has one's pride."

"Was it your pride or Mr. March's pride that concerned you last night?" Emeline asked dryly.

"It makes no matter now. The upshot is that I am without a client this morning."

"Never fear. Another one will soon come along."

Emeline's sunny optimism could be extremely irritating at times, Lavinia reflected.

"It occurs to me," she said, "that Mr. March will no doubt collect his fee from his client. In which event, he really ought to split it with me, don't you think?"

"Indeed," Emeline said.

"I believe I will mention the matter to him." Lavinia munched eggs and absently listened to the muffled clatter of hooves and carriage wheels in the street. "Do you know, as difficult as he proved to be on occasion, Mr. March was of some use in the affair. When all is said and done, he was the one who discovered the valet's diary."

Emeline eyed her with interest. "What are you thinking, Lavinia?"

She gave an elaborate shrug. "It strikes me that it might prove beneficial to both Mr. March and myself to occasionally collaborate in the future."

"Well." A strange expression appeared in Emeline's eyes. "Well, well, well. Indeed. A fascinating thought."

The thought of future partnerships with Tobias was exhilarating and quite terrifying, Lavinia decided. Best to change the subject.

"First things first," she said firmly. "Today we must concentrate on your evening at the theater tonight."

"*Our* evening at the theater."

"Indeed. It was very kind of Lady Wortham to invite me also."

Emeline's brows rose. "I believe she is somewhat curious about you."

Lavinia frowned. "I trust you have not mentioned any of my former careers to her?"

"Of course not."

"And you haven't told her anything of my new business venture either, I hope?"

"No."

"Excellent." Lavinia relaxed slightly. "I do not believe that Lady Wortham would find any of my professions suitable."

"In her circles, there *are* no suitable professions for females," Emeline pointed out.

"Quite true. Tonight I shall make certain to drop a hint to the effect that you have a modest but secure inheritance."

"That's not exactly a hint, Aunt Lavinia. It's more in the nature of a lie."

"Details." Lavinia waved that aside. "Now then, do not

forget we have our final fittings at Madame Francesca's this morning."

"I will not forget." Emeline hesitated, a worried frown marking her usually smooth brow. "Aunt Lavinia, concerning this evening, I trust you will not get your hopes too high. I'm quite sure that I will not take."

"Nonsense. You will look beautiful in your new gown."

Emeline grinned. "Not nearly so beautiful as Priscilla Wortham, which, of course, is the real reason her mother has been so kind to me and well you know it. She believes that having me in the vicinity shows Priscilla off to advantage."

"I don't care a fig for Lady Wortham's schemes—" Lavinia broke off, appalled. She cleared her throat and tried again. "It makes no matter to me that Lady Wortham is plotting to display Priscilla in the best possible light. As Priscilla's mother, that is her duty. But in the process, she has provided us with a golden opportunity, and I intend to make full use of it."

The door of the breakfast room opened without warning. Mrs. Chilton loomed. There was a marked glint of excitement in her eyes.

"Mrs. Dove is here, ma'am," she said loudly. "Are you seeing callers at this early hour?"

"Mrs. Dove?"

Panic roared through Lavinia. Tobias had been wrong when he had assured her there were no stains on the carriage cushions. In the poor light, he had no doubt missed an incriminating spot. She wondered if Joan Dove had come to demand payment for damages done to the seat of her expensive equipage. How much did it cost to re-cover a carriage cushion?

"Aye, ma'am. Shall I put her in the parlor or yer study?"

"What does she want?" Lavinia asked warily.

Mrs. Chilton looked startled. "Well, as to that, I couldn't say, ma'am. She asked to speak with you. Do you want me to send her away?"

"No, of course not." Lavinia took a deep breath and braced herself. She was a woman of the world. She could deal with this sort of thing. "I will see her. Please show her into my study immediately."

"Aye, ma'am." Mrs. Chilton removed herself from the doorway and disappeared.

Emeline looked thoughtful. "I'll wager that Mrs. Dove has come here this morning to insist upon paying you for your services."

Lavinia's spirits rose. "Do you really think so?"

"What other reason could there be?"

"Well—"

"Perhaps she wishes to apologize for her actions."

"I doubt it."

"Lavinia?" Emeline frowned. "What is wrong? I should think you would be thrilled that she has come here today to give you the money she owes you."

"Thrilled." Lavinia went slowly toward the door. "Absolutely thrilled."

She managed to keep Mrs. Dove waiting for four full minutes before the suspense became unbearable. She tried to look politely unconcerned and unhurried as she walked into the study.

A woman of the world.

"Good day, Mrs. Dove. This is a surprise. I was not expecting you."

Joan stood in front of the bookcase, where she had apparently

been perusing the handful of volumes on the shelves. She wore a dark gray gown that Madame Francesca had obviously designed to discreetly display her elegant figure and to accent her blond and silver hair.

The veil of the clever black hat was crumpled attractively on the brim. The expression in Joan's eyes was, as always, unreadable.

"I see you read poetry," Joan said.

Caught off guard by the remark, Lavinia glanced quickly at the handful of books. "I do not have many volumes at the moment. I was obliged to leave a great many behind when we returned somewhat hurriedly from a recent tour of Italy. It will take me some time to replenish the contents of my library."

"Forgive me for disturbing you so early in the day," Joan said. "But I did not sleep at all last night and my nerves would not tolerate any further delay."

Lavinia forged a path toward the fortress that was her desk. "Please be seated."

"Thank you." Joan chose a chair in front of the desk. "I shall come straight to the point. I wish to apologize for what occurred last night. My only excuse is that I did not entirely trust Mr. March. I felt it would be best to keep an eye on him."

"I see."

"I came here today to insist upon paying you the fee I owe you. You and Mr. March were successful, after all. It is not your fault the diary was destroyed."

"Perhaps it's for the best," Lavinia said carefully.

"You may be correct. However, it still leaves a rather glaring question."

"You wish to know who sent you that dreadful little waxwork, I suppose."

"I cannot rest until I know the answer," Joan said. "I wish you to continue your inquiries into the matter."

Joan had not come here today to complain of ruined carriage cushions. She was here to pay her bill and to request further services.

Lavinia sat down rather more abruptly than she had intended. Quite suddenly the morning seemed much brighter in spite of the rain. She made an effort to conceal her relief behind a professional facade. Very deliberately she clasped her hands on her desk.

"I see," she murmured.

"I will understand if you feel it necessary to raise your fees to compensate for what you feel was my failure to be completely forthright in the matter of the diary."

Lavinia cleared her throat. "Under the circumstances."

"Yes, of course," Joan said. "Name your price."

If she had any sense at all, Lavinia thought, she would seize the opportunity of a second chance, pluck a handsome sum out of the air, and let bygones be bygones. But the memory of Tobias's close call last night insisted upon getting in the way.

Against her better judgment, she fixed Joan with a steady gaze.

"If we are to continue to do business together, Mrs. Dove, I must make it plain that there is to be no more spying on your part. I will not have Mr. March followed about as if he were a thief and a villain. He is a professional, just as I am."

Joan elevated one brow. "Mr. March is important to you, is he not?"

She would not rise to that bait, Lavinia vowed silently. "I'm sure you will understand when I tell you that I feel a strong sense of *obligation* toward Mr. March because he is my business associate."

"I see. A sense of obligation."

"Indeed. Now then, Mrs. Dove, may I have your promise that

you will not send a man to skulk about in the shadows while Mr. March is performing his inquiries?"

Joan hesitated and then inclined her head slightly. "You have my word that I will not interfere again."

"Very well." Lavinia smiled coolly. "I shall send a message to Mr. March immediately. If he has no objection to resuming inquiries on your behalf, I will accept your new commission."

"Something tells me that Mr. March will not be at all hesitant to continue on in his capacity as your associate in this affair. I gained the distinct impression last night that he was not in favor of the manner in which you hurled my money back in my face."

Lavinia felt herself grow very warm. "I did not throw it back in your face, Mrs. Dove. Not literally."

Joan smiled. She said nothing.

Lavinia sat back in her chair. "Very well, I believe you are correct when you say that Mr. March will be only too pleased to resume his efforts in this matter. Going on that assumption, I may as well ask you some questions. It will save time."

Joan inclined her head. "Yes, of course."

"We must assume that whoever burned the diary and left it for Mr. March to discover is trying to tell us that the blackmail is finished. I suspect you will not receive any more notes from the person who sent that waxwork to you. I believe he has lost his taste for blackmail."

"You may well be right. The knowledge that I had employed professionals to make inquiries into the matter no doubt alarmed him greatly and drove him back into the shadows. Nevertheless, I must know who he is. I'm sure you understand." Joan smiled humorlessly. "I cannot tolerate strangers sending death threats."

"No, of course not. In your shoes, I would feel the same way

about the matter. Last night in bed I thought about some aspects of this situation. It occurred to me that there might be more to this than ordinary blackmail. Please do not be offended, but I must ask you something."

"What is it?"

"Before you answer, I hope you will think carefully and be honest." Lavinia hesitated, searching for the most polite way of asking the question. "Is there any reason why someone might wish to harm you?"

No emotion flickered in Joan's eyes. Not surprise or outrage or fear. She simply nodded, as if she had anticipated the question.

"I cannot think that anything I have done would make someone want to murder me," she said.

"You are a very wealthy woman. Have you conducted any business dealings that might have caused someone great financial distress?"

For the first time, a whisper of emotion appeared in Joan's eyes. It was a sad, wistful expression that was quickly veiled.

"For many years, I was married to a very wise, very clever man who managed my affairs and his own quite brilliantly. I learned a great deal about investments and financial matters from him, but I do not believe I shall ever become as proficient as he was in such things. I have done my best since Fielding's death. But it is all enormously complicated."

"I understand."

"I am still struggling with many aspects of the investments and business affairs he left to me. It is all quite arcane. Nevertheless, I feel certain that nothing I have done since his death has caused anyone to lose money."

"Forgive me, but is there anything in your personal life that might be involved? Something of a romantic nature perhaps?"

"I was deeply in love with my husband, Mrs. Lake. I was true to him during the whole of our marriage, and I have not formed any connections of an intimate nature since his death. I do not see how there could be any personal reason for someone to threaten me."

Lavinia met her eyes. "Nevertheless, a death threat is a very personal thing, is it not? More personal, when you think about it, than blackmail, which is more in the nature of a business transaction."

"Yes." Joan rose from the chair. The beautifully cut skirts of her gown needed no adjusting. They fell instantly into graceful folds. "That is why I am asking you to continue your inquiries into the matter."

Lavinia got to her feet and started around her desk. "I shall send a message to Mr. March at once."

Joan went toward the door. "You and Mr. March are very close, are you not?"

Quite inexplicably, the toe of Lavinia's shoe snagged on the carpet. She stumbled and was obliged to grab hold of the side of the desk to steady herself.

"Ours is a business connection," she said. Her voice was a little too loud, she realized. A bit too forceful.

She straightened and rushed forward to open the door.

"You surprise me." Joan looked politely bemused. "Judging by your concern for his safety and well-being last night, I would have guessed the two of you had a personal as well as a professional relationship."

Lavinia yanked open the door. "My concern for him is nothing

more than the feeling anyone would have for a business associate."

"Yes, of course." Joan walked out into the hall and paused. "By the way, I very nearly forgot. This morning my coachman told me he had found something on the seat of the carriage."

Lavinia's mouth went dry. Her hand locked on the doorknob. She knew she had probably turned a dreadful shade of pink, but there was nothing she could do.

"On the seat, you say?" she managed weakly.

"Yes. I believe it belongs to you." Joan opened her reticule and removed a folded square of muslin. She held it out to Lavinia. "It certainly isn't mine."

Lavinia stared at the cloth. It was the fichu she had worn last night. She had not even noticed it was missing. Her hand went to her throat.

"Thank you." She hastily plucked the fichu from Joan's fingers. "I had not realized I lost it."

"One must take care in a carriage." Joan lowered the veil of her hat. "Especially at night. In the shadows it is often difficult to see clearly. It is easy to lose something valuable."

She sent the message to Tobias minutes after Joan departed in her elegant maroon carriage.

Dear Sir:
    I have been offered a new commission from our former client, who wishes us to continue making inquiries on her behalf. I have her firm promise that she will abide by certain strict requirements. Are you at all interested in

resuming your position as my business associate for the purpose of continuing on in this affair?

Yrs.

Mrs. L.

His reply came back less than an hour later.

Dear Mrs. L.,

Rest assured I will be delighted to assume whatever position suits you in this affair of ours, madam.

Yrs.

M.

Lavinia studied the short note for a long time. Eventually she concluded it would be best if she did not attempt to read any hidden meaning into what Tobias had written. He was not given to subtlety and nuance in his communications with her.

The man was not a poet, after all.

"Destroyed, you say?" Neville looked thoroughly confused by the news. "Bloody hell. Completely burned?"

"If I were you, I would lower my voice." Tobias glanced meaningfully around the lightly crowded club room. "One never knows who may be listening."

"Yes, of course." Neville shook his head in bewilderment. "I forgot myself. It is just that I am quite startled by this turn of events. There was nothing left?"

"A few pages had been spared. I believe that was done to allow me to confirm that I had discovered the diary I sought."

"But all of the pages containing the entries pertaining to the members of the Blue Chamber—they were all unreadable?"

"I went through the ashes very carefully," Tobias assured him. "There was nothing of interest left."

"Damnation." Neville's hand closed into a fist, but the gesture had a theatrical quality to it. "This means the affair is finished, does it not?"

"Well—"

"It is all quite frustrating, of course. I very much wanted to know the name of the one surviving member of the Blue Chamber, the man who turned traitor during the war."

"I understand."

"With the diary destroyed, we shall never know his name, nor will we ever learn the real identity of Azure."

"Given that he is dead and has been for nearly a year, perhaps that does not matter," Tobias said.

Neville frowned and reached for the bottle of claret. "I suppose you are right. I would have given a great deal to have got my hands on that diary. But in the end, the crucial thing is that the Blue Chamber no longer exists as a criminal organization."

Tobias leaned back in his chair and put his fingertips together. "There is one small problem."

Neville paused in the act of pouring his claret and looked up sharply. "What is that?"

"Whoever destroyed the diary may well have read it first."

Neville started visibly. "*Read* it. Bloody hell. Yes, of course. I had not thought about that aspect."

"Someone out there now knows who Azure really was. That same person also knows the identity of the one remaining member of the Blue Chamber."

The claret bottle shook a little in Neville's hand. "Hell's teeth, man. You're right."

"Whoever he is, he may have no intention whatsoever of revealing the secrets of the diary. In fact, I assume that is what he was attempting to tell us when he arranged for me to find the burned pages." Tobias paused deliberately. "Nevertheless, he knows the answers to our questions. That makes him dangerous."

"Well." Neville set the bottle down very carefully. "Well, yes, it does. What do you suggest?"

"I am prepared to continue my inquiries into the matter." Tobias smiled. "If you are prepared to continue paying my fees."

thirteen

*T*here was no denying that Priscilla Wortham was an extremely attractive young lady. But tonight, in Lavinia's opinion, she was a bit overdone in her fashionable gown of pink muslin.

Her experiences at Madame Francesca's establishment in the past few days had taught her a great deal, she reflected. The modiste held very precise views on the subject of fashion, and she was not at all hesitant to impart them. Thanks to what Lavinia had learned in the course of ordering gowns for herself and Emeline, for example, she could tell at a glance that there were too many scallops at the hem of Priscilla's dress.

In addition, Priscilla's pale hair was piled a bit too high in a profusion of artfully arranged curls ornamented with a number of satin flowers that matched the gown. Her gloves were also very pink.

All in all, Lavinia concluded, Priscilla resembled a rich cream cake covered in pink icing. Emeline more than held her own in the theater box.

Seated next to Priscilla, as Lady Wortham had insisted, Emeline was a striking contrast to her friend. Lavinia was relieved to note that the tyrannical Madame Francesca had been correct when she had insisted upon the simple gown in an unusual Egyptian green gauze. Emeline's dark hair was pinned up in an elegant, uncluttered style that emphasized her fine, intelligent eyes. Her gloves were a few shades darker than the dress.

The sacrifice of the Apollo had been worth it, Lavinia thought proudly as the lights came up between acts. Earlier in the evening her chief concern had been that Lady Wortham might view Emeline as competition rather than a suitable prop against which to display Priscilla. But those fears had proved groundless. Lady Wortham had taken one look at Emeline's simple, elegantly cut gown and had not troubled to conceal her relief at the knowledge that Priscilla's gown had not been overshadowed.

The two young women had drawn their share of admiring glances this evening. Lady Wortham was clearly pleased. She obviously believed the looks were directed at her daughter. Lavinia was quite certain a good number had been aimed at Emeline.

"An excellent performance, don't you think?" Lavinia said to Lady Wortham.

"Tolerable." Lady Wortham lowered her voice so that Emeline and Priscilla could not hear her above the background noise of conversation humming through the theater. "But I feel I should mention to you that your niece's gown is much too severe for a young lady. And that odd shade of green. Not at all the thing. I must remember to give you the name of my modiste."

"Very kind of you." Lavinia injected a note of regret into her voice. "But we are quite satisfied with the one we have."

"How unfortunate." Lady Wortham's disapproving gaze rested briefly on Lavinia's own satin gown. "A good modiste is worth her weight in gold, I always say."

"Indeed." Lavinia snapped open her fan.

"I'm sure mine would never have recommended that particular shade of purple for you. Not with your red hair."

Lavinia gritted her teeth. She was saved from the necessity of responding when the heavy velvet curtains at the back of the box parted.

Anthony appeared, looking extremely handsome in his fashionably cut coat and elaborately tied cravat.

"I hope I'm not intruding." He executed a graceful bow. "I wished to pay my respects to all of the lovely ladies in this box."

"*Anthony.* I mean, Mr. Sinclair." Emeline gave him a glowing smile. "How lovely to see you."

Lady Wortham nodded pleasantly. There was a sparkle of satisfaction in her shrewd gaze. "Do sit down, Mr. Sinclair."

Anthony drew up a chair and positioned it precisely between Emeline and Priscilla. The three young people immediately launched into a lively discussion of the play. In the neighboring boxes, heads turned.

Lavinia exchanged a knowing look with Lady Wortham. They would never be close friends, she thought, but in this they were united. They were both well aware that, in the marriage mart, nothing aroused interest in a young lady as effectively as seeing a presentable young man pay court to her. Anthony was an asset to the box.

"Where is Mr. March?" Emeline asked during a short break in the conversation.

"He'll be along in a moment." Anthony cast a sidelong glance

at Lavinia. "Said something about wanting to have a word with Neville first."

That caught Lavinia's attention. She had been curious about Tobias's client. "Lord Neville is here tonight?"

"In that box across the way." Anthony angled his head very casually toward the balcony on the other side of the theater. "He is sitting with his wife. Tobias is with them now. I expect he'll make his way over here when he's finished."

Lavinia raised her opera glasses and followed his direction. Tobias came into view and she caught her breath. It was the first time she had seen him since the encounter in Mrs. Dove's carriage last night. She was appalled by the distinct thrill of excitement that swept through her.

He had just entered Neville's box. As she watched, he bent politely over the hand of a woman dressed in a low-cut blue gown.

Lady Neville appeared to be in her early forties. Lavinia studied her for a moment and concluded that she was one of those females for whom the phrase "a handsome woman" had been coined. She was a tall, stately lady who had no doubt been considered plain in her youth. She possessed the sort of features that achieved a patrician quality with maturity. Her gown was cut in an elegantly strict style that made Lavinia wonder if she was another one of Madame Francesca's clients. Even at this distance, the jewels at her throat and ears sparkled as brightly as the theater lights.

The looks of the large, heavily built man who sat beside her appeared to have matured in a manner that was the direct opposite of his wife's. Lavinia had no doubt but that Lord Neville had cut a dashing, athletic figure in his younger days. But his well-sculpted features had begun to thicken and coarsen in an unbecoming fashion that spoke of debauchery and self-indulgence.

"Are you acquainted with Lord and Lady Neville?" Lady Wortham inquired with unconcealed interest.

"No," Lavinia said. "I have not had the pleasure."

"I see."

Sensing that she and Emeline had fallen a notch or two in their hostess's opinion, Lavinia sought to recover whatever territory she could.

"But I am very well acquainted with Mr. March," she offered. Good heavens, she must be desperate indeed. Who would have thought she would find herself tossing out Tobias's name in a frantic bid to raise her own social standing?

"Hmm." Lady Wortham eyed the other box with a speculative look. "Mr. March is the gentleman who is conversing with Neville?"

"Yes."

"I have never met him, but if he is on such familiar terms with Lord Neville, he must be acceptable."

"Hmm." Lavinia wondered what Lady Wortham would think of Tobias's acceptability if she knew what he had done in the carriage last night. "Are you acquainted with Lord and Lady Neville?"

"Over the years, my husband and I have received invitations to several of the same balls and parties as Neville and his wife," Lady Wortham said, coolly vague. "We move in the same circles."

Rubbish, Lavinia thought. Receiving invitations to the same social affairs hardly counted as a proper introduction, and they both knew it. Desperate hostesses routinely sent out invitations to everyone in Society. It did not follow that everyone accepted.

"I see," Lavinia murmured. "Then you really don't know Lord and Lady Neville?"

Lady Wortham bristled. "As it happens, Constance and I were launched the same Season. I remember her well. She was quite

ordinary, to say the least. If it hadn't been for her huge inheritance, she would have remained on the shelf."

"Neville married her for her money?" Lavinia asked curiously.

"Of course." Lady Wortham snorted genteelly. "Everyone knew it at the time. There was certainly nothing else to recommend Constance. She had no looks and no sense of fashion."

"She appears to have acquired a considerable amount of the latter," Lavinia said.

Lady Wortham raised her quizzing glass and peered across the theater. "Diamonds will do that for a woman." She lowered the glass. "I see your Mr. March has left their box. When he arrives, we shall have quite a nice little gathering here, won't we?"

Lady Wortham was almost rubbing her hands together and chortling in anticipation of having a second gentleman to display in the vicinity of Priscilla, Lavinia thought.

The velvet curtains behind her parted again. But it was not Tobias who entered the box.

"Mrs. Lake." Richard, Lord Pomfrey, gave her a smoldering look that was somewhat marred by his obvious air of inebriation. "I thought I saw you from across the theater. What luck running into you again. You have been on my mind since Italy."

His words were slurred and he was a little unsteady on his feet.

The shock of seeing him again after all these months froze Lavinia in place for a few seconds. She was not the only one who was stunned into immobility by Pomfrey's entrance. Beside her, she sensed Lady Wortham turning to stone.

Her hostess was clearly well aware of Pomfrey's reputation as a debauched womanizer, Lavinia thought. He was definitely not the sort of presentable gentleman she wanted here in the box with her innocent daughter. Lavinia did not blame her. She did not particularly want Pomfrey anywhere near Emeline.

It was Anthony who rose gallantly to the rescue. He took one glance at Lavinia and got to his feet. He put himself in Pomfrey's path.

"I don't believe we've met," Anthony said.

Pomfrey looked him up and down and apparently made the decision to dismiss him out of hand.

"Pomfrey," he drawled. "I'm a *very* good friend of Mrs. Lake." He turned to give Lavinia a smile that was little more than a sickening leer. "One might even say an *intimate* friend. We knew each other well in Italy, did we not, Lavinia?"

Lady Wortham gasped.

It was past time to take control of the situation, Lavinia thought.

"You are mistaken, sir," she said brusquely. "We were not at all well acquainted. You were a friend of Mrs. Underwood, I believe."

"She was, indeed, the one who introduced us," Pomfrey agreed in tones fraught with sensual implications. "For that, I am deeply indebted to her. Have you heard from her since she ran off with the count?"

"No, I have not." Lavinia smiled coldly. "As I recall, you are married, sir. How is your *lady wife* these days?"

Pomfrey was not put off stride by the reference to his long-suffering spouse. "At a country house party, I believe." He glanced at Emeline and a wide-eyed Priscilla. "Won't you introduce me to your lovely companions?"

"No," Lavinia said.

"No," Anthony said.

Lady Wortham's eyelid twitched. "That will not be possible."

Anthony took a step forward. "As you can see, the box is crowded, sir. Kindly take your leave at once."

Pomfrey looked irritated. "I don't know who you are, but you are in my way."

"And that is where I plan to stay."

More heads turned. Lavinia caught the glint of light glancing off lenses at several points around the theater. People were aiming their long-handled lorgnettes and opera glasses in this direction. She doubted anyone could overhear what was being said, but there was no mistaking the air of tension that hung over the Wortham box.

Lady Wortham's growing horror was also unmistakable. Lavinia could almost feel her hostess cringing at the realization that a scene was taking place and the lovely Priscilla was center stage.

"Step aside," Pomfrey said rather casually to Anthony.

"No," Anthony said. His voice was low and steady in a way that was reminiscent of Tobias. "You must depart at once, sir."

Pomfrey's eyes squeezed into an angry glare.

Lavinia's stomach knotted. Anthony was taking a stand that, if worse came to worse, could get him challenged to a duel. She had to put a stop to this.

"Leave, Pomfrey," she said. "Immediately."

"I wouldn't think of leaving until you honor me with an invitation to pay a call upon you," Pomfrey said. "Tomorrow afternoon would be convenient. Why don't you oblige me with your address, madam?"

"I don't think tomorrow would be at all convenient for me," Lavinia said.

"I can wait until the following day to renew our *intimate* connection. After all, I have already waited for some months."

Lady Wortham made a valiant attempt to take command. "We are expecting another guest, Pomfrey. We really do not have room to allow you to remain here. I'm sure you understand."

Pomfrey surveyed Emeline and Priscilla with an unpleasant expression. Then he turned back to Lady Wortham and bowed somewhat unsteadily.

"I wouldn't think of leaving without paying my respects to these exquisite young ladies. Indeed, I insist upon an introduction. Who knows? We may meet again at a ball or a soiree. I may wish to request a dance."

The thought of having to introduce this well-known debauchee to her daughter caused Lady Wortham to turn an unbecoming shade of puce.

"I'm afraid that is impossible," she declared.

Anthony clenched his fists at his sides. "Leave, sir. Immediately."

Pomfrey's rage surged in his eyes. He turned on Anthony with the air of a vicious hound confronting an irritating pup.

"Do you know, you are really quite annoying. If you do not get out of my way, I shall be forced to teach you a lesson in manners."

Lavinia went cold. This was getting out of hand.

"Really, Pomfrey, you are the one who is becoming extremely tiresome," she said. "I cannot imagine why you would wish to make such a nuisance of yourself."

She knew immediately that she'd gone too far. Pomfrey was not the most stable of men, she reminded herself. When he drank, he was unpredictable and inclined to violence.

Rage flashed in his eyes, but the curtain parted before he could respond to Lavinia's insult. Tobias entered the box.

"Mrs. Lake is not entirely correct, Pomfrey," Tobias said casually. "You are not *becoming* tiresome. You have advanced far beyond tiresome to the state of being a complete bore."

Pomfrey started at the unexpected attack. He recovered swiftly but his scowl held astonishment as well as raw fury. "March. What the devil are you doing here? This is none of your affair."

"Ah, but it is very much my affair." Tobias gave him a direct man-to-man look. "I'm sure you take my meaning."

Pomfrey was incensed. "What's this? You and Mrs. Lake? I never heard a word about a connection between the two of you."

Tobias gave him a smile that was so cold, Lavinia was surprised Pomfrey did not freeze to the carpet.

"Well, now you have heard about our connection, have you not?" Tobias said.

"See here," Pomfrey blustered. "I knew Mrs. Lake in Italy."

"But not very well, obviously, or you would have been aware that she considers you a complete bore. If you are unable to exit this box on your own two feet, I shall be happy to assist you in your departure."

"Bloody hell, is that a threat?"

Tobias considered that briefly and then inclined his head. "Yes, I believe it is."

Pomfrey's face worked. "How dare you, sir?"

Tobias shrugged. "You'd be amazed at how easy it is to threaten you, Pomfrey. Not difficult at all. I'd say it comes quite naturally."

"You will pay for this, March."

Tobias smiled. "I believe I can afford the price."

Pomfrey turned red. His hands bunched. Lavinia was suddenly terrified that he was about to issue a formal challenge.

"No." She was halfway out of her chair now. "No, wait. Pomfrey, you must not do such a thing. I will not permit it."

But Pomfrey was not paying any attention to her. He was intent only on Tobias. Instead of making her worst fears come true with an offer of pistols at dawn, he stunned everyone by launching a sudden, powerful blow aimed at Tobias's midsection.

Tobias must have been expecting the swing because he stepped back, barely avoiding Pomfrey's fist. The sudden movement affected his balance, however. Lavinia saw his left leg falter. He seized the edge of one velvet curtain for support, but the heavy drapery proved

unable to withstand his full weight. It tore free of several of the rings that secured it to the rod and sagged.

Tobias staggered back against the wall.

Priscilla uttered a little shriek. Emeline leaped to her feet. Anthony swore softly and put himself in front of the two young ladies in a futile attempt to shield them from the view of masculine violence.

Tobias slid down toward the floor just as Pomfrey's fist crashed into the wall with a jarring thud. Pomfrey uttered a muffled groan of pain and cradled his injured hand in his palm.

Lavinia heard a strange roaring noise. It took her a few seconds to realize that the crowd was cheering and applauding the spectacle. Judging from their shouts of encouragement, they seemed to find this better entertainment than anything seen onstage this evening, she thought.

She heard a choked groan followed by a heavy thump. When she glanced to the side, she saw that Lady Wortham had fallen out of her chair and was lying flat on her back on the floor.

"*Mama.*" Priscilla hurried toward her. "Oh dear, I do hope you remembered to bring your vinaigrette."

"My reticule," Lady Wortham gasped. "Hurry."

Tobias grabbed the railing and used it to haul himself to his feet. "Perhaps we should finish this in a more appropriate place, Pomfrey. The alley outside would do nicely."

Pomfrey stood blinking at Tobias. He seemed to become aware of the wildly screaming crowd. The rage in his eyes metamorphosed into a dazed expression. Several men in the pit yelled up at him, urging him to strike another blow.

Rage did battle with humiliation as it began to dawn on Pomfrey that he was involved in a public spectacle.

In the end, the forces of humiliation won.

"We will settle this another time, March."

Pomfrey sucked in a shuddering breath, then whirled and stumbled out of the box.

The crowd voiced its disappointment with a chorus of boos and hisses.

On the floor, Lady Wortham groaned again.

"Mama?" Priscilla waved the vinaigrette beneath her mother's nose. "Are you all right?"

"Never so humiliated in my life," Lady Wortham moaned. "We won't be able to go out in public for the rest of the Season. Mrs. Lake has utterly destroyed us."

"Oh dear," Lavinia said.

It was all his fault, Tobias thought. Again.

A funereal silence filled the hackney. Anthony and Emeline sat opposite Tobias and Lavinia. No one had said a word since they had left the theater. From time to time, everyone looked at Lavinia and then looked away again, helpless to find words of comfort.

She sat stiffly on the seat, head averted, and stared out the window into the night. Tobias knew she blamed him for everything.

He forced himself to do the manly thing.

"I apologize for ruining your plans for the evening, Lavinia."

She made a small, inarticulate sound and jerked a hankie out of her reticule. He stared, stunned, as she dabbed at her eyes with the lacy square.

"Bloody hell, Lavinia, are you *crying*?"

She made another odd noise and buried her face in the hankie.

"Now see what you've done," Anthony said. He leaned forward. "Mrs. Lake, Tobias and I cannot tell you how much we regret what

happened tonight. I swear, we never intended to cause you such distress."

Lavinia hunched her shoulders. A shudder went through her. She did not raise her face from the hankie.

"Pomfrey is a perfectly dreadful man, Lavinia," Emeline said gently. "You know that better than most. It was unfortunate he chose to show up tonight, but given that he did make a pest of himself, I really do not know what else Mr. March and Anthony could have done."

Mutely, Lavinia shook her head.

"I know you had hopes of attracting some attention in my direction this evening," Emeline added.

"If nothing else, we were successful in that regard," Tobias said dryly.

Lavinia sniffed loudly into the hankie.

Anthony glared at him. "This is hardly an appropriate time to indulge yourself in your decidedly odd notion of humor. Mrs. Lake believes she is confronting nothing less than an unmitigated disaster, and not without reason. I think it is safe to say the scene in Lady Wortham's box tonight will be the main topic of conversation over every cup of tea served tomorrow. To say nothing of the gossip in the clubs."

"Sorry," Tobias muttered. He could not think of anything else to say. He had seen Lavinia in a variety of moods, but there was a resiliency in her that he realized he had begun to take for granted. This was the first time he had seen her cry. He would never have imagined that she would succumb to a bout of tears simply because of a social fiasco. He was at a loss, far out of his depth, and he knew it.

"Well, it certainly isn't a disaster so far as I'm concerned," Emeline said bracingly.

Lavinia mumbled something incomprehensible.

Emeline sighed. "I know you worked hard to encourage Lady Wortham to invite me to the theater tonight, and you did sacrifice the Apollo for these lovely gowns. I regret that events did not transpire in quite the way you had anticipated. Nevertheless, I did tell you I was not particularly keen to be put on display."

"Mumph," Lavinia said into the hankie.

"It wasn't Mr. March's fault that Pomfrey made an ass of himself," Emeline continued. "Indeed, it is not fair for you to blame him or Anthony for what occurred."

"Please don't cry, Mrs. Lake," Anthony said. "I'm sure the gossip will die down very quickly. It is not as though Lady Wortham occupies a particularly elevated position in the Polite World. The entire affair will soon be forgotten."

"We are m-m-most certainly ruined, just as Lady Wortham said," Lavinia mumbled into the hankie. "That cannot be h-he-helped. I doubt if a single eligible gentleman will call on Emeline tomorrow. But what's done is done."

"Tears will do no good," Emeline said worriedly. "Really, it is not like you to weep over this sort of thing."

"Her nerves have been under a great deal of strain lately," Anthony reminded them all.

"Don't cry, Lavinia," Tobias muttered. "You are affecting the nerves of everyone present."

"I fear I cannot help myself." Lavinia slowly raised her head to reveal damp eyes. "Th-the expression on Lady Wortham's face. I vow I have never seen anything so entertaining in my entire life."

She collapsed into the corner of the seat, convulsed by another fit of laughter.

They all stared at her.

Emeline's mouth curved at the corner. Anthony started to grin.

In the next moment they were all laughing uproariously.

Something deep inside Tobias relaxed. He no longer felt as if he were being driven to a funeral.

"There you are, March." Crackenburne lowered his newspaper and peered at Tobias over the tops of his spectacles. "I heard you were responsible for a very entertaining diversion at the theater last night."

Tobias lowered himself into a neighboring chair. "Wild rumors and unsubstantiated gossip."

Crackenburne snorted. "You won't be able to make that version of events float for long. There was an entire theater full of witnesses. There are some who believe Pomfrey will call you out."

"Why should he do that? He was clearly the victor in the match."

"So I was told." Crackenburne looked thoughtful. "How did that come about?"

"The man has taken instructions in boxing from the great Jackson himself. I never stood a chance."

"Humph." Crackenburne's bushy brows came together over the bridge of his impressive nose. "Make light of the matter if you will, but watch your back around Pomfrey. He has a reputation for becoming violent when he is in his cups."

"I thank you for your concern, but I don't believe I am in danger of being called out by Pomfrey."

"I agree. I'm not worried that he will invite you to a dawn appointment. Pomfrey would work up the nerve to issue a challenge only if he were inebriated. Even if he managed that, I'm quite certain he would immediately retract the invitation as soon as the effects of the drink wore off. At heart he is not only a fool, he is a coward."

Tobias shrugged and reached for his coffee. "Then what is it that concerns you?"

"I would not put it past him to find some underhanded means of avenging himself on you." Crackenburne raised his paper in front of his face again. "I advise you not to take long walks alone at night for a while—and do try to stay out of dark alleys."

fourteen

avinia pulled the voluminous cap low over her eyes and arranged the woolen scarf so that it veiled her features. The apron she wore over the much-mended gown was the one Mrs. Chilton always used when she scrubbed the floors. Thick stockings and sturdy shoes completed the disguise.

She looked at the woman seated on a stool near the hearth, a woman she knew only as Peg.

"You're certain Mr. Huggett is away for the afternoon?" Lavinia asked.

"Aye." Peg munched a meat pie. "Huggett takes his treatments every Thursday. The only one who'll be there is young Gordy. No need to fret about him. He'll be out front sellin' tickets, assumin' he's not entertainin' his girl in one of the back rooms."

"What treatments does Mr. Huggett take?"

Peg rolled her eyes. "Goes to one of them quacks what use animal magnetism to ease aching joints and such."

"Mesmerism."

"Aye. Huggett's afflicted with rheumatism."

"I see." Lavinia hoisted the bucket of gray water. "Well, then, I'll be off." She paused, turning slowly on her heel. "Will I do, Peg?"

"Yer a sight, ye are." Peg picked up another meat pie and squinted at Lavinia with rheumy eyes. "If I didn't know ye was a fine lady, I'd be worrying that ye was after takin' my place."

"Never fear, I don't want your post." Lavinia gripped the handle of the dirty mop. "As I told you, my only intention is to win the wager I made with my friend."

Peg gave her a knowing look. "A lot of the blunt at stake, eh?"

"Enough to make it worth my while to pay you to let me carry out this masquerade." She started up the steps that led from Peg's tiny room to the lane. "I'll return your things within the hour."

"Take yer time." Peg settled back on her stool and stretched out her swollen ankles. "Ye ain't the first to want to borrow me bucket and mop for an hour or two, although yer the first to say she only wanted me things in order to win a wager."

Lavinia halted on the top step and turned quickly. "Someone else asked to take your place?"

"Aye." Peg gave a phlegmy chuckle. "I've got a regular arrangement with a couple of ambitious girls. I'll let you in on a little secret. Old Peg has made more renting out that bucket and mop and those keys than she's ever received in wages from that closefisted Huggett and that's a fact. How d'ye think I managed to obtain me own little room?"

"I don't understand. Why would someone pay you to let her scrub floors in your place?"

Peg winked broadly. "Some of the gentlemen customers get downright frisky when they tour the exhibits in that special gallery at the top of the stairs. The displays generally put 'em in the mood for a bit o' sport, and if there's a willin' lass about, well, they're happy to give her a few coins to let them lubricate her, if ye know what I mean."

"I think I understand." Lavinia stifled a shudder. "You don't need to go into further detail. I'm not interested in renting your bucket and mop to promote that sort of business. I'm not in that line."

"No, course not." Peg swallowed some pie and wiped her mouth with the back of a grimy hand. "Yer a *lady*, ain't ye? Yer just renting me bucket for a lark and a wager, not because yer next meal depends on it."

Lavinia could not think of anything to say to that. Without a word, she went up the stairs and stepped out into the dingy lane.

It did not take long to walk the short distance to Huggett's Museum on the fringes of Covent Garden. She found the alley behind the establishment. The back door was open, just as Peg had promised.

Clutching the mop and the bucket of filthy water, Lavinia took a deep breath and let herself inside. She found herself in a darkened hall. The door on the left, the one Peg said Huggett used as an office, was closed and locked.

She released the breath she had been holding. The museum proprietor did indeed appear to be gone for the afternoon.

The dimly lit ground-floor gallery was nearly empty, just as it had been the other day when she and Tobias had perused the

exhibits. None of the small handful of customers so much as glanced her way.

She walked beyond the grave-robbing scene and passed the gallows with its waxwork hangman. At the far end of the room, she found the spiral staircase in the shadows.

For the first time since the notion of investigating Huggett's mysterious upstairs gallery had occurred to her this morning, she hesitated.

From where she stood, she could not see the door at the top of the staircase that Peg had described. It was lost in the heavy gloom. A prickle of unease whispered through her.

This was no time for an attack of nerves, she thought. It was not as if there were any danger present. She was simply going to take a look inside the gallery.

What could possibly go wrong?

Annoyed with herself, she shook off the tingle of uncertainty, tightened her grip on the bucket and mop, and went briskly up the twisting stairs.

When she reached the landing, she found the solid wooden door. It was locked, just as Peg had predicted. The scrubwoman had explained that Huggett's gentlemen customers were allowed inside only after they had paid an additional fee. Apparently no one had done so this afternoon.

That would make things easier, Lavinia assured herself.

She dug the iron ring out of one of the pockets in her apron and fitted a key into the lock. There was a harsh, grating sound as the door opened. The hinges squeaked loudly.

Hesitantly she moved into the room, allowing the door to swing closed behind her.

The displays were unlit but there was enough light coming

through the high, narrow windows to allow her to make out the sign directly in front of her.

SCENES FROM A BROTHEL

The hulking shapes of five life-size waxwork tableaux loomed in the shadows around her.

She set down the bucket and mop and walked to the first display. In the gloom she could make out the muscular back of a nude male figure. He appeared to be engaged in a violent struggle with another figure.

She looked closer and saw with shock that the second figure was that of a partially clothed woman. She stared, baffled, for a few seconds. It finally dawned on her that the figures were engaged in a sexual act.

Neither figure appeared enraptured by the experience. In fact, there was an air of violence about the scene that made Lavinia's skin prickle. It was an image of rape and lust. The man looked quite savage. The woman seemed to be in agony. Horror twisted her features.

But it was not the expressions on the faces of the figures that drew her eye. It was the fact that they were so skillfully modeled. Whoever had done these waxworks was far more talented than those who had sculpted the morbid exhibits downstairs.

This artist rivaled Mrs. Vaughn in talent.

Lavinia felt excitement explode within her.

This artist could well have crafted the waxwork death threat that had been sent to Joan Dove. No wonder Huggett had appeared startled when she and Tobias had showed him the little picture.

She must not leap to conclusions, Lavinia cautioned herself. She needed clear evidence, something that linked these works to the death threat.

She moved to the next display and stopped to study it. The scene was that of a seminaked woman kneeling in front of a nude male. The man was in the process of ravishing her brutally from the rear.

Lavinia looked away from the huge, elaborately rendered genitals of the man and searched for small clues that could confirm her growing suspicions. It was difficult, partly because of the differences in scale. The death threat was so much smaller than these life-size figures. Nevertheless, something about the lushly sculpted female figure was reminiscent of the image of the woman in the green gown lying dead on the ballroom floor.

I should have brought Mrs. Vaughn with me, Lavinia thought. With her trained eye, the artist would no doubt have found it easier to discern similarities between these figures and the one in the death threat.

If there were, indeed, similarities.

Lavinia started toward another exhibit. She must be very, very sure of her deductions before she confronted Tobias with her theory, she thought.

The muffled clang of booted feet reverberated outside the chamber. Jolted, Lavinia jerked her attention away from the display and whirled to face the door.

"No harm in seeing if it's open," one of the men said. His voice was muffled by the door. "Save ourselves the price of an extra ticket. The lad out front will never know."

Lavinia hurried toward the bucket and mop. She heard a rasping, metallic sound as the knob was turned.

"What ho! We're in luck. Someone forgot to lock up."

The door swung open before Lavinia could reach for the bucket. Two men sauntered into the room, chuckling with anticipation.

She froze in the shadow of the nearest display.

The shorter of the two men ambled toward the nearest exhibit. "The lamps are unlit."

The taller man closed the door and stood gazing into the gloom-filled chamber. "As I recall, there's a lamp at each waxwork."

"Here we go." The short man stooped to strike a light.

The flaring lamp danced on the bucket and caught the trailing edge of Lavinia's apron and skirts. She tried to slink deeper into the shadows, but it was too late.

"Well, now, what do you think we have here, Danner?" In the glow of the lamp, the tall man's leer was plain to see. "A waxwork come to life, mayhap."

"Looks more like a lively little baggage to me. You did say you had met some very obliging charwomen working in this particular gallery." The short man eyed Lavinia with growing interest. "Hard to see what she looks like in those clothes."

"Then we must persuade her to remove them." The tall man jingled some coins. "What do you say, sweetheart? How much do you charge for a bit of sport?"

"Beggin' yer pardon, sirs, I must be off now." Lavinia edged toward the door. "I'm finished with the floors, ye see."

"Don't rush off, wench." The tall one jingled his coins more loudly in what he no doubt assumed was an enticing manner. "My friend and I can offer you more interesting and more lucrative employment."

"No thank you." Lavinia seized the mop by the handle and held it in front of herself as though it were a sword. "I'm not in that line, so I'll leave you two fine gentlemen to enjoy the displays."

"I really don't think we can allow you to depart so soon." Danner's voice held an unmistakable threat. "My friend here tells me that the nature of these sculptures is such that they are more appreciated when one has a pretty wench conveniently at hand."

"Show us your face, wench. Take off that cap and scarf and let's have a look at you."

"Who cares how pretty she is? Lift your skirts for us, lass, that's a good girl."

Lavinia groped for the doorknob. "Don't touch me."

His lust clearly whetted by the chase, Danner started forward. "You're not leaving until we've sampled your wares."

"Never fear." The tall one tossed one of the coins in Lavinia's direction. "We're prepared to make it worth your while."

Her fingers closed around the iron doorknob.

"I do believe she intends to run off," the tall one said. "Must be something about you that offends her delicate sensibilities, Danner."

"A cheap little light-skirt like her hasn't got any business having delicate sensibilities. I'll teach her to turn her nose up at me."

Danner launched himself at Lavinia. She jabbed the dirty, wet end of the mop at his midsection.

"Stupid little whore." Danner scrambled to a halt and stepped out of range. "How dare you try to attack your betters?"

"What the devil's the matter with you, lass?" The tall man sounded as if he were losing patience. "We're willing to pay for your services."

Lavinia said nothing. She kept the mop pointed at him while she opened the door.

"Come back here." Danner moved in on her again, eyeing her makeshift weapon warily.

She stabbed the mop in his direction one last time, causing him to swear viciously and dance backward.

"What the bloody hell do you think you're doing?" the tall one growled. Nevertheless, he elected to remain out of reach of the mop.

Seizing the opportunity, Lavinia dropped the mop and dashed through the doorway toward the spiral staircase. She grabbed the railing as she vaulted down the twisted steps.

Behind her, Danner snarled furiously at the top of the staircase.

"Bitch! Who do you think you are?"

"Let her go," his companion advised. "There are plenty of other whores in the neighborhood. We'll find you a more willing lass after we've viewed the displays."

Lavinia did not pause when she reached the ground-floor gallery. She rushed along the rear hall, yanked open the back door, and ran out into the alley.

It started to rain just as she went up the steps of Number Seven, Claremont Lane. The last straw, she thought. A fitting end to an extremely trying afternoon.

She used her key to let herself into the front hall. The perfume of roses was so strong she nearly choked.

"What in heaven's name is going on here?" She glanced around as she untied the woolen scarf. Baskets and vases of freshly cut flowers were arranged on the table. A small plate filled with white calling cards sat nearby.

Mrs. Chilton appeared, wiping her hands on her apron. She chuckled. "They started arriving soon after you left, ma'am. Appears Miss Emeline attracted some notice after all."

Lavinia was distracted by that heartening news. "These are from her admirers?"

"Aye."

"But that is *wonderful.*"

"Miss Emeline does not seem to be impressed," Mrs. Chilton observed. "The only gentleman she talks about is Mr. Sinclair."

"Yes, well, that is neither here nor there." Lavinia tossed the scarf aside. "The point is, that dreadful scene in Lady Wortham's box obviously did not ruin my plans after all."

"So it seems." Mrs. Chilton surveyed Lavinia's clothing, frowning in disapproval. "I hope no one saw you come through the front door, ma'am. My, but you look a fright."

Lavinia winced. "I suppose I should have gone around to the kitchen door. The thing is, I had a most unpleasant afternoon and then, on the way home, it started to rain, and by the time I got here, all I could think about was getting into my nice, warm study and pouring myself a large glass of sherry."

Mrs. Chilton's eyes widened. "You'll be wanting to go upstairs and change first, ma'am."

"No, I don't think that's necessary. Only the cloak and scarf are wet. The rest of my clothes are dry, fortunately. A medicinal dose of sherry is vastly more important at the moment."

"But, ma'am—"

Foosteps sounded overhead.

"Lavinia." Emeline leaned over the upstairs balcony. "Thank heavens you're back. I was starting to worry. Was your scheme successful?"

"Yes and no." Lavinia slung the tattered cloak on a hook. "What is going on with all of these posies?"

Emeline made a face. "Apparently, Priscilla and I are mildly

fashionable today. Lady Wortham sent a message an hour ago. I collect that all is forgiven. She invited me to accompany her and Priscilla to a musicale this evening."

"That is excellent news." Lavinia paused, thinking quickly. "We must consider which gown you will wear."

"It is not as if I have a great choice to make. Madame Francesca designed only one that would be suitable." Emeline picked up her skirts and started quickly down the stairs. "Never mind my gown. Tell me what happened at the museum."

Lavinia snorted softly. "I shall tell you the whole of it, but you must swear to me that you will never, under any circumstances, repeat any of it to Mr. March."

"Oh dear." Emeline came to a halt at the foot of the steps. "Something went wrong, did it not?"

Lavinia stalked down the hall toward her study. "Let's just say that things did not proceed according to plan."

Alarm flashed across Mrs. Chilton's face. "Ma'am, please, you'll want to change before you go into your study."

"I need that glass of sherry more than I need a change of clothing, Mrs. Chilton."

"But—"

"She's right, Lavinia," Emeline said, hurrying to follow. "You really must go upstairs first."

"I regret that my costume offends both of you, but this is my house and I will bloody well wear what I wish in my own study. Do you want to hear my tale or not?"

"Of course I want to hear it," Emeline said. "Are you certain you are all right?"

"It was a near thing, but I am happy to report that I got away unscathed."

"*Unscathed?*" Emeline's voice rose in mounting concern. "Good heavens. Lavinia, what happened?"

"An unanticipated problem presented itself." Lavinia swept through the doorway of her study and headed directly toward the sherry cabinet. "As I said, you must not breathe a word of the tale to Mr. March. I shall never hear the end of it."

Tobias looked up from the book he was perusing near the window. "This promises to be an interesting story indeed."

Lavinia halted a step away from the sherry cabinet. "What the devil are you doing here?"

"Waiting for you." He closed the book and glanced at the clock. "I arrived twenty minutes ago and was told you were out."

"That is precisely where I was." She jerked open the cabinet door, seized the decanter, and poured herself a large glass of sherry. "Out."

He gave her attire a leisurely appraisal. "Attending a masquerade ball perhaps?"

She sputtered on the mouthful of sherry. "Of course not."

"Have you decided to augment your income by taking a position as a scrubwoman?"

"Not enough money in it." She took another swallow of sherry, savoring the warmth. "Not unless one is willing to polish something other than floors."

Emeline gave her a troubled look. "Please do not keep us in suspense. What happened when you went to Huggett's Museum?"

Tobias crossed his arms and leaned against the bookcase. "You went back to Huggett's? Dressed in that odd costume?"

"Yes." Lavinia carried her glass across the room and dropped into a chair. She stretched her legs out in front of her and examined the thick stockings. "It occurred to me that it might be informative to discover what sort of waxworks were displayed in the upstairs gallery. Huggett seemed quite secretive about them, I thought."

"He was secretive because of the artistic theme of the displays." Tobias's voice was edged with impatience. "For obvious reasons, he did not care to explain to a lady that he had a gallery full of erotic waxworks upstairs."

"Erotic waxworks?" Emeline looked intrigued. "How unusual."

Tobias shot a frown in her direction. "Forgive me, Miss Emeline. I should not have mentioned the subject. It is not the sort of thing one discusses around unmarried young ladies."

"Think nothing of it," Emeline said blithely. "Lavinia and I both learned a great deal about such matters during our sojourn in Rome. Mrs. Underwood was very much a woman of the world, you know."

"Yes," Tobias said a bit too evenly. "I know. Everyone in Rome was aware of her proclivities."

"We stray from the topic," Lavinia said crisply. "It was not just Huggett's reaction when I asked him about the waxworks in his upstairs gallery that struck me as unusual. You and I both believed he recognized something about the death threat, if you will recall. This morning I woke up wondering if it was because he had some of the same modeler's sculptures on display in the locked chamber."

Tobias stilled. "You went to Huggett's to view those sculptures?"

"Yes."

"Why?"

She moved the hand in which she held the glass in a vague motion. "I just told you. I wanted to examine the quality of the modeling. I paid the regular scrubwoman to let me use her keys, and I entered the chamber in this disguise."

"Well, then? Obviously you saw the sculptures. Do you believe the statues you saw were modeled by the same artist who crafted the death threat?"

"To be frank, I could not say for certain."

"In other words, this nonsense of a masquerade was a complete waste of time, was it not?" Tobias shook his head. "I could have told you that if you had bothered to ask my opinion on your scheme before you carried it out."

"I didn't say it was a complete waste of time." She met his eyes over the rim of the glass. "Huggett's figures are life-size. The difference in scale made it difficult for me to be sure of my conclusions. But I think there were some similarities."

Tobias was beginning to look intrigued in spite of himself. "Indeed?"

"Enough to convince me that it would be worth our while to ask Mrs. Vaughn to study them and give us her opinion," Lavinia said.

"I see." Tobias moved toward the desk. He propped himself on the corner and absently massaged his left thigh. "Such a viewing would be difficult to arrange. Huggett is unlikely to cooperate with the request even if he has nothing to hide. After all, it would mean allowing a lady into his upstairs gallery. Very awkward, even if she is an artist."

Lavinia leaned her head against the back of the chair, thinking of Peg and her side business. "Huggett's scrubwoman is willing to rent out the keys to the gallery on the days when Huggett takes his treatments for rheumatism."

"I don't understand," Emeline said. "Why would anyone pay her for the use of her keys in order to sneak into the gallery when they could simply purchase a ticket?"

"She doesn't rent the keys to visitors who wish to examine the sculptures," Lavinia said very precisely. "She rents them to women

who make their living selling their favors to the gentlemen who purchase tickets to the upstairs gallery."

Emeline's brows shot skyward. "Prostitutes, do you mean?"

Lavinia cleared her throat and carefully avoided Tobias's gaze. "According to Peg, gentlemen who tour the upstairs gallery frequently find themselves in a mood to be entertained by those in the demimonde who ply their trade in such places. Something to do with the excitement induced by the displays, I believe."

Tobias gripped the edge of the desk and raised his eyes to the ceiling, but he said nothing.

"I see." Emeline pursed her lips and pondered that for a moment. "It is certainly very fortunate that there were no gentlemen about in the gallery when you went into it in your disguise, is it not? They might have mistaken you for a prostitute."

"Mmm," Lavinia said noncommittally.

"How extraordinarily awkward that would have been," Emeline continued.

"Mmm." Lavinia took a sip of sherry.

Tobias watched her closely. "Lavinia?"

"Mmm?"

"I am assuming there were no customers about in the upstairs chamber when you entered."

"Quite right," she agreed readily. "There was no one inside when I entered."

"I have also been laboring under the assumption that none of Huggett's gentlemen customers entered while you were inside. Am I mistaken?"

Lavinia exhaled deeply. "I think it would be best if you left us, Emeline."

"Why?" Emeline asked.

"Because the remainder of this conversation will not be suitable for your innocent ears."

"Rubbish. What could be more unsuitable than the subject of erotic waxworks?"

"Mr. March's language when he vents his temper."

Emeline blinked. "But Mr. March is not in a temper."

Lavinia swallowed the last of the sherry and set down the glass. "He will be soon."

fifteen

Tobias was still seething when he walked into his study an hour later. Anthony, seated behind the desk, looked up with interest. The expression on his face transmuted first into alarm and then amused resignation. He tossed aside his pen, then leaned back in the chair and gripped its arms.

"You have been quarreling with Mrs. Lake again, have you not?" he asked without preamble.

"What of it?" Tobias scowled. "By the bye, that is my desk. If you don't mind, I would like to have the use of it this afternoon."

"It must have been a particularly heated argument this time." Anthony rose leisurely and moved out from behind the desk. "One of these days you will go too far and she will dissolve your partnership."

"Why would she do that?" Tobias took command of his desk and sat down. "She knows very well that she needs my assistance."

"Just as you need hers." Anthony walked over to the large globe positioned on a stand near the fireplace. "But if you keep on in this fashion, she may decide she can get along very well without you."

A flicker of unease went through Tobias. "She is reckless and impulsive but she is not a complete crackbrain."

Anthony leveled a finger at him. "Mark my words, if you do not learn to treat her with the polite respect to which she is entitled as a lady, she will lose all patience with you."

"You believe she is entitled to polite respect from me because she is a *lady*?"

"Of course."

"Let me tell you a thing or two about the proper behavior of a lady," Tobias said evenly. "A *lady* does not don a scrubwoman's costume and sneak into a chamber full of erotic waxworks that are meant only for the viewing of gentlemen. A *lady* does not deliberately put herself into a situation in which she may be mistaken for a cheap street whore. A *lady* does not take foolish risks that oblige her to defend her honor with a mop."

Anthony looked at him, eyes widening. "Odd's teeth. Are you telling me Mrs. Lake was in danger this afternoon? Is that why you are in such a ferocious temper?"

"Yes, that is precisely what I am telling you."

"Damnation. This is terrible. Is she all right?"

"Yes." Tobias ground his teeth. "Thanks to the mop and her own presence of mind. She was forced to fend off two men who took her for a prostitute."

"Thank God she is not inclined to swoon in a crisis," Anthony said in heartfelt tones. "A mop, eh?" Admiration lit his gaze. "I must say, hers is a resourceful nature."

"Her resourceful nature is not the issue here. The point I am trying to make is that she ought never to have put herself into such an untenable position in the first place."

"Yes, well, you have often remarked that Mrs. Lake is inclined to be independent-minded."

"Independent-minded is a gross understatement. Mrs. Lake is ungovernable, unpredictable, and headstrong. She will not take direction or advice unless it suits her. I never know what she will do next, and she feels no particular need to inform me until it is too late for me to stop her."

"From her point of view, you no doubt possess similar faults," Anthony said dryly. "Ungovernable. Unpredictable. I have not noticed that you feel any particular need to inform her of your actions until after you have taken them."

Tobias felt his jaw lock. "What the devil are you talking about? There is no point in advising her of every move I make in this affair. Knowing her, she would insist on accompanying me whenever I wished to speak with one of my informants, and that would frequently be impossible. I certainly cannot take her with me when I go into establishments such as The Gryphon, and she cannot accompany me into my clubs."

"In other words, you do not always inform Mrs. Lake of your actions because you know there is likely to be an argument."

"Precisely. An argument with Lavinia is frequently an exercise in futility."

"That means that you sometimes emerge the loser."

"The lady can be extraordinarily difficult."

Anthony said nothing but his brows rose in silent comment.

Tobias picked up a pen and tapped it on the blotter. For some reason, he felt obliged to defend himself.

"Mrs. Lake very nearly got assaulted this afternoon," he said quietly. "I have every right to be in a temper."

Anthony contemplated him for a long while and then, to Tobias's amazement, he inclined his head in an understanding manner.

"Fear sometimes has that effect on a man, does it not?" Anthony observed. "I do not blame you for your strong feelings on the matter. You will no doubt have nightmares tonight."

Tobias said nothing. He was afraid Anthony was right.

Lavinia looked up from her notes when Mrs. Chilton ushered Anthony into her study.

"Good day to you, sir."

He gave her a very proper bow. "Thank you for seeing me, Mrs. Lake."

Lavinia managed a welcoming smile and tried not to let him see that she was holding her breath. "You are quite welcome. Please sit down, Mr. Sinclair."

"If you don't mind, I would prefer to stand." Anthony's expression was one of resolute determination. "This will be somewhat difficult for me. Indeed, I have never done this before."

Her worst fears were confirmed.

Lavinia stifled a sigh, put aside her notes, and braced herself to deal with a formal offer for Emeline's hand.

"Before you begin, Mr. Sinclair, please let me say that I find you to be a very admirable gentleman."

He looked startled by that remark. "Very kind of you to say so, madam."

"You have only just passed the one-and-twenty mark, I believe."

He frowned. "What does my age have to do with this?"

She cleared her throat. "It is quite true that some people are mature beyond their years. That is certainly the case with Emeline."

Anthony's gaze shone with sudden admiration. "Miss Emeline is, indeed, astonishingly clever for a person of any age."

"Nevertheless, she is barely eighteen."

"Indeed."

This was not going well, Lavinia thought. "The thing is, sir, I would not want Emeline to rush into marriage."

Anthony brightened. "I could not agree with you more, Mrs. Lake. Miss Emeline must take her time about the matter. It would be a grave mistake for her to become engaged too quickly. A bright spirit such as hers must not be too quickly extinguished by the constraints of marriage."

"We are agreed on that point, sir."

"Miss Emeline must be allowed to set her own pace."

"Indeed."

Anthony squared his shoulders. "But as much as I admire Miss Emeline and although I have dedicated myself to her happiness—"

"I had not realized you had done so."

"It is my great pleasure," Anthony assured her. "But as I was saying, I did not call upon you today to speak of her future."

The sense of relief Lavinia felt left her almost giddy. It appeared she would not have to find a way to thwart young love after all. She relaxed and smiled at Anthony.

"In that case, Mr. Sinclair, what was it you wished to speak to me about?"

"Tobias."

Some of her relief evaporated.

"What about him?" she asked warily.

"I am aware that he quarreled with you earlier this afternoon."

She moved her hand in a casual gesture. "He lost his temper. What of it? It was hardly the first occasion."

Anthony nodded unhappily. "Tobias has always had a tendency to be somewhat brusque, and he has certainly never suffered fools gladly."

"I do not consider myself to be a fool, Mr. Sinclair."

Horror lit Anthony's eyes. "I never meant to imply any such thing, Mrs. Lake."

"Thank you."

"What I am trying to say is that there appears to be something in the nature of his association with you that has an unusually provocative effect on his temper."

"If you have come here to ask me not to annoy him further, I fear you have wasted your time. I assure you, I do not deliberately set out to irritate him. But as you just noted, there does appear to be something in the nature of our association that has an abrasive effect on him."

"Indeed." Anthony paced back and forth in front of the desk. "The thing is, I would not have you judge him too harshly, Mrs. Lake."

That gave her pause.

"I beg your pardon?" she ventured.

"I promise you that beneath his somewhat rough exterior, Tobias is a fine man." Anthony stopped in front of the window. "No one knows that better than I."

"I am well aware of your fondness for him."

Anthony's mouth twisted. "I wasn't always so fond of him. Indeed, back at the beginning when my sister married him, I think I actually hated Tobias for a while."

She went quite still. "Why was that?"

"Because I knew that Ann had been forced to wed him."

"Indeed." She did not want to hear that Tobias had married his wife because he had first made her pregnant, she thought.

"She married him for my sake as well as her own, you see. I resented the fact that she felt obliged to sacrifice herself. And for a while I made Tobias the villain of the piece."

"I'm afraid I don't understand," Lavinia said.

"After our parents died, my sister and I were taken to live with our aunt and uncle. Aunt Elizabeth was not at all pleased to have us. As for Uncle Dalton, he was the vile sort who took advantage of chambermaids and governesses and any other helpless females who were so unfortunate as to cross his path."

"I see."

"The bastard tried to seduce Ann. She refused his advances but he was very insistent. She avoided him by hiding in my bedchamber at night. We barred the door every evening for over four months. I believe Aunt Elizabeth knew what was happening, because she became determined to see Ann married off. One day Tobias came to visit my uncle on a matter of business."

"Mr. March was acquainted with your uncle?"

"In those days, Tobias made his living as a man of business. He had a number of different clients. Uncle Dalton had recently become one of them. Aunt Elizabeth used Tobias's visit as an excuse to invite some of the neighbors to join us for dinner and cards. She insisted they spend the night under her roof rather than brave the roads. Ann thought she would be safe with so many people in the house, so she spent the night in her own room."

"What happened?"

"The long and the short of it is that Aunt Elizabeth arranged for my sister to be found in what she claimed was a compromising position with Tobias."

"Good heavens. How on earth did she manage that?"

Anthony stared out into the garden. "Aunt Elizabeth gave Tobias the room next to Ann's. There was an adjoining door. It was locked, of course. But early the next morning my aunt entered Ann's room and unlocked the door. Then she staged a great scene in which she announced to the entire household and her guests that Tobias had obviously entered Ann's bedchamber in the middle of the night and had his way with her."

Lavinia was incensed. "But that's utterly ridiculous."

Anthony smiled bitterly. "Yes, of course it was. But every-one knew Ann was ruined in the eyes of the neighbors. Aunt Elizabeth insisted upon an offer of marriage. I fully expected Tobias to refuse to be coerced into the arrangement. I was only a boy yet it was very clear to me, even then, that he was not the sort of man who would allow himself to be forced into doing anything he did not wish to do. But to my surprise, he told Ann to pack her trunk."

"You're quite right, Mr. Sinclair," Lavinia said gently. "Tobias would not have gone along with your aunt's demands had he not been willing."

"The fact that he took Ann away was not the most astonishing thing. The truly astounding thing was that Tobias told me to go and pack also. He rescued both of us that day, although I did not realize it until later."

"I see." She thought of how it would have been for a small boy to be taken away by a stranger. "You must have been frightened."

Anthony grimaced. "Not for myself. As far as I was concerned, anything was better than living with our relatives. But I was ex-tremely anxious about what Tobias might do to Ann once he had her in his power."

"Was Ann afraid of Tobias?"

"No. Never." Anthony smiled at some private memory. "He

was her knight in bright armor, right from the start. I think she fell in love with him before we were halfway down the drive, certainly before we struck the main road to London."

Lavinia propped her chin on her hand. "Perhaps that was one of the reasons why you did not take to Tobias immediately. Until that day, you were first in your sister's affections."

Anthony looked bemused for a moment and then he frowned. "You may be correct. I had not considered it from that point of view."

"Did Mr. March marry your sister straight off?"

"Within the month. He must have fallen in love with her at first sight. How could he not? She was very beautiful, inside and out. She was the gentlest of creatures. Kind, gracious, loving, sweet-tempered. More of an angel than a woman of flesh and blood, I think. Certainly too good for this world."

In short, a woman quite the opposite of me, Lavinia thought.

"But Tobias feared that her feelings for him were based only on gratitude and would soon fade," Anthony continued.

"I see."

"He told Ann she was under no obligation to become his wife, nor did he expect her to play the role of his mistress. But regardless of her decision, he made it clear he would find a way to take care of us."

"But she loved him."

"Yes." Anthony studied the pattern on the carpet for a moment and then looked up with a bleak, sad smile. "They had less than five years together before she and the babe both died of a fever in childbed. Tobias was left with a thirteen-year-old brother-in-law."

"Losing your sister must have been extraordinarily difficult for you."

"Tobias had been very patient with me. By the end of the first year of the marriage, I idolized him." Anthony gripped the back of a chair. "But I went a little mad for a time after Ann died. I blamed him for her death, you see."

"I understand."

"To this day, it is a wonder to me that he did not send me back to my aunt and uncle at some point during those months after the funerals or, at the very least, ship me off to school. But Tobias tells me it never crossed his mind to get rid of me. He claims he had become accustomed to having me around."

Anthony turned back to the window and fell silent, apparently lost in his own recollections.

Lavinia blinked several times to get rid of the moisture that was blurring her vision. Finally she abandoned the effort and took a hankie out of the top desk drawer. She dabbed quickly at her eyes and sniffed once or twice.

When she had composed herself, she clasped her hands on the desk again and waited. Anthony made no attempt to resume the tale.

"Do you mind if I ask a question?" she said after a while.

"What is it?"

"I have wondered about Mr. March's limp. I am quite certain he had no such difficulty when I met him in Rome."

Anthony glanced at her in surprise. "Did he not tell you what happened?" His mouth twisted ruefully. "No, knowing Tobias, he would not have done so. Carlisle lodged a bullet in his leg that night. It was a fight to the death. Tobias barely survived. As it was, he spent several weeks recovering from the effects of his wound. I suspect he will have that limp for a long time, perhaps for the rest of his life."

Lavinia stared at him, stunned.

"I see," she whispered eventually. "I had not realized. Dear heaven."

There was another lengthy silence.

"Why are you telling me these things?" she asked eventually.

Anthony gave a small start and looked at her. "I wanted you to understand."

"Understand what?"

"Tobias. He is not like other men."

"Believe me, I am well aware of that."

"It is because he has had to make his own way in the world, you see," Anthony continued earnestly. "He lacks a proper polish."

Lavinia smiled. "Something tells me that no amount of polishing would alter Mr. March's character."

"What I am trying to explain is that even though his manners are not always what they should be when he is in the company of ladies, he has many excellent qualities."

"Pray do not trouble yourself to give me a list of all of Mr. March's outstanding qualities. You will likely bore both of us."

"I fear you will not make allowances for his shortness of temper and his occasional lapse of manners."

Lavinia flattened her palms on the desk and pushed herself to her feet. "Mr. Sinclair, I assure you that I am quite comfortable with Mr. March's temper and his poor manners."

"You are?"

"Indeed, sir." She came out from behind the desk to show him to the door. "How could it be otherwise? I myself exhibit those very same character flaws. Just ask anyone who knows me well."

sixteen

She had hoped he would change his mind, but she had been in the business too long to expect such a happy event. In her experience, when a gentleman ended a liaison with his mistress, he rarely resumed the affair. The wealthy rakehells of the ton were easily bored, she reflected. They were forever seeking more fashionable denizens of what they liked to call the demimonde.

But once in a while a wise man realized he had been too hasty in ending a relationship.

Sally smiled with satisfaction and dropped the ticket into the pocket she had sewn inside her cloak. It was a very fine cloak, a gift from him. He had been quite generous with her. He had paid the rent on the pleasant little house where she had been living for the past few months, and he had given her some lovely jewelry. She kept the bracelet and the earrings in a safe place in her

bedchamber, knowing full well they were all that stood between her and a return to the brothel in which he had found her.

She refused to sell the jewelry to pay the rent. These were her best working years and they would not last long. She intended to spend them industriously. Her goal was to collect a large number of valuable gifts from a number of men. When her looks and youth were gone, she would use the trinkets to finance a comfortable retirement.

She was proud of her businesslike view of her finances. She had struggled hard to get herself off the streets of Covent Garden, where one was obliged to service the customers in carriages or the nearest doorway. Life was very dangerous and often brutally short at that end of the profession. She had worked her way into the relative security of a brothel, and now she had joined the lower ranks of the more fashionable courtesans. The future looked bright. Perhaps she would one day have her own box at the opera the way some of the most glittering members of her profession did.

She had begun discreetly shopping around for a new protector in the last day or so, hoping to secure one before the rent came due at the end of the month. But she had promised herself that she would not rush into a new connection, even if refusing to do so meant moving out of the little house. She had known other women who had made the mistake of leaping at the first offer in their haste to keep afloat financially. In their desperation, they sometimes agreed to connections with men who proved to be violent or who used them in ways that everyone knew were unnatural. She shuddered when she recalled an acquaintance who had taken up with an earl who forced her to entertain his friends with sexual favors.

She hurried down a shadowy aisle, paying little attention to the eerily lit displays on either side. She was here on business. She

glanced at a gallows scene and grimaced. Even if she had been in a mood to tour a waxwork museum, this was not the one she would have chosen. In her opinion, these exhibits were all extremely depressing.

At the end of the gloomy chamber, she found the cramped, circular staircase. She collected her skirts and the long folds of her cloak and went quickly up the steps. The instructions she had received had been very precise.

The heavy door at the top of the staircase was unlocked. It groaned on its iron hinges when she pushed it open. She walked into the dimly lit chamber and glanced around. Although the downstairs displays were not to her taste, she was curious about this room. She had heard that Huggett's boasted a very unique gallery, one that was open only to gentlemen.

The sign placed near the entrance was painted in elegant blue and gold. She took a step closer and bent down slightly to read it in the poor light.

SCENES FROM A BROTHEL

"Well, now, if that isn't a dull subject," she muttered to herself. But perhaps she was jaded because she was in the business.

She walked to the nearest illuminated display and studied the sculptures of a man and a woman writhing on a bed, engaged in a lustful embrace. The man's face was fierce and intent, almost brutal as he neared his climax. He surged against his partner, the muscles in his buttocks and back straining in a highly realistic manner.

The body of the woman had been modeled with a voluptuous abandon that was no doubt guaranteed to interest the average male viewer. Large breasts and well-rounded hips that could have

graced an ancient Greek statue were paired with tiny, elegant feet. But it was the woman's face that caught Sally's attention. There was something familiar about the features.

She was about to move closer to get a better look when she heard the faint scraping sound in the darkness behind her. She jerked her attention away from the waxwork.

"Who's there?"

No one spoke or moved in the thick shadows. For no discernible reason, her heart started to pound. Her palms went cold and damp. She knew these signs. She had experienced them from time to time in the old days on the streets. Some of the men who had approached her had triggered this odd reaction. She had always heeded her intuition and declined to service those who made her feel this way, even when it had meant going hungry for a day or two.

But this was no stranger trying to lure her into a dark hackney. Surely this was her protector, the man who had paid her rent for the past few months. He had sent for her, asked her to meet him here. There was no need for this anxiety.

A small chill went through her. For some reason, she suddenly recalled the old gossip that had circulated in the brothel about his previous mistress having committed suicide. Some of the more romantic among her associates had claimed the woman's heart had been broken and viewed the event as a great tragedy. But most had shaken their heads at the foolishness of allowing one's sensibilities to overwhelm common sense.

She herself had wondered about it all at the time. She had had a passing acquaintance with his former mistress. Alice had not struck her as the type to make the mistake of falling in love with her protector.

She shook off memories of poor, foolish Alice. But another

whisper of dread shivered through her. It was the nature of the displays, she thought. They had affected her nerves.

There was no call to be alarmed. He was playing one of his games.

"I know you're here, my handsome stallion." She forced a coy smile. "I got your message, as you can see. I've missed you."

No one stepped out of the shadows.

"Did you send word to have me meet you here so we could act out some of these scenes?" She giggled a little, the way he liked. Then she clasped her hands behind her back and started down the aisle between the waxwork tableaux. "How very naughty of you, my stallion. But you know I am always happy to oblige."

There was no response.

She stopped in front of a dimly lit exhibit of a woman crouched on her knees in front of a man whose member did a great deal of credit to the artist's imagination. She pretended to examine the rigid pole with an air of grave consideration.

"Now, in my opinion," she declared, "your cock is even larger than his." It was a lie, of course, but lying to the customer was an essential skill in her profession. "Of course, I may have forgotten the *exact* dimensions, but I would be delighted to measure it again for you. Indeed, I cannot think of a more fascinating way to spend the evening. What do you say to that, my fine stallion?"

No one spoke.

Her pulse was not slowing. If anything, it had picked up the pace. Her hands were clammy. It was impossible to fill her lungs with air.

Enough. She could no longer fight the old street fears. Something was very wrong.

Instinct took over. She stopped resisting the impulse to escape. She no longer cared whether or not her former protector

wanted to resume their liaison. She wanted only to escape from this chamber.

She whirled and fled back down the aisle. The door was invisible in the heavy darkness at the far end of the gallery, but she knew where it was.

There was a sudden stirring in the deep pool of shadows to her right. Her first, crazed thought was that one of the waxwork figures had come to life. Then she saw the weak light glint on a length of heavy iron.

A scream rose in her throat. She knew now that she would never make it to the door. She turned, raising her hands in a vain attempt to ward off the blow. She stumbled backward. Her foot struck a wooden bucket sitting on the floor. She lost her balance and fell. The bucket tipped over, spilling filthy water across the floor.

The killer moved in, the poker raised high for the murderous blow.

In that instant, Sally suddenly understood why the waxwork prostitute in the first display had seemed familiar. The figure had Alice's face.

seventeen

*T*he Gryphon was warm and dry but that was about all that could be said in favor of the smoky tavern. Nevertheless, as he made his way through the crowd, Tobias thought those qualities were definite assets on a damp, fog-bound night.

The fire on the massive hearth blazed with hellish good cheer, illuminating the establishment with an evil, flaring light. The serving maids were all large, buxom, sturdily built wenches. The similarities in their figures were not a coincidence. Smiling Jack, the proprietor, liked them that way.

Tobias had changed his clothes for this venture. Garbed in a dockworker's well-worn trousers, ill-fitting coat, shapeless cap, and heavy boots, he drew little attention as he passed among the rough patrons of The Gryphon. The annoying catch in his stride was a good complement to his disguise, he thought. Most of those around him made their livings in injury-prone ways, not all of which were legal. Limps such as his own were common. So were scars and missing fingers. Eye-patches and wooden legs were also sprinkled liberally about the premises.

A broad-bosomed serving maid blocked Tobias's path. She gave him an encouraging grin. " 'Ere now, me 'andsome man, what'll ye 'ave tonight?"

"Got business with Smilin' Jack," Tobias muttered.

He made it a point to converse as little as possible with the staff and patrons of The Gryphon. The rough, dockside accents he adopted for these visits saw him safely through short exchanges. He was not certain they would hold up in longer, more involved discussions.

"Jack's in 'is room at the back." The maid nodded toward the hall that led to the rear of the tavern and winked. "Best knock afore ye open the door."

She moved off through the crowd, her tray of mugs held high overhead.

Tobias worked his way along rows of tables and benches. At the far end of the tavern, he found the dingy hall that led to the room Smiling Jack was pleased to call his office. He went down the passage and stopped in front of the door.

A muffled shriek of feminine laughter reverberated through the heavy wood paneling. Tobias rapped loudly.

"Begone, whoever ye are out there." Jack's voice rumbled like a load of coal. "I've got business in here."

Tobias wrapped one hand around the knob and twisted. The door swung inward. He lounged against the jamb and looked at Smiling Jack.

The huge proprietor of The Gryphon was seated behind a battered desk. His face was buried in the large, naked bosom of the

woman perched astride his thighs. The wench's skirts were hiked up to her waist, displaying plump buttocks.

"I got your message," Tobias said.

"Is it you then, Tobias?" Smiling Jack raised his head and squinted. "Bit early, aren't ye?"

"No."

Jack groaned and gave his companion a playful pat on her bare backside. "Off with ye, lass. My friend here's in a hurry and I can see he's a mite short of patience tonight."

The woman giggled. "Don't mind me, Jack." She wiggled her bottom. "I'll just sit here and carry on with what we started while the two of ye discuss yer business."

"Afraid that's not possible, sweetheart." Jack heaved a regretful sigh and gently eased her off his lap. "You're a distraction and that's a fact. I can't concentrate on me business affairs with you workin' yer wiles."

The woman laughed again, stood, and shook out her skirts. She winked broadly at Tobias and took her time exiting the room. Her generous hips moved in a rolling motion that held the undivided attention of both men until the door closed behind her.

Her laughter echoed in the hall.

"A new employee." Jack closed his trousers. "I think she'll do nicely."

"She does appear to be possessed of a cheerful disposition." Tobias dropped the dockside accents. He and Jack knew each other too well.

Tobias knew, for instance, the tale behind the grotesque scar responsible for the name Smiling Jack. The stitches that had closed the knife wound had been set by a poor seamstress. They had healed into a death's-head grin extending from the corner of Jack's mouth to his ear.

"Aye, that she does." Jack heaved his bulky frame erect and waved Tobias to one of the ladder-back chairs near the hearth. "Sit down, man. It's a mean night. I'll pour ye some of my good brandy to ward off the chill."

Tobias took one of the unforgiving wooden chairs near the hearth, reversed it, and sat down. He folded his arms on the back and tried to ignore the ache in his leg.

"The brandy will be welcome," he said. "What news do you have for me?"

"There are a couple of matters that may interest you. First, you asked me to look into the backgrounds of some of Neville's women." Jack poured brandy into two glasses. "I have turned up one or two items of interest on that subject."

"I'm listening."

Jack handed one of the glasses to Tobias and lowered himself back into the chair behind his desk. "You told me Neville is in the habit of selecting his women from the brothels rather than from the ranks of the fashionable high-flyers. You were right."

"What of it?"

"I'm not certain why he prefers the less expensive sort, but I will tell you one thing. When women plucked out of the brothels throw themselves into the river, the authorities don't take much notice." Jack grimaced. The expression twisted the scar into a ghastly imitation of amusement. "There are even a few who will say good riddance. One less whore selling her favors."

Tobias tightened his fingers around the glass. "Are you telling me that more than one of Neville's light-skirts have ended up in the river?"

"I cannot say how many of his women have drowned themselves after he cast them aside, but two, at least, seem to have been unable to endure their broken hearts. A woman named Lizzy

Prather killed herself a year and a half ago. Several months back a wench named Alice was also dragged out of the river. There are rumors that three more are dead by their own hand."

Tobias sipped the warming brandy. "Hard to credit that so many females would succumb to severe melancholia after Neville was through with them."

"Aye." Jack's chair squeaked in protest when he leaned back. He ignored the warning and laced his hands on top of his expansive belly. "Make no mistake, it happens now and again. There's always a few foolish girls who actually believe they've found true love with a wealthy man and get their hearts broken. But most of the wenches know what they're about when they get involved with a man from Neville's class. They milk him for all the baubles they can get and move on to the next cove when they find themselves havin' to pay their own bills again."

"A business arrangement on both sides."

"Aye." Jack took a hefty swallow of brandy, put down the glass, and wiped his mouth. "Listen well now, because here's the most interestin' bit about this particular affair."

"Yes?"

"Neville's latest doxy, Sally, has also disappeared. No one has seen her since yesterday afternoon."

Tobias did not move. "The river?"

"Too soon to say. I haven't heard of her body being pulled out of the water, but that can take a while. All I can tell ye at this point is that she's gone. And if my sources can't find her, no one can."

"Damn it to hell." Tobias rubbed his leg.

Smiling Jack allowed that news to sink in before he continued. "There's one more thing you might want to know."

"About Sally?"

"No." Jack lowered his voice even though there was no one else in the room. "It concerns the Blue Chamber. There are some rumors circulating."

Tobias stayed very still. "I told you, the Blue Chamber is finished. Azure and Carlisle are both dead. The third man has gone to ground but not for long. I'll have him soon."

"What you say may be true enough as far as it goes. But what I'm hearing on the streets is that there's a private little war being waged."

"Who is involved?"

Jack shrugged. "Can't say. But I hear the victor intends to take control of whatever is left of the Blue Chamber. Word is, he plans to rebuild the empire, which fell apart after Azure died."

Tobias looked at the fire for a long time, thinking about that.

"I owe you for this information," he said eventually.

"Aye." Jack smiled his grisly smile. "You do. But I'm not worried. You've always been one to pay your bills."

The fog had grown more dense while he had been inside The Gryphon. Tobias paused on the step. The lights of the tavern were reflected by the swirling mist hovering in the street. The eerie orange glow was oddly bright, but it revealed nothing.

After a moment he started across the street, resisting the urge to pull the high collar of the ancient coat up around his ears. The thick wool would block some of the chill, but it would also limit his side vision and muffle the small sounds of the night. In this neighborhood it was only prudent to take full advantage of all of one's senses.

He moved quickly through the weak glare created by the fog

and slipped into the deep darkness beyond. There appeared to be no one else about. Hardly surprising on such a night, he thought.

Once free of the weird glow of The Gryphon, he was able to make out a small, dim circle of light suspended high off the ground. Judging it to be the lantern of some conveyance, he made for it, staying in the center of the street, well clear of unlit alleys and darkened doorways.

Nevertheless, for all his precautions, the only warning he got was the soft, sliding rush of a man coming up very swiftly behind him. *Footpad.*

He fought the instinct to turn and confront the assailant, knowing all too well that this one was probably only a distraction. London footpads frequently hunted in pairs.

He veered to the side, seeking the protection of the nearest wall to put at his back. Pain shafted through his left leg but the sudden change of direction served its purpose. It caught the man behind him by surprise.

"Bloody hell, I lost 'im."

"Light the lantern. Light it, mate. 'Urry or we'll never find 'im in this bloody fog."

That settled the question, Tobias thought. There were indeed two footpads working together here. The angry voices pinpointed their positions.

He drew the pistol from his pocket and waited.

The first man swore loudly, struggling with the lantern. When the light sputtered and flared, Tobias used it as a target. He pulled the trigger.

The roar of the gun boomed in the street. The lantern shattered.

The footpad yelped and dropped the light. The oil flared high as it spilled onto the paving stones.

" 'Ell's teeth, the bastard's got a pistol." The second man sounded aggrieved.

"Well, he's fired it now, 'asn't he? So it's no more use to 'im."

"Some coves carry two."

"Not unless they're expectin' trouble." He moved into the flickering light cast by the burning lantern oil, grinning demonically, and raised his voice. "You, hidin' there in the fog. We come to deliver a message to ye."

"Won't take long," the other man said loudly. "Just want to make sure ye realize it's a very serious message."

"Where is he? I can't see a bloody damn thing."

"Quiet. Listen, ye great, blatherin' fool."

But the vehicle at the end of the street was in motion now. The rattle of wheels and the clatter of shod hooves on stones sounded very loud in the night. Tobias used the noise to cover his movements.

He shrugged out of the tattered greatcoat and draped it loosely over a nearby iron railing.

" 'Ellfire, the bloody nightman's comin' this way," one of the footpads snarled.

Not a nightman's wagon, Tobias thought, moving to intercept the oncoming vehicle. *Please, don't let it be a nightman's wagon. Anything but that.*

The jiggling lamp was almost opposite him now. The figure on the box shouted and slapped the reins against the horse's rump, urging the animal into a brisker trot. Tobias grabbed a handhold as the wagon rumbled past.

The foul smell of the cart's contents hit him with the force of a blow. The nightman had been hard at work going about his business of emptying privy cesspools and collecting rubbish from the households and businesses of the neighborhood.

Tobias tried to hold his breath as he hauled himself aboard the moving wagon.

"Couldn't you have found some other equipage?" he demanded as he dropped onto the seat.

"Sorry." Anthony gave the horse another encouraging slap. "By the time your message reached me, there was very little time. I couldn't find a hackney. On a night like this they're all taken."

"There he is," Tobias heard one of the footpads shout. "Over there by the railing. I see his coat."

"I was forced to start out on foot." Anthony pitched his voice above the clatter of hooves. "Came across a nightman and offered him some money for the use of his vehicle. I promised to return it within the hour."

"Now we've got you," came another shout from the footpads.

Steps echoed on the paving stones.

"What the bleedin' 'ell? He got away. He must be on the bloody nightman's cart."

A shot thundered in the night. Tobias winced.

"Don't fret," Anthony said. "I'm sure you will be able to secure another coat as unfashionable as that one."

A second shot thundered in the fog. The nightman's horse had had enough. This was most certainly not part of the normal routine. The beast flattened its ears, lurched forward, and broke into a canter.

"He's gettin' away, I tell ye. We'll not get paid for this night's work if we don't catch him."

After the footpad's words died down, Tobias said to no one in particular, "It seemed like such a simple, sensible plan. All I asked was that you secure a hackney and wait in the street outside The Gryphon, just in case there was a problem that necessitated my hurried departure."

"An excellent precaution, given the nature of the neighborhood." Anthony worked the reins, playing the role of coachman with enthusiasm. "Just think what might have happened if you hadn't sent me the message to meet you here."

"Do you know, for some reason, it never occurred to me that you would choose a nightman's wagon."

"A man's got to work with whatever is available. You taught me that." Anthony grinned. "When I couldn't find a hackney, I was forced to make do. I thought I demonstrated initiative."

"Initiative?"

"Right. Where do we go now?"

"First we return this splendid coach to its rightful owner and pay him for the use of it. Then we shall head straight home."

"It's not that late. Don't you want to go to your club?"

"The porter would never let me through the door. In case you have not noticed, we are both sorely in need of a bath."

"You have a point."

An hour later Tobias got out of the tub, dried himself with a towel in front of the fire, and put on his dressing gown. He went downstairs and found Anthony, also freshly scrubbed and garbed in the spare shirt and trousers he kept in his old room upstairs.

"Well?" Anthony lounged in a chair, feet stretched out to the hearth. He did not turn his head when Tobias entered the room. "Let's have it. Do you think they were genuine footpads?"

"No. They said something about having been paid to deliver a message." Tobias shoved his hands into the pockets of the dressing gown.

"A warning?"

"Apparently."

Anthony tilted his head slightly. "From someone who does not want you making any further inquiries?"

"I did not hang about long enough to ask. It's possible the message was from someone who wants me to cease my investigation. But there is another suspect."

Anthony gave him a knowing look. "Pomfrey?"

"I didn't put much credence in Crackenburne's warning about him. But he may have been correct when he told me that Pomfrey might seek revenge for what happened at the theater."

Anthony thought about that for a time. "Makes sense. Pomfrey's not the sort to do things in an honorable fashion." He paused. "Will you inform Mrs. Lake about what happened tonight?"

"Bloody hell, what do you take me for? A lunatic? Of course I'm not going to inform her about this evening's adventure."

Anthony nodded. "I thought you might say that. Naturally you wish to keep her in the dark because you do not want to make her overanxious for your safety."

"That's got nothing to do with it," Tobias said with feeling. "I'm not going to tell her about the encounter with those two men because I am quite certain she would use the occasion to read me a lengthy lecture."

Anthony did not bother to conceal his amusement. "Rather like the one you read her when you discovered that she had gone off to Huggett's disguised as a scrubwoman and got into a bit of a scrape?"

"Precisely. It strikes me that it would be extremely unpleasant to be on the receiving end of that sort of tongue-lashing."

Lavinia was halfway through breakfast when she heard Tobias in the hall.

"Don't bother, Mrs. Chilton. I know my way around the place. I can announce myself."

Emeline picked up the butter knife, smiling. "It would appear we have an early visitor."

"He has certainly given himself the run of our house, has he not?" Lavinia forked up a mouthful of eggs. "What the devil can he want at this hour? If he thinks I'll listen to another lecture on how I must not make a move without informing him, he can think again."

"Calm yourself."

"It is impossible to be calm where Mr. March is involved. He has a talent for roiling the waters." Lavinia stopped munching as a thought struck her. "Good heavens, I wonder if something terrible has happened?"

"Nonsense. Mr. March sounds quite fit and in excellent health."

"I meant, I wonder if something terrible has happened regarding our investigation."

"I'm certain he would have sent word if that had been the case."

"Do not depend on it," Lavinia said darkly. "As I pointed out in Italy, Mr. March plays a deep game."

The door opened. Tobias strode into the breakfast room, filling the small, cozy space with the energy and force of his masculine presence. Lavinia swallowed her eggs very quickly and tried to ignore the little thrill of awareness ruffling her nerves.

What was it about him that sent these little chills of excitement through her? she wondered, not for the first time. He was not a big man. No one would describe him as handsome. He rarely bothered to employ the refined manners one expected of a gentleman, and he clearly needed a new tailor.

On top of everything else, although he seemed to be interested

in her in an earthy fashion, she was not at all sure that he liked her very much. It was not as if they shared some ethereal, meta-physical bond, she thought. There was no poetry in their associa-tion; on the contrary, it was a matter of business and a rather spectacular sort of lust. At least it was spectacular from her point of view, she amended. She was not at all certain that it was any-thing out of the ordinary for Tobias.

Lavinia wondered if the strange sensation she felt when she was near Tobias was an indication of an attack of nerves. It would not be the least bit surprising, she thought, given the strain she had been under lately.

Irritated by that possibility, she crumpled her napkin fero-ciously on her lap and glared at him. "What are you doing here so early, Mr. March?"

His brows rose at the peremptory greeting. "Good day to you, too, Lavinia."

Emeline made a face. "Pay no attention to her, Mr. March. My aunt did not sleep well last night. Do sit down. Would you care for some coffee?"

"Thank you, Miss Emeline. A cup of coffee would be very wel-come."

Lavinia watched the cautious way he lowered himself into a vacant chair. She scowled. "Did you strain your leg again, sir?"

"A bit too much exercise last night." He smiled at Emeline and took the cup she had just filled for him. "No need to concern yourself."

"I wasn't concerned," Lavinia assured him in lofty tones. "Merely curious. What you choose to do to and with your leg is entirely your own affair."

He gave her an amused look. "I am in complete agreement with that statement, madam."

Quite suddenly the memory of how his legs had slid between her own that night in the carriage flashed through her brain. She met his eyes across the table and knew with horrible certainty that he was also thinking of the passionate interlude.

Fearing she was turning an embarrassing shade of pink, she hurriedly forked up some more eggs.

Emeline, blithely oblivious to the undercurrents, smiled graciously at Tobias. "Did you dance last night, sir?"

"No," Tobias said. "My leg does not take well to dancing. I engaged in another form of exercise."

Lavinia tightened her fingers around the fork until her knuckles whitened and wondered if Tobias had been with another woman last night.

"I have a busy day planned," she said brusquely. "Perhaps you would be so good as to explain why you felt compelled to visit us at this extremely early hour?"

"As a matter of fact, I too have plans for the day. Perhaps we should compare notes."

"For my part, I intend to speak to Mrs. Vaughn and ask her if she would be willing to give me her opinion of the waxworks in Huggett's upstairs gallery," Lavinia said.

"Indeed." Tobias gave her a politely inquiring smile. "And just how do you intend to smuggle her into that chamber if she does agree to examine them? Will you disguise her as a scrubwoman?"

His condescending attitude goaded her. "No, as a matter of fact, I have thought of another way to get into the gallery. I believe it may be possible to bribe the young man who sells the tickets."

"You're serious about this, aren't you?"

"Indeed, sir." She gave him a bright little smile.

He set the coffee cup down hard onto the saucer. "Damnation,

Lavinia, you know very well I don't want you going into that gallery alone."

"I won't be alone. I will be accompanied by Mrs. Vaughn." She paused delicately. "You are invited to join us, if you wish."

"Thank you," he said dryly. "I accept."

There was a short silence. Tobias reached across the table and helped himself to a slice of toast. Lavinia caught a flash of white teeth when he took a bite.

"You have not said why you came here this morning," she reminded him crisply.

He munched thoughtfully. "Came by to see if you would like to accompany me while I make inquiries about a woman named Sally Johnson."

"Who is Sally Johnson?"

"Neville's most recent mistress. She disappeared the day before yesterday."

"I don't understand." He had her attention now, however. "Do you think there is some connection to our investigation?"

"I cannot say yet." Tobias's eyes were shadowed. "But I have got a very nasty feeling that there may be a link."

"I see." Lavinia thawed slightly. "It was good of you to stop here this morning to inform me of your plans and to ask me to accompany you."

"As opposed to the secretive manner in which you handled your inquiries at Huggett's yesterday, do you mean?" Tobias nodded. "Indeed. But then, perhaps I take our agreement to work as *partners* more to heart than you do."

"Not bloody likely." She tapped the tines of her fork against the edge of the plate. "What is this all about, Tobias? Why are you asking me to join you today?"

He swallowed another bite of toast and fixed her with a steady look. "Because if I am so fortunate as to find Sally, I will wish to speak with her. I have no doubt but that she will be more forthcoming with a woman than with a man."

"I knew it." Bleak satisfaction settled in the pit of her stomach. "You came here this morning not because you wished to work as partners but because you need me to help you conduct your own inquiries. What do you expect me to do? Put Sally into a mesmeric trance and coax her to speak freely?"

"Must you always question my motives?"

"Where you are concerned, sir, I prefer to proceed with utmost caution."

He smiled faintly, eyes gleaming. "Not always, Lavinia. I have known you to make one or two exceptions to that rule."

eighteen

The house was a narrow structure with two floors aboveground and kitchens below. The neighborhood was not the best, Lavinia thought, but it was clear of the stews.

It had not taken long to determine that Sally Johnson was not at home. Tobias had come prepared for that eventuality.

She stood with him in the tiny front area below street level and watched him insert the end of a metal tool between the kitchen door and its frame.

"Neville appears to have been only moderately generous to Sally," she observed. "This is certainly not the grandest of houses."

Wood and iron groaned as Tobias applied judicious force to the bar.

"When you consider that Neville took her out of a brothel, this place no doubt looked like a mansion to her," he said.

"Yes, I suppose that's true."

The door popped open.

Lavinia wrapped her cloak more securely around herself and peered into the darkened hallway. "I do hope we will not stumble across another body. I have had quite enough of corpses."

Tobias led the way into the house. "If Sally has met with the same fate as her two predecessors, her body will likely be found in the river, not here."

Lavinia shuddered and followed him across the threshold. "It makes no sense. Why would your client murder his mistresses?"

"There is obviously no reasonable answer to such a question."

"Even if he did dispatch the women, what does it have to do with the death threat that was sent to Mrs. Dove or the Blue Chamber?"

"I cannot say yet. Maybe nothing. Maybe a great deal."

Lavinia came to a halt in the center of the kitchen, wrinkling her nose at the scent of rotting meat. "You do realize what you are saying? That your client may be a liar and a murderer."

"I told you, all clients lie." Tobias opened a vegetable basket and glanced inside. "That is one of the many reasons why it is wise to obtain an advance on one's fees when one accepts a commission."

"I shall remember that in future." She opened a cupboard and peered inside. "But you must have some theory as to why Neville would be in the habit of murdering his mistresses."

"One possibility is that he is quite insane."

She shuddered. "Yes."

"But there is another possible motive." Tobias dropped the lid of the basket and looked at her. "A man who keeps a woman tucked away in a little house such as this does so because he wishes to spend a fair amount of time in her company."

Lavinia made a face. "Probably a good deal more time than he spends in the company of his wife."

"Precisely." Tobias slanted her an enigmatic glance. "Given that most marriages in the ton are made for reasons of money and social connections, it's hardly surprising for a man to discover that his relationship with his mistress is far more intimate in many ways than the one he has with his wife."

His point finally struck home. Lavinia swung around, frowning. "Do you really believe that when Neville tires of his mistresses he murders them because he fears they know too much about him? What sort of secrets does he possess that would make him kill three women in order to ensure their silence?"

"I will be truthful with you." Tobias closed a drawer and started up the stairs leading to the main floor of the house. "I do not know what to think at the moment. I only know that at least two and quite possibly three women with whom Neville has enjoyed a very close connection during the past two years are dead. Supposedly by their own hand."

"Suicide." Lavinia glanced uneasily around the kitchen and hurried after him. "We do not know for certain that Sally Johnson followed the other two into the river."

Tobias reached the hall and disappeared into the parlor. "I think that, under the circumstances, we must assume the worst."

Lavinia left him to the ground floor. She continued on up the narrow staircase and emerged in a small hall.

It required only about two minutes inside Sally's bedchamber to conclude that Tobias was wrong on one point. She whirled and rushed back to the top of the stairs.

"Tobias."

He appeared in the hall below and looked up at her. "What is it?"

"I do not know what happened to Sally, but I can tell you one thing for certain. She packed up her things before she

disappeared. The wardrobe is empty and there are no trunks under the bed."

Tobias mounted the steps without comment and came down the hall to where she stood. She stepped aside to let him move past her into the bedchamber. When she walked into the room behind him, she found him gazing at the interior of the empty wardrobe.

"It's possible that someone who knew her and was aware she was missing came here and stole her possessions," he said quietly. "It would not surprise me to learn that Sally's friends are nothing if not opportunists."

Lavinia shook her head. "If a thief had come here, he or she would most likely have left the chamber in a state of disarray. Everything is too neat. Whoever packed Sally's things knew the room well."

Tobias studied the furnishings with a considering look. "Neville would have known this chamber intimately. Perhaps he wished to conceal some evidence of murder."

Lavinia went to the washstand and glanced into the large bowl. "But if that was the case, surely he would have got rid of this bloodstained cloth and the water in this basin."

"What the devil?" Tobias crossed the room in three strides and looked at the dark stains on the cloth and the reddish brown water. "I wonder if he killed her here and then tried to clean the blood off his hands."

"There is no sign of blood anywhere else in the room. Everything is quite neat and tidy." Lavinia hesitated, thinking. "There is another possibility, Tobias."

"What is it?"

"Perhaps there was an attempt made on Sally's life. But what if

she survived it? She might have returned to her house, washed her wound, packed her belongings, and then disappeared."

"Gone into hiding, do you mean?"

"Yes."

He surveyed the room. "You're right about one thing. There is no sign of a struggle in this chamber."

"Which only makes sense if she was attacked somewhere else." Warming to her theory, Lavinia went quickly toward the door. "We must speak with the neighbors. Perhaps one of them saw Sally return home and leave again."

Tobias shook his head. "A waste of time. My informant assured me no one has seen Sally since she vanished."

"Perhaps your informant did not speak to everyone in the neighborhood. It is often necessary to be extremely thorough about this sort of thing."

"Jack is a thorough man."

Lavinia went toward the stairs. "I know you will find this difficult to credit, Tobias. But men do not always think of everything."

To her surprise, he did not quarrel with that. He followed her back down the stairs, and they left the house through the kitchen door.

Lavinia halted on the street and contemplated the two rows of small houses.

The neighborhood was quiet at this hour. The only person in sight was an old woman dressed in a cloak. She carried a basket full of flowers on her arm. She did not look at Lavinia and Tobias when she trudged past. Her attention was on a conversation she appeared to be conducting with an invisible companion.

"The roses are too red," she mumbled. "I tell ye, the roses are too bloody red. Red as blood, they are, red as blood. Bloody red.

Can't sell roses that red. Makes people nervous. Can't sell them, I tell ye. . . ."

The poor woman was quite mad, Lavinia thought. There were many like her on the streets of London.

"A candidate for Bedlam," Tobias said quietly when the flower seller was out of earshot.

"Perhaps. On the other hand, she likely does not go around murdering people the way your client apparently does."

"An excellent point. I wonder what that says about Neville's state of mind?"

"Perhaps only that he is able to disguise his insanity better than that poor woman can hide hers."

Tobias's jaw tightened. "I must tell you, Neville has always appeared quite sane to me."

"Which only makes him all the more fearsome, does it not?"

"Perhaps. It occurs to me that we have begun to speak of him as if we are quite certain he murdered these women," Tobias said. "But in fact we do not yet know that."

"You are right. We are rushing ahead of ourselves." Lavinia studied the array of front doors. "The housekeepers and maids are our most likely source of information. I trust you brought a goodly number of coins with you."

"Why is it that I am always the one who must produce the money when it is required in this investigation?"

Lavinia walked briskly toward the first of the kitchen doors. "You can put it on your client's bill."

"It appears increasingly likely that my client will prove to be one of the villains in this affair. If that is the case, it may be extremely difficult to collect my fee from him. We may have to put these sorts of miscellaneous expenses on *your* client's bill."

"Do stop grumbling, Tobias." Lavinia went down the steps. "It distracts me."

He stayed on the walkway, watching her. "One point before you knock. Try not to make it obvious that you are willing to pay for information unless you feel certain you will gain something useful. Otherwise, we shall likely be out of coins before we reach the end of the block and have nothing useful to show for it."

"I have had some experience with bargaining, if you will recall, sir." She raised the knocker and dropped it smartly.

The maid who responded was willing enough to gossip about the woman across the street who had been in the habit of entertaining a gentleman at night. But she had not seen her in two days.

Lavinia got the same results at the next door and the next.

"This is hopeless," she declared forty minutes later, after talking to the last maid in the last house on the street. "No one saw Sally, yet I am convinced she came back long enough to tend her wound and pack."

"She may not have been the one who came back." Tobias took Lavinia's arm and steered her along the street toward Sally's small house. "Perhaps it was Neville who collected her belongings so it would appear that she had gone on a journey."

"Nonsense. If he had wished to make it appear that she had left for the country, he would have removed the food from the kitchen. No woman closing up a house for an extended period of time would leave meat and vegetables to rot."

"Neville is a man of means. He has always had servants and housekeepers about to see to the running of his household. He has probably not entered a kitchen for the last twenty years."

She pondered that. "You may be right. But I still think it was Sally who came home that night."

He tightened his grip on her arm. "Have you concocted your version of events because you do not want to imagine Sally dead?"

"Of course."

"You do not even know the woman," Tobias pointed out. "She's a prostitute who, from all accounts, made her living in a brothel before she managed to attract Neville's attention."

"What does that have to do with it?"

The corner of his mouth twisted slightly.

"Nothing at all, Lavinia," he said very softly. "Nothing at all."

Absently she watched the mad flower seller. The old woman had paused in front of Sally's small house. The conversation with her invisible companion had grown more heated.

"Cannot sell roses that red, I tell ye. There's no selling the ones that are blood red. No one wants 'em, ye see. . . ."

Lavinia stopped suddenly, forcing Tobias to halt.

"The flower seller," she whispered.

He glanced at the old woman. "What of her?"

"No one wants the bloody roses. . . ."

"Look at her cloak," Lavinia said. "It is very fine, is it not? Yet she is obviously a poor woman."

Tobias shrugged. "Someone no doubt took pity on her and gave her the cloak."

"Wait here." Lavinia freed her arm from his grasp. "I want to speak with her."

"What good will that do?" he muttered behind her. "She's mad."

Lavinia ignored him. She walked slowly toward the flower seller, not wanting to alarm the old woman. "Good day to you," she said gently.

The flower seller started and then glared at Lavinia, as if she objected to having her one-sided conversation interrupted.

"Only got bloody roses for sale today," she announced. "No one wants blood-red roses."

"Did you sell roses to the woman who lived in this house?" Lavinia asked.

"No one wants bloody roses."

How did one conduct a conversation with a crazed flower seller? Lavinia wondered. Mad as she might be, however, the old woman had somehow managed to keep herself from being dragged off to Bedlam. That implied she was capable of making a living selling her flowers. Which, in turn, meant that she possessed some rudimentary bargaining ability.

Lavinia jingled some of the coins Tobias had given her.

"I would like to purchase your bloody roses," she said.

"No." The woman gripped her flower basket very tightly. "No one wants 'em."

"I do." Lavinia held out the coins.

"No one wants to buy bloody roses." A crafty gleam appeared in the woman's eyes. "I know what ye want."

"You do?"

"Yer after me new cloak, aren't ye? Ye don't want the red roses. No one wants bloody roses. Ye want me bloody cloak."

"Your new cloak is very lovely."

"Hardly any blood on it at all." The flower seller smiled proudly, displaying a quantity of missing teeth. "Just a bit on the hood."

Dear heaven, Lavinia thought. *Stay calm. Do not confuse her with too many questions. Just get the cloak from her.*

"There's no blood on my cloak," she said very carefully. "Why don't we trade?"

"Oh ho, so ye want to trade, eh? Well, now, that's mighty interestin'. *She* didn't want it because of the blood, ye see. No one wants bloody roses, either."

"I want them."

"She used to buy me roses." The flower seller gazed down into her basket. "But she didn't want 'em that night. It was the blood, y'see. Told me she barely escaped with her life."

Lavinia's pulse raced. "She escaped?"

"Aye." The flower seller grinned. "But she's afraid now. She's hiding. Wanted me old cloak. No blood on it, y'see."

Lavinia reached up and unfastened her own cloak. She swung it off her shoulders and held it out to the woman together with the coins.

"I will give you this excellent cloak plus these coins for your cloak."

The flower seller squinted warily at the garment Lavinia held. "Looks old."

"I assure you, it is still quite serviceable."

The madwoman cocked her head. Then she snatched the cloak from Lavinia's hand. "Let's have a good look at what yer offerin', dearie."

"There's no blood on it," Lavinia said smoothly. "Not a single drop."

"That may be as may be." The woman shook out the cloak and reversed it so she could view the inside of the cloth. "Aha. Appears to be a stain of some sort here." She peered closely. "Looks like someone tried to scrub it out."

Lavinia heard a smothered sound that might have been laughter coming from Tobias's direction. She was careful not to look at him.

"Hardly noticeable," she said firmly.

"I noticed it."

"That small stain on my cloak is a good deal less objectionable than the bloodstains on your cloak," Lavinia said through her teeth. "Are you interested in trading or not?"

The flower seller's wrinkled face tightened with scorn. "D'ye think I'm completely mad, dearie? This grand cloak I'm wearin' is worth a good bit more than yer offerin' and that's a fact."

Lavinia took a breath and tried not to show her desperation. "What else do you want?"

The flower seller cackled. "Yer cloak, the coins, and yer pretty half boots will do."

"My half boots?" Automatically, Lavinia glanced down at them. "But I need them to walk home."

"Don't fret, dearie, I'll let ye have me old ones. No blood on 'em at all. None at all. Not like the roses." The spark of crafty awareness faded from the madwoman's eyes. The dreamy fog rolled back. "No one wants to buy any roses with blood on 'em, y'see."

"I have reconsidered my diagnosis." Tobias assisted Lavinia up into the hackney. "I am no longer convinced the flower seller is entirely mad. On the contrary, I believe you may have met your match when it comes to the business of bargaining."

"I'm glad that you are amused." Lavinia dropped down onto the seat and morosely examined the battered old shoes she wore. There were holes in the soles and the stitching was gone at several points. "Those half boots were nearly new."

"You are not the only one who came out on the bad end of the shrewd bargain you made." Tobias hauled himself up into the cab and shut the door. "Was it necessary to give her so many of my coins?"

"I decided that since I was losing both my cloak and my shoes, you may as well contribute."

"I hope you are satisfied with your purchase." Tobias dropped

onto the opposite seat and eyed the cloak in her hands. "What do you think you will learn from that garment?"

"I don't know." Lavinia searched through the folds. "The flower seller was right about the bloodstains, though." She turned the hood inside out and drew in her breath. "Look. The marks of a head wound, do you think?"

His eyes narrowed at the sight of the dried blood. "So it would seem. Head wounds tend to bleed freely, even when the injury is slight."

"Thus my theory that Sally survived the attack and returned home to collect her things before she went into hiding may be right."

"It makes sense that she exchanged cloaks with the flower seller too," Tobias said thoughtfully. "Sally came out of the stews and that is where she would return to hide. An expensive item of clothing would only serve to call unwanted attention to her in such neighborhoods."

"Yes. Tobias, I do believe we are on to something here."

Lavinia saw the pocket attached to the inside of the cloak and put her hand inside. Her fingers brushed a scrap of paper.

"All we know now is that Neville's last mistress may have escaped the fate of the others," Tobias said. "The cloak helps to verify the conclusions you reached in her bedchamber, but it does not give us new information or lead us in a new direction."

Lavinia stared at the ticket she had just removed from the pocket.

"On the contrary," she whispered. "It leads us straight back to Huggett's Museum."

nineteen

Rage and pain," Mrs. Vaughn said very quietly. "Pain and rage. Astonishing."

The words were spoken so softly that Lavinia could barely hear them. She glanced at Tobias, standing beside her at the far end of the ill-lit gallery. He said nothing, his attention fixed intently on Mrs. Vaughn.

Huggett hovered anxiously near the door, a skeleton prepared to rattle back into the shadows at the first opportunity.

"Most improper," Huggett mumbled. "Never meant these statues to be viewed by respectable ladies. This gallery was intended only for gentlemen, I tell you."

They all ignored him. Mrs. Vaughn moved slowly to the next waxwork tableau and paused to study the features.

"I do not recognize the faces of these women, but I can tell you they are taken from life." Mrs. Vaughn hesitated. "Or, perhaps, death."

"Death masks, do you mean?" Tobias asked.

"I cannot say. There are three ways to achieve a likeness in wax. The first, the one I employ, is to sculpt the features, just as one would sculpt stone or clay. The second involves taking a wax impression of a living person's face and using it as a model for the sculpture. The third, of course, is to fashion a death mask."

Lavinia studied the face of the woman writhing in pain or ecstasy in the nearest exhibit. "Wouldn't the features of a death mask be less, uh, animated? A corpse would surely not be so lively looking."

"An expert modeler in wax could, perhaps, take the frozen features of a death mask and use the impression to re-create the image of a still-living face."

"Not at all proper." Huggett wrung his bony hands. "Ladies shouldn't be here."

No one glanced at him.

Tobias moved closer to one of the waxworks and examined the face of one of the male figures. "What of the men in these displays? Would you say that they are modeled from life or death?"

Mrs. Vaughn glanced at him with raised brows. "The features of the male figures are all taken from the same model, hadn't you noticed?"

"No." Tobias looked at one of the masculine figures more closely. "I hadn't observed that."

Startled, Lavinia peered up into the violently contorted features of one of the male figures. "I do believe you're right, Mrs. Vaughn."

"I doubt if most of the men who come into this chamber bother to spend much time examining the faces of the masculine

statues," Mrs. Vaughn said dryly. "Their attention is no doubt on other aspects of the tableaux."

"But the faces of the women are distinctive." Lavinia walked to another display. "They are individuals. All five of them."

"Yes," Mrs. Vaughn said. "I would say so."

Lavinia looked at Tobias.

He raised a brow. "The answer is no. I do not recognize any of them."

She flushed and cleared her throat. "What of the male figure?"

Tobias shook his head once, decisively. "I am not acquainted with him," he said. He turned abruptly to confront Huggett. "Who sold these waxworks to you?"

Huggett flinched. His eyes widened in their sockets. He slithered back until he came up sharply against the door.

"No one sold them to me," he said, sounding both terrified and aggrieved. "I swear it."

"You got them from someone." Tobias took a step toward him. "Unless, of course, you are the sculptor?"

"No." Huggett swallowed and made a stab at regaining control of his nerves. "I am no artist. I certainly did not model these figures."

"What is the name of the modeler who created them?"

"I do not know, sir, and that is the plain truth," Huggett whined.

Tobias closed the distance between himself and Huggett. "How did you come by them?"

"There is an arrangement." Huggett started to babble. "When one is ready, I receive a message to go to a certain address and fetch it."

"What is the address?"

"It is never the same," Huggett said. "Usually a warehouse somewhere near the river but never the same warehouse."

"How do you pay for them?" Tobias asked.

"That is what I am trying to explain to you, sir." Huggett cringed. "I do not pay for them. The arrangement is that I may have them free of charge provided I display them publicly."

Tobias gestured toward the collection. "Which of these was the last to be delivered to you?"

"That one." Huggett pointed a quivering finger at a nearby tableau. "Got a message about four months ago telling me that it was ready."

Lavinia glanced at the figure of the woman frozen in some dark ecstatic horror and shuddered.

"There have been no new messages from the artist?" Tobias asked.

"No," Huggett said. "None."

Tobias pinned him with a cold look. "If you receive any further communication from the modeler, you will send word to me immediately. Do you comprehend?"

"Yes, yes," Huggett squeaked. "Immediately."

"I warn you, there is murder involved in this affair."

"I want no part of murder," Huggett assured him. "I am merely an innocent business proprietor attempting to make a living."

Lavinia exchanged a glance with Mrs. Vaughn. "You said that an artist of this caliber would want his work exhibited to the public."

Mrs. Vaughn nodded. "It is only natural. Apparently this modeler is not obliged to make a profit on his creations, however."

"We are looking for a person of some financial means then," Tobias said.

"I would say so." Mrs. Vaughn looked thoughtful. "Only someone with another source of income could afford to create and give away such large and well-modeled works."

"One last question, if you would be so kind," Lavinia said.

"Of course, my dear." Mrs. Vaughn beamed. "I do not mind in the least. Indeed, this has been a most interesting experience."

"Do you think the modeler who created these waxworks might be the same one who sculpted the death threat I showed you?"

Mrs. Vaughn looked at the anguished face of the nearest figure. A shadow passed across her own face.

"Oh, yes," she whispered. "Yes, indeed. I think it is quite possible that the artist is one and the same."

Tobias leaned against one of the stone pillars supporting the roof of the artfully designed Gothic ruin and gazed out at the overgrown garden.

The ruin had been constructed several years earlier. The architect had no doubt intended it to be a graceful addition to this remote region of the large park. A place for peaceful contemplation of nature's soothing essence.

But this portion of the extensive grounds had never proved popular with the public. As a result the ruin and the surrounding hedge and gardens had been allowed to fall into a decline. The unchecked greenery had grown wild, creating a natural veil that shielded the ruin from the sight of anyone who might happen to wander into this isolated section of the park.

Tobias had stumbled onto the shrouded ruin a long time ago. He came here sometimes when he wanted to think without any distractions. This was the first time he had brought anyone else to the place he had come to think of as his private retreat.

It had stopped raining for a time, but the trees still dripped. The hackney he had managed to flag down after leaving Huggett's Museum waited on a path elsewhere in the park.

At least he hoped it waited there. He did not relish the notion of walking all the way back to Lavinia's house. His leg ached today.

"We've got several seemingly unrelated things going on here," he said. "The deaths or disappearance of some of Neville's mistresses, the waxworks, and the rumors of war being waged for control of what is left of the Blue Chamber. They must be linked."

"I agree." Lavinia stood near one of the other pillars, her arms folded. "I think the links are obvious."

"Our clients."

"Both of them have lied to us from the start of this affair."

Tobias nodded. "Yes."

"Both of them are attempting to use us for secret ends."

"Evidently."

She glanced at him. "The time has come, I believe, to confront them."

"I suggest we start with yours."

"I was afraid you would say that." She sighed. "I do not think Mrs. Dove will be pleased. She will very likely dismiss me."

Tobias straightened and took her arm. "If it is any comfort to you, I do not expect to collect any money from Neville."

"I suppose I can always sell another statue to pay the rent and Mrs. Chilton's quarterly wages," Lavinia said.

"One of the things I admire about you, Lavinia, is that you are never without resources."

Joan Dove sat so still on the striped sofa that Lavinia decided she could have been easily mistaken for one of Mrs. Vaughn's elegantly modeled waxworks.

254

"I beg your pardon," Joan said in the icy tones of a woman not accustomed to being questioned. "What are you implying?"

Tobias said nothing. He looked at Lavinia, letting her know that he trusted her to deal with the unpleasant scene. This was her client.

Lavinia met his gaze and then rose from her chair. She went to stand at one of the drawing-room windows. Her red hair was a vivid contrast to the dark green velvet drapes.

"I thought the question quite straightforward," she said quietly. "I asked you if you were once involved in an affair with Lord Neville. Is he the one who seduced you and cast you aside twenty years ago?"

Joan did not respond. The frozen silence emanating from her threatened to chill the entire room.

"Bloody hell, Joan." Lavinia spun around, anger flaring in her eyes. "Do you not comprehend what is at stake here? We have good reason to believe that Neville has murdered at least two of his former mistresses. Perhaps many more. The latest one may be alive, but if so, it is only due to luck."

Joan said nothing.

Lavinia began to pace. "We know that Sally Johnson visited Huggett's Museum shortly before her disappearance. There is a special gallery there devoted to the display of some brilliantly executed waxworks. The threat you received was crafted by an expert modeler in wax. We believe the artist who created them all is one and the same. Now, just what in the name of heaven is going on here?"

"That is quite enough." Joan's mouth thinned. "You do not need to rage at me, Lavinia. I am your client, remember?"

"Answer my question." Lavinia stopped in the middle of the carpet. "Did you have a liaison with Neville?"

Joan hesitated. "Yes. You are correct. He was the man who seduced me all those years ago and then abandoned me."

For a moment no one in the room moved or spoke.

Then Lavinia exhaled deeply. "I knew it." She collapsed into the nearest chair. "I knew there had to be a connection."

"I fail to see how that very old indiscretion can possibly have any bearing on this matter of murder," Joan said.

Tobias looked at her. "Neville appears to be in the process of getting rid of his former mistresses. At least two women he had been intimate with in the past two years are dead. Three more are rumored to be dead, and one has gone missing."

Joan frowned. "Why on earth would he kill them?"

"We cannot be certain," Tobias said. "But we believe it's possible he fears they know too much about him."

"What could they possibly know that would make him believe he had to murder them?"

"I will be blunt, Mrs. Dove," he said. "I am almost certain that Neville was a member of a criminal organization known as the Blue Chamber. The gang was very secretive and very powerful for many years. It was controlled by a man who called himself Azure and his two lieutenants."

"I see." Joan watched him without expression. "How very odd."

"The Blue Chamber began to fall apart after Azure's death several months ago. One of two lieutenants, Carlisle, died three months ago in Italy."

Joan frowned. "You know this for a fact?"

Tobias smiled coldly. He did not take his eyes off her face. "Yes. I am absolutely certain of his death."

Joan glanced fleetingly at Lavinia. "So now there is only one

member of the Blue Chamber left, and you think that man is Lord Neville."

"Yes," Lavinia said. "Tobias hoped the valet's diary would provide him with proof."

"But the diary was conveniently destroyed before anyone could read it," Tobias said.

Lavinia studied her fingertips. "It's possible that Neville killed Holton Felix, destroyed the diary, and arranged for Tobias to find it. But it's equally possible that someone else committed those acts."

"Who?" Joan asked.

Lavinia met her eyes. "You."

There was a moment of shocked silence.

"I don't understand," Joan whispered. "Why would I do those things?"

"Because you were desperate to conceal one particular secret hidden in the diary," Lavinia said.

"The fact that I had an affair with Neville?" Joan's eyes glinted with scornful amusement. "I'll admit I want very much to keep the liaison secret, but I assure you, I would not risk committing murder to do so."

"It is not gossip about the liaison with Neville that concerns you," Lavinia said. "It is the fact that your husband was Azure."

Joan stared at her. "You're mad."

"You loved him very much, didn't you?" Lavinia continued almost gently. "You must have been stunned when you got the first blackmail note from Holton Felix telling you that Fielding Dove had been the leader of a secret criminal organization. You would do anything to keep the information buried, would you not? Your husband's honor and good name are at stake."

All of the color drained from Joan's face for a few seconds. Then it returned in an angry rush.

"How dare you imply my husband was involved with this . . . this Blue Chamber? Who do you think you are to even *hint* at such an accusation?"

"You told me that when your husband died, you were suddenly plunged into an exceedingly complicated financial tangle. You mentioned that you are still sorting out the various threads," Lavinia said.

"I explained that he was a brilliant investor."

"A host of complex business investments could well have masked his criminal activities," Tobias said quietly.

Joan closed her eyes. "You're right. Holton Felix did send me a note threatening to expose Fielding's role as the head of a vast criminal empire." She raised her lashes to reveal the bleak certainty. "But the threat was based on a lie."

"Are you sure of that?" Lavinia asked softly.

"It's not possible." Tears glistened in Joan's eyes. "Fielding and I were together for twenty years. I would have *known* if he was a criminal. He could not have hidden such a thing from me for that length of time."

"Many wives remain ignorant of their husbands' financial activities for the entire duration of their marriages," Lavinia said. "I cannot tell you how many widows I have known who found themselves at a complete loss after the funeral because they had no understanding of their own finances."

"I refuse to believe that Fielding was this Azure you speak of," Joan said evenly. "Do you have any proof?"

"None at all," Tobias agreed easily. "And as both Azure and your husband are dead, I have no interest whatsoever in pursuing the matter. But I would very much like to bring down Neville."

"I see," Joan whispered.

"Preferably before he murders you too," Lavinia said.

Joan's eyes widened. "You really think he sent the death threat?"

"It's a distinct possibility," Tobias said. "He is no artist, but he may have commissioned a worker in wax to create that little picture you received."

"But why would he give me warning of his intentions?"

"The man appears to be a murderer," Lavinia said. "Who can say how his mind works? Perhaps he wishes to torment you or punish you in some manner."

Tobias turned away from the window. "More likely he is seeking to draw you into a more vulnerable situation. You have a small army around you, Mrs. Dove. Your footmen are obviously trained to do more than carry glasses of champagne on silver platters."

She sighed. "My husband was very wealthy, Mr. March. He took care to employ men who could protect us and our possessions."

"It's possible Neville sent the death threat in an attempt to rattle your nerves," Lavinia said. "He may hope that you will become anxious and careless and do something foolish that will put you in his power."

"But he has no reason to want to murder me," Joan insisted. "Even if he is a criminal, I had no knowledge of his activities twenty years ago. He must know that."

Tobias looked at her. "If we are correct, if you were indeed married to Azure, then Neville has every reason to fear that you know far too many dangerous secrets."

Joan's hands clenched in her lap. "My husband was not Azure, I tell you."

The denial was spoken more hesitantly this time, Lavinia thought.

"We suspect he was," she said. "And if we're right, you are in great danger."

Much of the pain and outrage faded from Joan's eyes. She unclenched her hands. "Do you really believe Neville murdered those women?"

"It certainly seems that way," Tobias said. "I'm beginning to think he commissioned those waxworks in Huggett's gallery as some sort of macabre souvenir of the killings."

Joan shuddered. "What artist would create such works?"

"One who was paid a sufficiently large commission might not ask too many questions," Lavinia said. "Or one who feared for his or her life. Remember, Madame Tussaud was forced to make those death masks while she was imprisoned in France."

There was a short silence.

"I plan to search Neville's house tonight," Tobias said after a while. "This affair must come to an end and quickly. I need proof of his involvement in criminal activities, and I can think of no other way to get it. Until this matter is finished, you must take no chances. I suggest you remain here in the safety of your home."

Joan hesitated and then shook her head. "The Colchester ball is tonight. It is the one event of the Season that I simply cannot miss."

"Surely you can send your regrets?"

"Impossible. Lady Colchester will be greatly offended if I do not put in an appearance. I told you, she is the grandmother of my daughter's fiancé and she is the tyrant in the family. If she becomes annoyed with me, she will take her petty vengeance on Maryanne."

Tobias saw the sympathetic understanding in Lavinia's eyes and groaned silently. It occurred to him that no one comprehended the perils and pitfalls of attempting to forge a good match more acutely than another who was engaged in a similar attempt. He knew before she even opened her mouth that he had already lost this small battle.

"Good heavens," Lavinia said. "Do you think Lady Colchester might go so far as to force Maryanne's fiancé to cry off?"

Joan's expression tightened. "I cannot say. I only know that I will not put Maryanne's future at risk simply because I am afraid to attend a ball tonight."

Lavinia turned quickly to Tobias. "Mrs. Dove will be in the company of her footmen traveling to and from the affair. Once in the Colchester mansion, she will be surrounded by people. She should be quite safe."

"I do not like it," he said, aware that he was wasting his breath.

Lavinia brightened. "I have an idea."

Tobias winced and absently rubbed his leg. "Of course you do," he said. "Bloody hell."

twenty

*T*he house was empty and silent when Tobias followed Lavinia through her front hall a short while later. All the better for the stern lecture he planned to administer, he thought.

"Mrs. Chilton is at her daughter's this afternoon," Lavinia explained as she slung her bonnet over a hook. "Emeline is attending a lecture on antiquities with Priscilla and Anthony."

"I am aware of that. Anthony said something about escorting them to the event." He dropped his hat and gloves onto the table and looked at her. "Lavinia, I wish to speak to you."

"Won't you come into the study?" She was already halfway down the hall. "We can light the fire. Such a pleasant, cozy setting for one of our little quarrels, don't you think?"

"Damnation."

There was no help for it. He followed her into the study. She

was right. The small room was a far more charming venue for an argument than the front hall. It occurred to him that he was becoming very comfortable with this snug, book-lined little chamber. When he entered it he had the oddest sensation of coming home.

Utter nonsense, of course.

He watched Lavinia settle lightly into the chair behind her desk. The thoroughly satisfied air that emanated from her was palpable.

He crouched in front of the hearth, wincing at the throb in his leg, and lit the fire.

"You are very pleased with that shameless bit of manipulative strategy, are you not?" he said.

"Come now, Tobias. Suggesting to Mrs. Dove that Emeline and I accompany her to the Colchester ball was a perfectly reasonable solution to a difficult dilemma. It was obvious she was quite determined to attend the affair. This way I will be able to keep an eye on her."

He smiled humorlessly. "What a stroke of good fortune for you that Mrs. Dove did not perceive any problem in securing additional invitations for some friends from Bath who just happened to be visiting her."

"You heard what she said. Even if she could not get additional invitations, it would not be a problem to bring two companions with her. The Colchester ball is such a huge crush that no one will notice a few extra guests."

"Could you try a little harder not to gloat? It is very irritating."

She gave him an innocent look. "I'm going to all this trouble to protect my client."

"Do not try to pretend that you made your gracious offer purely for the sake of keeping an eye on Joan Dove." His leg

protested again when he got to his feet. "I know you too well, madam. You took advantage of the opportunity to seize an invitation to a ball for your niece."

She smiled smugly. "It really is an incredible coup, is it not? Just imagine, tonight Emeline will attend one of the most important social events of the Season. Wait until Lady Wortham hears about this. So much for her little innuendos about all the *favors* she is doing for Emeline."

Tobias was almost amused in spite of his mood. "Remind me never to get in between a matchmaking woman and an invitation to an important social affair."

"Come now, Tobias. At least this way we know that Mrs. Dove will be safe tonight." Lavinia paused. "Not that Neville is likely to try to murder her in the middle of the grandest ball of the Season."

Tobias considered that closely. "It does seem an awkward situation in which to attempt murder, does it not? Nevertheless, given Mrs. Dove's reclusive nature and the fact that when she does leave her house she is always accompanied by those large footmen, a desperate killer might think he had little choice."

"Don't fret, Tobias. I will not let her out of my sight at the Colchester ball." Lavinia sat forward and rested her chin on her palm. The expression in her eyes grew somber. "Were you serious when you told her that you plan to search Neville's house tonight?"

"Yes. We must have some answers quickly, and I do not know where else to look for them."

"But what if he is home?"

"This is the height of the Season," Tobias said. "Given their social standing, Neville and his wife are out of the house nearly every night. I know for a fact that Neville rarely goes home before dawn even during the quiet months."

Lavinia wrinkled her nose. "It is rather obvious that Neville and his lady do not take much pleasure in each other's company."

"In that regard, they have much in common with other couples in the ton. Be that as it may, in my experience, when the servants in a large house know their employers are going to be away for most of the evening, many of them slip out for a few hours also. Odds are the mansion will be almost empty tonight. The few members of the staff who are there will likely be occupied in their own quarters. It should be easy to get in unobserved."

She said nothing.

He looked at her. "Well? What is it?"

She picked up a pen and tapped the end of it against the palm of her hand. "I don't like this plan of yours, Tobias."

"Why not?"

She hesitated and then put down the pen. She got to her feet and looked at him, unease clear in her eyes.

"This is not the same as searching Sally Johnson's little house," she said quietly. "We have as much as concluded that Neville is a murderer. The thought of you prowling through his mansion alone at night disturbs me greatly."

"Your concern is touching, Lavinia. And not a little surprising. I had no notion you cared so much for the safety of my person. I was under the impression that I have been something of a nuisance to you."

Without warning, she bristled. "Do not make light of this. We are dealing with a man who may have murdered several women."

"And quite possibly commissioned the murder of Bennett Ruckland," he said softly.

"Ruckland? The man who was killed in Italy?"

"Yes."

"But you said Carlisle arranged for his murder."

"Neville and Carlisle knew each other well because of their connection to the Blue Chamber. I suspect Neville paid him a great deal of money to see to it that Ruckland never returned to England."

"You are so determined to find the information you want, I fear that you will take foolish risks. Perhaps you should take Anthony with you. He could serve as a bodyguard."

"No. I want Anthony to attend the Colchester ball. He can help you keep watch on Joan Dove."

"I am perfectly capable of keeping an eye on Joan. I think Anthony should go with you."

He smiled faintly. "It's kind of you to be so concerned on my behalf, Lavinia. But console yourself with the thought that if anything does go wrong, it will be entirely my fault. As it always is, in your opinion."

"Damnation, sir, you are trying to avoid the issue."

"Well, yes, I am. I don't see the conversation going anywhere useful."

"Tobias, do stop provoking me, or I will not be responsible for my actions."

The clenched fists at her sides and the sudden storm in her eyes told him instantly that his poor attempt to lighten the mood had misfired.

"Lavinia—"

"This is not a matter of affixing blame. We are talking about common sense here."

He caught her face between his hands. "Has it escaped your notice, madam, that where you and I are concerned, common sense is a very uncommon commodity?"

She gripped his wrists with her fingers. "Promise me that you will be extremely careful tonight, Tobias."

"You have my word on it."

"Promise me that you will not enter the house if there is any sign that Neville is at home."

"I can assure you, Neville will most certainly not be home tonight," he said. "In fact, it is highly likely that he and his lady will put in an appearance at the Colchester ball. You will probably see more of him than I will."

"That's not good enough. Promise me you won't go in if there is anyone at all in the house."

"Lavinia, I cannot do that."

She groaned. "I was afraid you would say that. Promise me—"

"I have had enough of promises for the moment. I would much rather kiss you."

Her eyes glittered, whether with temper or passion, he could not say. He hoped it was the latter.

"I am attempting to conduct a serious conversation," she said.

"Do you want to kiss me?"

"That is not the subject of this discussion. We are talking about you risking your neck."

He stroked his thumbs along the line of her jaw. The soft, smooth feel of her skin riveted him.

"Kiss me, Lavinia."

She put both palms on his shoulders, fingers digging into the fabric of his coat. He could not tell if she wanted to push him away or pull him close.

"Promise me that you will be sensible," she said.

"No, Lavinia." He lightly kissed her forehead, then her nose. "You cannot ask that of me. It is not in my power to make such a promise."

"Rubbish. Of course it is."

"No." He shook his head slightly. "I have not been sensible

where you are concerned since the first time I saw you on a street in Rome."

"Tobias." She caught her breath. "This is madness. We do not even particularly like each other."

"Speak for yourself, madam. As for me, I find I am growing rather fond of you in spite of your ability to infuriate me so easily."

"Fond?" Her eyes widened. "You are *fond* of me?"

A twinge went through him. He could almost hear Anthony lecturing him.

"Perhaps 'fond' is not the appropriate word under the circumstances," he said.

" 'Fond' is a word one uses to describe one's feelings for a good friend or a doting aunt or . . . or a pet dog."

"Then it is most certainly the wrong word," he said. "Because my feelings for you have nothing in common with my feelings for friends, aunts, or dogs."

"Tobias—"

He touched the exquisitely sweet place at the nape of her neck where a few strands of unruly hair had come free of the pins. "I want you, Lavinia. I cannot ever remember wanting a woman this badly. It is an ache in my gut that will not go away."

"Wonderful. I give you a bellyache." She closed her eyes. A shiver went through her. "I have always dreamed of being able to affect a man in such a thrilling manner."

"Anthony tells me that I am not very good when it comes to dealing with women. Perhaps it would make things simpler if you would cease talking and kiss me."

"You really are the most impossible man, Tobias March."

"Then we are indeed well matched. You are certainly the most impossible woman I have ever met in my life. Will you kiss me?"

Something flashed in her eyes. It could have been outrage or

frustration or passion. Her hands moved off his shoulders, wound around his neck. She stood on tiptoe and kissed him.

He opened his mouth on hers, tasting her, searching for the wildness he had uncovered the other night in the carriage. She shuddered and tightened her arms around him. Her desire ignited the smoldering fire in his blood.

"Tobias." She slid her fingertips through his hair and kissed him with rising urgency.

"There is something about you that makes me feel I am in the grip of a powerful drug," he whispered. "I fear I am becoming an addict."

"Oh, *Tobias*."

This time his name was a choked, strangled cry, muffled against his throat.

He tightened his hands around her ribs, just beneath her breasts, and lifted her up against his chest. She made a soft, erotic sound that fanned the blaze sweeping through him.

He moved forward with her. She braced her palms on his shoulders again and continued to pelt him with damp, heated little kisses.

When he got her to the desk, he lowered her until she was sitting on the edge. He used one hand to steady her and opened his trousers with the other. When his sex sprang free, she reached down and took him in her soft fingers.

He closed his eyes and set his teeth against the hunger threatening to consume him. When he had himself back under control, he opened his eyes and saw that she was flushed with excitement, trembling with anticipation.

He eased her legs apart and put his hands on the soft, bare skin just above her stockings. He went down on one knee in front of her and kissed the inside of her right thigh. Then he went farther, closing relentlessly on his goal.

"Tobias." She clenched her hands in his hair. "What are you . . . ? No, no, you cannot kiss me *there*. For goodness sake, Tobias, you must not . . ."

He ignored her shocked protests. When he touched the tender, sensitive nubbin with the edge of his tongue, she finally stopped talking. The last of her protests died in a choked gasp.

He slid his fingers into her and deepened the kiss. She came in near silence, as if she had no breath left. He felt the tightness within her dissolve in a series of tiny shivers.

When the crisis had passed, he stood up and held her in a close embrace. She went limp against him.

"Did you learn that in Italy?" she mumbled into his neck. "They do say there is nothing like the Grand Tour to put a polish on an education."

He did not think the question required a reply. Just as well. He did not trust himself to carry on a lucid conversation.

He moved between Lavinia's legs and wrapped his hands around her lushly curved buttocks. She lifted her head off his shoulder and smiled slowly. Her eyes were like seas a thousand miles deep and filled with warm, enticing currents. He could not have looked away if he had tried.

"The eyes of a practitioner of mesmerism," he whispered. "You have indeed put me into a trance."

She touched the lobe of his ear with one fingertip. Then she touched the edge of his mouth. She smiled and he plunged deeper into the spell.

He readied himself to plunge into her as well.

The sound of the front door opening followed by muffled voices in the front hall stopped him cold just as he was about to sink himself into Lavinia's snug warmth.

She stiffened in his arms. "Oh dear," she said urgently. "Tobias—"

"Hell's teeth." He rested his forehead on hers. "Don't tell me—"

"I do believe that Emeline has returned home somewhat earlier than expected." Panic infused Lavinia's voice. She batted at him ineffectually. "We must put ourselves to rights at once. She will be here in a moment."

The trance was broken.

He stepped back, fumbling with his trousers. "Calm yourself, Lavinia. I do not think she will notice anything amiss."

"We need some fresh air in here."

Lavinia bounced off the desk, shook out her skirts, and rushed to the window. She opened it wide. A cold, damp breeze rushed into the study. The fire flickered wildly.

Tobias was amused. "It's raining, in case you had not noticed."

She whirled around and shot him a repressive glare. "I am very well aware of that fact."

He smiled. Then he heard a familiar voice coming down the hall.

"I thought the portion of Mr. Halcomb's lecture devoted to the ruins of Pompeii was rather weak," Anthony said.

"I agree. I doubt very much he went farther than the British Museum to conduct his researches."

Lavinia stiffened. "What do they think they are doing? Good heavens, if any of the neighbors saw them enter an empty house together, Emeline will be ruined. Utterly ruined."

"Uh, Lavinia—"

"I will handle this." She marched to the door of the study and flung it open. "Just what is going on here?"

Anthony and Emeline, halfway down the hall, stopped.

"Good afternoon, Mr. March," Emeline said.

"Miss Emeline."

Anthony looked wary. "Is there something wrong, Mrs. Lake?"

"Have you no common sense?" she demanded furiously. "Emeline, it is all very well to allow Mr. Sinclair to escort you as far as the front door, but to invite him into the house when there is no one about? What on earth were you thinking?"

Emeline looked baffled. "But, Lavinia—"

"What if any of the neighbors saw you?"

Anthony exchanged a look with Emeline. Then a knowing expression appeared in his eyes.

"Let me make certain I have this plain," he said. "You are concerned because I may have been seen escorting Miss Emeline into a house where there is no one present to act as a chaperone. Correct?"

"Precisely." Lavinia fitted her hands to her hips. "Two unmarried young people entering the house together? What will the neighbors think?"

"Allow me to point out the small flaw in your logic," Emeline murmured.

Lavinia glowered. "And what is that, pray tell?"

"The house is not empty. You and Mr. March are both here. One could hardly ask for more appropriate chaperones."

There was a short, brittle silence while that observation took hold.

Tobias managed to swallow his laughter. He glanced at Lavinia, wondering when it would dawn on her that she had violently overreacted to Anthony and Emeline's innocent homecoming.

A close call sometimes had that effect on the nerves, he reflected.

Lavinia sputtered, turned very pink, and then launched into the only argument left.

"That is all very well, but you did not *know* we were here, Emeline."

"Well, as to that," Anthony said diffidently, "we *did* know you were home. Lady Wortham's footman escorted Miss Emeline to the front door. When she opened it with her key, she saw Tobias's hat and gloves and your cloak. She assured Lady Wortham that you were both present, and the good lady gave her approval for me to enter the house with Miss Emeline before she and Miss Priscilla drove away."

"I see," Lavinia said weakly.

"Evidently you did not hear us arrive in Lady Wortham's carriage," Emeline said. "Nor did you hear me tell her that you were home."

"Uh, no." Lavinia cleared her throat. "We heard nothing. We were occupied in the study."

"You must have been concentrating on a very important matter," Anthony said with a deceptively innocent smile. "We made a fair amount of noise, did we not, Miss Emeline?"

"We certainly did," Emeline said. "Indeed, I cannot imagine anyone failing to hear us."

Lavinia's mouth opened but no words emerged. She closed it quickly. The pink in her cheeks turned to red.

Mischief sparkled in Emeline's eyes. "Whatever were you and Mr. March conversing about that was so fascinating you did not hear us arrive?"

Lavinia took a deep breath. "Poetry."

twenty-one

Lavinia stood with Joan in the relatively quiet shelter of a window alcove and surveyed the crowded ballroom. She was torn between her concern for Tobias and a sense of triumph. Since there was nothing she could do about the former, she allowed herself to revel in her latest social coup.

The Colchester affair was everything she could have asked for in the way of a setting for Emeline. The ballroom had been decorated in the Chinese style, with a mix of Etruscan and Indian motifs. Mirrors and gilt had been used in glittering profusion to enhance the effect. Dressed in the deep turquoise gown that Madame Francesca had stipulated for such an occasion, her dark hair swept up in a clever style and trimmed with small ornaments, Emeline looked as elegant and exotic as her surroundings.

"Congratulations, Lavinia," Joan murmured. "That young man

who just asked to escort Emeline out onto the dance floor is in line for a title."

"Estates?"

"A number of them, I believe."

Lavinia smiled. "He appears to be quite charming."

"Yes." Joan watched the dancers. "Fortunately, young Reginald does not take after his father. But that is not surprising, under the circumstances."

"I beg your pardon?"

Joan's smile was cold. "Reginald is Bolling's third son. The first was found dead in an alley behind a brothel. It was assumed he was murdered by a footpad who was never arrested."

"I collect that you do not believe the tale?"

Joan raised one shoulder in the smallest of graceful shrugs. "It was no secret he had a fondness for very young girls. There are some who believe he was stabbed by a relative of one of the small innocents he had debauched. Perhaps an older brother."

"If that is the case, I cannot feel any pity for Bolling's first heir. What happened to the second?"

"He was in the habit of drinking heavily and going into the stews in search of entertainment. One night he was found face-down in a gutter outside a notorious hell. Drowned in a few inches of water, they say."

Lavinia shuddered. "Not a happy family."

"No one ever dreamed that young Reggie would inherit the title, of course, certainly not Lady Bolling. Indeed, having done her duty by giving her husband an heir and a spare, she went her own way after the birth of her second son."

Lavinia glanced at her. "She took a lover?"

"Yes."

"Are you implying that the lover is Reginald's father?"

"I think it quite likely. He has his mother's brown hair and dark eyes, so it is impossible to be certain of his sire. But I seem to recall that Bolling's first two sons both had fair hair and light eyes."

"So the title is likely going to the offspring of some man other than Bolling."

Such incidents occurred more often than anyone acknowledged, Lavinia reflected. Among the ton, where marriages were made for a variety of reasons, none of which involved affection, it was only to be expected that a certain number of heirs came into their inheritances via somewhat indirect paths.

"Frankly, in my opinion it is all for the best in this case," Joan said. "There is something in the blood of the men of Bolling's line that is not wholesome. They have a history of coming to a bad end through their own weaknesses. Bolling himself is hopelessly addicted to the milk of the poppy. It is a wonder he has not done himself in with an overdose."

Lavinia gave her a quick, searching glance. This was not the first such gossipy tale she had heard from her companion to-night. Perhaps it was a certain sense of boredom induced by their enforced association that had inspired Joan to relate a series of rumors and secrets concerning their fellow guests. Lavinia had learned more about the foibles and scandals of the ton in the past hour than she had in the past three months.

"For a lady who does not go out much into Society," Lavinia said cautiously, "you appear to be exceptionally well informed about those who move in the highest circles."

Joan tightened her gloved fingers around her fan. There was only the smallest of hesitations before she inclined her head. "My husband made it a point to acquaint himself with information

and rumors that he thought might affect his financial affairs. For example, he looked very thoroughly into the background of Colchester's heir before he accepted the offer for Maryanne's hand."

"Naturally," Lavinia said. "I would do the same thing if a young man showed a strong interest in my niece."

"Lavinia?"

"Yes?"

"Do you really think it's possible that my husband may have kept the truth about his criminal activities from me for all those years?"

The wistful quality of the question brought a shimmer of moisture to Lavinia's eyes. She blinked rapidly to clear her vision.

"I think he may have gone to great lengths to keep his secrets from you because he loved you so much, Joan. He would not have wanted you to know the truth. Indeed, he may have thought you would be safer if you did not know it."

"In other words, he wished to protect me?"

"Yes."

Joan smiled sadly. "That would have been so very like Fielding. His first concerns were always for the welfare of his wife and daughter."

Anthony materialized out of the throng. He had a glass of champagne in each hand. "Who the devil is Emeline dancing with now?"

"Bolling's heir." Lavinia took one of the glasses from him. "Are you acquainted with him?"

"No." Anthony glanced over his shoulder toward the dance floor. "I assume he was properly introduced?"

"Of course." She took pity on him. "Don't be too concerned. She has not promised the next dance to anyone in particular. I'm sure she would be delighted to take the floor with you."

Anthony's expression cleared immediately. "Do you think so?"

"I am almost certain of it."

"Thank you, Mrs. Lake. I am very grateful." Anthony turned away to scrutinize the floor.

Joan lowered her voice so only Lavinia could hear her beneath the swell of the music. "I thought I heard Emeline promise the next dance to Mr. Proudfoot."

"I will take full responsibility. I shall say I made a mistake when I made a note of the names for Emeline."

Joan studied Anthony, who was intent on the dancers. "Forgive me for offering advice, Lavinia, but I feel I should point out that if you find Mr. Sinclair unacceptable as a future nephew-in-law, you are not doing him a kindness by encouraging him to dance with Emeline."

"I know. There is no money, no title, and no estates in that direction, but I must confess, I rather like him. In addition, I can see how happy he and Emeline are when they are together. I am determined to give my niece a Season or two and a chance to meet a variety of eligible young men. But in the end, she will make her own decision."

"And if she chooses Mr. Sinclair?"

"They are both really quite clever, you know. Something tells me that, between the two of them, they will not starve."

The big house was drenched in darkness save for a small fire burning dimly down below in the vicinity of the kitchens. Tobias stood in the shadows at the rear of the main hall and listened for a moment. He heard muffled giggles and a man's drunken laughter in the distance. Two members of the household staff had obviously found something more entertaining to do than to slip away for the evening.

Their presence downstairs would not be a problem, he decided. He had no reason to search that portion of the mansion. A man of Neville's class would have little interest in the area of the house that was the domain of his servants. It would certainly never occur to him to conceal his secrets in a realm he seldom if ever entered.

In point of fact, Tobias thought as he moved through the gloom-filled hall, Neville had no reason to go to extraordinary lengths to hide anything in this house. Why would he bother? He was lord and master here.

"Bloody hell," Lavinia said to Joan. "I just saw Neville and his wife in the crowd."

"Not surprising." Joan looked almost amused by Lavinia's scowl. "I told you, everyone who is anyone will put in an appearance tonight or risk offending Lady Colchester."

"I still cannot believe the sweet old lady who greeted us at the door has the power to terrify everyone in Society."

"She rules with an iron fist." Joan smiled. "But she seems to be quite fond of my daughter. I'd like to keep things that way."

For her part, Lady Colchester would not want to lose the large inheritance Maryanne would bring into the Colchester coffers, Lavinia thought. But she decided not to mention the obvious. The higher one went in the ton, the higher the marriage stakes. While she schemed to scrape together a taste of a real Season for Emeline, hoping to attract the eye of a young man who could support her niece in some degree of comfort, Joan was engaged in a strategy more akin to an affair of state.

She caught another fleeting glimpse of Neville in the crowd and decided it was a good thing he was here. It meant he was not at home in his mansion, where Tobias might accidentally encounter him in the middle of the search.

She wondered what it was about Neville that had attracted Joan's interest at one time.

As if she had read her mind, Joan answered the question. "I know he has the unpleasant look of a hardened rake who has spent too many years pursuing meaningless pleasures, but I assure you that when I first met him he was a very dashing, very handsome, thoroughly charming man."

"I understand."

"Looking back, I should have seen the streak of greed and selfishness just beneath the surface. I pride myself on being an intelligent woman. But the long and the short of it is that I did not realize his true character until it was too late. Even now I find it difficult to imagine him killing those women."

"Why?"

A small, thoughtful frown drew Joan's brows together. "He was not the sort to get his hands dirty."

"It is often difficult to see into the hearts of others when one is very young and has not had much experience of the world." Lavinia hesitated. "Do you mind if I ask you an extremely personal question?"

"What is it?"

Lavinia cleared her throat. "I realize you do not go out into Society very much, but obviously there are occasions when you must meet Neville in public. How do you handle such moments?"

Joan smiled with what appeared to be genuine amusement. "You will soon learn the answer to your question. Lord and Lady Neville are coming this way. Shall I introduce them to you?"

Nothing.

Frustrated, Tobias closed the journal of household accounts and dropped it into the desk drawer. He stepped back, lifting the candle higher so that it cast its light deeper into the shadows of the study. He had searched every corner and crevice of this room, but he had uncovered no hint of murder or conspiracy.

Neville had secrets. They had to be someplace in this house.

It was very odd to find oneself being introduced to a murderer. Lavinia took her cue from Joan. A cool smile and a few murmured words that dripped with ennui. She could not help but notice, however, that Neville never quite met Joan's shuttered gaze.

Constance, obviously blissfully unaware of the past her husband shared with Joan, launched immediately into a cheerful conversation.

"Congratulations on your daughter's engagement," she said warmly to Joan. "It is an excellent match."

"My husband and I were very pleased," Joan said. "It is my greatest regret that Fielding did not live to dance at her wedding."

"I understand." Constance's eyes lit with sympathy. "But at least he had the satisfaction of knowing her future was assured."

Lavinia studied Neville's averted face while she listened to Joan and Lady Neville. He was looking at someone, she realized. There was something unpleasant in his eyes. Very discreetly she turned slightly to follow the path of his gaze.

Shock clenched her stomach when she saw that he was watching Emeline, who was standing some distance away with Anthony and a small group of young people. As if sensing danger, Anthony glanced toward her. His eyes narrowed when he saw Neville.

"What a lovely gown, Mrs. Lake." Constance smiled. "It looks like one of Madame Francesca's creations. I vow her work is quite unique, is it not?"

Lavinia managed a smile. "Quite. I take it you are one of her clients?"

"Indeed. I have patronized her establishment for years." Constance gave her a politely inquiring look. "You say you are visiting from Bath?"

"Yes."

"I have traveled there many times to take the waters. A charming town, is it not?"

She would go mad if she had to continue this inane conversation, Lavinia thought. Where was Tobias? He should have returned to the ball by now.

The giggles and laughter downstairs could not be heard up here on the floor where Neville's bedchamber was located. Tobias set the candle on the dressing table. Swiftly, methodically, he began opening and closing drawers and cupboards.

Ten minutes later he found the letter in a small drawer built inside the wardrobe. He removed it and carried it to the dressing table where the candle stood.

The letter was addressed to Neville and signed by Carlisle. It itemized expenses, costs, and fees for the commission accepted and carried out in Rome.

Tobias realized he was looking at the business contract that had been Bennett Ruckland's death warrant.

Neville took his wife's arm. "If you ladies will excuse us, I believe I see Bennington over there near the staircase. I have been wanting to have a word with him."

"Yes, of course," Joan murmured.

Neville whisked his wife away through the crowd.

Lavinia watched, trying to keep an eye on the pair. It soon became clear that Neville was not headed toward the staircase. Instead, he deposited Constance with a small cluster of women who were conversing near the entrance to the buffet and made his way toward the far side of the room.

"Forgive me," Lavinia murmured, "but I cannot help wondering if you went so far as to invite Neville and his wife to your daughter's engagement ball?"

To her surprise, Joan actually chuckled. "Fielding told me that Lord and Lady Neville need not receive invitations. I was quite happy to leave Neville off the guest list."

"I can understand that."

"Well," Joan said, "now you see how one handles the vexing problem of dealing socially with a former lover who may well be a murderer."

"You act as if nothing ever happened."

"Precisely."

Tobias tucked the letter inside his jacket, put out the candle, and crossed the room to the door. He listened intently for a moment. When he heard no sound out in the hall, he let himself out of the bedchamber.

The cramped staircase designed for the use of the servants was

at the far end of the corridor. He found it and started down into the deep well of shadows.

When he reached the ground floor, he paused again. Silence emanated from the floor below. The two people he had overheard earlier had either fallen asleep or found some other occupation that did not inspire them to giggles and laughter. He rather suspected the latter.

He had just opened the door of the conservatory when one of the heavy shadows looming in the hall detached itself from the wall. There was just enough moonlight to see the glint of the pistol in the man's hand.

"Halt, thief!"

Tobias dropped to the floor, rolled through the opening, and came up hard against a stone planter. Pain stabbed through his left leg but it was not from a bullet, just the all-too-familiar protest of his old wound, so he ignored it.

"Thought I heard someone on the back stairs."

The pistol exploded, shattering a nearby clay pot. Tobias flung an arm across his face to protect his eyes.

The man dropped the empty gun and launched himself through the doorway. Tobias staggered to his feet, barely avoiding the charge. Another jolt of pain was all the warning he got before his left leg collapsed on him. He pitched forward, groping for purchase.

The man was already back on his feet. The massive hands on the ends of his outstretched arms looked like claws.

"There'll be no more of yer tricks."

Tobias managed to catch himself on the edge of a workbench. His knuckles struck a large pot planted with a voluminous fern. He hoisted the heavy object in both arms.

The man was less than two paces away when Tobias slammed

the fern pot into his shoulder and the side of his head. He went down like a felled ox.

An unearthly silence gripped the conservatory. Tobias steadied himself against the workbench and listened. There were no footsteps. No cries of alarm.

After a moment he pushed himself away from the bench and limped toward the door that opened onto the gardens. A short time later he reached the street. There was no hackney in sight.

Just his bloody luck. It was going to be a long walk to the Colchester mansion. On the bright side, it was not raining.

twenty-two

Bloody hell, where is he?" Lavinia stood on tiptoe, trying to peer over the heads of the crowd. "I cannot see Neville. Emeline?"

Emeline did not have to go up on her toes in order to get a view. "No. Perhaps he went into the buffet room."

"A moment ago when I caught a glimpse of him, he was speaking with one of the footmen." Lavinia's palms tingled. "Now he is gone. He may have left the house."

"What is so surprising about that?" Joan asked. "Neville no doubt intended to put in only a brief appearance here at the ball. Events such as this are exceedingly boring for most gentlemen. By now he will be on his way to a gaming hell or perhaps to a brothel to search for a new mistress."

A vivid picture of the blood on the hood of Sally's cloak flashed through Lavinia's brain. "What a dreadful thought."

"Calm yourself." Joan watched her with an expression of concern. "I vow, you have become extremely anxious during the past half hour."

Because I cannot stop worrying about Tobias, Lavinia thought. But there was no point in voicing her private fears aloud. There was no reason to be overly concerned about Neville's sudden disappearance from the ballroom either. Joan was no doubt correct in her assessment of the situation.

Nevertheless, it made her uneasy to have lost track of her quarry.

Anthony materialized in front of her, a glass of lemonade in his hand this time. He handed it to Emeline.

Lavinia frowned at him. "Did you see Neville inside the buffet room?"

"No." Anthony turned slightly to examine the crowd. "Saw Lady Neville on my way back here, but not her husband. I thought you said you would keep an eye on him while I fetched the lemonade."

"He has disappeared."

Anthony's face tightened. She knew he was no happier with the news than she was.

"Are you certain?" he asked.

"Yes. I do not like this," Lavinia said quietly. "It is nearly one-thirty. Tobias should have finished his task and met up with us here by now."

"I agree," Anthony said soberly.

"I *told* him he ought to take you with him tonight."

Anthony nodded. "You have mentioned that once or twice this evening."

"He never listens to me."

Anthony winced. "If it is any comfort, Tobias is in the habit of doing as he likes."

"That is absolutely no excuse. We are partners in this affair. He ought to pay attention when I give him the benefit of my opinion and advice. I will have a few things to say to him when he finally does decide to put in an appearance."

Anthony hesitated. "He may have stopped off at his club on the way back here to confer with a friend."

"What if he is not there?"

"We must be reasonable about this. The search may have taken longer than Tobias expected." Anthony paused, frowning. "I could find a hackney and drive past the mansion to see if there is any sign he is still inside. If he is not there, I might check for him at his club."

She was not the only one who was growing alarmed, Lavinia thought. Anthony was trying to appear coolheaded but he was also uneasy.

"An excellent notion," she said. "Given the crowd here tonight, there are bound to be hackneys hanging about in the street hoping for fares."

Anthony looked relieved to have her make the decision.

"Very well then, I'm off." He made to turn away.

Emeline touched his sleeve, her eyes grave with concern. "You will be careful?"

"Of course." He took her hand and bowed gallantly over it. "Do not be anxious on my behalf, Emeline. I will be very careful." He turned to Lavinia. "I'm sure that all is well, Mrs. Lake."

"It will not be at all well for Mr. March if I discover he stopped off at his club instead of coming directly here."

Anthony smiled wryly and hurried away through the crowd.

Joan frowned. "Do you really believe something has gone wrong in the course of Mr. March's search?"

"I don't know what to think," Lavinia admitted. "But the fact

that he is not here at the appointed hour, together with Neville's sudden disappearance, makes me extremely worried."

"I do not see how you can connect the two. Neville could not possibly know Mr. March is at his house at this moment."

"It is something about the way Neville left after he was approached by that footman a moment ago that worries me," Lavinia said slowly. "Almost as if he had received a message and was responding to it."

"The waiting is going to be intolerable," Emeline said. "There must be something we can do."

"There is," Joan said with authority. "We must act as if nothing out of the ordinary has occurred. You have promised the next dance to Mr. Geddis, have you not? He is coming this way."

Emeline groaned. "Dancing is the last thing I want to think about at the moment. I could not possibly manage polite conversation with Mr. Geddis while I am worrying about Anthony."

"Gossip has it that Mr. Geddis is worth nearly fifteen thousand pounds a year," Joan said dryly.

Lavinia choked on her champagne. When she had recovered, she smiled pointedly at Emeline. "It will not hurt you to dance with Mr. Geddis. Indeed, it is necessary you do so."

"Why?" Emeline asked.

"To keep up the appearance that there is nothing wrong, just as Mrs. Dove suggested." Lavinia made surreptitious little shooing motions with her gloved fingertips. "Go on, dance with him. You must behave as any other young lady is expected to behave at such an affair."

"If you insist."

Emeline summoned a brave smile for the handsome young man who had just come to a halt in front of her. He stammered politely and led her out onto the floor.

Lavinia sidled a little closer to Joan. "Fifteen thousand a year, you say?"

"So I'm told."

Lavinia watched Geddis sweep Emeline off to the dance floor. "He appears to be a very nice young man. Any bad blood in that family?"

"None that I know of."

"That's good."

"I don't think he stands a chance against young Anthony," Joan said.

"I think you're right."

The waltz came to an end a few minutes later, leaving Emeline and her partner on the far side of the floor. Lavinia glanced at the tiny watch pinned to her reticule while she waited for the pair to return to the alcove.

"Calm yourself," Joan said quietly. "I'm certain that Mr. March is safe. He seems quite adept at taking care of himself."

Lavinia thought of Tobias's left leg. "He has been known to miscalculate."

Joan looked thoughtful. "You are genuinely concerned about him, aren't you?"

"I did not like this plan to search Neville's house," Lavinia admitted. "In fact, I was very much—" She broke off abruptly when she saw who had stepped into Emeline and Mr. Geddis's path. "Bloody hell."

"What is it? What's wrong?"

"Pomfrey. Look at him. I do believe he's attempting to persuade Emeline to dance with him."

Joan followed Lavinia's gaze to where Emeline and Mr. Geddis stood confronted by Pomfrey. "Yes." Her mouth tightened. "I do

hope he's not drunk. Pomfrey is quite capable of making an ass of himself when he's in his cups."

"I am very well aware of that. I cannot allow him to make another scene. Not here in Lady Colchester's ballroom." Lavinia snapped her fan closed and moved out of the alcove. "I must put a stop to this. I will be right back."

"Try to stay calm, Lavinia. I assure you that Lady Colchester won't allow any unpleasant behavior to occur in her ballroom."

Lavinia did not respond. She pushed her way through the crowd as discreetly as possible. Her progress was not an easy affair. She lost sight of her objective on several occasions when large persons loomed in front of her.

When she finally emerged, a trifle breathless, on the far side of the dance floor, she saw that Emeline had matters in hand. Pomfrey was already turning away. He did not even notice Lavinia bearing down on him.

Emeline's eyes lit with amusement. "It's all right. Pomfrey merely wanted to apologize for the events at the theater the other evening."

"As well he should." Lavinia came to a halt and glowered at Pomfrey's retreating back.

Emeline smiled at the confused-looking Mr. Geddis. "Thank you, sir."

"My pleasure." Geddis collected himself, bowed over her hand, and quickly hurried off into the crowd.

Lavinia watched him depart. "He seemed very nice."

"Try not to look so wistful," Emeline said. "It is embarrassing."

"Come, we must return to the alcove where Mrs. Dove is waiting."

She led the way around the edge of the dance floor, forging a trail through the crowd. Emeline followed close behind her.

When they broke through the last barrier of guests, however, she saw that the alcove was empty save for a harried-looking footman who was collecting used glasses on a tray.

Lavinia halted, a shock of panic washing through her. "She's gone."

"I'm sure she's somewhere nearby," Emeline said soothingly. "She would not have left without telling you where she was going."

"She's gone, I tell you." Lavinia grabbed a nearby chair and hopped up onto it. "I cannot see her anywhere."

The footman stared at her, appalled.

Emeline turned on her heel, searching the crowd. "Neither can I. Perhaps she went into the card room."

Lavinia clutched her skirts and jumped down from the chair. She pinned the footman. "Did you see a lady in a silver-gray gown? She was standing here in this very spot a few minutes ago."

"Yes, ma'am. I gave her the message and she left."

Lavinia and Emeline exchanged a glance. Then they both moved in on the footman.

"What message?" Lavinia demanded.

The hapless footman was clearly terrified. Sweat beaded his brow. "I don't know what it said, ma'am. It was written on a piece of paper. I didn't read it. I was instructed to give it to her and I did. She glanced at it and left immediately."

Lavinia took another step toward him. "Who gave you the message to give to her?"

The footman swallowed and took another step back. His nervous gaze switched from Lavinia to Emeline and then returned to Lavinia.

"One of the footmen hired for the evening gave me the message. I don't know him. He didn't say who gave him the note."

Lavinia turned to Emeline. "I will take that side of the room. You take the other. We shall meet at the far end."

"Yes." Emeline started to turn away.

"Emeline." Lavinia grabbed her arm to get her attention. "Do not leave the ballroom under any circumstances, do you understand?"

Emeline nodded and plunged headlong into the crowd.

Lavinia whirled and threaded her way into the throng on the terrace side of the long ballroom. She was halfway toward the buffet when it occurred to her that she would have a much better view of the room from the interior balcony that encircled the chamber.

She changed direction and veered toward the staircase. A few eyebrows rose when she pushed her way determinedly through the crush. There were some rude remarks, but for the most part, people ignored her.

She gained the stairs and managed by an effort of will not to break into a run. When she reached the balcony, she gripped the railing and looked down.

There was no sign of Joan's silver-gray gown among the hundreds of glowing satins and silks below. She forced herself to think logically. What if there had been something in the message that had provoked Joan to leave the safety of the ballroom?

She turned and crossed to the windows overlooking the vast gardens. She opened one and leaned out. The hedges and shrubs nearest the house were flooded with the light spilling from the French doors that lined the terrace side of the ballroom. The illumination did not extend far, however. Most of the heavily planted landscape lay in darkness. She could just make out the looming shape of a large stone monument. A tribute to Lady Colchester's late husband, no doubt.

A flash of movement near a hedge caught her eye. She turned

her head quickly and glimpsed pale satin skirts. In the shadows it was impossible to make out the color of the gown, nor could she see the woman's face, but something about the long stride and the fact that the lady was alone told Lavinia everything she needed to know.

She thought about calling out to the hurrying figure, but she doubted that Joan would be able to hear her over the laughter and music.

She whipped around, spotted a smaller staircase at the end of the balcony, and rushed toward it. A footman carrying a tray of canapés appeared just as she was about to descend.

"Can I get outside into the gardens from here?" she asked.

"Yes, ma'am. There's a door at the foot of the steps."

"Thank you." She grabbed the banister and used it to steady herself as she plunged downward.

She found the door at the bottom of the small staircase, opened it, and stepped out into the chilly darkness. There was no one about. Those guests who sought a breath of fresh air had confined themselves to the terrace.

It occurred to her that if the woman in the pale gown continued in the direction in which she had been headed a moment ago, she would intersect with the monument. The stone memorial would be a natural choice for a meeting point in this vast garden.

She picked up her skirts and hurried away from the lights toward the monument. The laughter and music faded as she moved deeper into the ornately cut hedges and plantings. The graveled path spun away into the shadows. She could feel the small pebbles through the thin soles of her dancing slippers.

She rounded the end of a hedge that was a foot higher than she was and saw the columns of the monument. Its cavernous interior was drenched in inky darkness. Something moved in the deep

river of night that flowed just inside the entrance. With the flap of a huge bat wing, it vanished.

She opened her mouth to call out to Joan but stopped before she uttered a word.

The bat-wing shape she had glimpsed could well have been the corner of a greatcoat. Whoever lurked inside the ruin was not Joan. She could not even be certain it was a woman. A man awaiting a lady with whom he had planned a tryst, perhaps.

She hovered in the thick shadows of the hedge for a few seconds, suddenly very conscious of the chill in the air. Out of the corner of her eye, she caught the glint of watery moonlight on pale satin.

Joan emerged from the dense foliage near the edge of the monument. She paused next to one of the stone columns. Then she started toward the dark entrance.

Suddenly Lavinia understood.

"Joan, no!" Lavinia hurried toward her. *"Don't go inside."*

Startled, Joan turned quickly. "Lavinia? What are you—"

There was a sudden rush of movement from the entrance of the monument.

"Look out!" Lavinia seized Joan's arm and hauled her away from the pillar.

A figure garbed in a greatcoat and hat rushed from the monument and disappeared into the deep darkness of the vast garden. Moonlight gleamed for an instant on what appeared to be a length of iron.

"I would not even think of giving chase, if I were you," Joan said. "Something tells me Mr. March would not approve."

twenty-three

$\mathcal{T}$here is, of course, only one reason why I would have rushed out into the garden without waiting to tell you what had occurred, Lavinia," Joan said wearily. "I received a message informing me that my daughter's life was in danger and that I must meet the messenger at the garden monument at once for further details. I fear I succumbed to panic."

"It never occurred to you the message was a lure meant to get you away from the safety of the ballroom?" Tobias asked.

Lavinia, seated on the velvet cushions opposite, gave him a look he recognized immediately. He ignored it. He knew very well his tone had been harsh, but he did not care a jot if he had offended Joan's sensibilities.

He was not in a good mood. When he had walked into the Colchester ballroom with Anthony a short time ago and discovered that both Joan and Lavinia had disappeared, he had been

ready to tear the house apart. It was Emeline who had prevented him from creating a truly memorable scene. She had been watching for signs of Lavinia and Joan from the balcony and had just spotted the pair slinking back through the gardens.

Tobias had whisked all of them away at once, commandeering Joan's elegant carriage without a by-your-leave. Joan had made no protest as he had bundled her, together with Lavinia, Emeline, Anthony, and himself, into the vehicle.

It was only after they were all secure inside the cab that Lavinia had given him a crisply rendered version of events in the ballroom and the garden. The cold satisfaction he had experienced upon finding the letter in Neville's wardrobe had immediately evaporated.

All he could think about at that moment was that Joan had not only placed herself at risk in the night-shrouded garden, she had caused Lavinia to rush into grave peril too.

Absently he flexed his hand on his thigh, seeking to ease the dull ache. Joan's elegant, well-sprung carriage was considerably more comfortable than the hackney Anthony had secured earlier to pluck him off the street, but the soft cushions did nothing to assuage his temper.

"I am not a stupid woman, Mr. March." Joan looked out the carriage window. "I realized the message might be bait. But it implied a threat to my daughter. I had no choice but to obey the summons. I was really quite frantic."

"A perfectly understandable response," Lavinia said bracingly. "Any parent would have done the same. And not just any parent, I might add." She shot a meaningful look at Tobias. "What would you have done, sir, if you had received a message indicating Anthony was in great danger?"

Anthony made an odd sound that might have been a smothered snort of laughter.

Tobias swallowed an oath. The answer to her question was obvious to all of them. What would he have done had he received a message indicating Lavinia was in jeopardy? He knew the answer to that question too.

There was no point in continuing this line of argument, he thought. Lavinia was firmly on the side of her client.

"It seems quite clear," Lavinia said, moving decisively to change the subject, "that Neville set the stage for all of the events this evening. I would not be surprised to learn that he even provoked Pomfrey into making the apology to Emeline because he wanted to create a distraction."

Emeline's brows drew together in a considering look. "Do you think he arranged to have a message delivered to himself as well as to Mrs. Dove?"

"It appears that way, does it not? It gave him the perfect excuse to leave the ballroom. If anyone inquires, there will no doubt be a number of people who can testify to the fact that he received a summons and was obliged to leave."

"But he left the house through the front door," Anthony said.

"Which meant one of the footmen would have brought him his greatcoat and hat," Lavinia said softly. "It also allowed him to go to his carriage to collect the poker or whatever it was he carried as a weapon."

Emeline nodded. "Yes, that makes sense. It would have been simple enough for him to make his way back into the Colchester gardens unseen. The grounds are quite extensive. There must be any number of places where one could go over the wall."

"When my body was eventually discovered, there would have been nothing to link Neville to the crime of murder," Joan said softly.

Tobias saw Lavinia give a small but distinct shudder.

"It all fits," Anthony said. "Neville tried to kill you tonight, just as he killed those other women. Perhaps he intended to dump your body into the river too. He could have hauled it there in his carriage easily enough."

Joan gave him an odd look. "Such a vivid imagination you have, sir."

Anthony grimaced with embarrassment. "Sorry."

Joan's mouth twisted wryly. "One cannot help but wonder if he intended to give his private artist a commission to create a death mask of me. Just imagine, my features might well have wound up on one of those erotic statues in Huggett's Museum."

For a moment no one spoke.

Joan turned to Tobias, her eyes grim and somber. "It would seem that you and Lavinia are correct in your analysis of this matter, sir. I am forced to conclude that Neville is indeed a murderer and quite possibly a member of this Blue Chamber you described. I can scarcely credit that my husband was the master of a criminal organization, but nothing else makes any sense. Evidently, Neville thinks I know too much and he wishes to silence me."

Lavinia sat down behind her desk a short while later. Anthony crouched in front of the hearth to light the fire. Emeline took one of the reading chairs. Tobias opened the sherry cabinet.

Lavinia watched him pour two glasses of sherry. Something about the way he moved told her his leg was aching badly. Little wonder. He had given it a great deal of exercise tonight.

"Do you think Joan Dove is telling the truth when she claims she never knew her husband was Azure?" Anthony asked of no one in particular.

"Who can say?" Tobias put a glass down on the desk in front

of Lavinia and took a swallow of sherry from his own. "Gentlemen in the ton rarely discuss any of their affairs, financial or otherwise, with their wives. As Lavinia said, widows are often the last to become acquainted with details of the family assets. It would certainly have been possible for Dove to keep his wife in the dark concerning his criminal activities."

"She knew," Lavinia said softly.

There was a startled pause. Everyone looked at her.

She shrugged. "She is a very intelligent woman. She loved him deeply and theirs was clearly a very close bond. She had to know, or at least suspect, that Fielding Dove was Azure."

Emeline nodded. "I agree."

"Whatever the case may be, she will certainly never admit it," Tobias said.

"One can hardly blame her," Lavinia said. "In her place, I would do anything I could to conceal the truth."

"For fear of gossip?" Tobias asked with mild interest.

"No," Lavinia said. "Mrs. Dove is perfectly capable of withstanding a storm of gossip."

"You are right," Tobias said.

"There are other reasons why a woman would do whatever was necessary to protect her husband's good name," Lavinia said.

Tobias elevated one brow. "Such as?"

"Love. Devotion." She studied the sherry in the glass in front of her. "That sort of thing."

Tobias watched the flames. "Yes, of course. That sort of thing."

There was another lengthy silence. This time Emeline broke it.

"You have not told us what you discovered in Neville's mansion tonight, Mr. March," she said.

He lounged against the mantel. "I found a letter that links Neville to Bennett Ruckland's death. It appears he paid Carlisle a

large sum of money to see to it that Ruckland was murdered in Rome."

Anthony whistled softly. "So it is finished at last."

"Almost." Tobias downed more sherry.

Lavinia frowned. "What do you mean? What is going on here?"

Tobias looked at her. "The time has come to give you a bit more background on this matter."

She narrowed her eyes. "Proceed, sir."

"Bennett Ruckland was an explorer and a student of antiquities. During the war, he spent a good deal of time in Spain and Italy. His profession occasionally put him in the way of being able to acquire information that was useful to the Crown."

"What sort of information?"

Tobias swirled the sherry in his glass. "In the course of his work, he sometimes learned the details of French shipping routes, heard rumors concerning the movement of military supplies and troops. That sort of thing."

Emeline looked intrigued. "In other words, he served as a spy?"

"Yes." Tobias paused a beat. "His contact in England, the man to whom he reported this information, was Lord Neville."

Lavinia went very still. "Oh my."

"The information Ruckland supplied to Neville via a chain of couriers was supposedly turned over to the proper authorities. And, indeed, much of it was."

"But not all of it?"

"No. But Ruckland did not discover the truth until after the war. About a year ago he went back to Italy to continue his scholarly research. While he was there, one of his old informants told him of some rumors concerning the fate of a particular shipment of goods that had been sent from Spain by the French late in the

war. The intended destination was Paris. Ruckland had obtained details of the secret route and had reported them to Neville at the time."

"Military supplies?" Emeline asked.

Tobias shook his head. "Antiquities. Napoleon was very keen on such things. When he invaded Egypt, for example, he brought along a host of scholars to study the artifacts and temples there."

"Everyone knows that. The Rosetta stone was among those artifacts, after all, and we have it now, safe and sound," Anthony said.

"Continue with your tale," Lavinia said. "What sort of antiquities were included in this shipment you mentioned?"

"Many valuable things. Among them was a collection of ancient jeweled objects that Napoleon's men had discovered concealed in a convent in Spain."

"What happened?"

"The shipment of jewels and antiquities vanished en route to Paris," Tobias said. "Ruckland assumed that Neville had arranged to have the shipment intercepted and taken to England. And, in a way, that is precisely what happened."

Lavinia frowned. "What do you mean?"

"The antiquities certainly disappeared on schedule," Tobias said. "But after talking to his old informant in Italy last year, Ruckland began to suspect that Neville had stolen the shipment for himself. He began to make inquiries. One question led to another."

Lavinia exhaled slowly. "Ruckland uncovered information about the Blue Chamber, didn't he?"

"Yes. Do not forget that he had had a great deal of experience as a spy. He knew how to conduct an investigation. He also had a network of old informants left over from the war. He started turning over stones and found snakes."

She took a quick sip of sherry. "One of which was named Lord Neville?"

"Ruckland learned that not only had Neville stolen any number of valuable cargos during the war, he had also betrayed his country on several occasions by selling British military information to France."

"Neville was a traitor?"

"Yes. And well connected to the criminal class because of his association with the Blue Chamber. He too had informants. A few months ago he learned that Ruckland was investigating his activities and getting close to the truth. He made arrangements with the other surviving member of the Blue Chamber, Carlisle, to get rid of Ruckland." Tobias's jaw tightened. "The business cost Neville ten thousand pounds."

Lavinia's mouth fell open. "Ten thousand pounds? To kill a man? But that's a fortune. We both know there are any number of footpads in any city in Europe, including Rome, who would have committed murder for a handful of coins."

"The ten thousand was not intended to cover the cost of murder," Tobias said evenly. "It was a premium charged because of Neville's delicate position. Carlisle knew Neville would pay any price for silence."

"Yes, of course," Lavinia muttered. "One criminal blackmailing another. There is a sort of irony in that, is there not?"

"Perhaps," Tobias said. "In any event, Neville must have been greatly relieved when the matter was settled. With Ruckland dead, he could proceed with his plans to take control of what was left of the Blue Chamber organization here in England."

Anthony looked at Lavinia. "But what Neville did not know was that Ruckland had already reported his suspicions to certain highly placed gentlemen. When he was murdered in

Rome, they immediately knew it had likely not been a random killing."

"Hah." Lavinia slammed both palms flat on the desk and looked grimly at Tobias. "I knew it. I knew there was more to this than you had told me. Neville never really was your client, was he?"

Tobias exhaled slowly. "Well, it depends on your view of the situation."

She leveled a finger at him. "Don't even think of trying to wriggle out of the truth here. Who hired you to look into Ruckland's death?"

"A man named Crackenburne."

Lavinia turned to Emeline. "I told you Mr. March was playing a deep game, did I not?"

Emeline smiled. "Yes, Aunt Lavinia. You did say something of the kind."

Lavinia switched back to Tobias. "How did your connection with Neville come about?"

"When rumors of the valet's diary began to circulate soon after Carlisle's death, I saw a chance to tighten the web around Neville. I approached him in my capacity as a man of business and an opportunist and told him of the dangerous gossip. I offered my services to locate it."

"Neville was desperate to find the diary," Anthony explained. "He had no way of knowing exactly what was in it, but he feared it could expose him."

"I suspect that shortly after he employed me to find the diary, Neville himself received one of Holton Felix's little blackmail notes," Tobias said. "He tracked Felix to his rooms, just as you and I did, Lavinia, but he got to him first, murdered him, and took the diary."

"He could hardly explain that to you, however, so he allowed

you to continue your inquiries, and when he judged the time was right, he arranged for you to find the thing burned to cinders," Lavinia concluded.

"Yes."

She met his eyes. "Tobias, when Lord Neville returns home tonight, he will learn there was an intruder in his house. That guard you fought with will inform him."

"No doubt."

"He will suspect you. He might well decide you know too much. You must end this thing now. Immediately. Tonight."

"Odd you should bring up the subject." He finished the last of the sherry and put down the glass. "I intend to do precisely that."

twenty-four

$\mathscr{A}$ gas lamp marked the front steps of the brothel. The weak ball of light was little match for the fog-drenched darkness. Tobias stood in the shadows and watched the door open.

Neville emerged. He paused long enough to pull the high collar of his greatcoat up around his ears and then he went down the steps without looking to the right or the left. He strode quickly toward the carriage that stood waiting in the street. The coachman, draped in a heavy, many-tiered coat, waited, unmoving and silent.

Tobias stepped from the shadows and stopped a few paces away from Neville. He was careful to stay just outside the small spill of light from the gas lamp.

"I see you got my message," he said.

"What the devil?" Neville started violently and whipped around. His hand went into the pocket of his greatcoat. When he saw Tobias, some of the tension seeped out of his stance.

"Bloody hell, March, you gave me a start. You ought to know better than to sneak up on a man in this part of town. You're liable to get yourself shot."

"At this distance and in this very poor light, it is unlikely your pistol would hit your target, especially if you tried to shoot through the fabric of your coat."

Neville scowled but he did not take his hand out of his pocket. "I got your message but I thought you were going to meet me at my club. What's this all about? Do you have some news? Have you found the person who killed Felix and took the diary?"

"I grow weary of this game," Tobias said. "You have no more time to play it, in any event."

Neville scowled. "What the devil are you talking about, man?"

"It ends here. Tonight. There will be no more killing."

"What's this? Are you accusing me of *murder*?"

"Several murders," Tobias said. "Including that of Bennett Ruckland."

"Ruckland?" Neville fell back a step. He yanked his hand out of his pocket to reveal the pistol he held. "You're mad. I had nothing to do with his death. I was here in London at the time he died. I can prove it."

"We both know you arranged for his murder." Tobias glanced at the pistol Neville was pointing at him and then switched his gaze back to the man's face. "When you return home tonight, you will learn there was an intruder in your house while you were out."

Neville frowned. Then his eyes widened in rage. "You."

"I found a certain letter that provides a great deal of evidence against you."

Neville looked stunned. "A letter."

"Addressed to you and signed by Carlisle. It summarizes the arrangements for Ruckland's death quite succinctly."

"No. Impossible. Absolutely impossible." Neville raised his voice to call to the coachman. "You there, on the box. Take out your pistol. Keep an eye on this man. He's threatening me."

"Aye, sir." The coachman eased aside the edge of his coat. Light glinted on the barrel of a gun.

The pistol in Neville's hand steadied. He was more assured now that he knew his coachman was prepared to defend him.

"Let me see this letter you claim to have found," Neville snarled.

"Out of curiosity," Tobias said, ignoring the demand, "how much did you make off your dealings with the French during the war? How many men died because of the information you sold to Napoleon? What did you do with that hoard of jewels you stole from the Spanish convent?"

"You can prove nothing. *Nothing.* You are trying to frighten me. There is no record of my dealings with the French. They were destroyed along with the letter you say you found. It no longer exists, I tell you."

Tobias smiled slightly. "I turned it over to a very high-ranking gentleman who expressed great interest in it."

"*No.*"

"Tell me, Neville, did you really believe you could assume Azure's position as master of the Blue Chamber?"

Something snapped in Neville's expression. Rage leaped. "Damn you to bloody hell, March. I *am* the new master of the Blue Chamber."

"You murdered Fielding Dove, didn't you? That sudden illness he suffered on the last visit to one of his estates—poison, I assume?"

"I had to get rid of him. Dove started making inquiries after the war ended, you see. I do not know what brought my dealings

with the French to his attention, but he was furious when he learned of them."

"He ran a vast criminal organization but he was, at heart, a loyal Englishman, is that it? He drew the line at treason."

Neville shrugged. "Mind you, during the war he had nothing against Carlisle or myself taking advantage of certain investment opportunities that came our way. There was money to be made supplying the military with weapons, equipment, grain, and women. And then there were the odd shipments of stolen gold and jewels to be had if one had access to certain information."

"Business was business. But Azure would not tolerate the selling of British secrets. He discovered what you had done."

"Yes." Neville tightened his grip on the pistol. "Fortunately, I learned in time that he had marked me for death, and I took action. I had no choice but to see him dead, and quickly. It was a matter of survival."

"Indeed."

"Had the advantage of surprise, you see. He never knew I had been warned that he was plotting against me. Even so, it probably would not have been possible to dispatch him so easily ten or fifteen years ago. But Azure was getting old, you see. Starting to lose his grip."

"Did you really think you could handle an organization like the Blue Chamber?"

Neville drew himself up. "I am Azure now. Under my guidance and direction the Blue Chamber will become far more powerful than it was when Dove was in charge. Within a year or two, I will be the most powerful man in Europe."

"Napoleon had a similar vision. You see where it got him."

"I will not make the mistake of engaging in politics. I shall stick to business."

"How many women did you kill?"

Neville tensed. "You know about the whores?"

"I am well aware that you have attempted to tie up a few loose ends and in doing so you have murdered several innocent women."

"Bah. They were not innocents. They were harlots. They had no families. No one even noticed when they died."

"You didn't want them to completely disappear, did you? You wanted trophies of your handiwork. What is the name of the artist you commissioned to make those waxworks in Huggett's upstairs gallery?"

Neville gave a crack of laughter. "You know about the waxworks? Amusing, are they not? I must say, I'm impressed with your thoroughness, March. I had no notion you were so good at your business."

"There was no need to kill them, Neville. They were no threat to a man in your position. No one would have listened to them. No one would have taken their word against that of a *gentleman*."

"I cannot afford to take any chances. Some of those light-skirts are a bit too clever for their own good. It's possible they learned too much about me in the course of our association." Neville's mouth twisted. "A man sometimes grows talkative after he's had a few bottles of wine and he finds himself with a lusty young woman who is so very eager to please him."

"You did not silence all of them. Have you seen or heard of Sally recently?"

"The bitch got away, but she will be found," Neville vowed. "She cannot hide in the stews forever."

"She is not the only one who eluded you. Joan Dove also survived the attempt you made against her."

That statement gave Neville serious pause. He tightened his

hold on the pistol. "So you know about her too? You have been digging deeply. So deeply, in fact, that you have succeeded in digging your own grave."

"You are right to fear her, Neville. Unlike the others, she is clever, powerful, and well guarded. She was careless tonight. You almost got to her. But she will not make the same mistake twice."

Neville grunted in disgust. "Joan is no better than the others. She was a whore by the time I finished with her, and not a very good one at that. I grew tired of her within a few months. I could scarce believe it when Dove married her. With his wealth and power, he could have had his choice of respectable heiresses."

"He loved her."

"She was his only real weakness. It is the reason I must get rid of her, you understand. It is likely that during the twenty years of their marriage she learned he was the head of the Blue Chamber. I must assume she knows a great deal about the workings of the organization."

"You do not have the time to fret about what Joan Dove knows," Tobias said. "For you, this matter is ended. Now, if you don't mind, my associate and I will be on our way."

"*Associate.*"

"Up here," Anthony called softly. "On the box."

Neville uttered a hoarse cry of alarm. He whirled around so quickly that he staggered and nearly lost his balance. He started to drag the barrel of the pistol toward the new target but froze when he saw the gun in Anthony's hand.

Tobias took out the pistol he had brought with him in the pocket of his greatcoat.

"It would appear that you have two choices, Neville," he said quietly. "You can go home and wait for some very highly placed

gentlemen who served at the highest levels during the war to call upon you tomorrow, or you can flee London tonight and never return."

Anthony held the pistol steady. "An interesting choice, is it not?"

Neville wobbled with impotent rage. His attention wavered back and forth between the two pistols trained on him.

"Bastard." He was nearly incoherent. "You tricked me right from the start of this affair. You set out to destroy me."

"I had some assistance," Tobias said.

"You will not get away with this." Neville's voice shook. "I am the head of the Blue Chamber. I have more power than you can possibly imagine. I will see you dead for this."

"I would be a good deal more anxious about that prospect were it not for the fact that I know you will be dead or on your way to France by tomorrow morning."

Neville cried out in incoherent rage. He turned and pounded off into the night. His boot heels rang hollowly on the stones.

Anthony looked at Tobias. "Want me to go after him?"

"No." Tobias eased his gun back into his pocket. "He is Crackenburne's problem now, not ours."

Anthony looked at the place where Neville had disappeared into the fog. "When you outlined his choices for him, you forgot to mention one. Most gentlemen in his position would put a pistol to their heads to save their families from the scandal of an arrest and trial."

"I'm quite sure that if Crackenburne's friends discover Neville at home tomorrow when they call upon him, they will make that suggestion in no uncertain terms."

Crackenburne lowered his newspaper when Tobias took the chair across from him. "He was not at home when Bains and Evanstone called upon him this morning. They were told Neville had left town to visit his estates in the country."

Tobias raised his brows at the rare, grim quality he detected in Crackenburne's voice. He looked into the faded eyes and glimpsed some of the cold steel that very few ever noticed beneath the benign, absentminded veneer.

Tobias stretched his legs out to the fire. "Calm yourself, sir. Something tells me Neville will soon turn up."

"Damnation. I told you I did not like your plans to confront him last night. Why was it necessary to give the bastard a warning?"

"I told you, the evidence against him is very thin. A single letter, which he could claim was forged. I wanted to hear some confirmation from his own lips."

"Well, you got your confession, but we have bloody well lost him now. The next thing you know, we will learn he is living well in Paris or Rome or Boston. Exile is not sufficient punishment for his crimes, I tell you. Treason and murder. By God, the man is a devil."

"It is finished," Tobias said. "That is all that matters."

twenty-five

*T*he tiny cottage behind the old warehouse looked as if it had not been used in years. Unpainted, its windows caked with grime, it appeared on the verge of collapse. The only indication that someone came and went regularly from the small structure was the lock on the door. There was no rust on it.

Lavinia wrinkled her nose. The smell of the river was strong and unpleasant here near the docks. The fog clinging to the old warehouses reeked. She studied the dilapidated structure in front of them.

"Are you certain this is the right address?" she asked.

Tobias examined the small map Huggett had sketched for him. "This is the end of the walk. There is no place left to go except into the river. It has to be the correct location."

"Very well."

She had been startled when Tobias had appeared at her front

door a short while ago explaining that he had a message from Huggett. The note had been brief and to the point.

Mr. M:

You said you would pay for information relating to a certain modeler in wax. Please visit this address at your earliest convenience. I believe you will have your answers from the present occupant. You may remit the fee you promised to me at my place of business.

Yrs.

P. Huggett.

Tobias refolded the note and walked to the door. "It's unlocked." He removed a small pistol from the pocket of his greatcoat. "Stand aside, Lavinia."

"I doubt Mr. Huggett would send us into a trap." Nevertheless, she did as she was told, moving to the left so she would not be a target for anyone who might be waiting inside the cottage. "He is far too anxious to receive the fee you promised him."

"I'm inclined to agree, but I do not intend to take any more chances. It has been my experience that nothing is quite as it seems in this affair."

Including you, she thought. You, Tobias March, have been the most astonishing surprise of all.

Tobias flattened himself against the wall, then reached out and opened the door. Silence and the eerily familiar odor of death wafted out of the cottage.

Lavinia clutched the cloak she had borrowed from Emeline more tightly around herself. "Oh, damn. I had so hoped there would be no more corpses in this affair."

He glanced inside the opening, then lowered the pistol. He

dropped the gun into his pocket, came away from the wall, and moved through the doorway. Lavinia followed reluctantly.

"There is no need to come inside." Tobias did not turn around.

She swallowed against the smell of death. "Is it Lord Neville?"

"Yes."

She watched him move farther into the cottage. He turned to the left and disappeared into the shadows.

She went as far as the threshold but did not enter. From where she stood she could see enough. Tobias was crouched beside a dark, crumpled shape on the floor. There was a pool of dried blood beneath Neville's head. A pistol lay on the floor near his right hand. A fly buzzed.

She looked away quickly. Her gaze fell on a tarp that covered a large, lumpy-looking object in the corner.

"Tobias."

"What is it?" He glanced up, frowning. "I told you there was no need for you to come in here."

"There is something over there in the corner. I think I know what it is."

She walked into the cottage and crossed the wooden floor to the shrouded form. Tobias said nothing. He watched intently as she pulled aside the covering.

They both looked at the half-finished waxwork that loomed before them. The roughly molded figure of a woman engaged in a lewd sexual act with a man was unmistakably similar to the sculptures in Huggett's upstairs gallery. The face of the female had not been completed.

An array of artist's tools and equipment were carefully arranged on a nearby workbench. The dead coals on the hearth testified to the recent fires that had been lit to soften the wax.

"Very neat and tidy, is it not?" Tobias rose stiffly. "The murderer and traitor is dead by his own hand."

"So it would seem. What about the mysterious artist?"

Tobias studied the unfinished waxwork. "I believe we are to assume there will be no more commissions taken for sculptures suitable for exhibition to gentlemen only in Huggett's special gallery."

Lavinia shuddered. "I wonder what sort of hold Neville had over the artist? Do you think she might have been one of his former mistresses?"

"I think it likely that we will never know the answer to the question. Perhaps it is just as well. I am more than ready for this affair to be finished."

"So it is finished at last." Joan Dove looked at Lavinia across the expanse of blue and gold carpet. "I am very relieved to hear the news."

"Mr. March has spoken with his client, who assured him the scandal will be kept to a minimum. It will be put about in certain circles that Neville suffered some severe financial losses recently and, in a fit of depression, took his own life. It will not be easy on his wife and family, but such gossip is certainly preferable to rumors of treason and murder."

"Especially when it is discovered that Lord Neville's financial reverses were not nearly so severe as he had believed them to be when he put the pistol to his head," Joan murmured. "Something tells me that Lady Neville will be greatly relieved when she realizes she is not facing ruin after all."

"No doubt. As it happens, Mr. March's client also made it clear

the scandal will be hushed up for reasons other than protecting Neville's wife and family. It seems that certain very highly placed gentlemen do not want it widely known they were so thoroughly outfoxed by a traitor during the war. They wish to pretend the entire affair never happened."

"Just what one would expect of highly placed gentlemen, is it not?"

Lavinia smiled in spite of herself. "Indeed."

Joan cleared her throat delicately. "And the rumors that my husband might have been the master of a criminal empire?"

Lavinia looked at her very steadily. "According to Mr. March, the rumors died with Neville."

Joan's expression lightened. "Thank you, Lavinia."

"Think nothing of it. All part of the service."

Joan reached for the teapot. "Do you know, I would not have thought Neville the sort to put a pistol to his own head, not even for the sake of protecting the honor of his family name."

"One never knows," Lavinia said, "what a man will do under extreme pressure."

"Quite true." Joan poured tea with elegant grace. "And I suspect the highly placed gentlemen who learned of Neville's treason applied a great deal of pressure."

"Someone certainly seems to have done so." Lavinia rose, smoothing her gloves. "Well, then, that is that. If you will forgive me, I will be on my way."

She turned to go toward the door.

"Lavinia."

She stopped and looked back. "Yes?"

Joan watched her from the sofa. "I am very grateful for all you have done for me."

"You paid me my full fee and in addition you introduced me to your modiste. I consider myself amply compensated."

"Nevertheless," Joan said very deliberately, "I consider myself in your debt. If there is ever anything I can do to repay you, I hope you will feel free to call upon me without hesitation."

"Good day, Joan."

She was reading Byron when he came for her the next day.

He asked her to walk with him to the park. She agreed, closing the volume of poetry and setting it aside. She collected her bonnet and pelisse and together they left the house.

They did not speak until they reached the hidden Gothic ruin. He sat down beside her on the stone bench and looked out into the overgrown garden. The fog had dissipated, allowing the sun to warm the day to a comfortable temperature.

He wondered where to begin.

It was Lavinia who spoke first.

"I went to see her this morning," she said. "She was very cool about the entire affair. Thanked me graciously for having saved her life, of course. Paid me too."

Tobias rested his forearms on his upper thighs and clasped his hands loosely between his knees. "Crackenburne arranged for my fee to be paid into my bank."

"Always nice to receive one's wages in a timely manner."

Tobias studied the profusion of flowers and bright green leaves that cascaded in the wild garden. "Indeed."

"Now it truly is finished."

Tobias said nothing.

She gave him a quick, sidelong look. "Is something wrong?"

"The business with Neville is finished, as you said." He looked at her. "But it strikes me that some matters between us remain unsettled."

"What do you mean?" Her eyes narrowed slightly. "See here, if you are unsatisfied with the fee you collected from your client, that is your affair. You were the one who struck the bargain with Crackenburne. You certainly cannot expect me to share my payment from Mrs. Dove with you."

It was too much. He turned and caught her by the shoulders. "Bloody hell, Lavinia, this is not about the money."

She blinked a couple of times but made no move to pull away. "You're quite sure of that?" she asked.

"Positive."

"Well, then, what is this unfinished business you feel stands between us?"

He flexed his hands on her, savoring the curve of her supple shoulders, and tried to find the right words. "I thought we did rather well working together as partners," he said.

"We did, did we not? Especially when you consider the extremely difficult problems we were obliged to overcome. We did get off to a rather nasty start, if you will recall."

"The meeting over Holton Felix's body?"

"I was thinking of the night you destroyed my little business in Rome."

"In my opinion, the events in Rome constituted something of a slight misunderstanding. We eventually straightened it out, did we not?"

Her eyes gleamed. "In a manner of speaking. I was obliged to invent a new career for myself because of the slight misunderstanding. But I must admit that my new profession is a good deal more interesting than my former one."

"It is your new career I wish to discuss today," Tobias said. "I assume you intend to continue in it in spite of my advice?"

"I definitely intend to stick with this new occupation," she assured him. "It is very stimulating and exciting, not to mention occasionally quite profitable."

"Then, as I was about to say, it will very likely transpire that, on occasion, you may be in the way of discovering future collaborations between us eminently useful."

"Do you think so?"

"I think it highly likely that we could be of some service to each other."

"As colleagues?"

"Indeed. I suggest we consider working together as partners again when the opportunities arise," he said, determined to wring some sort of affirmative response from her.

"Partners," she said in a perfectly neutral voice.

A woman like her could drive a man mad, he thought. But he controlled himself. "Will you give my suggestion some thought?"

"I shall give it very serious consideration."

He pulled her close. "I shall accept that for now," he whispered against her mouth.

She framed his face with her gloved hands. "Will you?"

"Yes. But I should warn you that I intend to do my best to convince you to give me an affirmative answer eventually."

He untied the strings of her bonnet and set it aside. One at a time, he captured each of her hands in his and stripped off the kid gloves she wore. He brought the inside of her right wrist to his lips and kissed the soft skin.

She said his name so softly that he could barely hear it and then she wrapped her fingers in his hair. She kissed him on the mouth. He pulled her hard against him and felt her respond,

vibrant and restless as the passion ignited. She nestled closer, filling him with a great, intense hunger.

He lowered himself onto the stone bench and pulled her down on top of him. He raised her skirts so he could revel in the sight of her stocking-clad legs. She untied his cravat and went to work on the fastenings of his shirt. When she flattened her warm palms against his bare chest, he took a very deep breath.

"I love the feel of you," she said. She bent her head and kissed his shoulder. "It is most invigorating to touch you, Tobias March."

"*Lavinia.*" He tore the pins from her hair and heard them scatter on the stone floor.

She nibbled on him for a while, inspiring him with the thought that perhaps, given a quill and some ink, he might actually be able to write poetry.

By the time he got the front of his trousers open, she was shivering in his arms. When he tumbled her gently off the bench onto the floor, she wrapped her elegant legs around him. He was no longer tempted to write poetry. There was, he concluded, no possible way to set down in words such a soul-stirring experience as this.

She moved against him languidly and raised her head. "Is this what you meant by doing your utmost to convince me to give you an affirmative answer to your suggestion of future partnerships?"

"Mmm, yes." He slid his hands into the tumbled fire of her hair. "Do you think I presented a convincing argument?"

She smiled and he was suddenly swimming in the deep, seductive seas of her eyes. "What you presented was extremely convincing. As I said, I will give the matter my closest consideration."

twenty-six

$\mathcal{L}$avinia studied her image in the fitting-room mirror with a critical eye. "Don't you think the neckline is a bit low?"

Madame Francesca scowled. "The neckline is perfect. It is cut to hint at madam's bosom."

"A rather broad hint."

"Nonsense. It is an extremely discreet nod in the right direction." Madame Francesca tugged at a ribbon decorating the bodice. "Given that madam's bosom is not so grand, I have designed the gown to raise questions, not to answer them."

Lavinia toyed uncertainly with the silver pendant. "If you're quite sure."

"I am positive, madam. You must trust me in these matters." Madame Francesca frowned at the young seamstress crouched on the floor beside Lavinia. "*Non, non, non,* Molly. You did not pay attention to the drawing I made. There is to be only one tier of

323

ribbon flowers at the hem, not two. Two would be entirely too much for Mrs. Lake. Quite overwhelming. She is on the short side, as you can see."

"Yes, madam," Molly mumbled through a mouthful of pins.

"Go and fetch my sketchbook," Madame Francesca ordered. "I will show you my design once again."

Molly scrambled to her feet and hurried away.

Lavinia eyed herself in the mirror. "I'm too short and my bosom is less than grand. Really, Madame Francesca, I find it amazing that you are willing to spend any time on me at all."

"I do it for the sake of Mrs. Dove, of course." Madame Francesca put a dramatic hand to her own very expansive bosom. "She is one of my most important patrons. I would do anything to please her." She winked. "Besides, you are a challenge to my skills, Mrs. Lake."

Molly walked into the fitting room, the heavy volume in her hands. Madame Francesca took it from her, opened it, and began to flip through the pages.

Lavinia glimpsed a familiar green gown. "Wait. That was the dress you designed for Mrs. Dove to wear to her daughter's engagement ball, was it not?"

"This one?" Madame Francesca paused to admire the sketch. "Yes. Lovely, isn't it?"

Lavinia studied it intently. "There are two tiers of roses. Not three. This sketch has been altered. You removed one entire row of roses, didn't you? I can see where you marked it out."

Madame Francesca heaved a sigh. "I still maintain that with her elegant height, Mrs. Dove could have carried off all three tiers very nicely. But she was adamant that one row must be removed. What can one do when such an important client puts her foot down? One must submit. In the end, I changed the design."

Excitement and a dreadful thrill of fear rushed through Lavinia. She whirled around. "Please help me out of this gown, Madame Francesca. I must leave at once. There is someone I must speak with immediately."

"But, Mrs. Lake, we have not finished with the fitting."

"Get me out of this dress." Lavinia struggled with the fastenings of the bodice. "I shall return another time for the fitting. May I beg a sheet of paper and a pen from you? I must send a note to my, uh, associate."

It was raining again. There were no hackneys to be had. It took nearly forty-five minutes to make her way to Half Crescent Lane.

Lavinia came to a halt outside Mrs. Vaughn's front door and raised the knocker. She had to be certain, she thought, banging loudly. There could be no more mistakes. Before she and Tobias made another move in this treacherous business, she had to talk to the one person who had been right all along.

It seemed forever before the partially deaf housekeeper opened the door. She squinted vaguely in Lavinia's general direction.

"Aye?"

"Is Mrs. Vaughn at home? I must speak with her immediately. It is very important."

The housekeeper held out her hand. "You'll have to purchase a ticket," she said loudly.

Lavinia groaned and reached into her reticule. She found some coins and placed them in the work-worn palm. "There. Please tell Mrs. Vaughn that Lavinia Lake is here."

"I'll take ye to the gallery." The housekeeper led the way down the dark hall, cackling happily. "Mrs. Vaughn will be along in a bit."

The housekeeper stopped in front of the gallery door and opened it with a small flourish. Lavinia went quickly into the gloom-filled room. The door closed behind her. She heard another muffled cackle in the hall and then all was silent.

Lavinia hesitated, giving her eyes a chance to grow accustomed to the low lighting. A trickle of unease tingled through her. She reminded herself that this was the same disturbing sensation she had experienced the last time. She looked around, willing her pulse to slow to a more normal pace.

The chamber looked much as it had when she had come here with Tobias. The eerily realistic waxworks loomed around her, frozen in their various poses. She moved past the man with the glasses who sat reading in his chair and looked toward the piano.

There was a figure seated on the bench, peering intently at a sheet of music, hands poised above the keys. But the sculpture was that of a man in old-fashioned breeches. A waxwork, Lavinia thought, not Mrs. Vaughn posing as one of her own creations this time. Perhaps the artist liked to vary the nature of her little jokes.

"Mrs. Vaughn?" She wove a path through the figures, searching the wax faces around her. "Are you here? I know you enjoy this charade and it is quite effective. But unfortunately, I do not have time to play the game today. I wish to consult with you again on a professional matter."

None of the waxworks moved or spoke.

"It is extremely urgent," Lavinia continued. "A matter of life and death, I believe."

She glanced at a statue that stood facing the hearth. A new sculpture, she thought, not remembering it from her previous visit. The waxwork was that of a woman wearing a housekeeper's apron and a voluminous cap, the ruffles of which hid her profile.

She was slightly bent at the waist, a poker in her hand, as if she were about to prod the dead embers of an unlit fire.

Not Mrs. Vaughn, Lavinia thought. Much too tall and not nearly round enough at the hips.

"Please, Mrs. Vaughn, make yourself known if you are in here. I cannot afford to linger." Lavinia circled the corner of the sofa and came to a sudden halt when she saw the figure sprawled face-down on the rug. "Dear God."

The utter limpness in the limbs told her at once this was no waxwork that had toppled from a standing position. A terrible dread stole Lavinia's breath.

"Mrs. Vaughn."

She dropped to her knees, tore off a glove, and touched Mrs. Vaughn's throat. Relief flowed through her when she detected the throb of life.

Mrs. Vaughn was alive but unconscious. Lavinia jumped to her feet, intent on rushing to the door to summon assistance. Her gaze went past the waxwork housekeeper bent toward the hearth. Her mouth went dry.

There was mud on the figure's shoes.

For an instant, Lavinia could not breathe. The only path out of the long, narrow chamber would take her within striking distance of the poker. Screaming would do no good, given that the real housekeeper was half deaf. Her only hope was that Tobias had received her message and would arrive shortly. In the meantime, she must distract the killer.

"I see you got here before me," Lavinia said quietly. "How did you manage that feat, Lady Neville?"

The figure at the hearth jerked and straightened with a sudden movement. Constance, Lady Neville, turned to face her, the heavy iron poker raised high. She smiled.

"I am not a fool. I knew you were still potentially a great problem, Mrs. Lake. I set a man to watch you." Constance moved to block the path to the door. "He intercepted the street lad you sent to find Mr. March. He paid the boy well to give your message to him instead and came straight to me with it. Do not delude yourself with false hope, Mrs. Lake. There is no help on the way."

Lavinia edged backward, seeking to place the sofa between herself and the other woman. She put her hand on the locket she wore beneath her fichu. "It was you all along, was it not? You are the artist. I saw your figures in Huggett's upstairs gallery. They were most unusual."

"Unusual?" Constance looked contemptuous. "You know nothing of art. My work is brilliant."

Lavinia tugged hard on the locket. It came free in her hand. She held it up in front of her, letting the bright silver catch the little light in the gloomy chamber.

"Brilliant like my locket, do you mean?" she asked in a gentle, soothing voice. "Isn't it pretty? See how it sparkles. So bright. So bright. So bright."

Constance laughed. "Do you think you can purchase your life with that trinket? I am a very wealthy woman, Mrs. Lake. I have chests full of far more valuable jewelry. I do not want your locket."

"It is so bright, don't you agree?" She let the silver locket swing gently. It glittered and sparkled as it moved back and forth in an arc. "My mother gave it to me. So bright."

Constance blinked. "I told you, I care nothing for such cheap goods."

"As I said, your waxworks are most unusual, but in my opinion they lack the lifelike quality Mrs. Vaughn achieves."

"You are a fool. What do you know?" Rage flashed across Constance's handsome face. She glanced at the swinging locket and

frowned as if the sparks of light annoyed her. "My waxworks are far superior to these mundane sculptures. Unlike Mrs. Vaughn, I am not afraid to capture the darkest, most extraordinary passions in my work."

"You sent the death threat to Mrs. Dove, didn't you? I finally realized that this afternoon when I saw the modiste's drawing of the original version of the green gown. You based your little wax-work image on that picture, which you saw before it was changed, not on the finished garment. As a patron of Madame Francesca's, you had an opportunity to study the design. You never saw the final version, though, because you did not attend the engagement ball. If you had, you would have known there were only two tiers of roses at the hem, not three."

"It no longer matters. She is a slut, no better than any of his other women. She will die too."

Constance moved closer.

Lavinia caught her breath but she kept the locket in motion, never altering the rhythm of its arc.

"It was you who arranged for Fielding Dove to die of poison, was it not?" she asked in soft, soothing tones.

Constance glanced at the locket and then looked away. As if she could not help herself, she looked at it once more, following it with her gaze. "I planned everything, each detail. I did it for Wesley, you see. I did everything for him. He needed me."

"But Neville never truly appreciated your cleverness and your unfailing loyalty, did he? He took you for granted. He married you for your money and then went back to his other women."

"The women he used as vessels for his lust were not impor-tant. What was important was that Wesley needed me. He under-stood that. We were partners."

Lavinia winced and almost lost the rhythm of the swinging

locket. *Concentrate, you fool. Your life depends on this.* "I see." The locket continued in its gentle arc. "Partners. But you were the clever one."

"Yes. *Yes.* I'm the one who realized Fielding Dove was investigating Wesley's activities during the war. I saw that Dove was growing old and weak. I knew it was time to act. Once Dove was dead, nothing stood in Wesley's path. Just a few loose ends to tie up. I have always taken care of that sort of thing for him."

"How many of his mistresses did you murder?"

"Two years ago I finally realized the necessity of getting rid of those cheap whores." Constance glared at the moving locket. "I began to track them down. It wasn't easy. I have taken care of five of them so far."

"You created those waxwork statues in Huggett's upstairs gallery to celebrate your achievements as a murderess, did you not?"

"I had to show the world the truth about those women. I used my talent to demonstrate that in the end there is only pain and anguish for women who become whores. There is no passion, no poetry, no pleasure for them. Only pain."

"But the last one got away, didn't she?" Lavinia asked. "How did that happen? Did you make a mistake?"

"I made no mistake," Constance shouted. "Some fool of a scrubwoman left a bucket of soapy water near the door. I slipped and fell and the whore escaped me. But I will get her sooner or later."

"Who is the model for the man in your sculptures, Constance?" Lavinia asked evenly.

Constance looked confused. "The man?"

Lavinia swung the locket. "The face of the man in all of the sculptures is the same. Who is he, Constance?"

"*Papa.*" Constance dashed the poker at the locket as if trying

to bat it out of the air. "Papa is the man who gives the whores so much pain." She slapped at the locket with the tip of the poker. "He gave me pain. Do you understand? *He gave me so much pain.*"

Lavinia had to duck the poker twice. This was not going well. She managed to keep the locket moving but she knew it was time to change the subject. "Things were going well until Holton Felix got his hands on the diary and began to send out his little black-mail notes," she said.

"Felix learned from the diary that Wesley was a member of the Blue Chamber." Constance was more calm now. Her eyes followed the locket. "I had to kill him. It was easy enough. He was a fool. I found him within days of getting the note."

"You killed him and took the diary."

"I did it to protect Wesley. *I did everything for him.*"

Without warning, Constance swung the poker in a vicious arc. Lavinia threw herself backward, barely avoiding the blow. The hooked iron rod thudded into the skull of a nearby waxwork. The sculpture toppled to the carpet, its head in ruins.

Lavinia hastily stood behind the figure of the coy woman holding a fan, putting it between herself and Constance. She extended her arm to the side and started to swing the locket again.

Constance glanced at the flashing silver metal with obvious irritation. She looked away but her gaze returned to it again and again. She was not in a complete trance, Lavinia realized, but the locket had managed to distract her.

"It was only after you read the diary that you discovered Mrs. Dove and your husband had once been lovers, wasn't it? That changed everything as far as you were concerned. You could ignore his other women, but you could not forgive him for that affair."

"The others did not matter." Constance advanced on her, face

knotted. "They were cheap whores. He took them out of the brothels, amused himself for a while, and then he sent them back to the streets. But Joan Dove is different."

"Because she was married to the master of the Blue Chamber?"

"*Yes.* She is not like the others. She is wealthy and powerful and she knows everything that Azure knew. When I read the diary, I understood at once that Wesley would not need me when he assumed Azure's position as the master of the Blue Chamber."

"You thought that he would want Joan?"

"She could give him everything that was Azure's, couldn't she? His contacts, his connections, the details of how he ran his financial affairs, and the Blue Chamber itself." Constance's voice rose to a keening wail of despair. "What could I offer to compare? In addition, Wesley had once lusted after her as he had never lusted after me."

"So you decided that she had to die too."

"If he had her, he would no longer need me, would he?"

Constance swung the poker again. But she seemed to aim at the swinging locket this time. Lavinia shoved the sculpture of the woman with the fan at her. The iron struck it, squashing the head, and the figure crashed to the floor.

"But I wanted her to suffer as she had made me suffer," Constance whispered, her eyes following the locket. "So I sent her the waxwork scene of her own death. I wanted her to contemplate it for a while. I wanted her to know fear."

She dragged the poker out of the wax skull and hoisted it into striking position again. But it seemed to Lavinia that the movement was slower this time.

"Why did you kill your husband?" Lavinia backed away slowly, one hand thrust out to feel for objects in her path.

"I had no choice. He had ruined everything." Constance gripped the poker with both hands. "Stupid man. Stupid, stupid, stupid, lying man." Her bosom rose and fell with the force of her agitated breathing. Her eyes snapped to the locket and back to Lavinia's face. "Tobias March set a trap for him and Wesley walked straight into it. I was home when he came back to the house that night after March confronted him. Wesley was stricken with an attack of nerves. He ordered his valet to pack his things, said he had to flee the country."

Lavinia's fingers brushed the piano. She stopped. "You knew then that all of your work had come to naught."

"I pretended to help him make good his escape. I went with him to the docks where a man he knew had promised to meet him and take him aboard a ship. I suggested to Wesley that we wait in the cottage."

"And you shot him dead."

"It was the only thing I could do. He had ruined everything." Constance's face worked. "I wanted to hit him hard, just as I had hit those whores, but I knew it had to look as if he had taken his own life. Nothing else would satisfy March and the others."

"Do you plan to become the mistress of the Blue Chamber now?"

"Yes. Now I will be Azure." Constance stared at the swinging locket.

"Of course you will. Bright, bright, Azure."

Lavinia suddenly tossed the locket toward the nearest waxwork. Constance followed the glittering silver with her eyes.

Lavinia seized the candelabra from the piano and hurled it at Constance. It caught her on the side of her head. She screamed, dropped the poker, and fell to her knees. She put her hands to her head and howled.

Lavinia bounded over Mrs. Vaughn's unconscious body, jumped up onto the sofa, and leaped over the back. She gained the floor and ran toward the door.

It slammed open just as she reached for the knob. Tobias filled the doorway. He looked very dangerous.

"What the devil?" He caught her, held her, and looked past her.

Lavinia turned quickly in his arms.

Constance was still on her knees, sobbing now.

"It was her all along?" Tobias asked quietly.

"Yes. She thought that she and Neville had a partnership, you see. In the end, she killed him because she believed he was getting ready to violate the terms of their agreement."

twenty-seven

*S*he knew he did not love her, but she thought they had a more important, more enduring bond," Lavinia said.

"A metaphysical connection?" Joan raised her brows in elegant disdain. "With a man of Neville's nature? The poor woman really was quite deluded."

"I do not know if she thought of their arrangement in terms of metaphysics." Lavinia put down her teacup. "I rather doubt it. She spoke of a partnership."

"Bloody hell." Tobias, sunk deep into the large wing-back chair, shot her a dark look. "She would have to use that word."

"She believed she had made herself indispensable to him and that he understood he needed her." Lavinia rested her hands on the curved arms of her chair and met Joan's eyes. "She saw herself as the guiding intelligence in the partnership. She crafted the strategy. She took care of all the loose ends."

"She poisoned Fielding." Joan studied her tea.

"As you said, she was quite mad," Lavinia murmured.

"Indeed." Tobias put his fingertips together. "Which is why her family has committed her to a private asylum for the insane. She will spend the rest of her life locked away. No one will pay any attention to her rants and ravings."

Joan looked up from her tea. "She was the one who murdered some of Neville's discarded mistresses and attempted to kill me the night of the Colchester ball?"

"For years she had been obliged to accept Neville's affairs," Lavinia said. "She pretended to herself they were meaningless to him."

Joan grimaced. "Which, in fact, they were."

"Yes," Lavinia said. "I think she convinced herself that her connection with Neville transcended the lust he felt for the other women. Lust is such a fleeting thing, after all. And, I think, for her it meant only pain. She did not want his passion."

Tobias muttered something unintelligible. She glanced at him inquiringly but he did not bother to repeat himself. He gazed into the fire with a dark, enigmatic expression. She turned back to Joan.

"Underneath it all," Lavinia said, "I believe Constance hated the other women, though. When she conceived her strategy to install Neville as the new master of the Blue Chamber, she suddenly had the perfect excuse to get rid of some of them. She simply explained to Neville that they were potential threats to his advancement."

"Neville knew what she was doing," Tobias said. "But it was fine by him. He no doubt accepted her rationale for the deaths. He even thought the sculptures quite amusing. Looking back on our meeting the night I tried to provoke a confession from him, I see

now that he did not actually admit to being the killer, only to knowing the women had been killed."

"He left that sort of thing to Constance." Lavinia fixed her gaze on the fire. "She was more than happy to handle the pesky details for him. But when she read the diary and discovered Joan had once had an affair with him, she could not control her fear and rage."

Joan shook her head in sad regret. "As I said, the woman is clearly a lunatic."

"Lunatics weave their own logic," Lavinia reminded her. "The long and the short of it is that she decided you were a serious threat to her own relationship with Neville. She was afraid the pair of you would resume your intimate connection once Neville took control of the Blue Chamber."

Joan shuddered delicately. "As if I would have wanted to resume any sort of relationship with that dreadful man."

"She loved him in her way," Lavinia said. "She could not imagine you would not want him too."

Tobias stirred, stretching his left leg out to the fire. "In her disordered brain, you were the only one of his former lovers who could lure him away from her, because you could offer him everything and more than she could offer."

Joan shook her head. "So very sad."

Lavinia cleared her throat. "Indeed. When she read the message I sent to Tobias this afternoon, she realized I was still making inquiries. She got to Mrs. Vaughn's establishment a few minutes before me because she had her own carriage. I was obliged to walk because of the rain. She succeeded in rendering Mrs. Vaughn senseless."

"It is fortunate she did not murder the artist," Joan said.

"Mrs. Vaughn told me her thick hair and cap cushioned the

blow to some extent. She fell to the floor, dazed, but she had enough wit left to pretend to be dead. I arrived soon after, forestalling a second blow."

Joan looked at Tobias. "How did you come to arrive at Mrs. Vaughn's in such a timely manner if Lavinia's message never reached you?"

Tobias smiled. "But I did receive it. The lad sold the information first to Lady Neville's spy but, being an astute young man of business, the boy sought me out after striking his first bargain. Unfortunately, that meant I got the message belatedly, but I did get it."

"I see." Joan rose and adjusted her gloves. "That is the end of it then. I am very glad you are unhurt, Lavinia. And I am exceedingly grateful for all that you and Mr. March have done for me."

"You are quite welcome," Lavinia said, getting to her feet.

Joan smiled. "What I told you yesterday stands. I consider myself to be in your debt. If there is ever anything I can do for either of you, I hope you will feel free to come to me."

"Thank you," Lavinia said. "But I cannot imagine there will be any need to call upon your assistance."

"Nor can I." Tobias was on his feet. He went to open the door for Joan. "But we both very much appreciate your gracious offer."

Joan's eyes gleamed with secret amusement. She went through the doorway and paused briefly in the hall. "I should be very disappointed if you do not include me in some of your future inquiries, you know. I think I would find them most entertaining."

Lavinia stared, speechless. Tobias did not say a word.

Joan inclined her head in an elegant farewell, then turned and went down the hall to the front door, where Mrs. Chilton waited to see her out.

Tobias closed the door of the study and walked to the sherry

cabinet, where he poured two glasses. He handed one to Lavinia without comment and lowered himself back into the big chair.

For a long time they sat in silence, watching the flames dance on the hearth.

"The night I found the letter from Carlisle that damned Neville, I considered myself exceedingly fortunate," Tobias said after a while. "But at the time it occurred to me that it could be a forgery placed in a location where anyone who searched seriously for it might discover it."

"Only someone who wanted Neville destroyed would have done such a thing."

"It's possible Lady Neville put the letter in a place where it might be discovered," Tobias said.

"At the start of this affair, Lady Neville wanted only Mrs. Dove to die. She didn't want her husband dead until it was obvious he had ruined all of her plans."

"There is someone else who knew I intended to search Neville's house that night. Someone who might conceivably have the sort of criminal connections it would take to arrange for a forged letter to be smuggled into the mansion and hidden in Neville's bed-chamber."

Lavinia shivered. "Indeed."

Silence fell.

"Do you recall my mentioning the other rumors relayed to me by Smiling Jack in The Gryphon?" Tobias asked eventually. "The ones concerning an underworld battle for control of the Blue Chamber?"

"I remember." Lavinia sipped sherry and lowered the glass. "But I suspect the fanciful tale Jack told you was nothing more than wild, unsubstantiated gossip from the streets and the stews."

"I'm sure you're right." Tobias closed his eyes, tilted his head

back against the cushions, and absently massaged his thigh. "But let us say, for the sake of amusing ourselves, that there was some truth to those rumors of a criminal war. One could draw a very interesting conclusion about the outcome of such a conflict."

"Indeed." Lavinia paused a heartbeat. "Of all those who had some connection to the Blue Chamber, Joan Dove is the only one left standing."

"Yes."

There was another long silence.

"She considers herself to be in our debt," Tobias said evenly.

"She wants us to feel free to call upon her if there is ever anything she can do for us."

"She thinks it might be *entertaining* to participate in another one of our inquiries."

The flames crackled on the hearth with malevolent good cheer.

"I think I need another glass of sherry," Tobias said after a while.

"So do I."

twenty-eight

Tobias walked into Lavinia's study the following afternoon, a large trunk in his arms.

Lavinia frowned at the trunk. "What have you got in there?"

"A little souvenir of our time together in Italy." He lowered the trunk to the carpet and set about opening it. "I have been meaning to give these to you, but we have been rather busy of late. Slipped my mind."

She got to her feet and came around the desk, curious now. "Some of the statues I had to leave behind, I hope."

"Not statuary." Tobias raised the lid of the trunk and stood back. "Something else."

Lavinia hurried forward to peer into the trunk. She saw the stacks of neatly packed leather-bound volumes. A great rush of delight swept through her. She went to her knees beside the trunk and reached inside.

"My books of poetry." She drew a fingertip across the embossed lettering on one of the covers.

"I sent my man Whitby to your rooms the next day. Couldn't go myself because of the damn leg. He packed up your books."

Lavinia got to her feet, clutching a volume of Byron. "I do not know how to thank you, Tobias."

"Least I could do, under the circumstances. As you have so pointedly observed on several occasions, what happened that night was all my fault."

She chuckled. "Quite true. Nevertheless, I am grateful to you."

He cupped her face between his hands. "I do not want your gratitude. I am far more interested in discussing a continuation of our partnership. Have you given any thought to the suggestion I made to you a few days ago?"

"That we should work together on certain inquiries? Yes, as a matter of fact, I have given the issue a great deal of contemplation."

"What is your considered opinion?" he asked.

She held the book of poetry very tightly in both hands. "It is my opinion that any further association between us would be marked by heated disagreements and loud quarrels, to say nothing of a great deal of frustration."

He nodded, eyes somber. "I'm inclined to agree. But I must admit I find our heated disagreements and loud quarrels oddly stimulating."

She smiled and put the book down on the desk. Her eyes never left his as she wrapped her arms around his neck.

"So do I," she whispered. "But what of the frustration I mentioned?"

"Ah, yes, the frustration. Fortunately, there is a remedy for it." He touched the edge of her mouth with his thumb. "The cure is

temporary, I admit, but it can be applied repeatedly as often as needed."

She started to laugh.

He kissed her until she stopped. Then he continued to kiss her for a very long time.